ABBOT'S MEADOW

ABBOT'S MEADOW

PETER KNIGHT

Copyright © 2024 Peter Knight

The moral right of the author has been asserted.

Apart from any fair dealing for the purposes of research or private study, or criticism or review, as permitted under the Copyright, Designs and Patents Act 1988, this publication may only be reproduced, stored or transmitted, in any form or by any means, with the prior permission in writing of the publishers, or in the case of reprographic reproduction in accordance with the terms of licences issued by the Copyright Licensing Agency. Enquiries concerning reproduction outside those terms should be sent to the publishers.

This is a work of fiction. Names, characters, businesses, places, events and incidents are either the products of the author's imagination or used in a fictitious manner. Any resemblance to actual persons, living or dead, or actual events is purely coincidental.

Troubador Publishing Ltd
Unit E2 Airfield Business Park,
Harrison Road, Market Harborough,
Leicestershire LE16 7UL
Tel: 0116 279 2299
Email: books@troubador.co.uk
Web: www.troubador.co.uk

ISBN 978-1-80514-426-7

British Library Cataloguing in Publication Data.
A catalogue record for this book is available from the British Library.

Printed and bound in Great Britain by 4edge Limited
Typeset in 11.5pt Adobe Garamond by Troubador Publishing Ltd, Leicester, UK

*Special thanks go to friends Sylvia and Rob for their advice and support,
and my wife, Pat, for her proofreading, endurance and understanding.*

CHAPTER 1

"Do you have an appointment?"

The conservatively dressed receptionist looked at me with an air of disapproval over the top of her horn-rimmed glasses and did her best to make it clear that she was the real boss around here. For some reason, my name had not found its way onto her appointments list, and evidently my somewhat casual clothing suggested that I was no one of significance.

"He is very busy, and doesn't usually see people without an appointment," she added for good measure.

"Yes, I've got an 11.30," I said hoping that I sounded confident.

In truth, I was far from confident I had even got the right day, and resolved yet again to enter appointments onto my phone calendar rather than jot them down on some convenient, but soon lost, piece of paper. I suddenly became conscious that I hadn't properly considered what would constitute 'appropriate' clothing for this meeting, and began to regret opting for jeans and trainers. I had, however, taken the trouble to iron my T-shirt. I figured that ought to count for something.

Just then the office phone rang, and the receptionist snatched up the handset quickly. A demonstration to me of her efficiency, no doubt. As she listened intently, the look of disappointment crossing her face suggested that she might have to let me pass into her jealously guarded territory after all.

"Yes, Mr Chisholm, he's here now. Very well." She replaced the handset slowly.

After a few moments' consideration she said, "You may go through now. It's the last door on the right."

And with that she returned to examining her computer screen to make it clear that I was dismissed. As I walked down the corridor I could feel her eyes burning into my back, trying to work out who I was, and more to the point, why I was there.

The old Victorian Council House building was, like most buildings of the period, grand and unnecessarily ornate. It was built in an era when aesthetics and function were given equal importance, and plain simply wasn't an available option for designers. The big oak door to the office was no exception, with inlaid marquetry strips of some lighter wood. I knocked once and entered into a large wood-panelled room that was imposing and at the same time remarkably drab and gloomy. There were several unoccupied desks in the room, and at the far end peering over one of them sat a small, balding, bespectacled man.

The uneven wooden floor creaked as I walked towards his desk. In an age when most district councils appeared to put plush new council office buildings at the top of their shopping list, Castlebridge Council House seemed something of an anachronism. Whether it was a display of frugality with the public purse, a lack of ambition among its councillors, or just an indifference to modernity and efficiency, was difficult to determine.

From the appearance of the elderly man before me, I could imagine it was all of the above. He was dressed in a crumpled and badly fitting dark double-breasted suit, which could have been made to measure, but maybe not for him. It was accompanied by a pink shirt and a flowery orange and blue tie that was as hideous as it was out of place, and I mentally awarded him maximum points for comic effect.

He examined me closely through a pair of rimless glasses, the lenses of which gave his eyes a slightly porcine appearance. I tentatively stretched out a hand, but he waved towards a seat in front of the desk, indicating that he was much too busy for any formalities. Busy doing what I wasn't sure because, while most of the vacant desks appeared to be cluttered with computers, in-trays and piles of paper, his desk was furnished with just a jotter pad and phone. I felt slightly intimidated as he sat back, folded his arms, and waited for me to say something.

"Mr Chisholm, good of you to see me. I'm Daniel Curran of the *Castlebridge Gazette*. I wanted to ask you about Abbot's Meadow and why the district council has decided not to sell it, especially when it would have provided much-needed housing for the town?"

"Oh, I see," he said leaning forward on both elbows. "Well, in that case I'm afraid you're wasting your time. The decision has been made in committee, and it's out of my hands." He opened his hands to emphasise the point, but it had the effect of making him look defensive – or was that my overactive imagination?

"Was there anything else?" he enquired disingenuously, raising his eyebrows.

So here I was on my first proper investigative assignment as a journalist for the local newspaper, and it looked as though I was about to crash and burn. My training at university, such as it was, hadn't even remotely prepared me for the real world of uninspiring people of dubious dress sense and, from first impressions, displaying all the hallmarks of a personality bypass. In a business where conversation plays such a pivotal role, I wondered whether I had what it took. Spotting what looked like a golfing trophy in a glass case behind his desk, I decided to try the indirect approach.

"Ah… a fellow golfer I see. Which course do you usually play at?" I enquired, pointing at the cabinet.

"I don't. Pointless game. That belonged to one of my predecessors," he said dismissively.

He evidently wasn't in the mood for small talk either. However, I had learned something useful already. If you are going to try to get a conversation going with some 'soft' questions, it's much too late after you've already dived in with both feet! Nevertheless, I wasn't about to give up just yet.

"I gather the guy who wanted to buy the meadow from the council was going to build a lot of starter homes, which I would have thought would be welcomed in Castlebridge. There must be lots of young couples finding it difficult to get on the housing ladder? From what I could see driving past, the land just seems to be left fallow at the moment. There is obviously a very good reason why you don't wish to sell. I simply want to know what it is?"

"Look, son," he said, making it clear that I was definitely the junior here, and therefore would need things spelled out very slowly and clearly. "You're wasting your time. There's nothing to see here. The decision is made in committee. We take our duties very seriously and we have taken all the salient facts into consideration in reaching that decision. That's how we do it. So, it's no longer for sale. It's as simple as that. It doesn't matter why."

And with that he stood up, revealing that this didn't in fact make him much taller than when he was seated. He extended a small bony hand.

"Sorry to disappoint."

"Maybe," I said, hoping that this sounded slightly ominous. I stood up and turned to leave without shaking his hand. Childish, perhaps, but it felt justified in view of his patronising manner. As I left the room, I half turned to see him writing something on the jotter.

"The name's Daniel Curran... of the *Gazette*," I reminded him, and left.

On the way out I again passed the receptionist's desk, but dragon-lady had now been replaced by a cheerful and very attractive young girl who was ferreting around in a voluminous black handbag. I noticed immediately her hair which was a lovely shade of auburn. She looked up and I blushed, recognising that she had caught me staring.

"Oh, hello," she said, glancing at a notepad on the desk. "Sheila left me a note saying that you've been in with our Mr Chisholm?"

"Yes, briefly," I replied. "He was charm personified."

"I couldn't possibly comment," she replied with a knowing smile.

"What happened to your colleague?" I enquired, not sorry in the least at the much-improved aspect.

"Sheila? Oh, she's taken an early lunch break, so I've come down from Accounts to hold the fort. Not that there's much to do at this time of day. It's like a morgue most days."

"A very ornate morgue though," I replied, glancing around. "I'm surprised that the council offices are so... um..."

"Dated?" she offered. "Tell me about it. Stifling hot in the summer, freezing cold in the winter. It's a nice old building, but it would make a better museum than a dynamic hub of local democracy."

I laughed and racked my brain for something to say to keep the conversation going. An inner voice told me I was punching far above my weight here, but she was so lovely, I was determined to enjoy her company for as long as I could. A sudden thought occurred to me.

"Tell me, is there such a thing as a printed list of councillors that I could have?"

Quite what I was going to do with it was a mystery, but it seemed like a good idea. Maybe I would have more luck approaching another councillor. A more sociable one perhaps.

"Er… yes, we've got a list of them all somewhere."

She rummaged around in the desk and produced a colour photocopied leaflet with pictures of all the councillors from the various wards. She did her best to smooth out a crease and handed it to me.

"It's a bit tatty, I'm afraid. We do have proper glossy ones… somewhere. I think this is reasonably up to date. But if you go onto our website, I'm sure you'll find them all listed somewhere."

There were a lot more people than I had expected and my heart sank a little. I wondered what they all did. No doubt the website would tell me.

"That's great," I said, as if I had a cunning plan and she had provided the key to its success. "If I needed any other information of this type, do you think you could help me out? I'm not sure that Sheila and I got on that well. Just to explain, my name is Daniel Curran, of the *Castlebridge Gazette*. I'm following up a story about some land owned by the district council."

"No problem, any time. We do have a communications department, but I'm more than happy to help if I can," she said with an endearing smile, and wrote her phone number on the top of the leaflet. "My name's Jenny… Jenny Swan."

I wasn't at all sure that Jenny was following council procedures, but I for one was certainly not going to complain.

*

I think I was still smiling as I made my way out of the council offices and back onto the market square. I sought out a coffee bar where I could take a few moments to plan the rest of my day, hoping for something positive to turn up before returning to the office. The barista was a young lad, maybe in his late teens, with close-cropped hair and a pair of tattooed 'sleeves'. I ordered a latte and found a seat by the window where I could see the council offices.

The editor's voice was still ringing in my ears: "Dan, there's probably nothing in it. The meadow's been owned by the council ever since I can remember. I expect they just want to hold on to it until the price is right."

He was probably correct in his assumption, but why wouldn't Chisholm just have said that? I know that councils are always strapped for cash these days, but that was nothing to be ashamed or secretive about. Or was I being a bit obsessed with this, maybe trying too hard to make a mark when I still hadn't properly got my feet under the desk? I mean, this was my first proper story for goodness' sake! I started to feel a bit ridiculous. Not every lead I followed was going to turn out to be the scoop of the year.

The young barista was collecting cups from the nearby

table. "I'm guessing lots of the people from the council offices come in here?" I enquired, looking out of the window at the building opposite.

"Some," he said. "But to be honest I don't know many of them. There are a couple of regulars like Sid Chisholm and that Eric somebody-or-other. Chisholm comes in here some days for lunch and a double espresso and often meets up with a hot young chick. They're really lovey-dovey, although you wouldn't think he had it in him. He must be seventy if he's a day. Don't know what she sees in him, although he's loaded from what I hear, so maybe I do see. And he's always okay with me. Even leaves a good tip most times."

I tried to conjure up the scene he was describing, but having just met him, my powers of imagination didn't seem to be up to the task.

"How did he make his money? Can't have been courtesy of the district council," I ventured. "I think all they get is a modest allowance."

"Dunno. I've heard folks say that in a previous life he used to travel a lot. Gotta go, sorry."

And with that the barista returned to the counter where a queue was developing. It was clear that there was nothing furtive about Chisholm's relationship with this girl. Maybe using a café on the office doorstep for his rendezvous was intended to attract the attention and envy of colleagues? Or maybe she was his granddaughter?

Intriguing as it was, I couldn't at the moment figure how this information added anything useful, so I began to consider my options for the rest of the day. I was reluctant to go back to the office with nothing.

The builder who intended to purchase Abbot's Meadow was

Robert Coldwell & Sons of West Lodgeford, a village only a mile or so outside the town. I wasn't sure what I was going to achieve, but I thought a quick visit couldn't do any harm. I went back to my car and drove to the village wondering whether journalism was going to be the exciting career I was hoping for.

*

West Lodgeford was a sleepy-looking place with just a pub, a church and a cluster of expensive-looking houses and cottages. I found the builders' yard adjacent to a large detached house on the outskirts bordering onto open fields. There was a brick-built office at the back of the yard which I made my way to, circumnavigating piles of bricks, breeze blocks, scaffold poles and assorted canvas bags of sand and gravel. I knocked on the door and it was opened by a huge, burly man, in his early thirties I guessed. He had a strong, square jaw and his broad face bore that healthy, suntanned glow that comes with a life spent outdoors doing manual work. Despite his imposing appearance, the warm smile was welcoming. In his massive hand was an equally massive mug which bore the legend 'I turn tea into houses'.

"Hiya," he said cheerfully. "What can I do for you, pal?"

"Hi. I'm looking for Robert Coldwell," I said.

"That'd be me," he said. "Though folks just call me Bob. Bob-the-Builder, like," and his face cracked in a huge grin. I don't know how many times he'd used this line, but he obviously still found it hilarious.

"Hello, Bob. My name's Dan Curran of the *Castlebridge Gazette*. I just wanted to ask you a few questions about Abbot's Meadow, if I could?"

"Best come in then," he said, and stood aside to let me in. "Expect you'd like a brew?" he enquired, and without waiting for an answer, switched on an ancient electric kettle.

"I see your company name is Robert Coldwell & Sons. If you don't mind me saying, you seem a bit young to have sons in the business. Or is your dad also called Bob?" I enquired, wanting to break the ice.

He indicated a photo on the wall behind him. It was a professionally taken studio photograph of himself with a woman, who I took to be his partner or wife, and two small boys, both of whom I would have said were under five.

"That's my wife, Michelle, with the '& Sons'. She's hoping that they'll become engineers or doctors, but I'm wanting them to follow me into the business… when they're old enough, like. The company name is just my way of preparing the ground, so to speak. Michelle still tells me off about it."

Again, his face lit up with a broad grin. I could see that Bob and I were going to get on famously.

While he made some tea I took the opportunity to look around the office. On one of the walls, I noticed a drawing of a housing development, and closer inspection showed it to be what was proposed for Abbot's Meadow. Obviously Bob had done a lot of work in anticipation of the purchase going through. Access appeared to be from the main road into town, and I wondered whether there was some problem with the planning department because of increased traffic.

"I see you've spotted the planned Abbot's Meadow housing estate," said Bob handing me a large mug of tea, confirming the oft-quoted adage that builders like it strong. Nearly black in fact.

He took a mouthful of tea and continued.

"I can tell you I was not a happy bunny to hear that they pulled out of the sale. No warning, no reasons given, just an email saying that the council had reconsidered the sale and decided not to proceed. The housing association and I spent a shedload working up that scheme with the architect. We had initial land surveys done and everything. About half the houses were going to be so-called affordable too, which is what the young ones around here desperately need. I was gutted, I can tell you."

"Who actually sent the email?" I asked out of interest.

"Well, it came from some committee, as I remember, but was actually signed by some chap called Chisholm, Sidney Chisholm I think it was. Why, do you know him?"

"Met him less than an hour ago as a matter of fact. He said the decision was made by some committee or other and it was out of his hands. Out of interest, how did you come to hear that the field was going to be sold off in the first place?"

"I'll show you," said Bob, fishing out a folder from his filing cabinet. Inside the folder, paper-clipped to the cover, was a two-column-wide notice of sale cut out from a newspaper. On the top of the notice, someone had written, 'From Castlebridge Gazette, 17th February'.

"Ah," I said feeling a little embarrassed, even though the newspaper had only run the advertisement. "And you don't have any theories as to what could be behind the sudden change of plan?"

"Nope. Complete mystery. Mind you, our councillors are a law unto themselves it seems. And I'll tell you this. There's folks around here, mentioning no names, you understand, who reckon that there are some on the council that probably shouldn't be, if you get my drift. So who knows what's behind it."

"Are you saying that some of them are… well, bent?" I asked, suddenly interested in what Bob knew.

"Let's just say that not everyone is as pure as the driven snow. But it's all hearsay so I'm not going to spread rumours." He paused, looking at me with a quizzical expression.

"You from round here?" he asked. "Can't imagine Castlebridge is that exciting for a young lad like you?"

"I've got to start somewhere… and it's got me out of Luton," I replied with a smile.

"I suppose so. Don't really know Luton, mind you. Tell you what… leave me your phone number and if I hear anything more I'll give you a bell."

I'd been away from the office for too long and decided it was time to go. I jotted down my mobile number, finished the tea and made my excuses. As I weaved my way back across the yard, Bob called out from the door of his office.

"If I were you, pal, I'd stop worrying about Abbot's Meadow and move on. My gut tells me that nothing good will come from it."

I waved in acknowledgement. *Not a chance*, I thought.

CHAPTER 2

I remember breaking the news to my father, William, that I had been offered a place at Cardiff University to study journalism. My father, it has to be said, was not a man prone to mincing his words. He always said his Northern blood obliged him to 'speak as I find', which was odd because as far as I was aware, neither he nor his family had ever ventured further north than Birmingham. By the age of eighteen, I should have grown used to his candour, but it still unsettled me. I explained that I fancied being an investigative journalist for a newspaper, but I could see that he was not really listening.

"What on earth do you want to go into newspapers for, lad?" he chided, aggressively raking out the bowl of his pipe into an ashtray. In an increasingly health-conscious world where smokers are commonly awarded pariah status, it was odd that my father still favoured the occasional pipe. I was convinced it was an affectation to reinforce his supposed Northern connections. It seemed to put in an appearance whenever he felt the urge to pontificate, and that urge was most definitely upon him.

"Journalism's not a dignified profession. Look at all the court cases over phone hacking and the paparazzi. It's just an excuse to invade people's privacy, get pissed every lunchtime and write second-rate sensationalist stuff which few will actually bother to read. Good only for tomorrow's fish and chips. And anyway, they say that newspapers have had their day now everyone has got these mobile phones and tablets. Besides, with your A-levels you could go on to be a scientist, or a health professional like your sister… or whatever you want really."

In my father's ranking of worthwhile professions, my older sister, Emily, being a nurse at a Stevenage hospital, was right up there in the elite group, whereas journalists were definitely in the 'unclassified' section – just below traffic warden.

Refilling his pipe from an ancient leather pouch he added, "Can't you find something to make your mark on the world instead of sitting on the sidelines watching? The world is your oyster, lad… that's what they say. Get a grip. Find yourself a career that'll make your mum and me proud."

And with that he set fire to a new charge of tobacco in his pipe, emitting great clouds of noxious-smelling smoke, and returned to studying the runners at Newmarket in the *Racing Post*. He didn't believe in sugar-coating his pearls of wisdom, that's for sure! I remember thinking that my dad's decision to become a welder at the Vauxhall factory must have come as a great blessing to the local pastoral care workers, not to mention the Samaritans.

What my father was trying to express, in his own inimitable, cack-handed way, was that journalism was all about observing the actions and achievements of others, not about getting involved and contributing to society, even if in a very small way. Does anyone ever talk about the great reporters of the nineteenth and twentieth centuries? People remember the great news scoops and the scandals, but probably don't have a clue as to who was involved in exposing them. Okay, Bob Woodward and Carl Bernstein of the *Washington Post* seem to have gone into the history books over Watergate, but for most people, other examples are harder to recall.

I must admit that a part of me had some sympathy with my dad's view, but at the age of eighteen, I was convinced that I would be the exception to the rule. The idea of investigative journalism seemed exciting, thrilling even. A bit like being a detective, but without the discipline and bureaucracy, and without having to call people 'Sir' or 'Ma'am'. Exposing and righting the wrongs in our society, supporting the underdog, holding our elected representatives to account, helping to solve crimes and proving that the pen is indeed mightier than the sword. What was not to like? More than I had expected, as it was to turn out.

While my dad was decidedly unimpressed, my mother was positively ebullient, waving my offer letter around like a flag on Coronation Day. She was convinced that my eventual degree in journalism was going to be just the start of a great career in the 'media', in which I would move quickly through the ranks at Fleet Street, and on to the BBC or ITV, where I would be anchorman on *News at Ten* or *Panorama*. After all, that's how they all started. There was simply no doubt in her mind. It was as good as done.

"I can't wait for you to get me an invitation to meet that lovely Trevor McDonald," she said, laughing… and I suspect only half-jokingly. I was guessing that by the end of the day, the entire neighbourhood would be congratulating me on my success, and her on raising such a soon-to-be famous child.

I just hoped that I would be able to get to the end of my three years at Cardiff and graduate. I simply couldn't afford to fail or drop out and give my father the satisfaction of being in some sense right all along. I knew myself well enough to realise that boredom was going to be my biggest enemy. The truth was that part of the appeal of journalism was that it offered an endless supply of new stories to tell, new people to meet and places to go. As a child I always struggled with any activity which required sustained interest over any period of time. I strived to play an instrument, but gave up on both piano and guitar after just a few months, weary of the repetition and grindingly slow pace of progress. I can't even remember finishing a jigsaw or game of Monopoly – although maybe I was not alone in that respect.

As it turned out, the three years at Cardiff passed tolerably quickly, and fortunately I did manage to get a degree of sorts. Although with more application I could have done a lot better, I was nevertheless quite pleased with myself. My father even congratulated me, after a fashion.

"Well, at least now you might be able to get a regular pay packet," he conceded. "Not that it'll buy you much. Pay's bound to be low."

But there were not many kids like me, from the terraced houses of Luton, who could aspire to a job for which a university qualification was actually needed. Although a lot of my friends also went to university, they saw this as just an enjoyable way of passing time, before getting a job stacking shelves in a warehouse, or working on the shop floor of a factory pressing a button every two minutes. I liked to think my father had a sneaking admiration for my achievement, although he never let on.

The news that I had managed to get a job as a junior reporter with the *Castlebridge Gazette* went down rather better with my father, once it had been explained to him where

Castlebridge was. Although we got on reasonably well, I think he was keen to put the 'absence makes the heart grow fonder' theory to the test as soon as possible. Maybe he felt a stint in the backwaters of the East Midlands would bring me to my senses and make me more appreciative of my hometown. Or maybe I was misjudging him completely and he just wanted me to become more independent. But I couldn't wait to properly flee the nest and start fending for myself, although I had to admit that twenty-one years of being housed, catered and laundered for had made me more than a little apprehensive.

Unlike my father, my mother was completely distraught at the prospect of me leaving home for good. My time away at university was bad enough, but she had consoled herself with the thought that at least that was only temporary.

"Couldn't you have found somewhere near here?" she asked, trying hard to hold back the tears. "You'll have to find somewhere to live, and you know how expensive it is to rent. And you have all your friends here." She was floundering, searching for more arguments against the move, but knew deep down that this was going to be a lost cause.

"Well, make sure you phone at least twice a week, and come back and see us at least once a month," she stipulated. The first item I was going to have to buy was obviously a calendar so that I could keep a tally of calls and visits.

After a lot of hunting I did manage to find somewhere to live. However, a small and rather scruffy one-bedroom flat above a charity shop in one of the shabbier suburbs of Castlebridge was all I could afford. As I prepared to leave home, packing my ancient Mini with suitcases and assorted bags and boxes, my father stopped me.

"I'm sure you'll find this useful to get started, lad."

He thrust an envelope into my hand in which there was £500 in notes, and I noticed that his eyes were moist. At that moment, we both recognised the unspoken love that existed between us, and again, as was often the case with my father, no other words were necessary. We shook hands, our eyes locked for the briefest of moments and I drove away to start the next phase of my life.

*

The *Castlebridge Gazette* occupied a reasonably spacious office above a row of shops on Castlebridge High Street, which went by the rather pretentious name of the Albany Suite. The paper's editor and owner, Jack Marston, had a long and enviable track record in the newspaper industry, having worked as a senior reporter for several of the Fleet Street nationals in his thirties and forties. Now at the age of fifty-seven, his ambition to own his own newspaper was fulfilled, but at a cost. The money he had managed to put by in earlier years was gradually being eroded propping up the newspaper. Although at least half of the newspaper was devoted to advertising, this did not bring in sufficient revenue to supplement the gradually dwindling sales. In the age of the smartphone and tablet, the call for paper copies was in decline, even among the older generation who had once been stalwarts of the sales figures. They were fast becoming silver surfers, getting their news for free online.

What Jack desperately needed was an experienced, dynamic reporter who could set the paper on fire with astonishing and audacious scoops and exclusives. Someone new, with a reputation for fearless and incisive stories that would galvanise the local community into proudly supporting their very own newspaper champion. Unfortunately, what he got was me.

During my first week I managed to turn in some acceptable if unremarkable copy on a local headteacher retiring after forty years' service, and a clash between neighbours over the height of a garden fence which ended in the police being called. However, my time spent investigating Abbot's Meadow was, it seems, totally wasted, something I was sure that Jack would be only too keen to point out as I entered the office.

"Hi, Dan," said Tracy on reception as I came through the door at the top of the stairs. To tell the truth, I quite fancied Tracy, but from what I could gather listening to snippets of phone conversations, she already had a boyfriend. Still, I was willing to bide my time.

"Jack wants to see you, and he's not in a very good mood today so I should tread carefully," she confided.

I thought I might know why, but settled for "Thanks, Tracy", and smiled in what I hoped appeared a nonchalant manner as I made my way to his office in the corner of the open-plan area. Surely he would cut me a little slack in my first week. Wouldn't he?

The door was open and he was sitting looking at his mobile phone, a concerned expression on his face.

"Hi, Jack. Tracy said you wanted to see me," I said as brightly as I could muster.

Jack had the bearing of a man totally at ease with himself. I supposed that all those years spent at the sharp end of investigations involving the great and the good, as well as the lowly and less good, had equipped him with a resilience to stand his ground and not be deflected by the coercion, bribery, false praise, abuse or threats which must come with the job. His dark complexion, smart clothes, silver-grey hair and well-groomed moustache gave him a dashing appearance, which no doubt made him popular with the ladies. I was not fooled by his debonair looks, however. There was real steel in those blue eyes. I suddenly felt like an eleven-year-old boy called to see the headmaster, shuffling nervously from one foot to the other in the doorway.

"Daniel. Come in and sit down," he barked. "There's something I want you to do for me. When Tracy and I got home last night, my wife was up in arms. A family of Travellers was camped on the verge right opposite our house."

I made a mental note that Tracy was Jack's daughter and so definitely off limits. I also began to relax. Maybe this wasn't going to be so bad after all. He showed me a picture of the offending encampment on his mobile phone.

"I want you to go and have a word with them. Suggest that it would be better if they move on rather than camp just there. Narrow lane, obstructing the view of approaching traffic from the bend, potential accidents, unwelcome publicity in the press – that sort of thing. I've nothing against them, you understand, just don't want them opposite my house. Do you think you could handle that? A little gentle persuasion, that's all."

I was not entirely sure that what I thought had any relevance in this situation, so I just nodded enthusiastically.

"No problem," I said, wondering what sort of trouble I was about to get into, and suspecting that my relaxation was going to be short-lived.

"How did you get on with the Abbot's Meadow investigation?" he said, seemingly genuinely interested and with no hidden agenda.

I recounted my meetings with Councillor Sid Chisholm and the builder, Bob Coldwell. He looked out of the window down onto the street for a few moments to gather his thoughts, and then turned back to face me.

"I think I'm with you on this one, Daniel. I reckon you've got a journalist's nose when it comes to sniffing out a good story. The fact that no reason has been given doesn't sit well with me. The council is accountable to the general public, and they should be open and honest about these sorts of things. But hey, we should be able to find out what's behind it. Have a look on the council's website to see if any meeting minutes were published – I'm not sure which would be the relevant committee. Failing that we can make a Freedom of Information request. Could take a while though."

I was still processing the 'journalist's nose' comment. Those few simple words were music to my young ears, and probably constituted the single defining moment in my early career. The day when I realised that this was definitely what I was destined to do with my life. I suddenly became aware that Jack was speaking again.

"But in the meantime, Dan, I do need copy from you. This paper takes a lot of feeding. Can you make sure that you cover at least one or two reasonably meaty local stories each day in addition to anything you want to do on Abbot's Meadow? Geoff on the news desk will give you the necessary leads to follow."

As I turned to go, Jack added, "Oh, and, Dan, just a word of advice. Take things slowly. When you pull on a loose thread, there's no telling what will start unravelling, or who you might upset in the process."

Wise words that would later come back to haunt me.

CHAPTER 3

Geoff Clarke was another seasoned veteran of Fleet Street. No one knew quite how old he was, but the general consensus was well past what might be considered the normal retirement age. He remained as sharp as a razor, although the passage of years had taken its toll physically, and he needed a stick to get around the office. Although he only ventured out occasionally to cover particularly interesting stories, it was nothing short of miraculous what he could accomplish with just a telephone and the internet, and the younger reporters, myself included, were in awe of his talent for sharp, pithy writing.

Geoff ran the news desk, which covered local and national/international news, although the latter warranted typically only a single page in each edition, and most of the copy was derived from agency feeds such as Reuters. Local news was covered by a handful of reporters, plus me. Each morning, Geoff would hold an all-hands meeting to review the 'daily news pipeline', which consisted of a spreadsheet shown on a large wall monitor, onto which all leads and potential news stories were entered together with the name of the allocated staff member. We reviewed it again after lunch in case any big stories were developing, so that we could make any last-minute changes necessary for the single daily evening edition. For each item there was a target edition date, the expected column inches if known, plus an importance ranking ranging from front-page lead story to 'filler'; these were stories of lesser importance that were not especially time restricted and could be used whenever there was available space. As junior reporter this was where much of my time was destined to be spent.

I was assigned two stories for the day, one on a proposed new extension to a local school, and one on fly-tipping in Marsh Lane on the outskirts of the town. Geoff was helpful as always.

"When you go to the school, get an illustration of the proposed extension that we could use, plus some nice quotes from staff. Maybe even a quote from a pupil if it seems appropriate and you can get one to say something interesting. Also find out how the school governors have been supporting the development – maybe interview the chair to the governors."

After a few moments' thought, he added, "And for the fly-tipping incident, take a few pictures yourself, talk to the local farmers on the impact it's had, find out what the local council environmental people are doing about clearing it up… oh, and get them to give you an estimate of what it will all cost. The public quite rightly get angry when they realise that they are indirectly going to foot the bill."

Geoff reached into his drawer and produced a box containing business cards printed with my name on: 'Daniel Curran, Staff Reporter'.

"You'll be needing these," he said with a smile. I took one out and admired it, thinking that I must put one in an envelope and send it to my parents. Well, my mother at least.

I set off on my day's assignments, deciding that the very

first stop should be the Travellers at the end of Jack's drive. Keeping Jack happy was a priority, although in truth I had no idea how exactly that was going to be accomplished. His suggested approach felt like bullying, or even racism, which didn't sit well with me.

It turned out that Jack lived in West Lodgeford, not that far from the builder Bob Coldwell. The spacious mock-Tudor house had a large front garden lined with shrubs and a semi-circular gravel drive giving access at each end from the road. Directly opposite the house was a wide grass verge on which was parked a long, remarkably clean, white and chrome caravan, plus a white, nearly new Mitsubishi Shogun 4x4. I pulled up onto the verge behind the caravan and sat for a few minutes to gather my thoughts.

The truth was that one of the values that I inherited from my father was 'live and let live'. He was a lifelong Liberal, and despite the outwardly blunt, no-nonsense demeanour, was a kind and generous man. I can remember, as if it were yesterday, his sense of disappointment when he heard that I and my classmates at junior school had been making fun of some Gypsy children who were temporarily inducted into the class. Their longish hair and lack of any item of clothing that even vaguely resembled the school uniform quickly set them apart, and children can be surprisingly cruel.

"None of us get to choose the circumstances into which we are born, lad," he said. "You'd do well to think on that. People have a right to be who they are, and you should learn to accept and embrace the differences that make us all unique. And I'm not just talking about people who choose a travelling life. It could be race, colour, religion… Don't pick on people because of the way they were born and who they are. It's not right.

You're better than that." I had tried hard to heed his advice ever since.

I couldn't see that the Travellers were doing any real harm, and the area appeared to be quite clean and tidy. A washing line had been rigged up between two steel posts, and a quick look at the garments pegged to it told me that there was at least one small child.

"Can I help you, chap?" said a stocky, muscular man who I guessed was in his late twenties.

He was dressed in a white short-sleeved shirt with red braces holding up a pair of faded jeans. He looked a picture of health, with a full head of jet-black hair and a deep suntan. I could see that he was working on a portable generator, some bits of which were strewn around him on the grass.

"Er… well, hopefully," I said wondering how this conversation was going to develop. "My name's Daniel Curran and I work for the *Castlebridge Gazette*. I've been talking with the council recently about vacant land, and as I saw you here I thought I'd just stop and see whether you've been offered a proper pitch anywhere, or whether the council has done an assessment of your children's needs? I believe it's supposed to do that." I had no idea what I was talking about, or whether this was actually true, but from the little I had read on the subject, it seemed as though it might be.

"You've got to be joking, chap," he replied with a look that said I must inhabit some different planet. "Any discussions we do have are about when we're moving on. To be fair, they have set up a permanent Traveller site on the far side of town, but it's ridiculously small, and always full. We're just here temporarily, like, waiting for some friends coming up from Dorset, and then we'll try to find a better place somewhere."

I started to feel guilty and wondered whether he had seen through my pretence of interest in his predicament. However, a plan was forming in my head which I hadn't really thought through, but which might solve the problem. Either that or create another bigger one.

"The council do in fact own quite a large field off Basset Lane which was going to be a housing development, but I gather that's now fallen through. The field is just left fallow at the moment. Might be worth looking into."

Just then, a small buxom woman, wearing a pale blue dress and a red headscarf, appeared from the caravan holding a baby of maybe six months.

"What's up, Mickey?" she enquired, looking at the child who appeared rather flushed and was crying intermittently, but without any real enthusiasm.

"This chap's from a local newspaper," he responded, but decided not to elaborate.

"Oh I see," she said with a disapproving look.

"I was just passing and thought I'd stop for a chat," I lied, getting more uncomfortable with each passing second. "Your child doesn't look too well," I ventured, desperately trying to keep things cordial. "Is he running a temperature?"

"No, he's fine. He's just teething," she said, and smiled as she gave the child a jiggle. "You got kids, have you?" she enquired.

I shook my head, flattered that someone should look at me and see a potential parent, rather than a somewhat awkward, gawky young man still trying to come to terms with adulthood.

"This field you're talking about… would that be called Abbot's Meadow?" Mickey enquired.

"Yes, do you know it?" I asked.

"Know it? We were thrown off it a few months back. Us and a couple of other families were set up there and this chap from the council comes. Went absolutely mental, he did. Threatens us with police eviction. He said the meadow was off limits to the general public and we had to leave immediately. He got so fired up, I thought he was going to hit me at one point. Well, either that or burst a blood vessel."

"Can you remember the councillor's name?" I asked, intrigued.

"Don't know his name, but Rosa took a picture of him on her phone she was so worried. Thought I was about to take a pop at him, I reckon."

Remembering that I still had the leaflet of current councillors given to me by the stand-in receptionist, Jenny, I asked, "Do you think I could see the picture if it's still on the phone?"

Mickey looked at Rosa, who nodded. "Sure. You'd best come in then." And with that, he led the way to the caravan door.

The caravan was neat and tidy inside and nicely, if somewhat garishly, furnished, with brightly coloured throws over the seating. I noticed there was a second child, probably three or four years old, sitting at the table doing some crayoning. She looked up as we entered.

"This is Liberty, our eldest," said Mickey proudly. "Going to be a brilliant artist one day, aren't you, Libby?" Liberty looked up and beamed a gap-toothed smile. I was struck by what a pleasant family they seemed to be, and wondered whether Jack had actually spoken with them.

I took a seat while Rosa found her phone and scrolled through the images. Eventually she found the one she wanted and showed me the screen.

"There, that's him," she said tapping the screen. "Nasty piece of work he was."

The man appeared to be heavily built and had a ruddy complexion, made worse by what was obviously blind rage. His mouth was open, caught mid-snarl, and his eyes were wide and appeared bloodshot. I took out the leaflet from my jacket pocket, opened it up and compared the phone image to the thumbnail images showing the current councillors for the fourteen wards which made up the district. After a few moments, I identified the man as Samuel Hepworth, and showed Mickey and Rosa.

"That's him, wouldn't you say?" I said. "He's a bit more smiley in the leaflet picture, but I'm sure it's him."

They agreed without hesitation. I couldn't help wondering why a Traveller encampment was of such importance to Hepworth and resolved to see whether I might be able to shed some light on that. Maybe he had a personal interest in the meadow? Or maybe he just hated Travellers.

"Well, as I say, the meadow is still empty, and likely to remain that way from what I gather," I ventured pointedly.

I wondered whether what I was doing was totally ethical. The original brief was to get them out of Jack's hair, not help them find a new place to set up camp. Was I trying to provoke a response from the council at the expense of these nice people?

"I'd a good mind to go back there so we can spread out a bit and have room when our friends arrive," said Mickey. "They'll have to come up with a better excuse now as to why we can't use it just temporarily, like. You sure they ain't gonna build on it?"

I nodded. However, I was starting to think that maybe I had done a really foolish thing and was stirring a hornets' nest. I was also wondering what I was going to tell Jack.

"If you do move there, please don't mention that you've spoken to me as it could look as though the newspaper has been involved," I asked, probably sounding slightly pathetic. I tried to make light of it. "I've only just joined the newspaper, and would like to last at least a few months before they throw me out," I smiled, but was only half joking.

"No problem, chap," said Mickey and offered his hand. "I appreciate you taking an interest," he said. "Makes a nice change. So many folks won't give us the time of day."

I handed him one of my new business cards. "If you do run into any trouble, I'd like to know. Maybe I can come to the meadow and cover the story of how the council is failing the travelling community."

And with that, I thanked Mickey and Rosa, and left… before my inexperience led me to say anything else stupid.

*

My two assignments for the day went well, all things considered. The school extension was a really big deal for the staff, who would get two extra classrooms and, importantly, a proper staffroom for the first time in five years. I managed to chase down the chair of governors who worked for a firm of accountants, and he was only too pleased to come to the school for a quick photo session with the headmistress. We taped an artist's impression of the extension to a whiteboard, which made a perfect backdrop for the photo. I even got a quote from a seven-year-old called Holly, who thought that having a new classroom was going to be 'totally wicked'. Quite how I would be able to use that eluded me for the moment.

I found the fly-tipping incident really depressing and

couldn't understand what sort of person would dump old furniture, mattresses, fridges and assorted junk on a charming country lane. A farmer came out to investigate while I was taking photos, complaining bitterly about the blocked access to his field. This was not the first occasion such a thing had happened and he had an air of tired resignation. Among the detritus I found an envelope with an address on it and handed this to the environmental protection officer who had agreed to meet me at the site. If someone could be prosecuted, I figured the follow-up on the story would have, if not a happy ending, at least a just one.

When I got back to the office, I typed up a first draft of both stories and emailed them through to Geoff, who would check them and pass them on to one of the sub-editors. I wanted to use the rest of the afternoon to do some digging into the Abbot's Meadow story, although I was acutely aware that for most people, the fate of an uncared-for field on the outskirts of town was unlikely to be of huge interest.

I began my digging by visiting the Castlebridge District Council website and trying to locate the minutes of the meeting where the decision was made, if indeed either the minutes or the decision had made it into the public domain. It took me the best part of half an hour going between the various committees, but I finally found a document by the Housing & New Homes Committee entitled 'Request to Sell Asset Ref. 09-51473 known as Abbot's Meadow'.

The report was difficult to interpret for those not well versed in the workings of local government, but under the Recommendation section it stated:

That Housing Committee recommend to Policy &

Resources Committee that the freehold sale of the subject land should be denied.

In the Context/Background section, under Factors Against Sale, it said:

The Douglas report concludes that, under the Ancient Monuments and Archaeological Areas Act 1979, Abbot's Meadow can be declared an Area of Archaeological Importance, and as such must be afforded protected status pending further investigation.

There didn't seem to be any mention of voting, so I was not sure whether this was the final document in the decision-making process, but nevertheless it seemed pretty clear that there was some historical association with the meadow which prevented its sale. This was getting more interesting by the minute. I still didn't understand why Sid Chisholm had not simply told me that. He must have known the reason. Maybe the Douglas report would shed more light, but I couldn't find any other reference to this document. Google came up with many hits, but so far as I could judge, all were completely unrelated. I dug out the phone number for Jenny, the pretty Council House receptionist, and decided to give her a call, pleased to have a pretext on which to make contact. After a few moments she picked up.

"Hi, Jenny. This is Dan Curran of the *Castlebridge Gazette*. We met yesterday when I came in to talk with one of the councillors."

I was hoping she would remember, and also that there wouldn't be that awkward pause that you get when people realise that the chance to not answer the phone has gone, and that they are committed to a call they would rather not have taken. Happily, in this instance that did not seem to be the case.

"Oh, hello, Dan," she said brightly. "Nice to talk with you again. What can I do for you?"

She was doing quite a lot for me already, but down to the business in hand.

"I was talking with Sid Chisholm yesterday about the sale of a piece of council-owned land called Abbot's Meadow, which has now fallen through. I've just been looking on your website at the minutes from a Housing Committee meeting on 10th June about the sale. It seems that the site is of archaeological interest and the meeting notes refer to a document called the Douglas report. Trouble is, I can't find that report on your website. Would you have any idea how I could get hold of a copy? I realise it's probably not really a finance department issue, but…"

She paused for a few seconds and I suddenly regretted putting her in an awkward position. However, when she replied, there was nothing in her voice that suggested any discomfort.

"Well, I could certainly dig around and see what I can find," she said. "It should be filed on our system, and I can't believe it's classified. Especially when it relates to a council meeting that anyone can attend. When do you need it by?"

"Well, whenever really," I said. "I'm just doing a bit of investigation in the background. There might be nothing in it from the news story perspective."

"Do you want me to do it quietly, so to speak, or are you okay with me asking someone in Planning or Housing outright?" she enquired.

This willingness to collude with me was both flattering and, suddenly, really worrying. I was sure that what was being proposed would not comply with any council code of behaviour.

"Look, I don't want to get you into any trouble," I said, and a vision of her getting fired for misconduct or some such thing flashed into my head. "Maybe I'll just write a letter to the council requesting a copy?"

"No, really, it's okay. Let me take a look. It's no problem, and you've got me interested. A bit of a break from boring figures."

"Well, alright then but very discreetly. I might be completely wrong, but, between you and me, something doesn't quite feel right. All I really want to know is how I can get a copy, so maybe just the name of someone there that I can talk to. If you can even tell me who wrote it, that would be a good start. I'm guessing it's someone called Douglas, but is this a consultant or someone at the council?"

"Okay. Leave it with me, Dan. I'll give you a call on this number when I know more. Is it alright if I phone you after hours? If I can find out anything, maybe we could meet for coffee, or something…" Her voice tailed off.

"That would be great," I said, perhaps a little too hastily. "I'll look forward to it."

I put the phone down and smiled to myself. I realised I was sweating. My usually clumsy advances to the opposite sex were invariably met with embarrassment and a string of unconvincing excuses. I was not used to girls being so forward, and it felt both exciting and slightly unnerving. Or had I just misread the situation entirely? It wouldn't be the first time. The sound of the desk phone ringing jolted me out of my reverie.

"Dan. It's Jack. Can you come in here, please?"

He sounded even more terse than usual and my anxiety level shot up. I crossed the office and knocked on his door before entering. Jack looked very serious and immediately I knew that something bad was coming.

"Did Sid Chisholm seem unwell or upset when you saw him yesterday at the council building?" he said, giving nothing away.

"He was fine as far as I know," I said. "I've never met him before. He wasn't particularly courteous and didn't really want to talk to me, but yes, he seemed alright. Why do you ask?"

"He died last night," said Jack. "Probably a heart attack, but the police have been involved while other causes are ruled out."

CHAPTER 4

Mr Jeffers, one of my old lecturers at Cardiff, used to say that bad things don't really happen in journalism, because it's all future copy. A somewhat callous viewpoint, I admit, but I could see what he meant. Nevertheless, the news of Sid Chisholm's death came as a massive shock to me. The thought that I was talking with him the day before and now he was gone was hard to comprehend. I replayed the visit over and over again in my mind, hunting for the clues about his state of health which I may have missed. Could the reason he was so abrupt with me be that he was concerned about his health?

Jack instructed me to drop my investigation into Abbot's Meadow until the results of the post-mortem were known. Maybe he thought I'd been heavy-handed in my meeting with Chisholm and put him under pressure, which in some way contributed to his demise. Whatever the reason, I did suddenly feel sorry that we had not had a friendlier, more constructive meeting, and I regretted my rather petulant departure.

The next morning Jack came to my desk and was seemingly very happy.

"Well done, Dan. The Travellers were gone when I left the house this morning. Did you run into any difficulties?"

"Not really. They were very friendly, on the whole," I replied somewhat obscurely.

It was a great relief to know that they had actually gone, as I didn't have the heart to ask them to leave directly. I thought it prudent to keep quiet about how the meeting actually went. I was keen to see whether the family were now camped on Abbot's Meadow, and resolved to drive past there at the first opportunity.

For the next couple of days, I worked hard on the filler stories assigned to me by Geoff and was pleased to see that these were now making it into print, albeit after some rewrites. I felt that I was starting to get a better understanding of the dynamic nature of newspapers. The editor needs to be able to reflect breaking news or rapidly developing stories, and so the positioning and relative importance of articles remains quite fluid right up to the print deadline. As a result, some filler stories which aren't timebound get bounced at the last minute. I told myself it was nothing personal, although not making the current edition was disappointing.

We ran a few column inches reporting the death of Sid Chisholm in the edition following his death, but Jack had it in mind to run a larger obituary piece later, looking back over his career and particularly his public service as a councillor.

We eventually found out via the police Corporate Communications Office that the coroner had requested a post-mortem and the preliminary results gave the cause of Sid's death as *coronary atherosclerosis*. A quick check on Google told me that this would be classed as natural causes. Jack asked me if I would like to write a draft of the obituary piece, being as I seemed to be the only member of staff to have actually met him. While I was contemplating how to begin, my mobile phone rang and I saw that it was Jenny Swan. My heart raced a little as I pressed the pick-up button.

"Hi, Jenny. Have you managed to find out anything?"

"Hi, Dan. Well, yes I have, sort of..." she said, with a vagueness that suggested that whatever she had discovered wasn't going to get me a whole lot further. She was also speaking very quietly and I guessed that there were other people nearby.

"I think it would be better if we met up somewhere after work," she suggested.

"No problem," I said, thinking that this was a great idea, whether or not Abbot's Meadow was on the agenda. "What time do you finish this evening?" I asked.

"I finish at five o'clock. There's a coffee bar right opposite us, but I think I'd prefer somewhere a bit further away. How about we meet at Harry's Place just off Market Street – do you know it?"

I didn't, but was sure I'd find it. "Great. I'll see you there at about 5pm, or just after."

We said goodbye and I put the phone down, feeling a little light-headed. Jenny seemed really nice, but whether I stood any chance with her I had no idea.

I wanted to maximise the possibility of getting some useful information from our meeting, so I took out the list of district councillors, and for the next hour or so I used Google and social media to see what I could find out about some of them. I was particularly interested in Samuel Hepworth, the man pictured on Rosa's phone who was involved in their previous eviction from Abbot's Meadow. Rosa described him as a nasty piece of work, but his Facebook posts showed him in quite a different light. There were pictures of him at a care home, at a charity event and with his family. If he did have a darker side, he kept it well hidden. He appeared to be of average height, but above average weight, and several posts showed him with a beer in his hand. I guessed he was probably in his fifties and therefore unlikely to have retired, so I did some searching to see if I could uncover a day job.

There were quite a lot of pictures based around gardens and building sites, although his clothing didn't suggest that he was engaged in the manual side. Perhaps he was running a building business. A further search on Google gave me 'Hepworth Landscaping Ltd, Birchwood Road, Castlebridge', and the website for the company confirmed that Samuel Hepworth was a director along with a Chris Hepworth. Maybe I would ask Bob Coldwell if he'd come across them.

Next, I turned my attention to the late Sid Chisholm. In common with a lot of people of his generation, he didn't appear to be a Facebook user, or indeed a user of any social media. I conducted a quick name search through the *Gazette*'s archives and found a piece written when he first won his seat ten years ago at the age of sixty-one. It came as something of a surprise to learn that Chisholm had previously worked as a widely respected senior geologist for a global oil company, during which time he travelled the world. The write-up said that he was married with a grown-up daughter, and I wondered whether the young lady that the coffee bar barista spoke of could possibly have been his daughter, although his age suggested that this was unlikely. He won his seat representing the Labour Party with a good majority, so evidently a sizeable number of people in his ward liked him. The more I read, the more I began to think that perhaps I had misjudged him. However, I kept coming back to his demeanour when I tried to get him to talk about Abbot's Meadow. It seemed very much as if he was hiding something.

*

As five o'clock approached, I left the offices and made my way down High Street towards Market Street. Harry's Place turned out to be a trendy independent coffee bar where there appeared to be a different variety of coffee for every day of the year. I was a little early, so I took a seat in the far corner which was less busy and did a bit of people-watching.

There were the usual students intently poring over laptops, making a single latte last for an hour, and a couple of young mothers with buggies doing their best to have a rational conversation while attempting to ignore needy babies. Several teenagers still in school uniforms were in a huddle, silently sucking on iced coffee concoctions, while delegating all responsibility for communication to fingers and thumbs which danced silently over the screens of their smartphones. I wondered idly whether I was watching Darwinism in action. After centuries of developing and enriching the art of human discourse into the language which gave us Shakespeare, Dickens and Austen, had our dialogue finally evolved into the mangled and horribly truncated text so enamoured by my generation? And if thumbing a few letters is simply too much bother, there is always an emoji for every situation, emotion or human condition.

Jenny arrived just after five looking very attractive in a yellow and orange floral print dress which complemented the softly curled shoulder-length auburn hair. Her make-up was expertly applied, but in an understated way, accentuating her natural good looks. As she sat down and made herself comfortable, I noticed that there wasn't a ring on her left hand, not that this meant very much these days.

"Hi, Jenny," I said, trying to compose myself and telling my racing heart to get a grip. "How about a coffee?"

"Oh, thanks, Dan. I'll have a small cappuccino if that's okay?" she said, opening her voluminous handbag to remove a notebook.

I heard the person in front of me at the counter order two triple venti, half-sweet, non-fat, caramel macchiatos, and it came as a great relief to be ordering something straightforward which even I couldn't get wrong. I brought two cappuccinos back to the table, wondering whether the Abbot's Meadow issue was the only reason for her wanting an in-person meeting.

"So, what did you manage to find out?" I asked, half hoping that there was going to be nothing in it, so that we could concentrate on getting better acquainted.

She took a sip of coffee and consulted her notebook.

"Well, I had a look on our server and found the meeting report fairly easily, and you were right, it does reference a Douglas report. Seems it was written by a firm of consultants. Among all the documents associated with that meeting is a file called 'Abbot's Meadow Survey Report and Findings', which I'm guessing is the document in question. Trouble is, when I tried to open it, I found it was password-protected, and I've not got a clue what the password might be. Now we do sometimes password-protect sensitive documents like payroll files, but these are usually kept in a restricted access directory anyway. In my admittedly limited experience, we never password-protect documents relating to the routine day-to-day committee meetings, which members of the public are entitled to attend. After all, isn't local government supposed to be the servant of the people – open and transparent?"

"I see," I said, feeling that this piece of information alone vindicated my conviction that there was more to all of this than met the eye.

"The other really strange thing is that the report found its way onto our system, but I can't work out how it got there. Normally we would raise a purchase order for an external piece of work to be done, and when it arrives there would be a transaction note which would be signed to receive in the goods or services. I'm presuming that it must have come electronically attached to an email, but I can't find any trace of it on our general office email account. That suggests it was sent to someone's personal email account. I did manage to uncover a paper copy of the receipt note, but it was signed off by Mia, one of the juniors in the office. She says that a councillor had confirmed that the order had been fulfilled and asked her to print and sign it. She can't remember who though. So the bottom line is, yes, it seems we have mysteriously got the report on our system, but we can't read it."

This was getting more intriguing by the minute.

"Is there someone on the council who was at that Housing Committee meeting who you think would be willing to talk to me about it? Someone you think is definitely conscientious and trustworthy? Someone who would be anxious to make sure that everything is above board?"

Jenny paused for reflection, and then her face lit up.

"Yes, I know just the person. You need to talk with Jim Symonds. He's been a councillor for years and is honest as the day is long. He's a real sweetie… and he sits on the Housing Committee."

"Great. Do you know if Jim knew Sid Chisholm?" I asked, trying hard to focus on something other than Jenny's engaging brown eyes. "I have to do an obituary piece on Sid, and I need someone who can tell me about him, both from a work perspective and personally."

"Yes. I'm pretty sure that Jim got on well with Sid. Well, to be fair, Jim gets on well with most people." She paused and a distant look crossed her face for a few moments. "You know, I still can't believe that one minute Sid was there talking to me, and the next, he's dead. He wasn't everyone's cup of tea and could sometimes be a bit short with people. But I liked him. He was always kind to me, especially when I first started and everything was new. It's all so sad."

"I feel just the same. The meeting I had with him wasn't especially constructive, but had I known that he was on borrowed time, I might have handled the situation differently and been a little less confrontational. I read on the council website that he was married with a grown-up daughter. Do you know much about the family, or about Sid?" I enquired.

"I know he was separated from his wife a long time ago, but he saw his daughter quite regularly. They would meet up at the office every month or so and go out to lunch. She seemed very pleasant, and obviously doted on her dad."

Something prevented me from talking about the conversation I had with the young barista in the coffee bar opposite the council offices. I didn't want Jenny to think that I traded in gossip, and maybe I was conscious that it would give Jenny the impression that I was always in journalist mode. However, while I was considering how to progress the conversation, Jenny came back with the lead I was hoping for.

"To be honest," she said blushing slightly, "Sid had a young girlfriend, early twenties like me, I would guess. Everyone knew about her and he never tried to keep it a secret. I think he was very well off, which I guess is always an attraction for some girls, but he seemed very happy, at least until recently, and who are we to judge?"

"Absolutely. Couldn't agree more. Do you know her name? I would quite like to interview her so that their relationship doesn't just stay the subject of gossip and tarnish the legacy he leaves." I said this in all sincerity, and I could almost feel my dad's hand on my shoulder saying, 'That's right, lad, live and let live.'

"I think it was Natalie Barker or Parker... something like that. I expect Jim Symonds will know." And with that she opened the notebook at the back page and copied down a phone number onto a paper napkin. "Here, this is Jim's mobile number."

There was something in what Jenny said that troubled me.

"You said until recently Sid seemed happy. Do you know what happened recently that might have had a bearing on his demeanour?"

"The other girls noticed it too, and the gossip was that he was being put under pressure of some sort over the course of the last two or three weeks. About what and by whom I've no idea," she replied. "Maybe something in his private life to do with his wife, but that's just speculation. Whatever it was, it was making him unhappy."

I wondered whether he was being put under duress not to talk about Abbot's Meadow. He was certainly very terse with me on the subject. There seemed to be a bit of a lull in the conversation at this point so I thought it was time to see if I could move things on from work. We both started to speak at the same time, and then both stopped awkwardly.

Jenny laughed and started again. "I was just going to ask how long you've been with the *Gazette*?"

"Oh, this is my first job after uni, so my whole career… which is now some ten… no, I tell a lie… eleven days."

Jenny laughed and replied, "Well, you must like it to have stayed so long. Are you living in Castlebridge?"

"Yes. I have a flat on the outskirts in a bit of a rough area, but it's fine for now. I lived in Cardiff for three years while I studied, but I guess home is still Luton where my parents live. What about you?" I asked, keeping the question deliberately vague in the hope that she would open up, and that we were not just engaged in polite conversation.

"Not a lot to tell," she replied. "I live with my dad in Thornton, which is a village a few miles south of the town. My dad's a design engineer for an engineering company here in Castlebridge. My mum passed away with cancer just over four years ago and I just couldn't bring myself to leave him on his own. He was in a very fragile state for the first year or two, but he's a lot better now and enjoying life again. Not that he will ever really get over it… they were really close since childhood. Soulmates, you might say. But Dad and I get along just fine."

"I'm so sorry to hear about your mum," I said. "That's really tough. What line of work was she in?"

"She was a radiographer. It's a bit ironic that the disease which she spent her working life helping hundreds of people recover from is what killed her. I must admit I did wonder whether the job was in some way responsible for her cancer, but I guess it was really just the luck of the draw. Very bad luck, as it happens."

"And what about your work at the council? How do you find that?" I hoped mentioning the council wouldn't lead us back into journalist interview mode, but I was keen to get to know as much as I could about Jenny.

"The council has been really good to me," she said. "I went straight into work after my A-levels, which was stupendously foolish, but at the time I just wanted to be earning money to help Dad out. After the best part of a year doing secretarial work in a really boring insurance office, I realised that I wanted more, and I did three years on day release to get my accountancy qualifications. If I could start over again, I think I might have done things differently, gone into medicine maybe…"

We chatted for a while longer and Jenny glanced at her watch. "Oh gosh, I need to go. I'm doing the shopping for dinner tonight on the way home."

"Can I give you a lift? My flat isn't far and I have a car there… of sorts," I offered.

"No, that's okay thanks. I also have a car… of sorts, which I hope is still parked where I left it this morning," she replied with a smile.

"Perhaps we could meet up one evening and have a meal?" I offered, surprising myself at my uncharacteristic boldness, and then instantly worrying that I'd overstepped the mark. When it came to the opposite sex, I was pretty hopeless at reading the vibes, as my sister was always reminding me.

"I'd like that, Dan," she said with a smile to melt the heart. "Call me."

As we stood to go, builder Bob Coldwell and his wife walked into the café. He recognised me immediately and came over to our table.

"Hello, Bob," I said. "Good to see you. You left the 'and sons' to run the business, have you?"

"Hello again," he said, laughing. "The lads are with their nan, just to give us a bit of together-time, like. This is Michelle, my wife." We shook hands and I turned towards Jenny.

"Jenny, this is Bob and Michelle. Bob's company was going to build houses on Abbot's Meadow before the sale was stopped. I met him at his yard a few days ago."

Jenny shook hands with them and commented, "The change of plans must have been disappointing for you."

I suddenly recalled the image of the man on Rosa's phone.

"Hey, Bob, there was something I wanted to ask you. What, if anything, do you know about a local chap called Sam Hepworth who has a landscaping company? He is the councillor who threw some Travellers off Abbot's Meadow last year."

Bob immediately lost his smile.

"Unfortunately, I do know Sam Hepworth, and his brother, Chris Hepworth. The pair of them run a business providing domestic and industrial landscaping, but it's the younger one, Chris, that calls the shots as far as that business is concerned. I wouldn't trust him as far as I could throw him, that one. He's trouble through and through. I had the misfortune to hire him and some of his team a couple of years back. Did a really shoddy job on a new build and then reneged on the price we agreed saying there were 'extras'. When I complained he as good as threatened me and my boys, saying that, with all the crime nowadays, it would be a shame if the site got vandalised. I paid him just to get him off my back. I don't know how true it is, but one of my guys heard that Chris had done time for GBH, or something. The pair of them are like the old 'good cop, bad cop', although of course they're as far from cops as you can get. Sam is allegedly the honest, respectable councillor, while Chris is running the dodgy family business which lines Sam's pockets. To be honest, I would keep clear of both of them if I were you."

"Er... Bob, you should perhaps know that Jenny here works for the council," I said.

"Oh. Sorry, Jenny. Speaking out of turn again as usual. Michelle is always telling me that the reason my mouth is so big is because it's had my foot in it so often." Bob glanced at his wife, who reprimanded him with a single look.

Jenny laughed. "Don't worry... my lips are sealed. But now I really do have to go. It's been nice meeting you."

I escorted Jenny to the door and turned to see that she was looking at me with a concerned expression.

"Mia, the girl who signed off the receipt note for the Douglas Report is quite new and doesn't know many of the staff yet. She couldn't remember clearly who asked her to do it... but she did mention that it might have been Sam Hepworth!"

CHAPTER 5

I awoke with a start to hear the phone ringing. It was Saturday and I had hoped to have a lie in, but it seemed someone was intent on robbing me of that pleasure. I picked up the phone and saw that it was a mobile number, but not one that the phone or I recognised.

"Hello," I said, for some reason trying to sound like I was wide awake and had been up for ages.

"Dan, this is Rosa. You met me and Mickey the other day."

I could tell immediately that all was not well with Rosa. She sounded breathless and upset.

"We're pitched on Abbot's Meadow, and I think that man from the council has sent some of his heavy mob to move us off again. Mickey doesn't take well to being pushed around and I'm afraid that he's going to get hurt."

"Okay. Don't panic," I said, while trying desperately to follow my own advice, and plainly failing. My oh-so-clever plan had backfired, and I was now regretting having mentioned Abbot's Meadow at all.

"I'll phone the police and then get straight over there. The police have no powers to force you to leave, but they do have powers to keep the peace. The main thing is to make sure that Mickey doesn't rise to the challenge and stays calm."

"Okay, thanks. I'll try to keep him in check, but please hurry!"

I ended the call, dressed quickly and then rang the police to alert them to the possible altercation. I explained to the police operator at a painfully slow pace exactly who I was and what was happening, but had zero faith that my plea for assistance would be acted upon. She didn't sound convinced that this was an urgent police matter.

I got in the car and set off on the ten-minute drive to Abbot's Meadow. I just hoped that I could get there before the situation got out of hand. Precisely what I was going to do I had no idea, but as I drove I recalled some of the internet research on Travellers' rights I had done before visiting Rosa and Mickey on the verge opposite Jack's house. Trespass on its own is not a criminal offence, so unless some form of criminal activity can be established, the police generally prefer to let the civil law run its course. I just hoped they would turn up.

When I arrived, I saw an unmarked white Ford Transit truck parked on the far side of the field close to a caravan. Rather than park by the entrance and walk across the field, I decided to drive straight in. The ground was none too even and I was forced to take it quite slowly. As I got close, I noted that the truck was loaded with a cement mixer, wheelbarrows and building materials of various sorts, and, as Rosa suspected, it seemed likely that Sam Hepworth was again involved, even if not in person.

I got out and walked towards Rosa and Mickey's caravan to find them being shouted at by three burly-looking characters who didn't seem to understand the concept of personal space. One had his face just inches from Mickey's and was giving his best impression of Sylvester Stallone on a really bad day.

Unfortunately, there was no sign of the police and I suddenly felt very inexperienced and vulnerable. I put on my bravest face and approached the group, setting my phone on video mode and holding it in front of me.

"What's going on?" I said loudly, mustering as much authority as I could.

"Who the fuck are you, and what the fuck do you think you're doing?" said one of the men, clearly taking exception to my phone.

He walked towards me threateningly. It was obvious that he was one tough cookie, with the sort of face that just wasn't built for smiling, and no neck at all to speak of. The shaved head and heavily tattooed bulging biceps did nothing to soften the image. But now I had committed to challenging him, there was no going back.

"I'm a reporter for the *Gazette* and it looks like I've come to witness intimidation of this family." I don't think I have ever been so scared, but strangely I was gaining confidence and warming to my theme. Who was it that said that bravery is being the only one who knows just how afraid you are?

He tried to grab the phone from my hand, but I pulled away and carried on videoing.

"I'm live-streaming this so that won't do you much good," I lied. "Staff at the office will be watching." I didn't really understand how to do that, but was bargaining on the fact that he would be equally clueless about such technology.

"By the way, I've called the police… and right on cue it looks as though they've arrived." I tried desperately not to let my relief show.

The man turned to see a police car drive into the field entrance and slowly make its way across the grass. Two police officers got out and sauntered towards us, taking their time to make it obvious how tedious they found this. I thought I'd better kick things off.

"Hi. I'm Dan Curran of the *Gazette*. I'm the one that called you because I was concerned that this family is being physically intimidated by these men."

"Right," said the older of the policemen. "I'm PC Griffiths and this is PC Walker." Turning to Mickey, PC Griffiths asked, "And who are you?"

Just then, Rosa appeared from the caravan holding the baby, with daughter Liberty hiding behind her skirt. Rosa looked across at me and mouthed a 'thanks'.

"I'm Mickey Boswell, and this is my wife, Rosa. We just need to stay here for a few days until we're joined by some friends and then we'll be moving on," Mickey explained. "I believe the land belongs to the council, and we don't have permission to be here, but as the official site on the other side of town is absolutely rammed and this meadow is lying fallow, we thought a few days wouldn't be no problem. But these characters here seem to have other ideas."

PC Griffiths took out his notebook and pen and started writing, before turning his attention to the three men.

"And who might you be?" he enquired.

The most mouthy of the three responded. "We work for Sam Hepworth, who is a councillor. He's asked us to help these pikeys move on quickly as this is council-owned land and they have no business pitching up here with all their crap."

"And your names are?" the PC enquired with pen poised.

"Is that really necessary? Can't you just do your job and move this scum on?" said Mouthy, who was beginning to look decidedly uncomfortable.

PC Griffiths was apparently not in the mood. He squared up to the man and looked him straight in the eyes. "I think perhaps I'm the best judge of that, and just at the moment, yes, I do think it's necessary… see? So, names?"

The mouthy one looked at his mates and then shrugged. "I'm Dean Lockwood, this is Simon Kendall and Josh Townsend. We all work for Hepworth Landscaping."

"Okay," said PC Griffiths putting away his notebook slowly. "So, none of you three is the owner of the land, and you are in fact just tradesmen. And, to be absolutely clear, you have no powers of eviction and no more right to be here than these good folks."

I liked this old-school PC. He had a nice, economical way with words that cut to the chase while somehow maintaining the congenial charm that goes with a soft Welsh accent.

"Furthermore, if the council wishes to remove these people from their land, there is a formal process which begins with obtaining a court order. It does not begin with you three also committing trespass and throwing your weight around trying to scare people. Have I made myself clear?"

I don't know whether PC Griffiths was expecting an answer, but Hepworth's men were not inclined to give him the satisfaction. They just looked sullenly at me, no doubt imagining what level of facial reconstruction would be appropriate.

"Now, I suggest that you all get in that truck of yours and leave right now, while I'm still in a good mood."

The three glowered at me one last time, turned around and started walking back to the truck. It was a fair bet that Dean Lockwood was going to cross me off his Christmas card list.

The policeman called out after them, "Oh, and you will be wanting to get that broken offside tail light repaired."

PC Griffiths turned to Mickey and Rosa.

"I think you should phone the council as soon as possible and formally ask them to consider allowing you to stay for a little while. If you can put a time limit on it, say one week, then it's odds on that the council will agree. It takes a while to get a court order and they would probably have to assess your needs and those of your children, and the risks to them if evicted. Just make sure you don't do any damage to the land as that could change things."

"Thank you, officer," said Mickey, obviously relieved by the policeman's sympathetic tone.

"And if the council agree to let you stay for a short period, ask them to tell this chap Hepworth, so those clowns don't keep giving you grief."

The policeman then turned to me and offered some advice.

"If I were you, sir, I'd keep well clear of those three. They didn't look very pleased with you and they won't like reporting back that they have failed. I'm not sure why this Sam Hepworth character thinks he can act independently of the council, but he presumably has his reasons."

And with that the policemen departed. I too was intrigued as to why this meadow was so important to Hepworth. Turning to Mickey I asked, "The last time you were here, when Hepworth came and railed at you, had you done any damage or given him reason to be so angry?"

Mickey looked offended. "We never do damage. I always respect the sites we use. The only thing I can think of which may have upset him is that I dug a latrine over in the corner near the hedge there. We don't need to do that now because there's a chemical toilet facility at the new canal marina which is just the other side of those trees. They let us use that."

Perhaps I had misjudged Hepworth. If the site did contain some archaeological secrets, maybe he was worried that Mickey's digging would disturb or damage whatever it was waiting to be uncovered. That Douglas report would shed some light on things, if only I could get hold of a copy.

*

I drove back home deep in thought, reliving my encounter on Abbot's Meadow. As I got near to my flat, I glanced in the rear-view mirror and noticed a white Transit truck behind me. Was it following me? Had it followed me from Abbot's Meadow… or was I being paranoid?

I took a random left and then right-hand turn, but the truck was still there. I was now fairly certain that Hepworth's men were following me, although I couldn't really make out any faces through the reflections in the windscreen. I drove past my road and onto an estate of old terraced houses where cars were parked along both sides of the already narrow streets. The gap between cars was no problem for my little Mini, but for the truck this gap was impossibly tight and it slowed to a crawl trying to avoid clashes with wing mirrors. I raced to the end of the road, back out onto the main road, and put a few miles between us as quickly as possible. My heart was pounding and any thoughts I'd had that Hepworth had good intentions were fading fast. I didn't know what I was getting myself into, but it was starting to feel a tad scary.

Just to be safe, I decided to leave it a little while before going back home, so I parked up and called the number Jenny had given me for her favourite councillor, Jim Symonds. Jim was at home and said he would be glad to see me. I entered his postcode into my phone satnav and after a short drive to the quaint village of Hinton Green, pulled up at an impressive old detached house with a beautiful front garden full of flowers and shrubs. On the block-paved drive stood an old, but immaculate, Volvo estate car, which was clearly someone's pride and joy.

I rang the bell, and the door was opened by an elegant, elderly lady with a neat grey permed hairdo, and sporting a flour-splattered apron protecting an expensive-looking frock.

"Ah, you must be Dan," she said with a welcoming smile. "Do come in. I'm just doing a spot of baking. Jim is expecting you. He's in the back garden, as usual. Spends so much time there I'm starting to think he's got another woman in his potting shed. I'm Jill, by the way. Lovely to meet you."

Her laugh was infectious and her easy conversation immediately made me feel relaxed.

"I expect you'd like a cup of tea," she said as we walked through the house to the back door. "How do you take it?"

I glanced at my watch and it was still only ten o'clock in the morning. "Milk no sugar, please," I replied, marvelling at that very British custom of requiring tea to be produced on all occasions, whatever the time of day.

Jim Symonds was hard at work in the back garden mowing stripes into a wonderfully green and weed-free lawn. The beautifully tended borders were a sea of colour, and at the back of the garden, partially hidden by some fruit trees, were a wooden-framed greenhouse and shed. I looked at the shed and thought about Jill's comment with a smile.

Jim stopped the mower and walked over to me, arm extended. We shook hands and I noticed that, even though he was probably in his late seventies, his grip was firm and eye contact steady. He still had a full head of neatly groomed grey hair, and was remarkably well dressed for gardening, with smart beige slacks and a check shirt.

"Hello, Dan," he said. "Good to see you. I had a phone call from young Jenny last night. She told me roughly what you wanted to talk about, but it'd perhaps be best if we sit down, and you can take me through it from the start."

I was touched that Jenny had taken the trouble to ring him. The fact that she felt comfortable doing that showed that she was happy that he could be trusted. We took seats on the patio that ran along the back of the house, and Jill appeared with two china cups of tea on a tray, together with a plate of chocolate digestive biscuits.

"I'll leave you boys to chat," she said. "If you want refills, just shout." I reckoned that Jenny's description of Jim as a 'sweetie' could also be applied to Jill.

"Thanks for sparing me the time, Jim," I said. "There are a couple of things I'd like to talk about, the first being the late Councillor Sid Chisholm. I have been asked to write an obituary piece for the *Gazette* and I'd like to find out as much as I can about him."

"Well, you've come to the right place," he replied. "I got to know Sid quite well over the years, and we often met up for a drink and a chat. It's sad that he passed away, but I guess he went in the way he would have wanted." Jim gave a rueful smile.

"I'm afraid I don't know much about his death – except that it was a heart attack," I replied.

"Ah," said Jim, clearly trying to decide how to start. "Well, I guess you know he had a girlfriend?" I nodded. "A young girlfriend called Natalie," said Jim with a smile. "He died… how can I put this delicately… in bed."

"Oh, I see," I said, slightly shocked as I thought back to our meeting in the council offices. I tried hard to reconcile the image that Jim was painting with the man I had met.

"Well, I suppose if you've got to go, it's as good a way as any," I offered.

Jim had a slurp of tea and carefully placed the cup back on the saucer while he considered how much to tell me. Although he continued to look at the cup, I was aware that I was being carefully scrutinised.

"I'm sure people will think that he was just a dirty old man, but it wasn't like that. There was genuine affection there on both sides, maybe love even. You see, Natalie had a very violent previous relationship which left her really scarred and Sid was tremendously kind to her. He confronted her boyfriend and threatened to report him to the police, which for a man of about five-foot six and advancing years, must have taken some courage. He eventually paid the fellow off on the condition that he never darkened her door again. Yes, Sid bought Natalie lots of nice things, but he also gave her money to buy a flat and a car in her own name, with no strings attached. It was a relationship that suited them both, and I'm certain that Natalie will be absolutely devastated that he's gone. She doted on him."

"What about Sid's wife?" I asked.

Jim's expression changed to one of real sadness. "Such a shame. She had an affair with Sid's best friend that he'd known since schooldays. Sid confessed to me that he had been heartbroken. It was all a very long time ago, mind you. They had only been married a few years. They tried to patch things up, but the hurt was just too deep. I don't think they ever divorced, but I believe Sid stayed single right up to the time he met Natalie about two years ago. I guess he couldn't face being hurt again."

Just then Jill appeared to see if we wanted anything and had obviously overheard some of the conversation.

"Nice girl, Natalie," she said. "We had a coffee together once when I was in town. She credited Sid with saving her life, you know, and with such a brutish boyfriend, she could have been right. It's just a pity that people can be so judgemental and say such horrid things."

Jim didn't have Natalie's phone number, but he was able to tell me the name of the bakery where she worked as an assistant. We then moved on to Sid's life story. With Jim's permission, I took notes while he talked.

Sid was born to quite poor parents who lived in London. He worked hard at weekends and in school holidays doing newspaper rounds, leaflet drops and odd jobs. At school he excelled and managed to get into university where he studied geology. Apparently, as a child he was fascinated by fossils and was always breaking rocks with a hammer to see what he could discover. After university he got a job with Shell Oil where he stayed right up to his retirement. He ended up in quite a senior position and travelled to oil fields all over the world to examine rock formations, drill core samples and sift through geological survey data. Jim thought that he was on a high salary for at least the last half of his working life, and didn't appear to be a big spender before meeting Natalie. Outside of work Jim thought his main hobby was repairing and collecting old clocks.

"Did he have any close relatives apart from his wife?" I enquired. "Jenny mentioned a daughter?"

"Yes, they had a daughter called Janice very early in the marriage who kept in touch with Sid. She was very fond of him,

I believe, and they got together every few weeks. Lives with her husband in the Cotswolds, I seem to recollect. I imagine she too will be very upset. And he had a brother called Rodney who is still alive as far as I know. I'm not sure they got on quite so well, but, from what I know of him, he will probably be the one to arrange the funeral and manage the estate. I'm guessing he will be keen to learn what Sid put in his will."

"Did you and Sid meet before you were elected to the council?" I enquired.

"Yes, we did as a matter of fact," said Jim. "Although we never got to know each other personally until we both became councillors. Before I retired I was a solicitor and I handled the conveyancing when he bought a house in Castlebridge. It must have been at least thirty years ago. Can't believe where the time has gone really."

"And what about his council years?" I enquired.

"Sid was a great councillor," said Jim. "He took his duties very seriously and was an active member of several committees – Housing, Audit and Standards, Licensing, and he chaired the Appeals Committee. His attendance record was probably one of the highest. The public loved him and he was re-elected several times."

We were now coming round to the principal reason for my visit and I wanted to be sure of my ground before possibly putting Jim in an awkward, if not compromising, position. However, Jenny thought that Jim was honest and trustworthy, and I couldn't detect anything which made me doubt that.

"Were you and Sid both at the Housing and New Homes Committee meeting when the Abbot's Meadow sale was discussed?" I asked.

"Ah. Jenny mentioned that you were interested in this,"

Jim replied with a knowing smile. "Yes, we were both there and I remember the meeting well."

"Could you explain to me exactly why the sale was refused?" I said, anxious not to lead Jim in any particular direction.

Jim leant forward a little and said earnestly, "I will tell you what I know, but you have to promise me that you will not publish anything without letting me read it first. Will you do that?"

"Of course I will," I said, somewhat relieved that he was being so candid. If I was starting to get into deep water, then having a wise and experienced confidant was going to be a definite plus.

"Fair enough," said Jim. "I'm keen to make sure that everything is as it should be, and Jenny, who I am very fond of, certainly is having doubts. We actually discussed the sale of the meadow at two meetings. At the first meeting about two months ago, it seemed that the sale would go through unopposed, but then at the last minute, Sam Hepworth introduced a note of caution. He said that talking with the local historians he had learnt that the meadow might actually be the site of an Anglo-Saxon burial ground and suggested that it was probably the council's duty to ask someone experienced in archaeological surveys to investigate before allowing bulldozers in. This seemed entirely sensible to everyone present, so the decision was shelved pending a review, which Sam agreed to organise after consulting the Cabinet Executive on correct procedure. So, we left Sam to it. I have no idea what process was followed, how the company was selected, or whether he got three separate quotes for the work according to the rules. At the second meeting about three weeks ago, Sam produced hard copies of a report he had commissioned, written by a firm of archaeological consultants in London called K. Douglas and Partners."

I found it impossible to keep quiet and jumped in. "Did you keep a copy of the report?"

"I'll get to that in a minute," said Jim, holding up a hand to try to quell my impatience. "The report appeared to be very thorough, and had maps and extracts from old reference works and ancient charters. Even aerial photos, as I recall. It concluded that there was a strong possibility that there was an ancient burial site where the field is today and recommended a ground-penetrating radar scan be conducted. Apparently, such a survey might inform archaeologists where to start digging, if indeed that was to happen. In view of this new information, the committee voted in favour of refusing the application, at least for the time being. This would give the council time to decide what should be done. One thing was clear: if we did have a radar survey done it wouldn't be any time soon, judging by the cost estimates in the report. There was simply nothing in the current budget to cover those sorts of costs."

It was all intriguing stuff, but I was dying to get to the nub of the issue. "Can I get hold of a copy of this report?"

"Sam Hepworth was keen not to let the reason for refusing to sell get into the public domain, because he said that the field would immediately be swamped with metal detectorists looking for buried treasures. Fortunately for Sam, there were no members of the public present at that meeting. I wish now that there had been, although to be fair we only get the public attending when there is something contentious or of great local interest. So, the reports were all collected up for safe-keeping when the meeting finished. I assumed that the report would be properly filed and accessible, although Jenny tells me that the file is locked in some way, which I find disturbing. In fact, I would say it is highly irregular. If you want to see the report you could always submit a request under the Freedom of Information Act, although it's possible that a request could be denied if it fails the prejudice test. Sam could presumably argue that negative consequences would arise from full disclosure, but I am no expert on these matters."

"Yes, I did consider making a request under the FOI Act," I said. "Tell me, did everyone accept the decision, or were there dissenters?"

"Now you mention it, at the first meeting Sid Chisholm was very sceptical that there would have been a burial ground on that site, because, according to him, the ground would have been totally unsuitable. He reckoned that the whole area was once a flood plain and even the Anglo-Saxons would have known that the ground geology was unfavourable as a burial ground. How on earth he knew this I've got no idea, but this was Sid's area of expertise after all. However, Sam was quite forceful and got his way for a study to be undertaken. At the second meeting when we saw the Douglas report, Sid never said a word. I did get the feeling that he wasn't happy, but he voted with the rest of us to turn down the application."

"That's interesting. Can I ask what your opinion is of Sam Hepworth?" I enquired, not too hopeful that Jim would wish to comment while he himself was still on the council. Jim looked at me for a few seconds while trying to make up his mind how to respond. He shifted his legs and his body language suggested he was feeling uncomfortable.

"On the face of it, Sam is a good councillor. He attends loads of meetings and probably has one of the best attendance records. He has declared the business he runs with his brother in the Register of Members' Interests, and is always keen to declare a conflict of interest if it ever seems likely that landscaping work might result from any decision made. The sale of Abbot's Meadow for development does seem to blur that line, but to be fair he did abstain from voting. Nevertheless, his concerns over the field did have a big impact on the outcome."

"I sense there is a 'but' coming?" I said, pen poised.

"Off the record... and again, I stress that this must remain absolutely between you and me, and I don't want you to write this down. I have never been comfortable with Sam. There is something a bit sinister about him that suggests to me that he always has a hidden agenda, and that being a councillor is in some way convenient rather than being an act of public service. However, I must stress that I have absolutely no proof that he is anything other than what he appears to be. And that, I'm afraid, is all I have to say on the subject."

This seemed to draw a line under our conversation. Jim went quiet and I sensed that he was feeling that he may have said too much. Perhaps breached his own personal code of ethical behaviour. It was time for me to go. I thanked him for taking the time to talk to me so openly.

"I don't know where that leaves me, but rest assured, if there is a story here worth telling, I certainly won't publish anything without your say-so," I promised.

I said goodbye to Jim, and to Jill on the way out, and drove back to my flat deep in thought. I now knew the reason why the council chose to stop the sale of Abbot's Meadow... and somehow, I didn't believe a word of it!

CHAPTER 6

When I got back home from Jim's house, I phoned Jenny.

"Hi, Jenny, it's Dan."

"Oh, hi, Dan. Can you just give me a moment?" Jenny left the phone and I could hear conversation in the distance. After a few moments, she came back on.

"Sorry about that. Dad and I are just saying goodbye to my brother and his wife. Dad was on holiday today. They came to see him this morning and stayed for lunch."

"I just wanted to thank you for briefing Jim Symonds," I said. "I went to see him and Jill this morning. You didn't tell me they were both real sweeties… to use your word. Jim was really helpful and I now know what happened during that committee meeting."

"That's great, Dan. After we parted I started to worry about what was going on, so I'm glad it proved useful. Both Jim and Jill are lovely, aren't they?"

"Yes, they are," I replied. "I don't want to say too much on the phone, but I'm now fairly certain that there's much more to this story than meets the eye. Also, I think I might be stirring up a hornets' nest because I'm pretty sure that some of Hepworth's heavies followed my car today."

"Oh no! Just be careful, Dan." Jenny had concern in her voice, which I found very touching.

"I will," I promised. "On a lighter note, you said yesterday I should phone you about going out for a meal. I was wondering whether you would like to go out this evening?"

There was a slight pause and I prepared myself for the disappointment I felt sure was coming. Although I had a few girlfriends while at university, I hadn't really had any serious relationships and always felt somewhat shy and awkward in the presence of women. Jenny did seem to be the exception, or so I hoped.

"Oh dear. I can't really make this evening," she said.

"Oh… okay, some other time maybe?"

"It's just that today would have been Mum's birthday. That's why Brian and Sarah, my brother and sister-in-law, came to see Dad this morning. I said that I would cook Dad a special meal tonight, and we would have a film show of family photos together.

"You could always come and have a meal with us," she continued enthusiastically before I had a chance to respond. "I'm not the world's greatest cook, but it's usually just about edible, and I haven't actually poisoned anyone yet. Not knowingly, anyway."

I was encouraged by the offer, but it felt too soon to be meeting her father when I hardly knew her, especially at such a sensitive time.

"That's nice of you, but no, I don't think I should intrude. It's a special time and it needs to be just you and your dad," I said, trying not to let my disappointment show.

"Okay. Well, how about Monday evening?" she said. "I'm free then."

"Great! It's a date. I'll pick you up at seven o'clock – well, I would if I knew where you lived."

She gave me her address and I rang off, suddenly feeling on top of the world. Was this the start of something really good in my life?

*

Saturday is supposed to be a non-working day, so I decided that the day would be devoted to me-time. After catching up on some housework, I had a light lunch and decided to go for a run, something I hadn't done in a month or more. I always found running remarkably therapeutic, a time where some of my most lucid and productive thinking took place. Equally, when needed, it was also a time when I could think of absolutely nothing and enter an almost meditative state. I am not one of those runners that needs to be wired for sound, and much prefer to let the sounds and general ambience of the places I pass through provide their own soundtrack to the pounding of my trainers on the ground. Besides, I seem to have the sort of ears that treat in-ear headphones as a foreign body to be expelled at the first opportunity.

I changed into my running gear and set off through the town centre, across the market square, and out along the side of the river towards the bridge that many years ago gave the town its name. The river front had become a mecca of trendy wine bars, restaurants and gastro pubs, all with their outdoor seating spilling out towards the riverbank path. Walkers and runners have to dodge the tubs of flowers, picnic tables and billboards advertising 'Happy Hour' or 'New Menu'. The sun was shining and the area was busy with people enjoying a lazy

Saturday afternoon. As I came to the bridge, I took the steps up onto the road and turned towards the countryside, beginning to feel really energised.

I turned to check on traffic and stopped dead in my tracks. There in front of me was Westbridge Bakery, a small artisan bakery shop selling fresh bread, cakes and pastries. According to Jim Symonds, this was where Natalie, Sid Chisholm's girlfriend, worked. Tomorrow being Sunday, the shop would be closed and this seemed too good an opportunity to miss. I went in and saw that there were two women serving, one I would have thought was in her twenties, and one probably nearer to sixty. There were a few people waiting to be served and I suddenly became self-conscious, standing there in my old running shorts and faded T-shirt which had sweat patches rapidly spreading under the arms. Fortunately, the queue seemed to be moving quite quickly, and after a short wait it was my turn to be served. The elder of the two women looked at me with just a flicker of wariness.

"Hello. I was looking for Natalie… I'm sorry, I don't know her second name, but I believe she works here?"

She turned towards her colleague. "Natalie… this gentleman wants to speak with you." The very slight pause before the word 'gentleman' was revealing, but perhaps not unexpected, especially as I could now feel my T-shirt beginning to stick to me after my exertions.

The young girl finished serving a customer and walked over to where I was standing.

"How can I help you?" she enquired, looking me over warily.

"Hi. I'm sorry for my somewhat unconventional appearance. I was out running and came across your shop quite by chance. My name is Dan Curran and I'm a reporter with the *Gazette*."

I realised that not only did I have no business cards with me, but also had no pen or paper to make any notes. I was beginning to feel a little foolish and cursed myself for not planning this more professionally.

"The *Gazette*?" she said, suddenly looking very worried. "What on earth do you want to talk to me about?"

"It's about Sid Chisholm," I said, trying to work out where to begin. "I gather you and he were close friends, and I have been tasked with writing an obituary piece about Sid in the *Gazette*."

At the mention of Sid's name, I saw her demeanour change to hostility.

"In that case I can't tell you anything," she said dismissively, her eyes darting to the floor, and she turned ready to go back to her station at the counter. Her older colleague looked across at me, concern writ large across her face.

"I can understand why you might feel that way, but please hear me out before you decide. I got your name from Councillor Jim Symonds who was a good friend of Sid's."

At the mention of Jim's name, she stopped and looked me over again. Maybe, if Jim had been prepared to reveal her name to me, I couldn't be all bad.

I could see she was reassessing the situation, so I continued, "Jim told me you were a big part of Sid's life, and I'm really sorry that you've lost him. But I do want the piece I write to reflect who Sid was and do him justice. You're probably the only person that can help me understand what made him tick."

I suddenly realised the unfortunate appropriateness of that

comment, given that Jim had told me Sid's hobby was clock repairing. However, now didn't seem to be the time for jokes.

Natalie again looked at the floor for a few moments, and then turned to her colleague. "Steph, can you hold the fort if I nip out for a little while?"

Stephanie, who was serving another customer further down the counter, said, "That's not a problem, Nat. You go."

I suspected that Stephanie possessed that uniquely female trait of being able to listen to every word of one conversation, while conducting a completely separate conversation with someone else.

Natalie took off her shop pinafore and pointed to the door. "Let's go over the road, down by the river. There are some seats there."

I followed her back down onto the river path and we made for a vacant bench. I wished I had brought a notebook with me, but I did have my phone, and Natalie said that she had no problem with me recording our conversation.

"So, tell me about Sid."

She was still unsure whether this was a good idea, and our initial conversation was somewhat laboured. However, she gradually let her guard down and it soon became obvious that she had been extremely fond of Sid and was still in shock after his death. Her long brown hair had a fringe which partially hid her face and eyes. I noticed that when her eyes were visible, she found it difficult to maintain eye contact and I suspected that this was a legacy of her previous abusive relationship. She had obviously been deeply scarred by the experience.

"How did you two meet?" I enquired.

"We actually met on that bench over there," she said with a hint of a smile. "He was out walking one lunchtime and sat next to me to eat a sandwich. He could see that I had been crying, and I was trying my best to hide a black eye. Ever since that day he took care of me and somehow got rid of my boyfriend at the time… thank goodness! Sid was so good to me. The kindest man I ever met. He saved my life…"

Her voice tailed off and I saw her eyes fill with tears. She looked small and vulnerable, and I wanted to put my arm around her shoulders but knew that, in these cold modern times, such displays of empathy were open to misinterpretation.

After a few moments she regained her composure and continued. "Everyone thinks that because of the age difference, Sid was after just one thing, but that couldn't have been further from the truth. If anything, it was me who had to encourage him as a way of saying thank you. It was probably three months before we actually… well, you know," she said, clearly embarrassed. "He got me settled in a flat of my own and bought me a nice second-hand car. I really liked him, you know. It may even have been love. I don't know. I haven't had much love in my life, not even from my parents, who divorced when I was five. I haven't seen my father since then and my mother rarely speaks to me these days. She's much too busy clubbing and drinking, even though she's almost fifty. Pathetic really."

We talked about Sid's hobby of clock repairs, his love of cricket, his dreadful dress sense and his work as a councillor, which he took extremely seriously. In his job Sid travelled the world and had many stories of scrapes with the locals when prospecting for new oil fields. He got involved with North Sea oil and gas fields and was even required to practise escaping from a sunken helicopter, definitely not something for the faint-hearted.

Remembering what Jenny had told me, I enquired, "Did

you notice any change in Sid over the last two or three weeks before his death?"

Natalie immediately looked suspicious and said, "How did you know about that?" Before I could explain, she continued, "Yes, he was very worried about something but wouldn't tell me what. He just said it was council business. It started when I told him about a strange man who came into the shop. He bought some sausage rolls, and as I was giving him his change, he said something about Sid and me being lucky and that he hoped our luck would last. I asked what that meant, and he just smiled and said Sid would know. When I told Sid his face went white and he was visibly shaken, but he just brushed it off saying he must have eaten something that disagreed with him. After that he seemed nervous and he kept phoning me throughout the day to check I was alright. Truthfully, I was more worried about him. He had a history of heart problems and was taking medication for high blood pressure, but he never told anyone else. I was really worried. He seemed to be much more tense than usual, which can't have been good for him."

"This man who came into the bakery. Can you remember what he looked like?" I asked.

Natalie nodded. "He was a thick-set bald man in what appeared to be builders' clothes… you know, with mud and dust over his trousers and filthy boots. Oh, and he had lots of tattoos on both his arms."

I thanked Natalie for taking the time to talk with me. I wanted to mention her in the obituary and asked, "Would you mind if I referred to you as Sid's long-term 'partner' in the piece I'm going to write? It seems appropriate, and I promise you it will be really kind and sympathetic."

She agreed, and I walked her back to the bakery. As we reached the door she stopped and turned to me.

"I just hope people don't see me as a gold digger, you know? Sid suspected that he might be living on borrowed time, and he often talked about his will and what would become of me when he died. He lived quite frugally but was actually a very wealthy man. I had to make him promise faithfully not to leave me a penny in his will. His kindness was worth more than any amount of money, and I don't want any members of his family to hate me."

After leaving the shop I resumed my run, thinking about our conversation. Natalie was indeed a remarkable young woman, and I could now see why Jim and Jill Symonds took a shine to her. I was now fairly sure that Sid was being leant on by one of Hepworth's men, the mouthy Dean Lockwood who had taken a dislike to me in Abbot's Meadow. Knowing what I now knew, it was obvious that Lockwood's veiled threats to Natalie would have been a dagger through Sid's poor, diseased heart.

*

Sunday passed uneventfully, if you exclude the phone conversation with my mother, who was positively bursting to tell me how my big sister, Emily, had been promoted to Senior Staff Nurse. Such a wonderful profession, what a credit to the family and so on. I also heard about the cat's worrying illness, my Aunty Marjorie's gallstones operation, and how Dad's car had failed its MOT. Apparently, Dad was convinced that the garage's exhaust measuring equipment was obviously faulty. Oh… and Dad's dahlias had won second prize at the local produce show. Eventually she did get around to asking how my work at the paper was going, but by this time I didn't really feel like displaying any great enthusiasm, and quickly changed the subject.

Next, I phoned my sister to congratulate her. Emily and I were close, and whenever I felt a bit low, she was always there with her gentle ribbing to chase away the black dog.

"It's no biggie really, but you know what Mum and Dad are like. I really worry for their blood pressures if I ever make it to Sister. Anyway, how's the job working out?" she asked.

"It's working out just fine, Em," I replied, wondering how much to say. "And I've met someone," I added, knowing that this was going to pique her interest more than any news story.

"Have you now? Tell me more. What's she like, and more to the point, when do we get to meet her?"

I laughed. "She's lovely… and not yet, that's for sure. I need to prepare her gently for meeting Mum and Dad. It's not something you can consider lightly. If I find them trying and eccentric, heaven only knows what Jenny would make of them!"

Emily pressed me for more details and we chatted effortlessly for over half an hour. I was sure that Jenny and Em would get on famously. However, first base was our date the following evening, and I just prayed that it was going to go well.

*

When I arrived for work on Monday morning, Tracy waved me over. "Dad was looking for you a few minutes ago. He's got a visitor and he wants you to go in and join them."

I knocked on Jack's door and entered. Sitting opposite Jack drinking a cup of coffee was Sam Hepworth.

"Dan, come in. I'm not sure whether you've met Councillor Sam Hepworth?" said Jack. "Sam wondered whether we're going to feature an obituary on Sid Chisholm, and has given me some background on his work at the council."

I recognised Hepworth immediately from his photo. He wasn't quite so hot and bothered as he appeared on Rosa's phone, but still had a ruddy complexion. He also had large, slightly protruding eyes, which seemed to be faintly bloodshot. I couldn't help but stare at his sandy-coloured hair which was shaved at the sides to leave a tuft on top, giving the impression of an extremely cheap toupee. On a younger man it might have looked trendy, but on a fifty-something with a wide face, it looked a touch ridiculous. As I had guessed from his social media posts, from what I could see he didn't appear to be especially tall, but was certainly overweight, with a paunch that bulged out from his jacket and overhung his trousers.

We shook hands and eyed each other knowingly. He knew that I had got the police to see off his heavies before they could evict Mickey and Rosa, and I knew that the real reason for his visit to our offices was to fire a warning shot across my bows.

"Pleased to meet you. Were you a friend of Sid's, then?" I said, trying to infuse the phrase with as much irony as I could muster.

"Oh yes. I like to think that Sid and I were close. I warned him to take it easy at his age. Unfortunate things happen when you don't take care of yourself," he said, looking me straight in the eye. "Jack tells me that this is your first job. How would you say it was going so far?" he said, his face a picture of amused innocence.

"I think it's going okay, all things considered, although I

guess that's more a question for Jack. There's certainly lots for me to get my teeth stuck into, if you know what I mean?"

The slight falter in his smile and flicker in the eyes told me that I had scored a direct hit.

"Jack here is a hard taskmaster, that's for sure, but he has great experience in sorting the winners from the losers when it comes to potential stories. I'm sure there's lots you can learn from him. Oh well, best be going. Nice to meet you. Jack here has made some notes which might be useful in your article about Sid."

And with that, Sam rose and shook Jack's hand.

"Good of you to see me, Jack. I was just passing and thought I couldn't let the chance of contributing to Sid's obituary go by. I'm sure young Dan here will be able to take my views into account." He gave me one final knowing look of barely concealed contempt and left.

After he had gone, Jack turned to me.

"What was all that about? It seemed like there was an atmosphere between you two, almost as if you were adversaries."

"We need to talk, Jack," I said, closing the door to the office.

We sat down and I went through the events of the past week, bringing him up to speed and leaving out nothing. Well, nothing apart from the fact that Jenny and I were going to have a meal together that evening, which I was hoping would stay private. I even showed him the video I had taken when being confronted by Dean Lockwood and his mates on Abbot's Meadow. While I spoke, he looked at me with unerring focus but devoid of any expression, and I couldn't tell what sort of reaction I was going to get. I was worried that I could be in line for an almighty bollocking for taking it on myself to play detective and potentially getting the paper involved in what might seem like a personal obsession.

When I finished, he just sat there in silence for what seemed like an eternity. He eventually broke the silence with an observation, his face stern.

"Don't you think that it's a remarkable coincidence that the Travellers I asked you to get rid of end up making camp on the field which you have been investigating… the field which it seems is not now going to be built on?"

He let me squirm for a few seconds and then broke into a broad grin.

"What was it I said… a journalist's nose. Now I understand why Hepworth came here. It was basically to let you know he's on your case. What I don't understand, however, is why this damn Abbot's Meadow is so important to him. It's just a bloody field for Christ's sake! But I must say, getting the Travellers to camp there was a master stroke. Sometimes you have to tweak the tiger's tail a bit."

"To be fair, I didn't exactly tell them to go there," I said. "I just dropped it into conversation that the meadow was empty and not being sold off. Mickey and Rosa are a really nice couple, and to be honest I now feel a bit guilty for getting them involved."

"Well, what's done is done. We need to find out what's behind all this. I suggest you next apply formally for a copy of that Douglas report through the FOI Act. They will need to come up with a bloody good reason if it's refused."

"I did think of that, but it could take a while," I replied. "Also, it will be a direct challenge to Hepworth if the report does contain something he wants to remain hidden. And it will confirm that I know about the report. If he managed to persuade the other councillors on the Housing Committee to keep it quiet, I think there's a good chance he'll be able to devise a reason for not disclosing it under the FOI. He'd probably reference the harm that might result to a site of archaeological importance. Anyway, I figured I would keep digging quietly for a day or two and see what turns up. Keep our powder dry for the moment. What do you think?"

"Well, okay," said Jack, who didn't sound all that convinced. "But you have got to promise me two things before I let you run with this story any further. One, you keep me informed of any developments, no matter how small. And two, you stay clear of trouble and don't take any chances. I suspect Samuel Hepworth and his friends might not be very nice people."

Jack was not wrong about that.

CHAPTER 7

Geoff called me over to the news desk.

"I know Jack has got you on this council story, but I need you to cover another story for me this morning. There's a lady called Gladys Parker at the Belle Vue Care Home who is a hundred years old today. They're having a bit of a 'do' at eleven o'clock and I'd like you to cover it. Apparently, she helped build Spitfires during and after the Second World War, so see if you can get an interview. If she got her card from the King, then a nice picture of her holding that surrounded by some family members would work well."

"No problem," I replied, slightly irritated that my next steps in the Abbot's Meadow investigation, whatever they were, would have to wait. In truth, I was beginning to feel that my lack of experience meant that those investigations were running out of steam, so taking a break might be no bad thing. I got the address of the care home, which was within walking distance, and set off.

Belle Vue Care Home was a large three-storey, 1960s property that had been much extended in a sympathetic, if much more modern, style, set back from the road and surrounded by lawns and gardens. From the outside it appeared to be well maintained and the flowers and shrubs well tended, but having been into care homes previously to visit elderly relatives, I was reserving judgement.

The first thing I noticed on entering was the smell... or rather, lack of smell. I was expecting that unpleasant whiff of disinfectant, ineffectually disguised by the sweet, cloying smell of so-called air fresheners. To my relief, it was more like entering a 5-star hotel lobby. The entrance area was beautifully decorated, with a spotless plush blue carpet and a large vase of fresh-cut flowers on the corner of a polished oak reception desk. I rang the bell and a lady in a pale blue uniform arrived, smiling warmly.

"Hello. Can I help you?" she enquired.

"Hi. I'm Dan Curran of the *Gazette*. I've come to cover Gladys Parker's birthday celebrations. I believe that it's all going to kick off at around eleven?" I said, hoping all the information I'd been fed was correct.

"Oh, that's great. Thanks so much for coming. Could I ask you to sign the visitors' book, Dan, and I'll take you through to the lounge to meet Gladys. You're in for a treat. She's one of our favourites... not that we should have favourites of course," she added hastily, looking slightly embarrassed. "But she really is such a special lady."

As we walked through, she told me that Gladys was no longer very mobile but was as sharp as a tack. Once I got her talking, I would very likely be there for the duration. She took me through to a large lounge, again beautifully decorated and sumptuously carpeted, with pictures around the walls, several vases of flowers and expensive-looking furniture. There were a handful of residents seated around the lounge, most of whom appeared to be reading or knitting. Again, the ambience was more hotel than care home.

"Gladys, this is Dan. He's from the *Castlebridge Gazette*, and he wants to talk with you." Turning to me she said, "I'm Pam, by the way. Anything you need, just shout… or ring the bell on the reception desk if I'm not there."

And with that, Pam picked up some discarded birthday card envelopes lying on the table and left us to it. Gladys was sitting in a high-backed chair next to a lovely marble fireplace, the mantlepiece of which was filled with birthday cards. She looked much younger than her age and was nicely dressed in a skirt and blouse. Her neatly curled hair had probably just been done for the big occasion. She looked up, smiling.

"Oh good. It's not often that I get a chance to chat up nice young men," she said with a twinkle in her eye. "My Arthur was always telling me that once I'm among men I could talk for England, you know. So, you have been warned. Now, take a seat here, nice and close as my hearing isn't so good these days."

I strongly suspected that her hearing was perfectly fine, but I was only too happy to draw up a chair next to her. We spent the next half hour talking and I discovered that Gladys, who was absolutely charming and incredibly garrulous, had a rather naughty sense of humour. In these days of seemingly rampant dementia, it was so great to see that the years had not taken their toll on her mental faculties, and as Pam had said, she was razor sharp.

She gave me a potted history of her life, which began in Birmingham, where she was born to working-class parents. Her father worked in a car factory and her mother was a midwife. The Second World War broke out not long after she left school to become a trainee secretary, but wanting to do her bit for the war effort, she applied for a job at the aeroplane factory in Castle Bromwich, where she learnt to operate a Herbert lathe making parts for the Spitfire. She spoke of those years with a mixture of happiness and great pride, and it was clear that the time spent in the factory remained very special to her, not least because that is where she met and was wooed by her husband-to-be, Arthur.

When hearing ordinary people talking about the extraordinary experiences that war brings, it is difficult not to feel a touch of envy, that they should have lived through a time when the entire population experienced such a sense of unity and camaraderie in the face of adversity. But even though those years were, quite understandably, etched into her memory, Gladys was equally knowledgeable and lucid about current affairs, politics, TV programmes, celebrities and such like. She flipped from one subject to another effortlessly, requiring only a single word or thought to launch her into a whole new subject.

As we talked, members of her family started to arrive, and she broke off only to greet them, before returning to her conversation with me. I sensed that she was mentally reliving her life and wanted to make sure that she didn't miss out anything important. The family took seats and listened in with a mixture of real affection and fascination, even though I suspected that they had heard much of this countless times. Gladys certainly knew how to hold an audience.

I could see the care staff starting to assemble in the lounge with a large cake and flowers, and this was a signal that I needed to make way for the main event. However, not wanting to let a good opportunity pass by, I asked Gladys how long she had lived in Castlebridge. I had in mind the comment made by Sid Chisholm at the council meeting that, long ago, the Abbot's Meadow area would have been a flood plain. I very much doubted that she would know anything about that, but it was worth asking.

She replied, "Well, Arthur and I got married as soon as the war ended and we moved here almost straight away because Arthur got a job at an engineering company in the town. Been here ever since, so that's... well, a lot of years. It's just me now, of course, since Arthur passed away about ten years ago. I can't believe I am one hundred years old today, you know."

"Well, I think you're just great, and I don't know what you're taking, but I want some," I said, only half joking. She really did look great.

"Can I just ask you one more question? If I wanted to know more about the history of Castlebridge going back years... maybe even to the Middle Ages, do you know anyone that might be able to help?"

Gladys barely needed to reflect on this.

"Yes, I do. Kevin Handleigh, the chairman of the Castlebridge Heritage Society. He is about the most knowledgeable person I know when it comes to Castlebridge history. I used to be a member of the society up until my hips and knees started to let me down. He actually teaches history at Castlebridge Grammar School over on Charnhill Avenue. Do you know it?"

I said that I didn't, but would find out without any difficulty, and then Pam returned to start organising people. The first task was a photo opportunity with Gladys surrounded by friends and family. Gladys proudly held her card from the King with a photo of His Majesty and a personally signed message. I used my phone to get some nice pictures, and then took some of Gladys on her own, and with some of the carers.

I thanked Gladys, wished her well and gave her a peck

on the cheek for good measure, having thoroughly enjoyed the encounter. Once outside I used my phone to Google the grammar school, found a phone number and rang.

"Mr Handleigh will be teaching till 12.30," said the school receptionist after I had explained that I was a journalist for the *Gazette* and was interested in talking with Mr Handleigh about the heritage society. "If you drop by then I'm sure he will be able to spare you a few minutes," she said helpfully.

*

I didn't have my car with me, but the walk to Charnhill Avenue only took me fifteen minutes or so. The school was much larger than I expected, with several fairly modern buildings leading off what I assumed was the original Victorian brick-built school in the centre. The receptionist asked me to sign in the visitors' book, provided me with a lanyard to wear and then gave me directions to Classroom 4b, where Kevin Handleigh had just finished the morning lessons.

Had I not known that he was a teacher, I think I might have been fairly confident in hazarding a guess, just based on appearances. He turned out to be a man of about fifty, with thinning hair but a full beard, wearing a pair of small wire-framed glasses. He wore slightly crumpled beige corduroy trousers, a check shirt with a button-down collar and a tweed sports jacket with leather patches on the elbows. All that was missing was a stick of chalk behind the ear. He was plainly excited by my visit, presumably thinking that his beloved heritage society had finally, and quite justifiably in his opinion, been noticed by the media. And not before time. His fifteen minutes of fame was surely beckoning.

"Ah, Dan. Can I call you Dan? Please take a seat," he gushed, indicating the front row of pupil desks. "I gather the *Gazette* is interested in our fantastic heritage society? We have over forty members, you know, not that they all turn up every month, of course, but when they do they usually enjoy themselves, because most times we manage to get great speakers, not always, of course, and they can talk about anything from buildings to famous people who lived in Castlebridge, to notable periods in the history of the town, and sometimes we bring along artefacts to discuss, and…"

I figured he would have to take a pause for breath at some point, and I finally managed to get a word in.

"Well, yes, and sometime we could maybe run a piece on the society. But I have been told that you are the go-to man when it comes to the history of Castlebridge, so I first wanted to pick your brains, if I may?"

By now he was positively bursting with enthusiasm and pride, his rather small eyes shining excitedly behind the wire frames. All those years poring over dusty records had not been in vain. He might even make the papers.

"Fire away," he said. "Hopefully I will be able to help. I don't know everything about the town, of course, but I have studied lots of references over the years, and dug through parish archives, and even went to the British Library two or three years ago to follow up leads, although that wasn't totally successful, but, interestingly, I did learn that in the fourteenth century, this area was renowned for being a major producer of leather goods. Nobody around here seemed to be aware of that fact, and…"

I could see that it might take me quite a while to get as far as asking an actual question, and aware that the pupils would presumably be returning to class for afternoon lessons at some point, I interrupted the flow.

"What can you tell me about a stretch of land to the south of the river called Abbot's Meadow?"

Quite suddenly, his demeanour changed, almost as if I had punched him in the stomach. He looked at me over the top of his glasses with wide eyes, a perfect example of the rabbit in headlights analogy.

"Abbot's Meadow?" he said hesitantly, which in itself was revealing, as he was a man who I didn't think had yet mastered slow speech. "Um… it's just a field like any other, nothing special as far as I know," he said unconvincingly.

In that moment, I knew beyond any doubt that our Mr Handleigh was up to his neck in something, but I hadn't a clue what that 'something' was. He reminded me of a child caught with his hand in the sweetie jar, anxiously pondering what he could possibly say to assuage his guilt.

I decided to press on with my questioning to see whether more pressure would make him open up, but I didn't want to mention the possibility of a burial site. If my suspicions were correct, he would know that such information could only have come via a council member.

"From what you know, could that field have been part of a flood plain in the distant past?"

He looked at me incredulously, probably wondering how on earth I knew this, and I sensed he was now inwardly praying for this all to go away. Desperately searching for some way of changing the subject, he said, "I very much doubt it. Now there is still a flood plain to the north of the River Bardon, which is not far from here. I don't believe that has flooded for at least thirty years though, although it did get close a few years ago…"

His voice tailed off, by now clearly getting the distinct feeling that I wasn't going to be deflected. He looked pointedly at his watch, no doubt for the first time in his life praying that the children would start arriving for their history lesson early. He decided that enough was enough.

"Look, I really wouldn't know about any of this," he said. "It's not something that the heritage society has ever researched into. I don't mean to be rude, but I need to get some lunch before the children come back. Would you like to know some more about our society?"

It was obvious that Handleigh knew a lot more than he was letting on, and given his lack of co-operation, I didn't feel that I needed to worry too much about being polite. "No, I'm sorry but I have to dash. More enquiries to make, people to see. A journalist's work is never done, et cetera."

Then, for some unfathomable reason, I felt slightly guilty and added, "If you've got any literature on the society, I'll take it with me." Perhaps I was going to have to learn to be more hard-nosed, but it wasn't going to come easily.

He rummaged through his briefcase and handed me a creased leaflet. I rose to go and the devil in me came up with a remark which was bound to cause him concern. "Thanks for your time. It's been most useful."

As I closed the classroom door, I hesitated outside for a few seconds and looked back through the window. Kevin Handleigh was staring blankly into space, probably wondering what he had said that was so useful, and maybe trying to work out exactly how much trouble he was in.

*

When I got back to the office, I dropped in on Jack to give him a quick update, as he had requested. I briefly ran through the meeting with Kevin Handleigh and told him of my suspicion that Handleigh was somehow involved in the Abbot's Meadow story.

Jack took it all in with his usual fixed, dispassionate expression, and then opened a notebook on his desk.

"After our discussion this morning, I did a bit of digging into the background of the Hepworth brothers. It seems that Chris Hepworth has quite a police record – grievous bodily harm, for which he got eighteen months, conspiracy to defraud, for which he got six months, and demanding money with menaces, for which he got a hefty fine and community service. But I understand he's been clean for the last nine years, or at least, hasn't been caught doing anything illegal. His brother, Sam, on the other hand is, it seems, a model citizen."

I was intrigued. "Can I ask how you managed to get this information?" It seemed to me incredible that such information could be freely available.

"Let's just say that you don't get to work in Fleet Street for more than twenty-five years without making a few friends in the right places. Mind you, none of what I have told you can ever be printed. Understood?" said Jack, fixing me with those intense blue eyes.

"Understood," I replied, still in awe of this man.

I went back to my desk and settled down to write up the story about Gladys, which was a delight to do, and I recalled our conversation with pleasure and amusement as I wrote. I finished this around 4.30pm and, as it was a bit late in the day to start on Sid Chisholm's obituary, thought I would use the remaining time for a bit of online research. Armed with search engines, online directories, social media, catalogues and various archives it is nowadays possible to uncover key background information in minutes, where once it might have taken a week. I wanted to know more about the Hepworth brothers and so began with Companies House.

The two Hepworth brothers, Sam and Chris, were listed as active directors of Hepworth Landscaping Ltd, but interestingly, there was a third director, Paul Connolly, who it seems resigned, or maybe was fired, a year ago. The most recent accounts that had been filed showed a balance sheet which, as far as I could judge with my very limited grasp of such things, appeared to show that the company was reasonably sound financially. However, the company was not signed up to any of the trader ratings schemes, and on both the internet chat sites and social media, there seemed to be quite a lot of unhappy customers. The most frequent criticisms appeared to be overcharging and poor quality work, as Bob Coldwell had found. There were pictures of shoddy paving, collapsing embankments and uneven lawns, but, to be fair, there were one or two pictures of what looked to me like quite acceptable landscaping jobs.

It also turned out that in the past, the company had experienced several brushes with the Health and Safety Executive and had received a number of improvement notices. These were for things like inadequate safety measures to protect employees and the general public, and unsatisfactory site control measures. I used Google Street View and Google Earth to look at the company premises expecting to see a run-down building in line with a company that really didn't seem to be trying too hard. What I saw was a shock. The business premises adjoined a very large modern detached house, with grounds seemingly occupying maybe two acres, backing on to Castlebridge golf course. Alongside the house was a small building which may have been the office, in front of which there was a yard with vehicles and material storage. I found that the business had a website with a photograph of the office, in front of which there were two white Ford Transit trucks and a mini-digger. But it was what was behind the house and office that was intriguing.

From the aerial view I could make out two very large greenhouses and a collection of outbuildings, one of which was substantial and probably of brick construction. Maybe the premises had previously been a garden centre or nursery? I wondered what these buildings were used for currently and whether the view from the golf course would provide any answers. There appeared to be some sort of track behind the property, and a quick look on a local website for runners showed me that the golf course did indeed have a public footpath along the boundary which would provide a good vantage point. Something to think about for a future run maybe.

I left the office much later than I intended, confused and no further forward. Hepworth Landscaping appeared to be making a reasonable living despite the apparent poor workmanship and negative reviews. The question was, how?

*

Jenny's father's house was a modest semi-detached house in the pretty village of Thornton, about two miles south of the town. I arrived a few minutes early and sat in my car contemplating the day's events. The more I found out about Abbot's Meadow it seemed like the less I knew, or perhaps more correctly, the less I understood. Why would this be such a big deal to the Hepworths? From what I could gather from Jim Symonds, it didn't appear to be a big deal for the council. As the Hepworths were in the landscaping business, it would have made more sense if they were trying to ensure that the meadow was in fact going to be developed, even if such action could have been a conflict of interest. But to try to stop it being developed made no sense, unless they were either avid tree-hugging environmentalists, or were anxious to preserve the site's historical significance and archaeological treasures – neither of which seemed very likely. And how did Kevin Handleigh fit into the picture? Was he on the Hepworth payroll in some way?

These thoughts were still buzzing around my head as I rang the doorbell. Jenny opened the door, and was looking so lovely that, for a moment, I froze like a teenager about to experience a first kiss. I was praying that her father wouldn't suddenly appear to look me over, as my imitation of a guppy fish might have given him cause for concern. Fortunately, she was ready to leave and shouted, "Bye, Dad," as she closed the door.

Jenny was wearing a simple pale blue summer dress with sandals in a matching colour, and looked gorgeous. I held the door for her to get into the Mini and tried to recover my composure. It is always said that women like their men to be confident and self-assured. The evening promised to be challenging, as I felt neither of these things and was, in fact, nervous and acutely self-conscious. It all felt slightly surreal, as if I were in a dream, except that even in my wildest dreams, I could never have imagined a date with someone so naturally beautiful.

"I booked a table at the Riverside Bistro," I said, hoping that Jenny approved.

"That's great. It's really nice there. I went once with the

girls from the office on a hen night. Not that hen nights are my thing really. I'm not a big drinker," she said, as though an apology was needed.

"Me neither, and if I'm driving, I stop at a half pint," I said. "Anyway, it's just a way of pouring money down the drain – almost literally when you think about it – and in my experience, it usually ends badly. I had a friend at university who nearly died from alcohol poisoning, and that was really scary. I was the one who found him and had to call the ambulance. It changed my attitude to alcohol overnight."

It only took a few minutes to get to the restaurant, and we parked up just opposite in a conveniently vacant space. The waiter showed us to a nice table for two in the window overlooking the river, and I could see the path that I ran along when I had met Natalie.

"There's something I need to get off my chest," I said, once we had got comfortable.

"Oh… this sounds ominous. What?" she said, looking apprehensive, as if there was bad news coming. "Don't tell me… you're vegan?"

I laughed nervously. "No, it's nothing like that."

"You're broke and want us to split the bill?"

"No, it's not that either. What I wanted to say was that, yes, I'd like to tell you about my ongoing investigations into 'Abbotsgate', and also to get your views, but when we've done that and it's out of the way, can we just be boy meets girl? A very bewitching girl in this instance."

Wow! I'm not sure what spell she was weaving, but that didn't sound like me, even to me. I cringed internally and wondered whether I'd blown it. Well-judged compliments were never my thing.

She laughed and I sensed that both of us relaxed.

"I'm not sure about the bewitching bit, but yes, I'd like that very much."

The waiter came up to the table, breaking the spell, and gave us menus. The food sounded really nice, if a little more expensive than my usual eating-out fare. After much deliberation, we both opted for Dover sole followed by cheesecake. I ordered a half of lager and Jenny had a mineral water.

"So, if we're going to do the work bit first, you had better have this," Jenny said, reaching into her big handbag. She slid a USB memory stick across the tablecloth.

"On there you'll find a copy of the report from Douglas and Partners, although, as you know, it's password-protected and I don't have the password. Maybe you can find a way of unlocking it? I've also included copies of the three written quotations for carrying out the study we received from companies, including Douglas, which our procedures require us to have. Those files are all readable, and it seems that the quotation from Douglas was in fact the cheapest."

"Jenny, that's great," I said. "I just hope I'm not going to get you into trouble." I felt my cheeks flush at the unfortunate phrasing. "If you'll forgive the expression," I added.

Jenny smiled and put her had on mine for a moment. "Don't worry. These documents should all be readily available – well, the report at least, if not the quotes. Talking to the press isn't perhaps the preferred approach to tackling such issues, but I have a feeling that something is wrong which needs exposing. And I trust you. Anyway, what's the worst that can happen?"

I had no idea what the worst that could happen might be, although I was certain that it would not be good for Jenny or her career. But I did have the feeling that getting a copy of the file was going to prove a breakthrough moment.

"When I was in Cardiff, I shared a flat with a guy who's an IT wizard. I'm pretty sure he'll be able to unlock the file," I said enthusiastically.

From that point the conversation flowed continually and easily between us, and we barely found time to eat. I brought her up to speed on my latest news, covering the meeting with Sam Hepworth in Jack's office, my trip to meet Gladys and the strange meeting with Kevin Handleigh. However, I decided not to mention what Jack had told me about Chris Hepworth's criminal record, partly because I think Jack would prefer it was kept between him and me, but also because I didn't want to worry Jenny. She listened intently, asking the occasional question which revealed a very sharp mind.

Eventually, our conversation moved away from work and on to more enjoyable topics. She spoke a lot about her late mother, whom she obviously adored. It was apparent that looking after her dad was her way of honouring her mum, and in some respects she was putting her personal life on hold to make sure he was okay. As she talked, I felt myself falling into those hypnotic brown eyes, and I had to make a determined effort to concentrate on what was being said.

I think we must have just about covered each other's entire life story, because we were the last people to leave the restaurant and the waiters were beginning to hover. I paid the bill, despite Jenny's request that we should go halves, and left a generous tip for the staff, who between them had provided us with a very special evening. We left by the rear door which opened out onto the terrace facing the river, just to take in the sights. The coloured lights from all of the businesses on the riverside were reflected in the water, and those few moments were magical and incredibly romantic.

We held hands and started to walk around the bistro to the road when a voice called out from the garden of the adjacent pub. I turned to see Dean Lockwood and his two mates sitting at a picnic table littered with glasses. They had undoubtedly been drinking heavily, probably for most of the evening.

"Well, look who it is! If it isn't that fuckin' arsehole who has to get the rozzers to protect him, and he's pulled some totty by the look of it."

It seemed that alcohol hadn't dulled Lockwood's natural charm or way with words.

"You want to watch out hangin' round with him, love. Our boss is not a happy bunny because of this tosser and his pikey friends."

Lockwood attempted to get up, but picnic tables are not designed for a rapid departure, especially when inebriated. Having got one leg over the bench seat, his trailing leg caught on the side trestle leg. He fell into a drunken sprawling heap on the grass, much to the delight of his friends who whooped and shouted raucously. Jenny pulled my hand and quickened her stride along the path towards the front of the bistro.

"Ignore him, Dan, please," she pleaded, recognising quickly that Lockwood's disparaging references to her might engender a degree of courage in me that, in reality, could not be backed up by physical prowess. It seemed that Lockwood wasn't finished, and called after us as he attempted to stand and recover his composure.

"You'd better watch your step and stop pokin' your fuckin' nose where it don't belong."

We walked to the car in silence, and as we got there I turned to check that we were not being followed. I looked at Jenny, but she had read my mind before I could speak. "Don't worry, Dan. I'm not easily scared, and certainly not by drunken louts like that."

"I'm just concerned about involving you in all of this," I said, wondering whether my obsession with this story was affecting my judgement. "Perhaps I should just move on to something else and let this story drop?"

I didn't mean that, of course. There was no way I could let this drop. But maybe I should distance myself from Jenny for a while, for the sake of her safety… which was a possibility I hardly dared contemplate having only just met her. She stopped in her tracks, gripped my arms and looked me in the eyes.

"Listen to me, Daniel Curran! If you want me to think less of you, then go ahead. But you may be on to something here, and whatever it is, it needs seeing through. And if I can help I will. Otherwise horrible people like that will think they're untouchable."

"Maybe you're right," I said, becoming more impressed by this girl every minute. She really was quite extraordinary.

"I am right, trust me," she said as we got into the car.

I drove us back to Jenny's house and accompanied her to the door. "Thanks for a lovely evening, Jenny. I can't tell you how much I've enjoyed your company."

She smiled and said, "Yes. I've really enjoyed it too, so thank you."

"Can we do something together later in the week?" I suggested. "Maybe a film, or some music, if I can find something?"

"That would be nice," Jenny said with a smile. "How about

Thursday evening? There's a nice pub I know that has live music on a Thursday."

"That sounds great. I'll pick you up around 8pm if that's okay?" I suggested.

And with that we shared a kiss, a perfect end to a perfect evening. Well, nearly perfect, I thought as I got back in the car.

CHAPTER 8

The next morning I called my friend and flatmate from Cardiff University days.

"Hiya, Vishal. It's Dan. How are you keeping?"

At university, Vishal was studying computer technology and was an absolute wizard with all things computer-related. Unfortunately, during our time together, his devotion to his subject had been total, to the exclusion of some of the social norms which make for a more harmonious cohabiting relationship. We used to have major rows about things like washing his socks and underwear in the dishwasher because the washing machine was broken, months-old pizza leftovers under the sofa, and treating any food he found in the fridge as something to be shared – or preferably, just eaten by him. Vishal could eat for England, but still somehow remained stick thin, much to the annoyance of all those who knew him. Despite these tribulations, we remained good friends throughout our university days and had kept in contact.

"Hi, mate. Haven't heard from you in a while. What are you up to these days?" he said through a mouthful of food. I tried hard not to picture him eating, but failed.

"I've got a job as a reporter for a newspaper – not one of the big nationals, more provincial, but it's a start."

I didn't mention Castlebridge because I knew he would immediately be searching in a browser while we were talking, and I wanted to keep him focused.

"Cool. I'm with a cyber security company in Birmingham. They have some really neat software, but their DevOps methodologies need a bit of sorting," he said.

"Ah," I said, not having the faintest idea what he was talking about, or what would constitute an appropriate response. "The thing is, I've got a favour to ask."

"Fire away, buddy," he said, and then added for good measure, "as long as it doesn't involve money, cos I'm broke."

"No, it doesn't involve money," I said. "I have a word-processed report which is password-protected so the file can't be opened. Any chance you could exercise your magic powers and unlock it?"

Vishal didn't even have to pause to consider this.

"If the author just used the standard built-in protection rather than some fancy separate encryption software, then sure, piece of cake most likely. Do you want to email the file to me and I'll take a look?"

I agreed and we talked for a few minutes about the usual man-stuff like women, football and cars, before ringing off. I smiled to myself as I remembered Vishal's predilection for strategically placed duct tape whenever anything broke on his ancient, food-ridden Ford Fiesta. Over my time in Cardiff, I'd been happy to receive many a lift in that old banger. He might have the social graces of a warthog, but he had a heart of gold and would do anything for anyone.

I copied the memory stick file containing the Douglas

report onto my computer, and emailed it to Vishal. There being little else I could constructively do for the moment, I went to see Geoff Clarke, who had a job lined up for me.

"Ah, Dan, I need you to go to the industrial estate on Brindley Road and cover a warehouse fire," said Geoff, opening a map of the area and jabbing a finger on the location in question.

"I gather the fire brigade are just damping down now, so if you're quick, you'll get to talk with them. The warehouse belongs to a paper merchant, Castle Cardstock Ltd."

*

I set off, following the directions provided by my phone satnav, and arrived at the industrial estate to see a plume of smoke reaching into the sky like a heavenly finger, pointing downwards to the source of the conflagration. There were two fire tenders and a police car present, and a large group of onlookers had gathered behind a tape strung between two portable stanchions. Yet again I was amazed how, for many people, any event which requires more than a few seconds of observation must, of absolute necessity, be viewed through the camera on a mobile phone. I just hoped this wasn't yet another Darwinian evolutionary adaptation whereby the bit of the brain responsible for human visual memory is becoming redundant.

Several hoses snaked from the two tenders into a relatively modern warehouse, the roof of which was partially missing, allowing a pall of thick grey smoke to be released into the otherwise blue sky. I made my way to what appeared to be the senior fire officer, who was busy talking to a policeman. As I approached, the policeman broke away to return to his car and I recognised him as the Welsh officer, PC Griffiths, who came to our rescue on Abbot's Meadow when I was with Mickey and Rosa.

"Ah, hello again," he said with a friendly smile. "Keeping out of trouble, are we?"

"Not exactly," I said. "I'm following up a story which involves those three guys that you talked to the other day. It's probably fair to say that we're not the best of pals at the moment."

"Ah… I did wonder. I checked our records, and let's just say that we are familiar with two of them. I guess in your profession you're like us in that mixing with undesirables is all part and parcel of the job."

It was more of a statement than a question, but it struck a chord with me. I was no longer a student. I was grown-up – a professional.

"Yes," I agreed. "To be honest, I don't really know how to handle people like that. Self-defence is not something that journalism training really covers in detail – or at all, in fact."

"Well, if you're ever in need of some advice, I'm happy for you to give me a call. Can't promise I can help, you understand, but I might be able to give you some pointers on the best way of handling the situation. You might have to leave a message though, depending on what I'm doing." He reached into the breast pocket of his tunic and handed me a slip of paper on which was printed 'PC 267 Evan Griffiths' and a mobile telephone number. I was sure his kindness was going way beyond the call of duty.

"Thanks for that, Evan. I really appreciate it. So, what's the story here then?" I said, indicating the smouldering warehouse.

"You'd best speak with the OIC," said the policeman. "His name's Tinsley. He's just over there talking to the owner, who's a bit angry, like."

I took some photos and then walked over to where the fire brigade officer-in-charge was engaged, not so much in talking to as being shouted at, by the owner, one James Harringley. Watching your business go up in smoke is going to be gut-wrenchingly upsetting for anyone, but Harringley was evidently not happy with the way that the firefighters were dealing with the fire, and not backward about expressing his feelings.

"What stock isn't burned is ruined with your bloody water!" he shouted, with flecks of spittle clearly visible, even from where I stood a couple of metres away. "Everything is a total write-off. If you'd got here even five minutes sooner, we could have saved the stock in the last bay, maybe two bays. What kept you? I pay my rates expecting better service than this, and I shall be talking to my MP."

Once the heat had died down for both the premises and its owner, I talked first to Officer Tinsley and then to Harringley, and got two different accounts of what had happened. It seemed that the only thing they agreed on was that there had been a fire, which was now extinguished.

Harringley insisted that it had taken the fire brigade over fifteen minutes to arrive, whereas Tinsley assured him that it was under ten. Tinsley reported that the fire brigade had reached a preliminary conclusion that the fire started in a faulty dehumidifier, although Harringley was convinced it was caused by a discarded cigarette from one of the warehouse staff. He said that he had found a cigarette butt a week or so ago, and that smoking in the warehouse was a sackable offence, given the highly flammable nature of the stock. Maybe he knew that the dehumidifier was faulty, or hadn't been serviced? My money would have gone on the fire brigade's version of events.

There was something objectionable about Harringley and his ungrateful attack on the very people putting themselves at risk to save his factory. He was only too happy to tell me how much stock was lost and its retail value. I wondered whether he was underinsured in terms of stock, which might help explain, if not forgive, his anger. Finally, I talked to a member of the public who claimed to have seen smoke rising before the fire brigade arrived and thought that the tenders were on scene quite quickly.

I reckoned that I now had enough material to write up a short story. As I walked back to the car, I noticed the staff from the adjacent warehouse unit gathered outside, anxiously watching the events unfold next door. The sign above the warehouse said 'Blaze Storage and Logistics'. Sometimes life itself provides all the irony you need.

*

When I got back to the office, I checked my emails and saw that my inbox contained one from Vishal. It had an attachment.

The accompanying note from Vishal was short and to the point.

Dan
Piece of cake. Looks dead boring though!
Mine's a pint when we next meet (… and a curry)
Take care, mate.
Vishal

To say that I was excited at the thought of getting sight of the Douglas report was an understatement. I clicked on the file, and after a few seconds it opened up to reveal a very professional-looking and comprehensive report of some twenty-five pages, neatly formatted and including a number of pictures and illustrations. The report was entitled, *'An investigation into the history of Abbot's Meadow, Castlebridge, and the implications for future development of the site'*. At the back of the report were two pages of references, all cross-linked to the main body of the text.

The first section of the report discussed the history of Castlebridge and the surrounding land. It seems that the Romans built a settlement on or near the location of present-day Castlebridge in about 70 AD, and this included a fortress overlooking the river, which had commanding views down the valley. The fortress was situated on the banks of the River Brant and was reached by a stone bridge from the south, which later gave the settlement its name. After the fortress became a colony in the second century, further stone walls and gates were added, as well as a stone quay beside the river. Most of the subsequent development was on the southern side, and outer stone walls were built in the fourth century to encompass and protect the growing conurbation. There was a hand-drawn map of the area indicating the location of the fortress and the subsequent developments during this period, but it was impossible to see precisely where Abbot's Meadow was in relation to these features.

The second section of the report dealt with the changes brought about by the Anglo-Saxon influx starting in the fifth century. There was evidence that a church was built to the east of the stone bridge, and some stone features of this were retained when St Cuthbert's Church was built on the same site in the late fifteenth century. The report suggested that the Anglo-Saxon community was sustained by a mixture of arable and pastoral farming, and a rather crudely drawn map thought to date from the late seventh century showed that housing in Castlebridge had grown substantially with farmed fields to the north of the river also. I could see roughly where Abbot's Meadow would be, although the boundaries were very different, and there were various dykes and earthwork features which I was guessing would be unrecognisable today. Importantly, one of the features highlighted by the report was the presence of a number of barrows in this area, barrows being a sort of burial mound. It was suggested that, with the growth in arable farming over subsequent years, many of these barrows would have been flattened.

The next section covered the growth of Castlebridge through the Norman period and the introduction of the feudal system, traces of which could still be seen in some of the surrounding fields as ridges and furrows. The fact that the Abbot's Meadow area did not show such markings was said to support the theory that the meadow was treated differently because of its history. Given that most of the English countryside no longer shows traces of the feudal system, this seemed to me to be a somewhat tenuous argument, but who was I to say, particularly as I failed both my geography and history GCSE exams quite comprehensively.

According to the *Domesday Book*, much of the land around Castlebridge was under the control of tenant-in-chief Sir William de Ferrers, and the report devoted two pages to the tracing of the land ownership through to the present day. The Douglas people had done a remarkable job tracing through the convoluted line of ownership, although inevitably there were some gaps where the records either didn't exist or couldn't be found. The area now known as Abbot's Meadow became part of a Blackfriars Farm in about 1790, which covered roughly 700 acres. In 1870, the farm was sold to a very wealthy businessman called Henry Abbot and was inherited by his son, James, in 1904 when Henry died.

It seems that, unlike his father who amassed great wealth, James was something of a philanthropist and gave two large fields at the edge of the farm to the local authority. These fields, which became known as Abbot's Meadow and Blackfriar Meadow, were intended to be used for allotments by the townsfolk, although in the event only Blackfriar Meadow was ever used for this purpose, and the council rented Abbot's Meadow to a local farmer, John Manthorpe, to be used as pasture. Manthorpe still owned the adjoining farm to this day, but ceased his tenure of the meadow in 2017. Since that date it had remained on the council's land and property register.

The final section of the report gave conclusions and recommendations. It was difficult not to feel a sense of disappointment as I quickly scanned through this section, hoping for something, anything, that would back up my suspicion that a conspiracy was afoot. My heart sank as I read on.

> *There is clear evidence that Castlebridge was for several centuries a growing Anglo-Saxon settlement. While most of the surrounding area has been developed or has been used for arable farming, the area known as Abbot's Meadow has been relatively undisturbed, used principally as pasture. Early maps show earthwork features consistent*

with a burial site on, or close to, Abbot's Meadow. While these features have largely disappeared, an aerial view of the plot does indicate some contour anomalies consistent with this theory.

It is concluded that, on the balance of probability, some part of the meadow was used as a burial site for the Castlebridge town populus. It is recommended that a ground-penetrating radar survey be conducted to ascertain whether this might produce corroborating evidence. Given the custom for Anglo-Saxon burials to inter belongings and treasures with the deceased, it is further recommended that, pending such a survey, the council refrain from divulging details of this report to deter metal detectorists disturbing what could be a site of major historic importance.

So, there we had it in black and white. No mention of flooding rivers or flood plains, and no reason to suggest that the story of Abbot's Meadow was anything other than had been leaked to me by Jim Symonds. I felt like a prize fool, wasting my time and energy on a fool's errand, which of course is what Sid Chisholm had tried to tell me when we met.

And yet… there was something not quite right. I couldn't put my finger on it, but I just didn't see Councillor Sam Hepworth and his unpleasant employees as pillars of the community, motivated purely out of a sense of duty to protect the town's heritage. I realised that I needed to bring Jack up to speed as he had requested, and was not looking forward to having to admit that I'd probably wasted my time.

However, Jack seemed to be in a good mood when I entered his office.

"Well, would you look at that!" he exclaimed waving a card

from the morning's post. "I've had an invitation for Sarah and me to attend the National Press Awards bash at the Lancaster in London next month. I've not been to that since I left Fleet Street. Last time I went there would have been around 1990. Got totally pissed as I recall. Great evening though."

"Is there a prize for the journalistic equivalent of the village idiot?" I asked. "If there is then I must be a strong contender, if not favourite."

"Oh dear," said Jack. "That doesn't sound too good. You'd better close the door and tell me all about it."

I produced the copy of the Douglas report and gave Jack a summary of its contents before reading out the conclusions and recommendations in full. When I explained how I had acquired the report, he raised an eyebrow, but made no comment.

Yet again, while I spoke, Jack remained impassive throughout giving nothing away. He took the report from me and flicked through the pages, pausing occasionally to look at some of the illustrations. He dropped the report back on his desk, stretched out in his chair and put his feet up on the desk. He stroked his chin pensively for a couple of minutes.

"Well, the way I see it, there are three possibilities," he said, somewhat unnecessarily holding up three fingers to drive home the point. "Possibility one is that this Douglas firm has, for whatever reason, fabricated evidence to ensure that the meadow isn't developed. Possibility two is that they wrote the report in good faith concluding that there is no reason to prohibit development, and that someone else has modified the report to suit their own purposes. This could have included removing any reference to flooding or other evidence which cast doubt over It being a burial site. Option three is that the report is genuine, and that there is a good reason not to send the diggers in. Have I missed anything?"

"No, that's about the long and short of it," I said, enthralled by this man's ability to grasp the situation and summarise so quickly and succinctly. At the same time, I wasn't quite sure where this line of thought was taking us.

"Well then, I suggest you go and see Messrs Douglas," he said. "You should be able to judge whether they seem professional and genuine, in which case possibility one can be ruled out. If they query how you got hold of the report and are uncomfortable answering any questions from the press without checking with the council, then it's likely that possibility three is in fact the true situation – i.e. the report is genuine. However, if they are quite happy to answer questions and don't see any need for secrecy, then it's probably a fair assumption that someone acting for the council, or a council member, has been tampering with the report. Whichever it turns out to be, my advice would be to keep your powder dry as much as possible. If someone has been misrepresenting their work, they are not going to be best pleased, so for the time being, it might be better for them not to know about it. Gives us chance for further investigations behind the scenes, as it were."

I sat there dumbstruck. "Er… great. I'll go and see them first thing tomorrow, if that's okay?"

"Good," he said with a grin. "We can be village idiots together, because, for what it's worth, I'm with you. Methinks there is some skulduggery going on here, so trust your nose, Dan, just trust your nose."

CHAPTER 9

The next morning, I awoke at 6.15 with so many thoughts buzzing around my head that any further sleep was impossible. I had booked a seat on the 9.30 train from Castlebridge to London, so there was plenty of time for a run. I changed into my running gear and set off towards the nearest countryside to my flat.

Within about ten minutes I was leaving the suburbs, and open countryside beckoned. The early morning sun gave everything a slightly orange tinge, and cast long shadows of the trees across the misty fields. Soon the pavements had given way to wild grass verges. I was glad that the roads were quiet, although mindful that this would change on my return journey as commuters went about their daily trips to work. I had in mind a visit to Castlebridge Golf Club to investigate the path which passed behind the Hepworths' property, but cursed myself for not printing off a map before setting out. Thankfully, a brief chat with an early morning cyclist confirmed that I was heading in the right direction.

The golf course was a bit further than I had anticipated and things would be a bit tight time-wise, but the opportunity was too good to miss. As I turned into the drive up to the club,

I noticed that there were already a handful of expensive cars in the car park. I remembered that the path was to the left of the clubhouse, and after exploring the frontage, I discovered a public footpath sign, partly hidden by foliage. I was guessing that the groundsmen were quite happy to leave the sign partly obscured, so as not to encourage walkers or other improperly dressed riff-raff onto their hallowed ground, lowering the tone for well-heeled club members.

The footpath followed the boundary of the course and ran behind a number of properties, most of which had six-foot-high wooden fences separating them from the course. The challenge I now had was to identify which one of these belonged to the Hepworths. I soon came to a newer section of fencing, over the top of which I could just make out the tip of a large brick building. From my exploration on Google Earth, I was sure that this was the Hepworths' property. Fortunately, there were several knot holes in the fence, and looking through one of the larger and more conveniently placed holes, I could see the brick building and part of a large greenhouse. The greenhouse appeared to be full of plants of some type, with dark masses of green foliage. Was that unusual in England during early September? I know that some fruit and vegetables are grown in greenhouses during summer, like tomatoes and cucumbers, but from what I could make out through my spy hole, these plants looked very different. And what did they do with them all? Surely landscaping involved planting whatever it was that the customer had specified? Even stranger, to my fevered imagination at least, was the presence of a CCTV camera mounted on a bracket off the side of the brick building, monitoring the doorway. What was in there that needed to be guarded?

By contrast, the property immediately to the right of the Hepworths' had a relatively low fence onto the golf course, which was in a poor state of repair. I could see that the newer high fencing ran down the boundary line between the two plots, both of which were maybe 200 metres long. Halfway up the neighbour's garden was an orchard which almost completely obscured the house, and close to where I was standing was a wood-framed compost heap against the party fence. It occurred to me that this wooden structure might provide relatively easy access into the Hepworths' plot. Whether I had the courage to act on this was another matter. Maybe today's visit to Douglas and Partners would help determine if there were any next steps to be taken.

I looked at my watch and realised that it was now past eight o'clock and I had a train to catch. I ran back more quickly than usual and was exhausted by the time I reached my flat. I just had time for a quick shower before driving to the station.

*

I arrived at Castlebridge station with five minutes to spare, which was just enough to grab a bacon roll and coffee to take on board the train. Thankfully the train was only half full, and I was spared the awkwardness of having to evict an interloper from my reserved seat. I took out a notepad from my rucksack and, after polishing off my breakfast, set about making some notes for the coming meeting.

K. Douglas and Partners had premises in Kensington, about a five-minute walk from South Kensington tube station. The company website described the business as archaeological consultants, established in 1987 by Kelvin Douglas, who was now the CEO. When I rang the previous evening to make an appointment, the receptionist was doubtful that anyone would be able to see me at such short notice, but after a few moments came back on the line to say that Mr Charles Proudfoot, a partner of Kelvin Douglas, could see me at 12.30, but for twenty minutes only. Taking a lead from Jack, I didn't say exactly what I wanted to talk about but said that it concerned some work done by the company recently.

I wrote down the three possibilities for the Abbot's Meadow report which Jack had so adroitly arrived at, and considered each in turn.

1. *Douglas have falsified the findings in the report*
2. *Douglas wrote the report in good faith and someone subsequently falsified the findings*
3. *The report is genuine and accurate*

Jack had presumed that if the Douglas people were in collusion with Hepworth, or someone acting for him, then I should be able to deduce that from first impressions, attitude to questions, the degree of professionalism on display, etc. However, I wasn't so sure. I had no experience of other such companies with which I could make a comparison. Also, what questions should I ask to draw out meaningful information in order to make any form of rational judgement? I wished I had Jack with me.

The possibility that someone else had tampered with Douglas's report was going to be interesting. If this was the case, I certainly didn't want to make them aware of it, so maybe the best approach would be to first explore the possibility that the report was genuine. I would not immediately produce my copy but would make it plain that I knew exactly what was in there. If they showed concern and wished to check with the council before making any comment, then maybe that would be the time to throw in the towel and admit I'd got it wrong. To say that I felt out of my depth was an understatement. I felt I was in great danger of drowning.

The announcement 'bongs' sounded, interrupting my thoughts, and a thick cockney accent informed passengers of the train's progress and estimated arrival time. *So nice to hear down-to-earth regional accents*, I thought. I wondered what Charles Proudfoot was going to be like, the name conjuring up a man with an altogether different accent.

We pulled into St Pancras station bang on time, and I got off to join the mass exodus down the station platform feeling as though I was being swept along by a tide of impatient and unfriendly humanity, where everyone had their own personal agenda which trumped all others. I made my way to the subway, following the signs for the Circle Line.

I had only been to London twice before, and the whole underground experience was still very new and strange to me. The first challenge was to negotiate the screens of the ticket machine, trying desperately to look like I knew what I was doing as the people in the queue behind me made tutting noises and looked at watches. There was something slightly dystopian about so many people swarming along tunnels and up and down escalators, mostly saying nothing and looking straight ahead. In fact, catching someone's eye appeared to be something to be avoided at all costs, for fear of giving offence or being challenged in some way. My heart immediately warmed to a well-dressed man standing at the entrance to one of the side corridors leading to the Circle Line platform. He had a box of man-size Kleenex under his arm, and was offering them for free to passers-by.

"Big Tissue, anyone? Get your Big Tissue here."

I laughed out loud and took one, delighted that someone was trying to bring a little levity into the lives of these automatons. We humans had to stick together.

South Kensington tube station was nine stops on the Circle Line, or considerably more if you took the train destined to branch off to Hammersmith once it got to Edgeware Road. I managed to get the right train and stood in the packed compartment counting off the stations, secretly willing the train to go faster, while being apparently totally absorbed by the wonders of a tube train ceiling.

Getting my bearings once I'd emerged into the daylight proved more tricky than I had anticipated, due mainly to the seeming lack of road name plates. However, a friendly traffic warden was on hand to help, while being very unfriendly to an illegally parked Range Rover. His smile suggested that the bigger and brassier the car, the sweeter the ticket.

"Take this road here on the left, just past that red car with a parking ticket on its windscreen, and it will bring you out on Cromwell Road. I think you then have to turn right," he said.

And he was correct. K. Douglas and Partners occupied the top floor of an elegant white four-storey Regency office building. The concierge in the lobby directed me to the lift and I emerged into another lobby area on the fourth floor, in which sat a receptionist behind a large modern reception desk. Behind her were professionally produced graphic panels advertising the business. Emblazoned across the top was a company strapline: 'Expert Archaeological Services – Uncovering the Past, Enriching the Future'.

"Hello," I said, offering the lady behind the desk one of my warmest smiles. "I'm Dan Curran. I have an appointment with Mr Proudfoot at 12.30. I'm a bit early, I'm afraid."

The receptionist was beautifully dressed, with perfect make-up and hair. She sat in that straight-backed, poised manner that suggests deportment classes and finishing school.

"That's no problem at all," she smiled sweetly looking at her computer screen. "If you could just fill in the visitors' book for me, Mr Curran, that would be wonderful. I'll let Mr Proudfoot know you're here, and maybe he can see you early. Unfortunately, he does have an important international call at one o'clock. Can I get you a drink?"

"Thanks. A coffee would be really welcome," I said.

The last drink I had was from the station café and although the man serving described it as coffee, I was not at all sure. She produced a pass for me to wear and directed me to a conference room at the end of the corridor.

"I will bring your coffee down to you," she said, still smiling.

My feet sank into the plush carpet as I followed her directions. The room was very grand, with a large, highly polished conference table surrounded by black and chrome, high-backed swivel chairs. On the walls were a collection of large photographs of archaeological sites, and a map of the UK covered with dozens of different-coloured pins. I was standing inspecting these when the door opened, and a tall man dressed in an immaculate blue pinstripe three-piece suit entered. I guessed he was about fifty, his black hair, greying at the temples, giving him a distinguished appearance. He exuded the charm and self-confidence that generally comes from a public school education.

"Mr Curran, is it?" he asked.

"Yes, Daniel Curran. Good of you to see me at short notice," I said.

He extended a hand. The handshake was firm but friendly, the smile seemingly genuine.

"My name is Charles Proudfoot. I'm a partner of Kelvin Douglas. I see you have already spotted our map. The coloured pins show the locations of archaeological surveys and such like carried out by our company over the last twenty-five years or so. The pins are colour-coded – red for desk-based assessments, blue for photographic surveys, yellow for excavations, and so on. And we've a very wide and prestigious client base. For the past five years we have been a preferred consultant to the Crown Estate, National Trust and English Heritage."

By now it was obvious to me that this was a well-established, well-respected, highly professional company, and as such, it was unthinkable that they would be involved in falsifying a survey report. I mentally crossed off this possibility from my list of three.

"Now. What was it you wished to discuss?" asked Proudfoot, anxious to get down to business.

"Firstly, thank you again for seeing me at such short notice. I know you have a one o'clock meeting so I'll try to be brief. I'm a reporter with the *Castlebridge Gazette* and as I was in London, I couldn't let the opportunity to meet you go by," I said, telling myself that half-truths were definitely not lies – and anyway, I was on the side of the good guys.

"I was reading a report that you produced for our district council on a field that we know locally as Abbot's Meadow, and it was just fantastic. We learned so much about the town's history that we were totally unaware of."

I watched Proudfoot's face carefully, looking for any signs of discomfort or concern, but there was nothing. Just then the door opened, and the receptionist came in with my cup of coffee.

"Would you like one, Charles?" she offered.

"No thanks, Penny. I've not long finished one. I'll be wired all afternoon if I drink any more. Could you do me a favour and fish out the file on Abbot's Meadow, Castlebridge? The customer was Castlebridge District Council," he said. Penny left the room, leaving behind the fragrance of an expensive perfume.

"I don't know too much about that project," he admitted. "It was actually compiled by one of our senior researchers. I did read it through before it was issued as part of our quality control procedure, but I'm afraid I can't remember too many details. Probably an age thing," he said, smiling.

We exchanged business cards while we were waiting, and a couple of minutes later, Penny reappeared with a buff-coloured folder. Proudfoot removed a printed document stapled together, and scanned through it quickly.

"Ah yes. I do remember this one. And you have received a copy of this from the council, you say?" he said, looking up at me.

I was trying to judge whether he was suddenly being very guarded, bearing in mind that the report advised against widespread circulation.

"Yes," I said, again conscious that I was being somewhat economical with the truth, although Jenny did work for the council. I reached into my rucksack for my copy of the report. I had not bothered to staple the pages together, and on the spur of the moment, grabbed all but the last couple of pages, which I left in the rucksack.

Proudfoot seemed perfectly relaxed, and I began to wonder whether we were now heading towards Jack's 'skulduggery afoot' territory. Maybe the report had been tampered with. I took a slurp of coffee while I worked out how to proceed.

I flicked through the pages of the report, as if reminding myself of the contents. "It was a shame about the result," I said vaguely, hoping he would give me something to work with.

He smiled and said, "Well, to be honest it's about par for the course actually. Probably nine out of ten such investigations end up with no conclusive evidence of archaeological significance. We carried out what we call a desk-based study, although we did get some aerial photos taken for us using a drone subcontractor. There were some aspects which were interesting, but we have to consider the balance of probability, and we couldn't find enough evidence to warrant a more in-depth study, like a radar scan. The fact that the whole area was prone to flooding right up until around the fifteenth century was for us a pretty convincing argument that the Anglo-Saxons would not have favoured using the meadow as a burial site. But, in cases such as this, it is usually best to let the developers make a start. If they do find something, then that's a whole different story. We are not infallible… although we come close," he said with a smile.

I was at a loss to know exactly what to say, and my heart was racing. I was sure that Proudfoot would be mortified to know that the document I had in my hand did not reach the same conclusion. Stalling to give me time to think, I said, "This ground-penetrating radar – is it expensive?"

"I guess it would cost in the region of £10-15,000 for the meadow," he said. "I think we mentioned it in the report. But as I say, on the evidence we could find, we wouldn't consider it worth spending the money… well, not at this point anyway."

"The background information on Castlebridge was really interesting. If we wanted to use any of it in a feature on the town's history at some point in the future, would we need to ask you or the council? Who owns the copyright?" I enquired, suddenly seeing a possible opportunity.

"We always retain the intellectual property on anything we write, although we would have given the council free rein to copy and use it for their own purposes. So, you having a copy from them is not a problem in itself, but we would want to have sight of any proposed use by the newspaper," he said with a hint of firmness in his voice. "Especially if our name is mentioned. We live or die by our reputation, so we have to be really careful that we are not misrepresented. I'm sure you understand?"

"That's fine," I said, adopting my best puzzled expression. "Were the references included in the report?" I asked, opening my copy of the report to show that the pages were not there. Again, I justified this ploy with the thought that, in the long run, he would thank me.

"Oh… the reference list should certainly be there," he said showing me the relevant pages in his copy. "Looks like someone has given you an incomplete copy. Here, take this one. I can always get Penny to run off another."

I took the report from him, hardly daring to believe my luck.

"Thanks, that's great."

Proudfoot looked at his watch, and I took this as a signal to beat a hasty retreat, which I was keen to do before he changed his mind.

"Well, I mustn't take up any more of your time. I really

appreciate you seeing me at short notice, and if we do decide to run a piece about Castlebridge history, you can rest assured that I will be in touch," I promised as I stood to shake hands. On the way out I thanked the delectable Penny for the coffee, and she smiled sweetly.

I descended back down to the ground floor and out into the sunlight on Cromwell Road feeling light-headed. I couldn't wait to compare the two versions of the Douglas report, and had no doubt that the Abbot's Meadow story had suddenly taken a dark and sinister turn. This looked like a clear case of deception, although I had absolutely no idea why Hepworth, or anyone else, would go to so much trouble and risk being found out.

*

Back on the train home I was grateful that the seat next to mine was unoccupied, allowing me to put the two reports side by side on the tray in front of me, without anyone looking over my shoulder – not that anyone would have been that interested. My initial excitement had by now given way to apprehension, and I looked at the identical front pages for a full minute while thoughts swirled around in my head. I felt my heart rate rise as I turned the pages over and started to compare each version. The first three pages tracing through the history of Castlebridge were identical, so it did look like there was a big Anglo-Saxon settlement which ultimately became the town. However, from that point there were differences, some small and subtle, some very significant.

The discussion about earthworks and burial mounds had all been added. However, it was on the next page that I felt a tingle down the spine as I read the words several times, making sure I had not misunderstood. Originally the River Brant was kinked, in oxbow fashion, and the local resistance to flow in times of heavy rainfall would often cause flooding across the fields to the east of the bridge. This feature had been removed from the early handdrawn map included in the report, which showed a fairly straight river going up to the bridge. In the fifteenth century, the course of the river had been straightened, cutting out the oxbow kink, and this allowed free flow without flooding. The flood plain land including the old riverbed was reclaimed as farming land as the years of deposited sediment made the area particularly fertile. And Abbot's Meadow was part of this flood plain.

I sat back and reflected on my meeting with Sid Chisholm during my first week with the paper, and felt a sense of sadness. Jim Symonds said that Sid had mentioned flooding during the council meeting, although exactly how Sid knew will probably forever remain a mystery. Once Hepworth had made veiled threats about Chisholm's girlfriend, Natalie, he would have felt desperately torn between doing the right thing and protecting Natalie from any further pain or danger. She had been through so much already.

Just as Proudfoot had described, the conclusion reached was that, while there would, in all probability, have been an Anglo-Saxon burial ground somewhere close to the town, it was most unlikely to be anywhere near Abbot's Meadow. Although more conclusive proof might be obtained by conducting further investigations, such as a ground-penetrating radar study, the expenditure of around £10-15,000 could not, in the opinion of the author, be justified. I checked the copy that Jenny gave me, and this gave the radar study cost as at least £60,000. So, not only did whoever altered the report want to prevent the land being developed pending further investigation, they also wanted to frustrate those investigations by artificially inflating the cost.

I sat back and let these revelations sink in. Sam Hepworth was instrumental in getting the council to reject the development application for the meadow and provided members with a report which had been doctored. It was probably safe to assume that he had a hand in falsifying the report findings, even if he didn't do it himself. From his reaction when I questioned him, my money was on the school history teacher, Kevin Handleigh, being involved in some way. He appeared to be the go-to local historian, and would have had the right background to be able to change and embellish the findings without it being obvious to the reader.

And then we had the brother, Chris Hepworth. How did he fit into the picture? It was his landscaping boys that tried to evict the Travellers, Mickey and Rosa, from the meadow. Mickey told me that on the first occasion when Councillor Sam Hepworth got so heated, they were digging a latrine. I suppose that could be considered as a 'development' of sorts, a fairly unpleasant one admittedly. I wondered whether the meadow was in some way linked to Chris Hepworth's landscaping business, but it was hard to see how.

I realised that I still didn't know which of the brothers lived in the house adjacent to the Hepworth Landscaping yard and office backing onto the golf course. I fished out my mobile phone and dialled Jenny. She picked up almost straight away.

"Hi, Dan," she said brightly.

"Hi, Jenny," I said, excited to hear her voice again. "I'm just on the train back from London, so if we get cut off, you'll know why. I was wondering whether you could tell me where Sam Hepworth lives... or if that breaches protocol, just confirm whether it's on Birchwood Road, out near the golf course?"

"Hmmm... I probably ought not to give out an address, but just wait a few secs," she said.

I could hear tapping on a keyboard, and then she came back on the line.

"No, Dan, he lives at a place called Brockwell. It's out in the suburbs. I would prefer not to say where. We're not supposed to give out private details."

"Sure, I understand. That's all I wanted to know. How are you? Still okay to go out tomorrow night?" I asked, keen to move the conversation on so that she didn't feel I was abusing our relationship.

"Yes, looking forward to it. It's funny you should call just now," Jenny said. "Sam Hepworth dropped by my desk about ten minutes ago. He seemed to know that you and I have been... well, you know, seeing each other. He was smiling and perfectly polite... but I think he was sort of warning me. To tell the truth, I can't even remember his exact words, but it was the look in his eye I found a bit scary," she said.

Having met Sam Hepworth, I knew exactly what she meant. I was suddenly too aware that I now also knew how Sid Chisholm felt!

CHAPTER 10

After the excitement of going to London and getting hold of the original version of the report, the next day was something of an anticlimax. I brought Jack up to speed on the visit to Douglas and Partners, although I decided not to mention going to the golf course to see the back of the Hepworth premises. I had it in mind to maybe take a closer look at the outbuildings and greenhouse sometime, and wasn't entirely sure that he would approve of me trespassing.

"You did well," said Jack, his blue eyes fixing me like a pair of lasers. "But, as you follow up leads, please do make sure that you don't tell untruths, even in the name of a good story. I don't want that."

Although Jack was not exactly accusing me of lying, I felt unjustly admonished, and was honour-bound to put the record straight.

"Hang on a minute, Jack! I was careful, as I always am, not to tell lies… although I do admit that I did perhaps use a little subterfuge. But there is a fine line between lying and withholding some information in the interests of uncovering the truth. I don't believe I crossed that line."

I like to think that my father had instilled into me a keen

sense of moral and ethical behaviour, and was offended that this was somehow being challenged.

"Fair enough," he said, drawing a line under the discussion. "Now, unfortunately Simon is off sick today, so I need you to follow up a story for me, urgently. There was a particularly nasty ram raid on Green Lane Post Office early this morning. A cash machine was stolen, and there's apparently a lot of damage been done to the shop front."

And so it seemed that the rest of my morning was pretty much mapped out. In truth, I wanted Jack to be more enthusiastic about what I had uncovered, and was disappointed that he seemed somewhat underwhelmed. Corruption by local council officials seemed to me to be a big story, although when you have spent many years in Fleet Street following up everything from bloody foreign wars to corrupt domestic MPs, perhaps Jack's restraint was understandable.

However, in terms of professional development, investigating an actual crime was a definite step up the journalistic ladder for me, and I was determined to prove to Jack that I could handle anything he chose to give me. The police Corporate Communications Office was helpful and provided as much information as it could without prejudicing police enquiries. Apparently, the post office thieves used a stolen JCB AGRI telehandler to wrench the cash machine out of the front wall of the post office, escaping with an estimated £30,000. As I was making notes, my ears suddenly pricked up at the mention of Manthorpe Farm, from which the vehicle was stolen in the early hours. According to the Douglas report, Manthorpe Farm was adjacent to Abbot's Meadow and was owned by a John Manthorpe. This story had now taken a much more interesting turn as I saw a perfect opportunity to talk to the farmer.

I drove to the post office and managed to catch the proprietor, who was visibly distraught as she surveyed the damage done to her property. She had tears in her eyes as she described finding her life's work lying in ruins before her. The post office appeared to have been a cottage at some stage in the past, but had been converted with the addition of a large plate glass window in place of the original bay window. The whole of the front wall to the left of the doorway was destroyed, and the vehicle, which amazingly looked dusty but relatively undamaged, was in the process of being recovered on a low-loader lorry. A couple of builders stood in front of the shop scratching their heads, wondering how on earth they could make the premises secure. The police were controlling the traffic around the low-loader, and I guessed they had already completed their investigations. I took some photos and knocked on a few doors locally to talk with those residents who weren't already standing round taking photos on their smartphones. You would have thought that someone would have heard a JCB wrecking a building in the early hours, but all of the folks I talked to seemed to have slumbered on, blissfully unaware. Unless of course it was a case of not wanting to get involved through fear of reprisals or unforeseen repercussions, which is, unfortunately, all too common nowadays.

There didn't seem any point in staying any longer, so I set off for Manthorpe Farm. It felt good to be back on the trail again.

*

The track leading up to the farm had seen better days, the numerous potholes proving to be a real challenge for the tired suspension on my little Mini. I pulled into a muddy yard in front of the old brick-built farmhouse and was immediately met by a black and white border collie which had obviously decided that I was going to be lunch. He was barking so menacingly that getting out of the car was probably not the wisest thing to do, so I sat there and hoped the commotion might attract someone's attention. Sure enough, an elderly man wearing a holed green woolly jumper, worn brown trousers and gum boots approached. He had a beard which could have been described as magnificent if it weren't so unkempt looking, with some areas matted from splashes of who knew what. He wore a tired-looking woollen bobble hat, and I couldn't help but wonder what lay beneath. The man shouted at the dog, which immediately stopped barking, sat down and looked around with total disinterest, accepting that I was unfortunately off the menu. Cautiously I got out of the car, keeping one eye on the dog.

"I was looking for John Manthorpe," I said, casting an eye around to see whether there were any other signs of life. The yard was surrounded on three sides by brick and corrugated steel barns, which were in need of some attention, and one of which had an open front revealing several farm vehicles. There didn't seem to be anyone else around.

"Who wants him?" said the man, fixing me with a suspicious glare.

"I'm Dan Curran from the *Castlebridge Gazette*," I replied, reaching for a business card.

"Well, that'd be me you want then. Had the police here earlier. Wondered whether you lot would show up," he said, clearly none too impressed. "Suppose you'd better come in then."

And with that he turned and walked towards the farmhouse

with the dog close at his heels. At what appeared to be the back door, he took off his boots and padded through to a large, very traditional kitchen in his socks. I followed, wondering about the protocol regarding my shoes, the soles of which were, even after only a dozen yards or so, quite muddy. I decided it would be considerate if I did the same.

The kitchen was large, with a flagstone floor, and featured a double Aga range set among oak units. Manthorpe gestured towards a large, well-used oak table in the middle of the room.

"Best take a seat," he said.

I sat down, only to see him disappear into another room. A few moments later he came back with a photograph of a JCB farm vehicle, which I assumed was the AGRI telehandler which had been stolen that morning.

"Showed it to the coppers," he said, casting it down onto the table dismissively. "They were 'ere earlier asking damn fool questions, like how did I discover the vehicle had been stolen? I says to them, it's bright yellow, weighs five ton, and stands 'bout nine foot high. You sort of get to know when it's not where it should be."

"How did the thieves start it up without keys?" I asked, unsure whether such vehicles actually had keys.

"That were Vince," he said, scowling. "Tosser! Told him to always hang up the bloody keys in the house, but he goes and leaves 'em in, like he keeps doing. Mind you, I've heard from other farmers that the bastards can still drive 'em away, even without the proper key."

"Does Vince work for you?" I asked.

"Well, I pays him, if that's what you mean. I think working for me is stretching a point. But he's our nephew, so I doesn't have much choice, does I?"

I didn't know Vince, so any form of comment seemed inappropriate, and probably likely to provoke an angry response.

"Well, for what it's worth, the vehicle is being recovered as we speak, and doesn't appear to be too badly damaged."

I pulled out my phone and showed him one of the pictures I had taken. He gave the briefest of looks and grunted dismissively.

"Not sure when you'll be allowed to have it back, mind you, as I expect they'll want forensics to have a look at it. What's a vehicle like this cost?"

"Best part of a hundred grand, new," he said. "Mine was second 'and, so I paid 'bout half that."

"I presume you didn't hear anything," I said, fearing that I was going to regret it.

"Aw… that's what the police said," Manthorpe replied with a sneer. "If I had heard 'owt, I would've been out there with me twelve bore, pronto!"

It was probably just as well he didn't hear anything in that case, I thought. I could well imagine him taking a potshot and landing himself in all sorts of trouble.

"Changing the subject a little, what do you know about Abbot's Meadow next door?" I asked as casually as I could muster, hoping not to arouse any suspicions. "It was going to be sold, but the council has changed its mind, I gather."

He gave me a sideways look, suspicion written across his face. He was clearly trying to fathom the sudden, rather clumsy change of tack.

"Yes, that's what I've 'eard. I rented that field from the council up until a couple of year ago. Used it for sileage or grazing mainly," he said. "Decided it weren't worth the rent.

The really daft bit is that they now pay me to do a cut once a year, usually around August or September time, and I gets to keep the hay. The field isn't being properly managed now, although they did send in a couple of guys with a mini digger a year or so back, clearing drainage ditches, I think."

I was suddenly very interested to know who these 'guys' were. Anyone digging in Abbot's Meadow could be a potential lead, but I needed to tread carefully.

"Well, I suppose the council's got these people on the books anyway, so they might as well put them to good use tending the ditches and suchlike. Save the ratepayers' money, and all that."

"Nah. They weren't no council employees, that's for sure. They were contractors. Spoke to one of them over the fence and he told me to mind me own fuckin' business. Rough bunch of buggers, if you ask me. Still, it's nowt to do with me."

"Suppose you haven't got a map that shows your farm and the adjacent fields, have you? I'm interested in what sort of impact the proposed new housing development would have on you and the surrounding countryside. I had a look at the building plans a while back."

It sounded lame to me as I said it, but if Manthorpe thought the same, he didn't let on. He padded across the kitchen and pulled out a rolled-up map from a cupboard.

Spreading it out on the kitchen table he prodded a particularly stained area with a dirty finger and said, "There. That's my farm boundary as it is now, and that there is Abbot's Meadow. You can see that there's only a small length of boundary between us, because of the odd shape of the fields round 'ere. Lord knows why they're like that. Just 'ow it's always been."

"So I guess it's just about there that you saw these contractors doing the ditches?" I enquired, pointing at the spot on the map.

"Aye," he said warily. "You seem very interested in this Abbot's Meadow for a man wot came to talk about my stolen JCB, if you don't mind me sayin'," he commented, looking me in the eye, trying to weigh me up.

"Interested in both actually," I said casually. "Following up another story involving cowboy contractors in the Castlebridge area, so two birds with one stone, so to speak. Did you get to see whether they had a name on their digger, or lorry if they had one?"

"Nope. Had a white truck and trailer as I recall, but I don't remember owt being written on them. The kit looked quite good as far as I could tell."

I couldn't think of any other questions, so I decided it was time to leave while he was still being friendly.

"Well, I need to be going," I said, standing up. "Thanks for taking time to talk to me. I really appreciate it. And I hope you get your vehicle back soon."

Manthorpe grunted, and gathered up the map and the photo. I put my shoes on at the door, and made my way back to the Mini, keeping one eye open for the dog.

On my way home I called in at a hardware shop near to the flat, and bought a couple of large, strong hooks and a length of nylon rope… accessories no respectable trespasser could do without. I also put in a quick call to Jenny, who picked up before the first ring had died away.

"Hi, Dan," she said. "No problem with meeting tonight, I hope…"

"No, nothing like that," I replied, pleased that she was

thinking about it. "I'm looking forward to it. I just wanted to ask a quick favour... another bit of info. Do you know if the council has ever placed a contract on Hepworth Landscaping... maybe for doing some ditch clearing, or something like that?"

"That's easy," she said. "If they have then the company will be on the approved supplier list. In the public sector you can't even buy a loo roll unless the supplier has been vetted to within an inch of their lives and gained approved status. Now... let me see." I could hear clicking sounds of a keyboard. "Er... no, they aren't on the list, so we've never placed any orders with them."

"Thanks, Jenny. See you later."

So, if it was the Hepworth men that Manthorpe saw in Abbot's Meadow, and I strongly suspected it was, they weren't there in any official capacity. Which begged the question, who paid them... and for that matter, just what were they up to?

*

I arrived at Jenny's house a little early and sat in the car wondering whether I should knock on the door and risk meeting her father. I don't know why I was being so shy. Clearly it mattered a great deal that he would like me, or at the very least, consider me a worthy suitor for his beloved daughter. I decided that faint heart never won fair lady.

There were two cars in the drive, a Ford Mondeo and a little Fiat, which I guessed was Jenny's. I rang the bell and the door was opened by a tall, lean man with floppy brown hair and glasses. He smiled warmly and said, "Ah, you must be Dan. I'm Harry."

We shook hands, and I noted that he had the firm grip

and direct eye contact of a man for whom I suspected such conventions were an important indicator of decency and integrity. I just hoped I had passed this first test.

"Please come in," he said. "Jenny's just doing whatever it is women have to do before going out. Never was too sure, but I do know from experience that it can't be rushed." He stood aside, indicating a room off the hallway. "Please go through to the lounge."

The house, although probably built in the 1960s, was quite modernly furnished inside, and showed the hand of someone with a flair for decoration. "This is a very nice room," I said, anxious to break the ice.

"Can't take the credit for it, I'm afraid," he said with a wistful expression. "My wife was the home-builder. I just did whatever she told me and it always seemed to work out."

It seemed like he wanted to talk about his loss, and I was happy to be given a chance to clear the air.

"Jenny told me about your wife. You must have both been very fond of her?"

"Debs was my life," he said. "Simple as that. But I have Jenny to remember her by. Jenny is like her in so many ways, and we get along together just fine. Don't know what I'd do without her, to be honest."

I was trying to work out whether this was some sort of veiled warning against growing too fond of Jenny, but Harry's expression remained warm and friendly. I wondered how he'd feel if he knew that his daughter had already been obliquely threatened by a councillor because of her association with me, and made a mental note to discuss the incident with Jenny at an opportune moment.

"So, Jenny tells me that you're a journalist?" he said with a smile. "I don't think I've ever actually met a journalist before. I'm afraid I move in the boring and deeply technical world of engineering, where we are big on stress calculations and manufacturing route cards, but rather limited when it comes to written words and narrative. And, as for engineers who can spell… well, they are still trying to find one. But a free press is really important, so I think what you're doing is great. Debs used to write short stories, you know, for a women's magazine mainly."

"Did she?" I replied, pleased that, unlike my dad, Harry was a fan of my chosen career. "I'm afraid I haven't got as far as writing for myself yet, but maybe one day… I joined the *Gazette* last month, so I'm still finding my feet."

Just then Jenny came into the room, looking radiant as usual. She had gone for the casual look with smartly cut blue jeans and an intricately embroidered white blouse. I shook hands with Harry once more and said goodbye.

"Nice to meet you, Dan," he said. "Have a good evening, both of you."

The drive to the pub which Jenny had picked took us a little over ten minutes, during which time she wanted to know how I got on with Harry and what we had talked about. I sensed that her father's approval was as important to her as it was to me.

The Black Horse pub was located out in the country about four miles downriver from Castlebridge and was reached by a narrow lane, which in many places was only wide enough for a single car. As we pulled into the car park, I was surprised to see that there were dozens of cars including lots of very big SUVs, all of which had managed to negotiate the tricky lane. The pub was chocolate-box quaint, with a thatched roof and white walls covered with climbing shrubs and hanging baskets, but the main thing I noticed was how small it seemed, relative to the apparent number of visitors. However, when we passed through the pub to the rear garden which extended down to the river, all became clear. Against the rear wall was a covered wooden stage with a professional sound system and lighting, and the garden was full of tables and chairs. Each table had a colourful umbrella, large enough to make it just about work as an all-weather venue, but on a fine late summer evening, it was perfect.

The place was really busy, but we found a table towards the back, which suited us fine, and I made my way to the bar to order drinks. As I suspected, the bar was very small and crowded and being slightly more than six feet tall turned out to be a major asset in the competition to catch the eye of the over-run bar staff. Armed with drinks and crisps I made my way back through the tables, noting that the crowd was mainly young and, seemingly, very friendly.

We sat side by side at a trestle table facing the stage. The touch of Jenny's warm arm against mine felt so good.

"This is a great place," I said enthusiastically. "How often do they put on music?"

"From June to September they have music twice a week. It's folk or jazz music on Thursdays, and on Saturdays they put on some good local bands," she said.

Once again, I found myself gazing into her eyes and with the added smell of perfume at close quarters, I had to make a conscious effort to listen.

"Do you know who's playing tonight?" I asked, although in truth, I wouldn't have cared if it were a tone-deaf, musically challenged busker on a ukulele.

Jenny began to look through the gig list on the table, and determined that it was an electric-folk band called Brewster. This consisted of five singer-musicians playing electrified acoustic instruments of various sorts, and as it turned out, they were really very good. Jenny and I sat mesmerised until the interval, enjoying the music and each other's company, without feeling the need to talk. However, once the music stopped we launched into earnest conversation, enjoying learning more about each other.

Although neither of us played an instrument we found that our tastes in music were very similar, and equally eclectic. I felt more relaxed in Jenny's company than I had with any previous girlfriends and was able to talk openly about so many aspects of my life that had remained a closed book for so long. The sometimes awkward relationship with my father, being overshadowed by my elder sister's success – though never resenting it for one minute – an over-possessive mother, the insecurity that comes with being academically mediocre. It all came out without any fear of being judged.

I think it was the same for Jenny, who talked a lot about her mother and the guilt she felt in hoping her father would eventually find some sort of happiness with someone else. We continued talking well into the band's second set, and resumed as soon as they had played their final number.

"So how are your enquiries into Abbot's Meadow going?" Jenny said, out of the blue.

"Ah. I was kind of hoping you weren't going to mention that," I said. "I'm having such a great evening, it seems a pity to spoil it with work."

But Jenny was having none of it. "Nonsense," she said dismissively. "We can do both. I'm interested… and I'm involved. Don't forget that Sam Hepworth has very subtly leant on me, by way of a warning to you, I would guess. And who was it that got you the copy of that report? Did you manage to read it, by the way?"

So I told her everything, holding nothing back. About how I managed to read the report, what it said, my trip to Douglas and Partners in London, acquiring a copy of the original version of the report, and how I discovered that the findings had been falsified.

"Wow!" she said, stunned for a few seconds. "So, was it Sam Hepworth who changed it, do you think?"

"Well, either that or he got someone else to do it. Maybe someone with enough knowledge of history to make the changes seem convincing. I'm not sure Hepworth would be capable. No, I reckon it was the history teacher at Castlebridge Grammar School, Kevin Handleigh, but why, I haven't a clue. And why would the Hepworths not want the meadow developed? That's the really strange bit. I'm guessing that somewhere along the line, money is involved."

"This is so exciting," said Jenny, her lovely face beaming with enthusiasm. "It's like a real-life detective story. I can see why you wanted to go into journalism."

We were still sitting side by side, but were now turned to face each other, and on impulse, I leaned forward and planted a soft, lingering kiss on her lips. I'd heard couples often talking about a kind of electricity flowing between them, and had always put that down to a misplaced sense of romanticism – well, either that or nylon underwear. But suddenly I was a believer.

"Wow, again!" she said as we parted a little.

"My feelings exactly," I said.

We sat in silence for a few moments, neither of us wanting to spoil the moment by saying anything.

"There's something else," I said, before I could check myself. I wasn't going to mention my trip to the golf course and what I discovered was behind the Hepworth Landscaping premises. If I was going to climb over the fence to get a closer look, I had thought that it might be best to keep that to myself, but now for some reason, I didn't want there to be any secrets between us.

"Chris Hepworth, who it seems runs the landscaping business of which they are both directors, has a house alongside the company office. The back of the plot extends right down to Castlebridge golf course, and, from the little I could see through the fencing, has some interesting outbuildings. Firstly, there are some large greenhouses full of some type of plant. What are they cultivating, and why? Secondly, there's a large brick building with no windows and a security camera pointed at the entrance. What is inside that needs CCTV surveillance?"

"All a bit mysterious, isn't it?" Jenny mused. "Okay, so what's the plan? How are we going to find out what they're up to, and whether it's connected with the sale, or otherwise, of Abbot's Meadow?"

"Whoa… hang on a second there! What's with the 'we'?" I asked, suddenly becoming very concerned at the way this was heading. "I plan to take a closer look at the rear of the premises, but I don't want you involved."

"Well, I am involved," said Jenny defiantly. "Get over it. And besides, it would be safer for you to have a lookout, just in case someone comes."

Before I could respond, one of the pub staff approached our table.

"I'm sorry to trouble you guys, but you're the last here… and we want to go home."

We were so engrossed in conversation we hadn't noticed everyone else leaving. On the drive home we were both very quiet. I think we both sensed that our relationship had suddenly become much closer, and for me it felt slightly scary, but in a good way.

CHAPTER 11

Was I really going to go through with this… breaking into someone else's property? I sat in my car outside Jenny's house and wondered just what trouble I was getting myself and Jenny into. I was both scared and excited. It was coming up to six o'clock on a Saturday morning and the streets were pretty much deserted as people recovered from the working week, or maybe the effects of Friday night. My logic, if that word isn't attaching too much coherence to my thought process, was that this would be an acceptable time to be out for an early morning run so as not to arouse too much suspicion. I was banking on Chris Hepworth and any family members being still asleep.

I watched Jenny close her front door quietly so as not to disturb her father. This was the same father that was entrusting his precious daughter to me, a trust which I was now callously abusing by leading her into possible danger, just to further a news story. She opened the car door and smiled that captivating smile that made my heart melt.

"Hi," she said cheerily as she got in, leaning over to give me a kiss on the cheek. "I told Dad that we would be going for an early morning run. He's still sound asleep… well, noisily asleep would be more accurate." Her behaviour was so nonchalant, as though this was an everyday occurrence.

I turned in the seat to face her, steeling myself for what I was about to say.

"Jenny, I've had second thoughts and I can't let you do this. It's not fair and I'm sure your dad would not approve. It could get difficult," I said.

She looked at me with a defiant expression, then put her seat belt on.

"Daniel Curran, just shut up and drive the bloody car! I'm involved already, and I'm going to make sure that you don't get into trouble. Or do you think that I'm a woman and therefore incapable of doing anything resembling 'man's work'?" she said, drawing air quotes with her fingers around those words. "Maybe you'd like me to sit by the fireside doing crochet, hoping that you'll return safely!" Her smile had been replaced by flushed cheeks and an angry stare.

"Okay, okay," I said, realising that I really didn't have a choice in the matter. If I were to insist that she didn't go with me, I could see that this would be the end of a very sweet but short-lived relationship. She was one determined lady, not to be messed with. In fact, despite being only five feet six or so, I was beginning to think she would be more than a match for the Hepworths.

I started the car and pulled away quietly. As we turned onto the main road out of town, Jenny reached across and laid a hand on my arm.

"Thank you for being concerned, but don't worry," she said. "It'll be okay… really."

It took us about ten minutes to reach the golf club. I parked the Mini in the club car park, which was deserted. Jenny was wearing black leggings, a grey sweatshirt and trainers, and looked like she was no stranger to working out. Around her waist she wore a zipped bum bag containing her mobile phone. I was in my normal scruffy running gear and trainers, with a small backpack containing the hook and ropes that I had bought from the hardware shop, plus my mobile phone. We found the public footpath and began jogging in case there was anyone in the clubhouse.

As we reached the back of the Hepworth property, I noticed a man with a dog further up the path, but fortunately he was walking away from us. We stopped and looked around, relieved that there was no one else in sight. The neighbour's wooden fence, which I had previously noticed was in need of repair, had a gate leading onto the golf course. Although this was locked, it was easy to slide one of the loose adjacent fence panels sideways just enough to allow me to put my arm through and work the bolt across. I opened the gate a short way and peered through into the garden, thankful that the orchard about fifty yards away made it impossible for us to be seen from the house.

We went into the garden, which at this end was largely grass covered, and moved twenty yards or so up to the wooden compost heap frame against the fence between the two properties. The sides of the frame were maybe four feet high, with a cross brace that made a convenient step up. I climbed up onto one of the sides and had a clear view over the fence into the Hepworth plot, which I could see now was tapered, and more of a field than a garden. The house was some way away, and I estimated that the entire plot covered between one and two acres.

In the middle of the plot were two very large greenhouses

and several sheds, and nearer to us was a large, flat-roofed brick building. It looked very much like a relic from the Second World War. Unfortunately, there was not a great deal of cover between the fence and any of the structures, and the back of the house was visible. Anyone looking out at the right moment would see us. I cursed myself for not bringing binoculars, but from what I could make out, all of the curtains appeared to be still closed. I turned to see that Jenny had climbed onto the other side of the compost frame to take a look over the fence for herself.

"How are you going to get over and get back again?" she whispered, not that there was anyone close enough to overhear her.

I took off my backpack and produced the hook and rope. I had already tied three lengths of rope to make hoops, one short, one medium and long, each hoop being threaded through a ring on the hook. I placed the hook over the top edge of the fence, allowing the three loops to hang down onto the Hepworths' side, forming a sort of three-rung rope ladder.

"I'm seeing a whole new side to you," she said with a smile.

We each set our mobile phones to vibrate mode so as not to have any untimely or noisy interruptions during our clandestine mission. With the backpack in position once more, I cocked my right leg over the top of the fence and lowered my foot into the first rung of my makeshift ladder. This allowed me to bring my left foot over and into the second loop, and soon I was standing in the Hepworths' field looking at the house for any signs that I had been observed. The grass near the fence was quite long, and I was concerned that where I had trampled it down would leave a tell-tale sign of my presence. However, there was little I could do about that, and as all seemed quiet, I moved quickly across the grass to the first of the two greenhouses.

The construction was quite substantial, with a brick wall around the edge about three feet high, supporting a wood and glass top section with a pitched glazed roof. I guessed that it was at least seventy feet long, running laterally across the garden. This meant that the access door at the end was in full view of the house, even though the latter was some distance away. I looked across to see Jenny crouched on the side of the compost frame peering over the top of the fence towards the house, and I realised how reassuring her presence was.

She gave me the thumbs-up sign, so I moved quickly to the door and entered the first greenhouse. The staging on both sides was completely filled with shrub-like potted plants. My knowledge of horticulture was slightly less comprehensive than my knowledge of particle physics, and hence I had absolutely no idea what they were. There seemed to be two different kinds of plant, both with variegated green foliage. When I had first set eyes on the greenhouses through the hole in the fence, I had it in my mind that they were growing drugs of some kind, but now I could see the plants up close, they looked pretty innocuous and I felt a bit foolish. However, I took out my phone and photographed them, and then for good measure, I broke off one leaf from each variety and slipped them into the backpack. As I walked the length of the greenhouse, I noticed that there were a number of large industrial electric fan heaters which all appeared to be wired back to a distribution board where there was a single thermostat. This seemed to be an expensive way of providing heat, although on closer examination of the fans, there appeared to be a large accumulation of dust on the blades, suggesting that their use had been infrequent at best.

I walked back to the door and, after getting the thumbs-up again from Jenny, exited the greenhouse and moved up the field to the second one. This greenhouse was seemingly identical but a little shorter, and was filled with more shrub-like plants in pots. These appeared to be the same two species as I had just seen, but I took more photos just in case I was mistaken. As I turned to leave, I felt my phone vibrate. My heart skipped a beat as I saw that Jenny had sent a text:

someone is coming!

I immediately ducked down, suddenly conscious of the glass around me. I peered towards the house through the bottom part of the window, which fortunately was quite dirty. Two men were walking down the central path which led to the greenhouses and outbuildings. From the bald head and tattoos I was pretty sure that one of them was Dean Lockwood, who I had previously encountered, in a none too friendly way, on Abbot's Meadow. I didn't recognise the other man, although I only got a fleeting glimpse. They were deep in conversation, which suggested that they hadn't seen me, but it was clear that I was not going to be able to get to the rope ladder and make my way back over the fence without being spotted. In fact, there was a good chance I would be caught, which was a frightening prospect. The Hepworths didn't seem to be the sort of people who would involve the law, and I was fairly certain that retribution would be swift and fierce.

I closed the door of the greenhouse and crawled under the staging on the door hinge side keeping myself as tight as possible against the corner of the brick wall. The area was a mass of cobwebs and I tried not to think about what I might be sharing my hiding place with. And then I remembered the rope ladder! Taking out my phone again I texted Jenny:

ladder!

With my phone in selfie mode I stretched out my hand and raised it just above the glass panel in the door to see the makeshift ladder slowly being retrieved by Jenny. Another text arrived:

BE CAREFUL!

I could now hear the men conversing outside the greenhouse. "If you want to go and check the systems are all good in the Block, I'll do the watering here."

And with that the door to the greenhouse opened wide boxing me in, and my heart rate rocketed. I watched the man's legs as he walked down the length of the greenhouse trailing a bright yellow hose, and from the sound I could tell that he had begun watering the plants from the far end, working his way back up towards the door. I figured that as long as the door remained fully open I was boxed in, but hidden from view. After a few minutes he had got to where I was and I was covered with a deluge of cold water running between the plants and through the slats of the staging, taking my breath away. Fortunately, he had aimed the hose around the door rather than close it, and while my spirits were definitely dampened, at least I was safe. For now…

As the man exited the greenhouse, he shouted out to his friend.

"Hey, Chris. Come and look at this!"

I was willing my racing heart not to explode, trying to imagine what 'this' might be. Could he see me through the side window? I was so scrunched up in the corner that I couldn't move, let alone turn around to see whether I had been rumbled. I kept perfectly still and offered up a silent prayer. After a few moments I heard more footsteps outside.

"Look at the flattened grass here. Something, or someone, has been here," said a voice.

"Maybe a fox, do you think?" said the second voice, presumably Chris.

"Dunno. Probably."

The door to the greenhouse opened again. I sensed that one of the men was standing in the entranceway looking and listening. I wanted to look up through the staging slats but was scared that any movement, however slight, might just give me away. And breathing seemed to be out of the question. After what seemed like an eternity the door closed once more.

"Everything looks okay," said the first. "The Block seems fine and there's nothing suspicious. Don't like that grass being trampled though. You know, I'm reckonin' on getting a second camera installed looking back up towards the house. What do you reckon? Can't be too careful."

The footsteps faded as the two men moved down the meadow to the other greenhouse, and the brick building which they called 'the Block'. I guessed they were in the mood to double check these as well. After ten minutes or so, they approached where I was once more, and this time carried on straight past back towards the house. I checked my phone to see if it was still working, which thankfully it was. I texted Jenny.

am ok... tell me when they are out of sight

A few minutes later, Jenny texted back:

back in the house

I opened the door and quickly moved to the back of the greenhouse keeping a low profile so that the low brick wall and dirty glass provided at least some cover. What I wanted to do was get the hell out of there as fast as possible, but I was drawn to the Block, a building with no windows and a security camera covering the door. I made my way down towards it, keeping as low as possible, and making sure that I was not in the field of view of the camera. Walking around the brick walls, which were getting on for twenty feet high, there was nothing to be seen apart from some power cables running up to a flat roof, and a couple of extractor fan outlets high up on opposite ends of the back wall. The building almost certainly dated back to the war years and seemed incongruous in its current setting. I texted Jenny again:

coming back, can you hook the ladder up again

I made my way back to the fence quickly and saw that the makeshift rope ladder was once more in place. As I climbed back up, I mentally congratulated myself on this masterpiece of improvisation, which had worked superbly. Safely back in the next-door neighbour's garden, Jenny threw her arms around me and gave me a hug.

"I was so worried they would find you," she said, her eyes moist. She noticed that I was soaked and asked, "What happened?"

"I got watered. Tell you about it later. I suggest we go." I was anxious to cease trespassing as quickly as possible.

"There's just one thing," she said with a serious expression.

"What's that?" I asked, worried that maybe I had missed something during my escapade. Or worst still, left something there.

"You might want to remove that big dead spider from your hair. It's not a good look," she said.

*

After an eventful half hour, which seemed so much longer, the only thing I could think of was a strong, hot coffee. It was still very early in the morning, but there was a twenty-four-hour McDonald's drive-thru on the outskirts of town. We parked up and drank coffees while I recounted what had happened to Jenny.

"What I don't understand is why would a landscape garden company grow lots of just two varieties of plant?" I said, fishing out the leaves from my backpack. "I mean, I could maybe understand growing something more generic like turf, which might be needed in abundance, but surely the plants used during a makeover would be dictated by the customer? I can't see anyone needing hundreds of these things… whatever they are."

"And you're sure these are just run-of-the-mill shrubs and not something wacky, like a leafy equivalent of magic mushrooms?" said Jenny, pointing to the leaves.

"No, I'm not at all sure," I said. "I haven't got a clue what they are, although for some reason I seem to think that they're not uncommon. Trouble is, I don't know who to ask about them. Do you think a garden centre might help?" I suggested.

"Hang on," she said excitedly, grabbing my arm. "I have a friend from school days whose parents own a garden centre on Bardon Road, about three miles south of town."

And with that Jenny took out her mobile phone, flipped through the contacts and pressed the dial button. After a few moments the call was picked up.

"Hi, Debbie, it's Jen," she said. "Er… oh yes, sorry. I got carried away and didn't realise what time it was… but now that you're awake, could you do me a massive favour and tell your folks that I need some help identifying a couple of plants?"

Jenny listened for a while. "No, really, I'm serious. This isn't a wind-up, honestly! Yes, I know it's a bit early, and no, I haven't been drinking. I'm helping a friend who's investigating something. I can't say what, but it's important. I was hoping we could call in on them when they open this morning."

Again she listened, wide-eyed, enthusiastic and utterly captivating. I felt that I could watch her all day and never tire.

"You're a star, Debs. I owe you big time. I'm not sure whether they will remember me, so if you could prepare them beforehand it would be great. Oh, and by the way, my friend and I are in our running gear… but don't ask. It's way too complicated."

The contrite look on Jenny's face suggested that she was getting another friendly reprimand from Debbie.

"Right… and sorry I woke you. Let's get together soon, hey?" Jenny ended the call looking pleased with herself.

"All sorted. I suggest a quick pitstop at the ladies… for me obviously… a half-hour run to work up an appetite, and then pig out with an unhealthy but scrummy Maccy Dee's breakfast."

Sounded good to me.

*

Bishops' Garden Centre had not followed the trend set by its bigger rivals of incorporating coffee shops, restaurants, bookshops, aquatic centres and chain store outlets. What it did have was a multitude of plants, gardening supplies and people who knew about them. This was definitely not an establishment for the occasional weekend gardener, looking for something to do on a rainy Sunday to stop the family killing each other. And it seemed that the public had taken the old-school approach to heart. Even at nine o'clock in the morning there were more than a dozen cars in the car park. I parked the Mini and we got out, very conscious of our inappropriate clothing. Fortunately, I had dried out after my soaking, although my shirt had acquired a few more unsightly and somewhat suspicious stains.

John and Sarah Bishop had been proprietors of the garden centre for a little over five years, and in that time they had made many improvements, one of which was a sort of horticultural library. It was equipped with several tall bookshelves packed with reference books on plants covering almost every imaginable variety, genus, species and cultivar. And if the library or garden centre staff didn't have the information, there was a computer desk for staff and customers to use with resources such as the RHS horticultural database.

John approached us as we entered the main building. No doubt our unconventional appearance had made us easy to identify. "You must be Dan and Jenny," he said warmly. "Debbie phoned me earlier and said that you needed a bit of guidance?"

"Hi, John. It's really good of you to see us. Just to explain, I'm a reporter on the *Castlebridge Gazette* and I'm following up a story which, strangely, involves some potted plants… unlikely as that may seem. I just need some help in identifying them."

"No problem. Any friend of Debbie is a friend of ours. Come over to the library and take a seat. I'm going to get Frank to join us. What he doesn't know about plants really isn't worth knowing."

And with that he disappeared into the building complex.

We made ourselves comfortable in the cane patio furniture provided, and after a few minutes, John returned with a short, elderly man wearing a brown smock coat. At a guess, he was well into his seventies, but still had the bearing and movement of a man half his age. Unfortunately, he was also sporting one of the worst toupees I have ever seen. It looked like some small brown furry creature had decided to curl up and sleep on his head. The colour of the hairpiece bore only a passing resemblance to the other hair that was visible, which seemed to be dyed in a completely different shade of brown. Jenny and I exchanged a glance, and I could see she was struggling to suppress a fit of the giggles. I gave her a gentle elbow in the side to make sure that she retained her composure. I just hoped that Frank's eyesight was up to the task I was about to entrust him with.

John introduced us and we shook hands.

"Frank is our resident expert on all things horticultural," said John proudly. Sensing that he was going to be centre stage, Frank took out his reading glasses from his top pocket and put them on with a little flourish that said, 'Make way for the expert'. I thought I would begin with the pictures on my phone.

"Have you any idea what these plants might be? There are two different types… this one, and this one," I said, swiping images on my phone.

Frank immediately lost some of his enthusiasm, and

seemed slightly offended that we should be challenging him with such a trivial task, which anyone who called themselves a gardener should know.

"Well… yes, I have. They are both varieties of *Euonymus fortunei*. To be more specific, this one's Emerald Gaiety and that one's Silver Queen." He looked back at us. "Was that it?"

"Oh, I nearly forgot. I also have a leaf from each, just in case the photos don't show enough detail," I said reaching into my backpack. I put the leaves on the table.

"There you go," said Frank. "Just as I said, *Euonymus fortunei*… a very common border plant in the UK." He emphasised this last remark as a way of pointing out my stupidity.

"How long would these typically spend in a greenhouse?" I asked, still trying to fathom out why these would be grown in such numbers.

Frank scoffed and looked at John as if to say, 'Why have you wasted my time with these clowns?'

"They don't need a greenhouse. They are hardy perennials that can cope with the British climate just fine. And the photo shows that they are mature plants, not mere seedlings. Why on earth would you want to stick them in a greenhouse? Especially at this time of year… assuming you came across these recently."

Why indeed, I thought. I thanked John and Frank for their help, and Frank made his excuses, quietly tutting to himself as he left us.

*

Jenny and I met up again that evening for a drink at one of the pubs by the river. She was in a plain denim dress and sandals, and looked stunning as usual. We chatted excitedly and with a sense of achievement about our morning adventure, both of us knowing deep down that it came so close to ending very differently.

"Was your dad okay when you got back?" I asked.

"He was fine," said Jenny, smiling. "He did make a passing comment, wondering why I had suddenly taken an interest in running again, but he had a glint in his eye which suggested he didn't expect an answer. Which is just as well, as he didn't get one.

"What will you do next?" Jenny asked. "I mean about Hepworth... and Abbot's Meadow?"

"To tell the truth, I haven't the faintest idea," I said. "I'm going to have to level with the editor and, to be honest, I'm worried that I may have overstepped the mark."

"Well, I think you did good," she said, still smiling. "And we make a great team, don't you think?"

We did indeed. I leaned over and kissed her. I didn't want the night to end, but I had promised to go and see my parents the next morning, and an early start was required for the trip to Luton.

"Tell you what... how about I come with you?" offered Jenny.

"Er... well, you could, if you really want to? My sister is also joining us for a family Sunday lunch. I'm sure you two would get on well together. I just hope Mum and Dad aren't too embarrassing."

"I'd like to come," she said with that irresistible smile. I desperately wanted my parents to like her and really couldn't see how they could possibly do otherwise. What she was going to make of them, however, was quite another matter.

CHAPTER 12

My parents lived in a large semi-detached house on the outskirts of Luton. In common with many houses built in the 1930s, it had a long rear garden which, in those days, was largely given over to growing vegetables and fruit as a way of making relatively low, working-class wages go further. Once the unfortunate butt of jokes advertising Campari, where Luton was seen as the antithesis of paradise, the town over recent decades had steadily grown in desirability, thanks to its proximity to London and its international airport. The rise in commuters fuelling the lucrative trend for property refurbishment had kept house prices high, and the neighbourhood around my parents' house had become firmly middle class, although my father hated such a description. He liked to think that his working-class roots had kept him grounded, and failed to recognise that while he might not have changed, the world around him certainly had.

The house, and particularly the big garden, brought back fond memories of my childhood. Moving there at the age of eight from a back-to-back terraced house with a yard rather than a garden, was like moving into some sort of spacious wonderland. I and my new-found neighbourhood friends could run around in the back garden to let off steam, and kick footballs to each other rather than against a red brick wall. My parents were by no stretch of the imagination well off, but my sister, Emily, and I never really wanted for anything and had a very happy childhood. As we turned into the housing estate and I spotted the houses of old friends, the memories seemed all the more poignant. I wondered what they were all doing now, and what careers they had chosen… or fallen into.

We pulled up at the kerb outside the house at around midday. Emily's Ford Fiesta was parked in the drive behind my father's Astra.

"Emily's here already," I said, turning to Jenny to see whether she was showing the same sort of nervousness that I had experienced meeting her father. I needn't have worried. She'd already got her door open.

"Come on then, let's go in," she said excitedly. In truth, I was obviously the only nervous one.

My mother was evidently keeping a watchful eye and had the door open before I could ring the bell.

"Hi, Mum," I said, giving her a hug. "This is my friend, Jenny."

Jenny was the first girlfriend I had ever introduced to my parents, and I wasn't entirely sure how the conversation was going to go. Knowing my mother, the possibilities for excruciating embarrassment seemed limitless.

"Hello, dear," she said, and gave Jenny a hug. "Lovely to meet you. Do come in. I'll put the kettle on."

We went through into the lounge where Emily was sitting reading a magazine. As children, we had always been really close, helped no doubt by the mere two-year difference in our ages, which became more irrelevant with every passing year. Perhaps unusually for siblings, we had rarely had a cross word when growing up, and I had always found that confiding in her came naturally. My mother had warmed her up to the fact that I would not be coming alone, and she was all smiles as she got up to greet Jenny. They shook hands slightly formally, both laughed and then followed it up with a quick hug.

"It's great to see my little brother's got such a good eye," said Emily, smiling. "Always been a bit of a dark horse, has Danny boy. Mum's excitement levels went into overdrive when she heard that you were coming. Just keep your fingers crossed that she doesn't start getting the family photo albums out. Could turn into a cringe-fest!"

Just then Mum appeared. "What's that you're saying about me?" she said, grinning conspiratorially at Emily. "Oh, never mind. Your dad's pottering in the garden as usual. Do you want to take Jenny out and introduce her to the dahlias? I'll be out with tea in a few minutes. We'll sit on the terrace."

Dahlias were one of my dad's two great passions in life, the other being his beloved Luton Town Football Club. There were long beds of different dahlia varieties on each side of the garden, and a greenhouse at the end of the garden in which he dried tubers, propagated seeds and tended cuttings with an extraordinary devotion that bordered on obsession. The flowers were now just about at their best, and the range of colours and flower shapes was, even to my untrained eye, simply breathtaking. My dad was busy removing the odd dead head and adjusting cane supports.

"Hi, Dad. I'd like you to meet my friend, Jenny," I said, catching him totally unaware of our presence.

"Oh... startled me a bit, did that," he said, turning and wiping his soil-covered hands on a piece of cloth.

"Hello, lass. It's nice to meet you." He proffered a still-grubby hand which Jenny shook without hesitation, smiling warmly.

"It's really lovely to meet you, Mr Curran," she said. "Dan didn't tell me that you were a dahlia man! You need to meet my dad. You two would get on famously. He's grown them for years, mainly cactus and pom-pom, I think. Nothing on this scale though. These are simply gorgeous."

Dad looked at me as if to say, 'You've chosen well, son', and positively beamed. I wondered whether by any chance Jenny's dad also supported Luton Town, but sadly, that was probably unlikely.

"I must admit, I do like my dahlias," he said. "Got a little problem with powdery mildew on those few at the back, mind you. I tend to use a weak solution of hydrogen peroxide, but I'd be interested to know whether your dad has tried anything that works better."

Jenny was gracious as ever, even though she was probably regretting having mentioned dahlias.

"I'll certainly be sure to ask him, and I'll let you know," she said. "Can I take some pictures of the problem to show him?"

Nicely done! Jenny had played the joker card early, and was definitely on a roll now. Dad led Jenny round the path to the back of one of the beds and indicated the diseased plants. They didn't actually look that bad to me, but to him, anything short of perfection was an abhorrence. Jenny produced her phone and took photos of the offending plants while Dad stood back with a look of admiration on his face. After a few minutes I thought a rescue was in order.

"Mum's just making tea. We'd better go up to the house," I interjected, for some reason pointing at the house as though my dad might have temporarily forgotten where it was located.

Why was it that when things were going well, I sometimes found it hard to enjoy the moment, and worried all the more about what could go wrong?

As we walked back to the terrace, where there was a garden table and chairs, I realised that I was actually very tense, conscious that my choice of partner was being quietly judged by the family. My mother had served up tea from our best china cups and was entreating everyone to sit down and drink while it was hot. Emily and Jenny sat side by side and immediately launched into an easy conversation.

"Dan tells me that you're a nurse. My mum was a radiographer at our local hospital, so I grew up with daily reports about the NHS. Where are you based?" Jenny enquired.

"I'm working at Lister Hospital in Stevenage, on the cardiology unit," Emily replied. "Sounds a bit heavy, I know, but in reality it's a fun place to work and I have some fantastic, dedicated colleagues. Yes, we do have a lot of very sick patients, but for most of them there is a good outcome, which is really rewarding."

My parents listened in, positively glowing with admiration. I glanced across at Emily, mindful that comparing Emily's and my careers was something my father needed no encouragement to do. Fortunately, she had read my mind and changed the subject quickly.

"So what about you, Jenny? What line of work are you in, and how did you meet my little brother?"

"I'm an accountant working for Castlebridge District Council," she said. "Sounds a bit boring, but I'm getting some good experience and I'll use it as a springboard to something better when the time is right. Mind you, it's also opened my eyes to the calibre of some local government officials. Unlike you, my admiration for some of my colleagues definitely does have bounds," she added with a laugh.

I was now worried that Jenny might go into detail about Hepworth, but she swiftly moved the conversation on before there were any probing questions.

"And Dan and I met in the council offices, quite by chance actually. I was covering for the receptionist during her lunch break when he came in to talk with one of our council elders."

So far, so good. The tea-drinking session passed without any major hiccups, and everything seemed to be going okay, despite some nervy moments. My mother disappeared to continue preparations for Sunday lunch, and my father quietly slipped back into the garden hoping no one would notice. The girls continued chatting earnestly about girls' stuff, and I could see that my presence was surplus to requirements. It seemed that I was faced with the prospect of either joining my mother in the kitchen and being quizzed about when we would be announcing our engagement, or joining my father in the garden and being quizzed about my responsibility to think seriously about the earning potential of my chosen career if I was considering settling down and starting a family. Briefly, I actually considered tossing a coin, but conceded that this might seem somewhat strange behaviour, even in my family, so I opted for the garden.

The greenhouse was my father's refuge from life. The world turned, governments changed, fashions came and went with equal speed, but in this one sacred place, nature continued to perform its miracles constantly and reliably, with timetable precision, year upon year. It was warmer and lighter than the shed, which just had a single window, and I had known him spend several hours in there just sitting reading, or listening to his trusty old Bush radio. He kept the radio and the camping chair close at hand in the shed, along with a collection of books and gardening magazines. I caught up with him brushing down the wooden staging after a session of potting up. Seeing the greenhouse gave me an idea.

"Hi, Dad. The girls are busy chatting, so I thought I'd take the opportunity to get your opinion on some plants," I said, taking out my phone.

"Oh really? Not like you to show an interest in gardening, but happen it's never too late…" he responded, obviously intrigued to see what I wanted to show him.

"Any idea what these are?" I said, showing him one of the photos from the Hepworths' greenhouse. At the time I thought a second opinion would be good, even though Frank at the garden centre seemed pretty unequivocal. I would soon come to see that this was a really stupid thing to do.

"Well, I'm no expert you know. Shrubs aren't really my thing. Much keener on flowers."

He took the phone from me and studied the picture more closely, zooming in with his fingers.

"I'd say that they are a *Euonymus* of some description."

"And would you expect these to be raised in a greenhouse?" I asked.

"Well, you could do, I suppose, maybe just to start them off. But I'm not sure why you'd want to. There are different types, but they're all very hardy plants and, as far as I know, they'll grow just fine outside in the UK, even from seed." He handed the phone back to me.

"Why on earth do you want to know?" he asked, by now genuinely perplexed at this uncharacteristic display of horticultural curiosity. "Have you got a garden at your flat that you want to do something with?"

"Oh, no, nothing like that… it's just in connection with a story I'm working on. I wanted to get a second opinion, that's all."

The immediate look of disappointment on my father's face said it all. How was writing a story about some plants in the provincial newspaper of a town he'd scarcely heard of going to make me a decent and worthwhile living? I could see that, in his mind, this was just confirmation of a life being wasted. I was trying to think of something I could say which would perhaps restore a little of the faith in me that he'd seemingly lost, when I heard the bell ring for lunch. My mother kept a large hand bell by the back door to communicate with my father when he was down at the bottom of the garden. She would ring it energetically, producing a sound that took me back to my school days when the end of playtime was signalled. What the neighbours made of this rather eccentric display of campanology was anyone's guess, but in my case I was definitely 'saved by the bell'. I cursed myself for having mentioned the bloody plants. As we walked back to the house my father was very quiet. I sensed that this might be short-lived and that he would be voicing his frustrations before very long.

*

Lunch was a splendid feast of roast beef, Yorkshire pudding, roast potatoes and a selection of fresh vegetables, all served up on the best dinner service. My mother was an excellent cook, but a hopeless judge of quantities. There was easily enough food for twice as many people, and although we were encouraged to 'dig in', there was always going to be plenty left. The conversation was a little awkward at first, but my mother soon got into her stride, and then there was no stopping her. In between each mouthful of food, she updated us all on the health problems of the complete family on both sides, then moved on to news about neighbours and friends, and finally, when she was visibly running out of steam, she turned to me.

"So, Dan, how is the new job going?" she enquired, letting the question hang in the air while I tried desperately to dispatch a large mouthful of beef without choking. Don't you just hate it when you somehow feel obliged to bolt your food as your audience silently awaits an answer to an ill-timed question! I chewed furiously, conscious of the lull in conversation.

"It's going okay," I eventually managed to say. "I'm settling in quite well I think and I've had quite a few local news stories printed. At the moment I'm working on something really interesting which could turn out to be quite big."

"He's writing a story about some plants," interjected my father, managing to infuse those few words with so much sarcasm. He just couldn't help himself, such was his displeasure. I was obviously turning out to be a huge disappointment.

"I mean… bloody plants for goodness' sake!" he added, just in case there was anyone still doubting his exasperation at the futility of my chosen profession.

"Take no notice, dear," said my mother, looking across disapprovingly at my father. "I'm sure it will be very interesting. After all, gardening is very popular these days."

I wasn't sure what was worse, my father's sarcasm or my mother's patronising response. However, my father wasn't finished yet, so I reserved judgement for round two.

"Aye. I'm sure it will be real gripping *News at Ten* or *Panorama* stuff," he replied. "Or should that be *Gardeners' World*?"

The room went quiet, save for the sound of knives and forks

as everyone started eating noisily to cover the deafening silence of embarrassment that ensued. Everyone, that is, except Jenny. She put down her knife and fork, and glared at my parents. I had a sudden dread that she might be about to say something that would not go down well, but before I could head her off, she launched into a speech.

"Actually, what Dan is working on is potentially going to be very big news, certainly in Castlebridge, and who knows, maybe even nationally. Dan is without question going to be a brilliant investigative journalist, and I'm sure that someday soon he will make you both very proud. I do think a little faith in your son might not go amiss… if I may be so bold."

And with that, Jenny picked up her knife and fork and resumed eating, while everyone else stopped and looked at each other. It was Emily who broke the silence this time.

"Well said, Jenny! Well said. I certainly have faith in Dan," she said, fixing my father with a frosty stare, willing him to make amends and recover the situation.

After a few moments, my father reluctantly rose to the challenge. It was his turn to put down his knife and fork.

"I'm sorry, lad. It's just that I really want you to be successful. You have such potential and I don't want you to end up in a dead-end job… like being a welder at Vauxhall… regretting roads not taken and opportunities missed. You only get one chance at life. There is no rewind button."

I could see the sadness in his eyes and it was as if a veil had been lifted, revealing a vulnerable, sad man, trying clumsily to do his level best for his kids… and hoping desperately that they would be more successful in life than he had been.

Emily saw it too. She reached across the table to him and laid her hand on top of his.

"It's okay, Dad. Don't worry about either of us. We're both following our own particular stars and isn't that what you always used to say was the most important thing?"

He considered this for a few moments.

"You're right of course… and I'm very proud of you both," he said with an apologetic smile. "And thank you, Jenny, for being gentle with me and my foolish ways."

"Think nothing of it, Mr Curran," she said earnestly. "Your love for your children does you proud. And anyway, jobs and the material things they bring aren't, in my view, a good measure of a successful life well lived."

I could see my father starting to well up. Love was not a word that came easily to his lips, and Jenny had exposed an unspoken truth.

My mother had some simple rules of life, and one of these was that there was no situation or experience so bad that it couldn't be improved by either a cup of tea, or the right choice of tasty home-made food. Obviously, this was one of those occasions just made for a large helping of apple pie and ice cream. Emily and I helped clear away the plates and serving dishes while she brought in an extraordinarily large pie and a bowl of ice cream. While we were in the kitchen, Emily grabbed my arm and pushed the door closed, obviously intent on a private discussion.

"I like her a lot, bruv," she said. "Are you two serious?"

"Er… I don't know. I am, and that's for sure. I think she's absolutely lovely, but I'm not sure how she feels," I said.

In truth, I was still in fear of the day that Jenny discovered that I wasn't handsome enough, smart enough, funny enough for her.

"Bloody boys!" said Emily in exasperation. "Can't see an

inch in front of their faces. Of course she's serious about you, you idiot! She wanted to meet your family, for goodness' sake! And she's sticking up for you when Dad gives you a hard time. We had a bit of a heart-to-heart earlier, and I gather she's been helping you with your investigation… although don't worry, she refused to give away any details. I tried hard, mind you. There's not much doubt that she's serious in my mind, so just don't screw up."

"Well, thanks for that vote of confidence, Em," I said, and leaned over to give her a kiss on the cheek. "If you get fed up with nursing, you can always fall back on being an agony aunt."

With copious quantities of apple pie consumed, the atmosphere became much more relaxed and we all spent an enjoyable couple of hours chatting in the garden. Maybe my mother's theories on food were perhaps marginally less daft than I had previously considered.

Later that afternoon on the drive home, Jenny and I chatted about the day, but Emily's observations kept running through my mind.

CHAPTER 13

Monday morning came around all too quickly and it was time to update Jack, something I was not looking forward to. If he thought that I had sailed close to the wind when I inveigled a copy of the report out of Douglas and Partners, what was he going to make of trespassing? However, having given it some thought I had decided to stand my ground if Jack took umbrage. I got him to open up Google Earth and zoom in on the Hepworth property so that I could point out the various buildings. As I explained the events of Saturday morning, Jack took his trademark silent treatment to a whole new level, making me so self-conscious that I found myself squirming in my seat and stumbling over words. I didn't mention Jenny or the part she played, probably because even to me, dragging her into my own private crusade seemed selfish and ungallant. Jack looked at me for what seemed like an eternity, and then got up and left his office without saying a word.

It looked like he wasn't at all happy with me. I sat in front of Jack's desk, mentally trying to prepare a defence, but not really coming up with anything which didn't sound feeble. Maybe he had just given up on me and gone to take some fresh air in exasperation? Or maybe this was his way of firing me? Gone to organise my P45 in a brown envelope? Suddenly a voice from behind me shook me out of my contemplation.

"Here. Take a look at this," Jack said, putting down an open copy of an old *Gazette* in front of me and jabbing a finger at a story entitled 'Castlebridge man arrested over cannabis farm'.

"I remembered this was big news about five years ago," he said.

I quickly read through the story which involved a car body repair business which had plenty of welding gear, but did relatively little welding it seems. The welding activity, or lack of, provided a convenient reason for the high electricity usage, which in reality was down to dozens of heat lamps in an attic keeping cannabis plants growing.

"That's what they're doing!" said Jack with a degree of animation which I had not previously encountered. "They're bloody well growing cannabis in this Block building! You can bet on it. The greenhouses are just a cover, so they can turn on the heaters should anyone come investigating where all the electricity is going. The average electrical supply man, or copper for that matter, isn't going to know whether or not those plants need a lot of heating."

He zoomed in on the Block to examine the roof.

"There, I thought as much! Those cables you described on the wall are coming from these roof solar panels which are, I would guess, hidden from view at ground level by the brick parapet. They are there just to try to minimise the electricity use. At least on the face of it they haven't done what a lot of these farms do and bypassed the electricity meter. In fact, it looks like they've spent some serious money setting this up."

By this point, Jack was positively beaming. "What was it I said when you started? A journalist's nose…"

"I was worried you were going to give me an almighty bollocking for trespassing," I said, as a sense of relief washed over me.

"I don't exactly condone it," said Jack seriously, but for only a moment. His smile then resumed as he added, "But I've lost count of the times I have literally crossed that line to get a story, particularly when you know that a wrong is going unpunished. I like us to stay firmly on top of the moral high ground and won't engage in any criminal activity, but civil law issues like trespassing I can live with."

"The bit that I don't get is how this relates in any way to the development of Abbot's Meadow," I said. "Maybe it doesn't, and it's just a coincidence that the very people helping Councillor Sam Hepworth to police Abbot's Meadow and prevent developers developing or intruders intruding, are also growing drugs, the proceeds from which may well end up in the pockets of Sam Hepworth."

"Well, for what it's worth, I'm with you on this. The likelihood is that it is connected, although I've no idea how," mused Jack, scratching his chin while deep in thought.

"I'm not even sure what law would have been broken in misleading the council by changing the Douglas report findings," I said. "It's not as though there was any financial gain involved – well, no obvious financial gain that I can see. On the other hand, it's certain that Sam Hepworth must have had something to gain from his actions. What, though? That's the question."

"There are a few possible offences I can think of," said Jack. "Misconduct in a public office, maybe obtaining pecuniary advantage by deception… and that's just for starters. There's also the whole Class B drugs thing. But although the brothers may be growing and selling cannabis, we have no proof, and certainly nothing that would give police sufficient evidence to obtain a search warrant. Plus we know nothing about how the cannabis is processed and distributed. The plants have to be dried, trimmed, cured, and it may be that the Hepworths have teamed up with someone else who takes charge of this side of the operation. Possibly on an even bigger scale."

Jack pondered some more, twiddling one side of his moustache.

"What we need to do is give them a nudge to break the status quo. Tweak their tail a bit. We could run an exposé on the council being deceived, but my instinct is to keep our powder dry and see if we can't uncover what's behind all this."

"Can we use our knowledge of the Douglas report in some way that makes it obvious to Sam Hepworth that we're on to him?" I ventured.

Jack considered this as he gazed out of the window.

Turning back to me suddenly he said, "How about you write an article for our occasional local history series on the rerouting of the River Brant at Castlebridge in… well, whatever year it was. You said that the Douglas guys had uncovered some references on this which you should be able to track down through the British Library or the National Archives. An article discussing how difficult it must have been to divert the course of a river with little more than shovels… that sort of thing. Maybe mention possible flooding, but don't mention Abbot's Meadow. We need to be a bit more subtle. We could then tip off Jim Symonds to look out for the article and raise it in the relevant council committee meeting, suggesting that Sid Chisholm's suspicions had been correct, and that the decision on Abbot's Meadow might need to be reviewed. What do you think?"

"That sounds like a brilliant plan," I said, again marvelling at the man's ability to assimilate facts and come up with an inspired plan of action. "Mind you, I think Sam Hepworth's going to be a bit pissed off when he has to explain how the report got it wrong."

"Let's hope that Sam's put on the spot, and that he and his brother panic into putting a foot wrong," said Jack. "I want us to nail these bastards!"

*

The Douglas report had so many references that after just a few minutes searching online databases and archives my head was reeling. Some of the references were from sources that required a subscription, and I just had no way of knowing which were going to be the most useful in writing an article about the river. Some were very old and the language, although ostensibly English, was very different from present-day language and difficult to decipher.

It was clear that I was going to need help, so I took a chance and called Douglas and Partners. The delectable Penny, who was equally as lovely on the phone as she was in person, put me through to Charles Proudfoot. I explained that I wanted in particular to read up about the rerouting of the River Brant, and after a few minutes' discussion with the actual author of the report, he was able to point me at the most useful sources of information and references.

"Glad to be of service," he said cheerily. "Are you going to mention us? If you do, I'll need to read it first. If you are simply doing your own research based on the reference list, I am happy for you to just go ahead."

"It will definitely be the latter," I assured him, and thanked him for his help. Any reference to Douglas and Partners would alert the Hepworths to the fact that we had access to the report.

Having located the right databases, two of which I had to subscribe to, I was able to read through several documents dating back to 1300 AD, and after a bit of cross-referencing, I was starting to build up a picture of what had transpired. Looking through the previous local history articles in the *Gazette*, I could see that the style was more like an essay than a straight factual report. I opened up a new document on my laptop and started to write:

Article for the 'Castlebridge Retrospective' section
Sir Robert's vision for the River Brant at Castlebridge
By Daniel Curran

As young children on a seaside family holiday, there was nothing my big sister and I enjoyed more than being on a beach playing in one of the streams that meandered down to the sea. This simple setting provided our enquiring and developing minds with hours of fun, building dams from the stones on the beach and quickly learning that, ultimately, nature always wins. But what really made it a special time was when we could dig channels in the sand and divert the stream for our own purposes, maybe around the moat of a sandcastle. Or we would create our own little pool on which to float driftwood sail boats. Here we could work with Mother Nature to our advantage.

Well, I've been trawling through historical records of the town, and it seems that our Castlebridge ancestors liked to do this also... but on a much more ambitious scale. In the early 1400s, the River Brant to the east of the bridge was not straight as it is now, but curved in a bow shape to the south, following the contour of the land. For reasons lost in the mists of time, it was decided to straighten out this section, no mean feat given that the section in question is around half a mile long.

Records show that the convoluted course of the river had caused it to flood at certain times of the year, so maybe the motive was to stop that happening. Because of the flooding, the ground would have been rich in nutrients, and so would have made good farming land. Another possibility is that the Lord of the Manor, Sir Robert Cuthbert, had something personally to gain from this diversion. Old maps show that a large manor house was built near to what is now the new section of river, and historical commentaries on the development of the town reference a previous water mill. So maybe it was the lure of water power. Unfortunately, nothing now remains of either building, and Sir Robert's motives will probably forever be a mystery.

Whatever the reason, Cuthbert put his men to work on the herculean task of digging a channel straight across the bowed section of the river. The records don't show exactly when this was completed or how long it took, but the sheer volume of earth to be moved with only hand tools would suggest it must have taken a good number of years. By the 1450s, maps show no trace of the original river course.

So, the next time you walk along the riverbank, or drink and dine at one of the many restaurants or pubs along the east side of the bridge, spare a thought for Sir Robert – a man with a vision. Who knows, he may have grown up playing in streams on the beach, preparing for the day when he could show Mother Nature who was really the daddy!

To go with this article, I located an aerial photo of Castlebridge town, and using a map from one of the references as a guide, marked the old course of the river with a thick red dotted line using a drawing program on the computer. I also found a stock photo of the riverside as it is now which could be included, space permitting.

Jack was fine with the article, so I sent it straight to the copy editor for proofing and inclusion in the Tuesday newspaper. The second part of Jack's cunning masterplan was to tip off Councillor Jim Symonds that the article was about to be published, so that he might consider how best to bring it to the attention of the Housing Committee. I rang his number and got through to his wife, Jill. She said that Jim was currently out on an errand but would be at home that afternoon and, she was sure, would be only too pleased to see me. Although with corruption on the council now confirmed, exactly how pleased he was going to be was another matter.

*

"Hello… do come in," said Jill, smiling warmly.

Once again, her hair was coiffed to perfection, and she was so elegantly dressed that I wouldn't have been surprised to see the local vicar walking up the path behind me.

"Jim's in the garden, of course… where else?" We walked through to the garden and I found him in the potting shed, tinkering with a motor mower engine.

"Ah, hi, Dan. Know anything about these?" he said,

pointing at the mower. "Damn thing won't start. I've checked the fuel and had the spark plug out. Looks okay to me, not that I really know what I'm looking for."

Fortunately, my complete lack of mechanical skills was not exposed. Without waiting for a response he continued, "Still, never mind. Let's go back up to the house."

I followed Jim back, noting that, as before, his clothing seemed much too smart for gardening, or playing around with engines for that matter. Having said that, I couldn't imagine him in anything so common as jeans. We sat in the conservatory, and Jill again brought us cups of tea and biscuits on a tray.

"Here you are, boys," she said, placing the tray on the coffee table between us.

Jim waited until Jill had disappeared before dunking a biscuit into his tea like a guilty pleasure.

"So, what have you got to tell me?"

"Well, the first thing you should know is that the Douglas report, which you and the rest of the Housing Committee were provided with by Sam Hepworth, had been tampered with. I won't go into the details of how I know. Suffice to say that I have been able to compare the report as originally written by Douglas and Partners, with the version you saw. Some fundamental changes have been expertly made to the body of the report and the conclusions. The Housing Committee would almost certainly have reached a different decision about Abbot's Meadow, had it known the truth."

"Seriously?" said Jim, looking at me for even a hint of a smile to suggest that this was some sort of ill-judged joke.

"Seriously," I replied. "Tomorrow, we are going to print an article in our local history section of the newspaper, which you might want to draw the committee's attention to." I pulled a copy of the article from my jacket pocket and gave it to him.

As Jim read, I could see his eyes widening. When he had finished, he sat there for a few moments trying to process the contents.

"And where is Abbot's Meadow in relation to the area which flooded?" he asked, although he already had guessed the answer.

"This is the original bend in the river," I said, pointing to the red dotted line on the aerial view of the town. "And this area here, in the middle, which contains Abbot's Meadow, is probably where it flooded."

"Well, I'll be damned!" he said, sitting back in his chair. "Sid Chisholm said that the Anglo-Saxons would have been unlikely to use a flood plain for burials. He was right all along, and nobody listened!"

"Certainly looks that way," I replied. "And we strongly suspect that Sam Hepworth knew all about this and was in some way instrumental in having the report changed. Of course, what we don't know is why he would go to such extreme lengths to try to stop the land being developed. However, we're hoping that, if you are prepared to show my article to the Housing Committee when they next meet, it may just provoke Hepworth into letting his guard slip."

Jim looked at me with a fire in his eyes that I had not seen before. "Just try stopping me! We've all been duped. I can't believe a fellow councillor would do this sort of thing. People have a right to expect better from their elected representatives."

"Or, would it be better to show the article to the leader of the council rather than wait for the next meeting?" I asked, anxious to move things on quickly and fearing that due process could be protracted.

Jim shook his head. "No need. As luck would have it, the committee meets the day after tomorrow. Leave it with me and I'll ring you to tell you what happens."

"I'd appreciate that," I said. "Also, just thinking about that meeting, it would be good to think about what we want the outcome to be… and I'll need to explain that. One scenario is that the committee will blame Douglas and Partners for missing vital information and want to make an issue of it. Maybe they will suggest withholding payment, if they haven't been paid, pending correction of the report. If that were to happen, then obviously Douglas would push back, and this would expose the fact that there has been some monkey business going on. That's perhaps not what we want to happen just at the moment."

Jim looked at me suspiciously. "I'm sorry, I'm not with you. You're going to have to explain that to me. I can't see why we wouldn't expose this deception for what it is as soon as possible. I certainly don't want to protect Hepworth."

"And neither do I," I replied. "But my editor and I are pretty sure that this whole Abbot's Meadow saga is just part of something much bigger, something which involves criminal activity. We want to nail him as much as you do, but we want you to trust us that we should not go in all guns blazing just yet. I'm afraid I can't tell you what we think he's up to, partly because we're still trying to figure out all the details, but also, it's best that you don't know for the moment so you can't inadvertently arouse his suspicion."

"Wow," said Jim, sitting forward in his chair. "This is getting more unreal by the minute! So just how do you propose we should deal with the issue of a falsified report?"

This is where I was flying by the seat of my pants, as I hadn't really got a strategy planned out.

"Well, the most likely scenario is that Hepworth appears shocked that Douglas and Partners apparently screwed up, and will take it on himself to sort it out with them. He will discourage anyone else getting involved so that the truth isn't exposed. My guess is that the next time the committee is presented with the report it will have been 'corrected' back to the original version, and Hepworth will take the credit for ensuring that a proper job has been done. However, we must remember that he didn't want the original version of the report to be seen, for reasons which are still a mystery, so presumably whatever problem that might have caused will now be a problem once again. We are hoping that his next moves after that will give us a clue as to what he is up to."

I could tell by the expression on Jim's face that he was not a happy bunny.

"And what if there are no next moves? What if the committee members realise that Abbot's Meadow is not after all an ancient burial site, and they approve its development? What if it all goes ahead without any further hiccup? Hepworth's subterfuge remains a secret, he gets away scot-free and continues to be a councillor. He may even get the credit for ensuring that a thorough job has been done on the survey. I can't in all conscience be a party to that!"

"It's a possibility," I admitted reluctantly. "But if he went to all that trouble once, there has to be a reason why he doesn't want the development to take place. He will be forced into some sort of 'Plan B'. Or at least, that's what we hope."

I could see Jim thinking this over, trying to weigh up in his own mind whether his conscience would allow him to go against his instinct. After a few moments he reached his decision.

"Okay. I'll agree to play it your way for now. If Hepworth is engaged in something more sinister, we need to expose it. However, if further down the line we don't detect a Plan B, then you must promise me that we will go to the leader of the council and tell him what we know. Lay all evidence out before him and let him decide. Agreed?"

"Agreed," I said, happy to have him on side… for now at least.

Jim sat back looking pensive. "There is one thing that's really worrying me though. Sam Hepworth may not be a good person to cross. Are you sure you know what you're doing?"

"Yes," I said, trying to look confident. What I really meant, of course, was no.

*

On the way back I passed a sign for West Lodgeford, the village where 'Bob the Builder' Coldwell lived, and on impulse took the turning. When we had first met a couple of weeks ago, I got the impression that Bob knew rather more about the Hepworths than he was letting on. Also, he tried to warn me off getting involved when we met in the cafe, and I was interested to find out if he could provide some vital piece of information which might give me a lead. And even if he couldn't help, I liked spending time with Bob.

The office in the builders' yard was closed, so I walked to the house alongside and rang the bell. Bob's wife, Michelle, answered the door, holding a tearful toddler with one arm. She had the look of someone preparing to deal brusquely with a cold-caller in the middle of a domestic crisis, but as she recognised me she broke into a welcoming smile.

"Oh hello. Just having a bit of bother with needy children. Sorry... I know we met briefly, but I'm afraid I can't remember your name," she said apologetically.

"It's Dan. I'm a journalist with the *Gazette*. Is Bob in?" I enquired, hoping that the timing of my visit wasn't too inconvenient. "Just wanted a quick word if I can?"

"Yes, of course, Dan. Do come in. Just step over the toys... haven't had a chance to tidy yet. You're lucky you caught him at home. He's usually on site, but I've got him on childcare, just while I go to the hairdressers."

The house was large and very modern, and had the lived-in feeling that comes from a love of children and a willing acceptance of the mess and chaos which comes as part of the deal.

Bob was sitting at the dining table in front of a laptop, and surrounded by building plans and Lego pieces. A boy of maybe four was on the floor playing with Lego. From the look of it he was building a house of some sort, planning to follow in his dad's footsteps no doubt. As I entered, Bob got up smiling and extended a huge hand.

"Hello again, pal... this is a surprise. What brings you here?" he said, beaming and indicating a seat. "Just put that stuff on the floor. I'm trying to catch up on some paperwork before joining the lads on site a bit later."

"Well... it's all a bit complicated, but I'm still looking into why your application to buy Abbot's Meadow was rejected. I've learned quite a lot, and there is just a possibility that we might be able to get the council to reconsider its decision to deny sale," I said, selecting my words carefully.

"If you can, that would be brilliant!" said Bob with a massive grin. "We'd given up on that, I must admit, even though the housing association and I sunk quite a bit of money into it."

"When we met in that coffee bar, I got the feeling that you might know more about Sam and Chris Hepworth than you were letting on," I said, hoping that Bob wouldn't think I was insinuating that he had deceived me. "You're probably like me and don't like trading in rumours?"

"Well, you're right to some extent," he said. "With the business I'm in, you get to hear a lot of stuff about other tradespeople, and Hepworth Landscaping has had more than its fair share of detractors over the years. I think I told you I used them some years ago, and that didn't work out well. Chris was, and is, just a rogue, pure and simple. But back when they started trading, the word is that they were okay. Mind you, they had another director then. Guy called Paul Connolly, who was a good lad. You know, hard working, did a fair job at a fair price. I didn't really know him that well, mind you, but what I saw, I liked. He would definitely be worth talking to."

"Do you have his address, or a phone number?" I enquired.

"No, I haven't. But a friend of mine, Kieron, who's a plumber, can probably help you. He does some work for me from time to time. He and Paul were best mates. Might be worthwhile tracking Paul down to see if he can give you the lowdown on the two brothers. It would be interesting to know what made him leave the company. I remember he left really suddenly."

"Do you have a contact number for Kieron?" I asked.

"I do," said Bob, taking out his phone and jotting a number down on a piece of paper. "But the best thing is to visit him on site. At the moment he's working every weekday on the new housing estate off the Bardon Road. They call it Bardon Pastures, I think."

Just then Michelle came into the room putting on a jacket and looking flustered.

"Any idea where the car keys are?"

"Last time I saw them they were on top of the fridge, in that bowl," said Bob.

Michelle came back a few seconds later, keys in hand.

"Right, I'm off to the hairdressers, Bob. You're holding the fort, okay? Don't let them just sit in front of the telly. Don't give them biscuits to keep them quiet. And don't give them that orange squash we bought last week. It makes them hyper. Oh, and the cat has tipped its milk all over the kitchen floor."

She gave Bob a kiss on the top of his head, said goodbye to me, and was gone.

Bob turned to me, with a smile of resignation. "Bless. She lets me wear the trousers on a Sunday… if I've been good." Then, thinking that this sounded like a criticism, he added, "Love her to bits actually. Can't imagine life without her… or the lads."

"You're a lucky man," I said, and meant it.

"You bet. Fancy a cuppa… or even a beer?" Bob asked.

"No thanks, Bob. I need to get back, and I'm driving. But a beer some other time sounds like a good plan."

"It's a deal," he said, his smile suddenly changing to a look of concern. "You know, Dan… be careful with the Hepworths. If it turns nasty and you find yourself in a fix or needing the cavalry, just give me a call. Happy to help, any time."

As I drove back I reflected on the fact that, over just the past hour, two people were having concerns for my safety… three, if you included me.

CHAPTER 14

Seeing my article about the river in print should have been something to celebrate. However, I couldn't help imagining what Sam and Chris Hepworth's reaction would be... not one of unalloyed celebration, that's for sure. I felt as though I had lit the blue touchpaper of a large, unpredictable firework; the explosion was just a matter of time and there was nothing I could now do to stop it. Several of my colleagues in the office complimented me on the piece, although they must have wondered what prompted me to write it. As far as I was aware, only Jack knew the full story behind the article.

My phone buzzed and I saw it was a text message from Jenny.

> Just had Sam Hepworth come into accounts! Was asking if Douglas and Partners have been paid yet. Any ideas why?

Shit! He must have seen the article already. I took a chance and called her, even though it was often difficult for her to speak privately in an open-plan office. She picked up straight away, speaking in little more than a whisper.

"Hiya. What's going on? Hepworth came in here looking

furious. Walked straight past me and asked Sandra at the next desk about the Douglas invoice, even though he knows that I usually handle that side."

I didn't want to go into too much detail on the phone, so I tried to summarise as quickly as I could.

"I've put an article in the paper today which proves that the Abbot's Meadow area used to flood, just as Sid Chisholm had said… so it's almost certain it wouldn't have been a burial site. Jim Symonds is going to raise it in committee tomorrow and suggest that the decision to sell the meadow is revisited."

"Gosh! No wonder he's livid. What will happen now?" she whispered.

"Not quite sure to be honest, but he will have to try to take charge of things and stop the committee asking difficult questions," I replied. "As a matter of interest, was the invoice paid?"

"Yes. They were on thirty days and we paid last week. Sandra, in all innocence, asked him if there was a problem, but he didn't really answer. He just… um… got to go, speak later, bye." She cut the call abruptly, and I guessed that someone was now within earshot.

No sooner had I rung off than my phone rang. This time it was Jim Symonds.

"Hello, Dan, it's Jim Symonds."

"Hi, Jim," I replied. "What's up?"

"I just thought I'd let you know that I have got a copy of the paper. Your article looks good, especially with the map and the photo."

"Thanks. Yes, I was quite pleased with it. Your call is quite timely. I've just had a call from Jenny to say that Sam Hepworth was asking whether the Douglas invoice had been paid, so from that I think we can safely assume that he's seen the paper also."

"Sounds like it's going to pan out as you predicted," responded Jim. "I'll be taking a copy of the paper with me to the Housing Committee tomorrow, so I think we can expect some sparks to fly. I'll give you a call tomorrow evening and let you know what happened."

"Thanks, Jim," I replied and rang off.

As Jack had given me leave to follow up this story as my principal task, I decided to try to make contact with the mysterious Paul Connolly, erstwhile director of Hepworth Landscaping, and, by Bob Coldwell's reckoning at least, all-round good egg.

*

The Bardon Pastures building site which Bob mentioned, was eventually destined to accommodate a hundred new two, three and four-bedroom houses, built on what was, until the bulldozers moved in, prime farming land. As is often the case, the relatively small number of 'affordable' two-bedroom semi-detached houses felt like a token gesture to appease the planners. Looking at the range of house prices on the advertising board at the entrance to the estate, I wondered whether the builders could be brought to task over their use of the term 'affordable', which was at best highly subjective, and at worst, downright misleading to most young first-time buyers. I certainly couldn't see myself being able to even cover the deposit any time soon. Still, there didn't seem to be any shortage of people prepared to buy large, expensive houses.

I parked in front of a couple of the more upmarket show houses and made my way along mud-covered temporary roads to a Portakabin which served as the site office. I knocked on the door but couldn't hear whether this produced a response, so I tried the handle and found that the door was locked.

"Can I help you, pal?" enquired a voice from behind.

"Oh, hello," I said, slightly taken aback by the owner of the voice, a mountain of a man in a yellow hi-viz jacket over orange overalls that were seriously struggling to contain his impressive bulk. A blue hard hat sat precariously on top of his large head.

"My name's Dan Curran. I'm a reporter with the *Gazette*. I was hoping I would be able to talk with a guy called Kieron who I believe is a plumber working here at the moment?"

"Hi. I'm Will, the site foreman. Can I ask what this is about? Kieron is working here, but he's kinda busy right now. We're up against a tight deadline."

I wasn't sure how much I should say, but realised I'd got some convincing to do.

"I believe Kieron can help me locate a person who may be able to shed some light on a story which I'm following up. I can't say too much, but rest assured it is important. I got Kieron's name from a chap called Bob Coldwell who runs his own building firm... you may have come across him?"

At the mention of Bob's name the man visibly softened.

"Well, if Bob thinks this is a good idea, I'm not going to argue. He and I go back a long way. But just don't keep Kieron talking too long... that's if he's happy to talk with you at all. He's working on the bathroom on Plot 144 three-bed which is just on the right at the end of that road there."

He pointed in the general direction of the back of the estate, and rather than ask for clarification and risk annoying him, I just thanked him and set off without really knowing quite where I was going. No doubt that was a classic male trait. I hadn't gone more than five steps when Will called out.

"Oi… where do you think you're going?"

I had a bad feeling that he was having second thoughts, and he really was too big to argue with. He disappeared into the site office, and a few seconds later, reappeared with a white safety helmet, a hi-viz vest, a leaflet and a notebook.

"Here," he said, holding out the helmet and vest. "You'll need to wear these, and sign in on this register, and read this leaflet. It tells you all of our site health and safety rules. When you've read it, sign the bottom to say that you understand and will abide by them, and then let me have it back, along with the register. Drop the hard hat and vest back in to me here when you go. Clear?"

I nodded vigorously, like an errant child being reprimanded, followed his instructions carefully and then set off again. Just what perils the hard hat was going to protect me from I couldn't imagine. As for the precautions to avoid 'slips and trips', it seemed to me that a pair of boots would have been much more appropriate, as my shoes and trousers were becoming increasingly muddy with each squelching step. Eventually I located Plot 144, a medium-sized detached house that, from the outside at least, looked pretty much finished. The front door was ajar, so I entered, went to the foot of the staircase and called out.

"Hello, anyone there?"

I heard footsteps on the floorboards above, and a man of about forty with close-cropped hair appeared at the top of the stairs holding a length of copper tubing.

"What's up?" he said, looking at me with suspicion written all over his face.

"Hi," I said, trying to sound as friendly as I could. "Are you Kieron?"

"Yes. What do you want?"

"I'm Dan, from the *Castlebridge Gazette*. I've spoken to Will and signed in. I'm trying to get in touch with a guy called Paul Connolly, and Bob Coldwell thought you might be able to tell me his whereabouts?" I said.

Again, at the mention of Bob's name, Kieron's expression became more relaxed and he said, "Best come up then." And with that he disappeared along the landing. Bob certainly seemed to be held in high regard in the building industry.

I climbed the bare wooden stairs, which were still littered with nails and assorted snack wrappers, and went into the bathroom where Kieron, lying on the floor, had resumed his task of fitting a section of pipe below the bath.

"So you do know Paul?" I asked, hoping that our entire conversation wasn't going to be conducted with me talking to a torso.

"Sure do… well, to be more accurate, used to." He slid out from under the bath and looked me in the eye. "To tell the truth, I haven't seen him in what must be getting on for a year now. Then again, he went to live in the States, so that's hardly surprising, I guess. But he's never written or called. His decision to emigrate came a bit out of the blue, like. I used to think we was best mates, but it seems I'd got that wrong big time."

"Was he married?" I enquired, wondering whether it was a case of the family seeking a new life abroad.

"Well, he was married, but he and Laura were separated. All a bit tragic really. Childhood sweethearts and all that, and then one day she just announces that she's been seeing some other bloke, and that it's all over. It really shook him up, poor guy. He used to dote on her. We was best buddies for years and it was horrible to see. Couldn't do much to help him, other than be a friendly shoulder in the pub while he got rat-arsed."

By now Kieron was sitting up on the floor alongside the bath staring into the distance, and presumably reflecting on the good times that they shared.

"Do you know anything about his job at Hepworth Landscaping? I gather he was a director?" I said, easing into the subject I had really come to discuss.

This question seemed to shake him out of his reverie, and he looked at me quizzically.

"Well, he used to like it there… at the start at least, but as time went on, he seemed to become more and more pissed off with them. I don't think he saw eye to eye with the two brothers, and, if you ask me, it was always destined to end badly. Blood is thicker than water and all that. I think after the job turned sour, his marriage going tits up was the straw that broke the camel's wotsit. I guess he had a sort of breakdown, and needed to just get away from it all. Can't really say I blame him. Just wish he'd kept in touch, that's all."

"Do you think Laura would have any insight into what was going on at Hepworths' and why Paul was so unhappy?" I asked.

"Might do. They were probably still together when he started to become really angry with the brothers. Anyway, told you all I can. Don't know what this is all in aid of… but I don't want to see my name in print, whatever it's about. Got me?" There was a touch of steel suddenly, which I hadn't expected.

"Sure. No problem. Just one more thing and I'll get out of your way. Do you know where Laura lives?"

Kieron tore off the end of a cardboard box of pipe fittings, got out his phone, scrolled through his contacts, and wrote down an address and phone number on the back.

"So far as I know, she's still at the family home here in Castlebridge. Whether she will want to talk to you is another matter. Probably wants to move on and not be reminded of what she's lost. She'll never get another bloke as good as Paul. This is the address and house phone number."

He thrust the piece of cardboard into my hand. "Right... nice talkin' and all that, but I need to get this job done. Got to finish everything in this house today or the gaffer will do his bleedin' nut!"

And with that he lay down and stretched his arm under the bath. Obviously this was the signal for me to go. I thanked him for sparing me the time and left a business card on the edge of the bath.

"If you think of anything else that might help me locate Paul, I've left one of my cards."

A mumble from under the bath told me that this was unlikely. I retraced my steps back to the site office and ditched the hard hat and vest, as instructed.

Back at the car I phoned the number Kieron had given me. To my relief it was picked up and a woman's voice answered.

"Hello?"

"Is that Laura?" I enquired.

"Speaking," she said, a note of caution in her voice.

"Hi. It's Dan Curran from the *Castlebridge Gazette*. I wondered whether you could spare a few moments to talk about Paul. I want to try and track him down, and got your number from Kieron... sorry, I don't know his last name... but he's a plumber."

I immediately sensed a tension and thought she was going to cut me off.

"Paul? He's not here. He's in the States. Why do you want to speak with him?"

"It's a bit complicated. I was kind of hoping that we could maybe do this face to face, rather than over the phone," I replied.

"Well, I don't know that I want to. We split up about twelve months ago. I expect Kieron told you?"

"Yes, I know. It wouldn't take long," I said, hoping that she would relent. "I'm trying to figure out why he left the Hepworths' business and was hoping you could shed some light?"

"Well, okay. I'm sort of pleased that, after all this time, someone is starting to ask questions about that pair of shits… pardon my French. I'm not sure how much I'll be able to help you, but come round anyway. I've tried a few times to get in touch with Paul. Maybe you'll have more success. Do you know where I live?"

"Is it still 40 Willowbank Close?" I asked.

"Yes, that's right. The house at the very end."

"I'll be there in about fifteen minutes," I said, and we ended the call.

*

Willowbank Close was on the outskirts of town in an area that probably was once quite prosperous, but now had a distinctly faded air. Some of the houses had an interesting line in garden furniture, like an old fridge or a settee, and many of the gardens were overgrown with weeds. Laura's house, however, was remarkably neat and tidy, with a well-kept front garden featuring a small lawn surrounded by flower beds. I had to park some way away as the area was a popular parking spot with town-centre workers looking to escape car park fees. Fortunately, I had some trainers in the boot and was able to change out of my muddy shoes.

I was not quite sure what to expect as I rang the doorbell. Was she remarried? Maybe she and Paul hadn't divorced? Would I be met by a burly male partner and have some very hasty explaining to do?

The door opened and I was confronted by an attractive woman with dark hair, maybe just into her forties, dressed in smart jeans and a pink T-shirt, emblazoned with a breast cancer charity logo and the word 'Survivor'.

"Hi, I'm Dan from the *Gazette*," I said, presenting her with my card. "We spoke on the phone just now. I'm trying to find Paul because I think he can help me in my investigations."

"Hello. Come in… go through," she replied, holding the door open and indicating a room just off the hallway.

The room was on the small side, but was nicely decorated with modern furnishings. On the table was a laptop computer with a large separate flat-screen monitor, and an expensive-looking laserjet printer. The remainder of the table was covered in sheets of paper, many seeming to feature drawings and photographs.

"Excuse the work mess," she said, pointing to a chair which was clear of paraphernalia.

"Looks like you work from home?" I said, trying to start the conversation gently.

"Yes. I'm a graphic artist working for an advertising company in town. I work mainly from home, but go into the office maybe two or three times a month. Doesn't pay a fortune, but thankfully Paul paid off the mortgage before we… well, while we were still together."

It seemed like she found it quite painful to discuss her life with Paul, which, if she was the cause of their splitting, was probably understandable.

"Kieron said that you knew Paul from school days. How long were you two together?"

"We got married at eighteen," she said with a smile. "Young love, hey? And we were madly in love back then, but after nearly twenty years of marriage things went a bit flat, and I met someone else. Kieron must have told you? I don't think he's ever really forgiven me. He and Paul were like brothers. I'm afraid that brief affair turned my head… and broke Paul's heart. Lasted all of a couple of months. The guy turned out to be a total arsehole, if you'll pardon my French. The bastard dumped me with a text message. Said that he wasn't looking for a serious relationship. There was a good reason for that of course… he was already married! And by the time I came to my senses, Paul had upped sticks and gone. Who could blame him? There's not a day goes by when I don't think about him and wish I could turn back the clock. Still, I've only got myself to blame."

I noticed that her eyes were moist. The look of despondency suggested that she still loved him.

"You didn't have kids, then?" I asked, hoping such personal questions weren't going to suddenly backfire on me. But she seemed happy to talk and I sensed that she was probably going to be able to provide some of the missing pieces in the jigsaw.

"No, unfortunately we couldn't. Not for the want of trying… if you know what I mean. Just never happened, you know? We did talk about IVF, but it's so expensive… and, well, you know, unnatural. So we just settled for each other's company. Maybe if we'd had kids we would have lived happily ever after, but…" Her voice tailed away.

"I'm sorry it didn't work out for you," I said, finding the whole thing incredibly sad.

"Anyway, enough of all this reminiscing. What's done is done. Do you fancy a cuppa?"

She was plainly now glad of the company, and disappeared into the kitchen without waiting for an answer.

A few minutes later, Laura returned with two mugs of tea, a bowl of sugar and a plate of biscuits. She caught me looking at a framed photo of her and Paul on their wedding day. They both looked so happy and so young.

"I can remember it as if it were yesterday," she said, staring wistfully at the image. "Now… you wanted to talk about the Hepworths. Fucking little shits the pair of them, if you'll pardon my French again. Gosh… listen to me! I don't normally swear, but in their case I make an exception. What did you want to know?"

"Why did Paul give up his directorship of the landscaping business?" I asked, coming straight to the point.

"Truthfully, I don't exactly know," she said, taking a slurp of tea. "At the start he really liked working there. They did some quite prestigious jobs and began to make a name for themselves locally. Paul seemed to be very well respected by customers and always strived to give them the best job he could. Picked up lots of work just on personal recommendation. But then Chris started throwing his weight around, and he got greedy. He began ripping people off, especially older folk. With every customer he had there were always problems. He took advantage of their good nature and their confusion, and always found what he liked to call 'little extras', which weren't at all little, and were never agreed up front. Often these extras came to several thousand pounds over and above the agreed price. Paul was being tarred with the same brush, and he hated it."

"Do you know if anyone tried to take them to court?" I asked, wondering how Sam would explain that away as a councillor.

"Don't think anyone ever dared. Some of the blokes employed by the firm were dead rough, and they were always threatening in their behaviour. Chris and his horrible brother were thick as thieves… well, they are both thieves in my book, even though Sam, with his seat on the council, acts all la-di-da and respectable-like. And they seem to get away with it. Paul was furious. He had stand-up rows with Chris and threatened to resign. Sam was the one who tried to be the peacemaker, but that's just because he couldn't afford to have anyone rock his gravy boat. And anyway, he struggled to keep his brother under control. Probably a bit frightened of him if truth be told. But underneath it all I think Sam is just as nasty and ruthless as Chris."

"Why didn't Paul just tell them where to stick their job and leave?" I asked.

"It wasn't that straightforward. You see, Paul left school at sixteen and went into gardening which he was a natural at, although the money was pathetic. Then, after years of hard graft and little reward, the chance to work with the Hepworths came up and it seemed too good to be true. They paid him really well… too well really. And when the business started to flow in they made him a director. Paul was dyslexic and didn't have any qualifications to fall back on so that was a big deal to him. But then things started to go wrong and he began to feel trapped. He couldn't afford to leave, and couldn't bear to stay. Sometimes when he came home the first thing he did was hit the bottle, just to try to calm down."

"But he did leave eventually, so I guess the overcharging just got to him?" I observed.

"No, there was something else going on, but Paul wouldn't tell me what. He just said that no way was he going to get involved in really dodgy stuff… illegal stuff. He told me that he had threatened to go to the police if Chris didn't stop whatever it was he was doing. Don't think he ever did, though. Paul wouldn't tell me what was going on though. He said it was better if I didn't know."

I reckoned that if Jack was right about the cannabis farming, that would explain why Paul was upset.

"And then, that was about the time we had a row about our marriage and I let slip that I had been seeing someone else. Paul quit Hepworths and left home, all in the space of a few days. Next thing I know a letter arrives saying that he was going to the US to start a new life… West coast, somewhere. And that was the last I heard of him. I tried phoning him, but his old number was discontinued, and he didn't leave a new number, forwarding address, anything. I can't tell you how many telephone calls and letters I've had with banks, credit card companies, insurance companies, the tax office and suchlike. Luckily we didn't have a mortgage as Paul wanted it paid off… and quite a lot of things including the house were in joint names. But it left me in a hell of a mess… took ages to get everything sorted out and put into my name."

Her voice tailed off, and I could now see tears welling up in her eyes.

"Have you still got that letter?" I asked, hoping that there might be more details, which, over time, she had forgotten.

"Yes, it's upstairs," she replied. "I'll fetch it."

A few minutes later she handed me a typewritten letter

on a sheet of A4 paper. This seemed like a very strange way to communicate with your wife… or even soon-to-be ex-wife.

"Did he normally type letters to people?" I asked.

"Paul didn't write much at all really. It was partly his dyslexia and, to be honest, his handwriting was not that brilliant. In fact, I can't ever remember him actually sending a letter to anyone. He would phone, or text… or email, but that was about it. But it's definitely from him, if that's what you're getting at. That's his signature on the bottom for sure."

The letter said that he needed to make a fresh start, and that he had a job offer from an old school friend who now runs an agricultural supplies business in Santa Cruz. Apparently, he had managed to get a work visa.

"Does your printer have a scanning function? I'd like to take a copy of this if you'll let me," I said.

"Sure," she said, switching on the printer and placing the letter on the scan table.

"Actually, can I have the original and you keep the copy? I promise I'll get it back to you."

"I suppose so," she replied, obviously a little reluctant. I could see that this letter represented her last contact with Paul and was, in some unfathomable way, precious.

"Have you got anything else from him with his signature on? Just so I can compare them."

"Now you are worrying me," she said with a look of concern. "You don't think he wrote this, do you?"

"I'm sure you're right and it was from him, but in my experience it's always best to check out assumptions wherever possible."

As the words came out, I couldn't help thinking that I was barely out of short trousers and already trying to talk like a seasoned Fleet Street hack. Fortunately, she seemed to think I knew what I was talking about. She rummaged around in a drawer and produced an old birthday card from Paul.

"You can have this. I don't know why I kept it really…"

It was obvious why she had kept it, and I suddenly felt a bit overwhelmed with sadness. I needed to go before I also started to well up. Boy was I going to have to harden up a bit! I really couldn't afford to get so emotionally involved in every story I followed up.

"Well, thanks for talking to me, Laura… and thanks for the tea. I'd best be getting back to the office. If I can locate Paul you'll be the first to know, and I will let you have his contact details."

"That would be nice," she said. "I'm sure we'll never be able to get back together. Too much water under the bridge. But I would like to have the opportunity to say how sorry I am and put things right between us. Life's too short… and all that."

"Never say never," I replied, but realised she was probably right.

*

When I got back to the car, I checked my phone which I'd set to silent, and found that there was a missed call. It was a number I didn't recognise, but thinking it might be important, I pressed the dial button.

"Hello?" said a man's voice.

"Hi, this is Dan Curran. I got a missed call from this number?" I said, hoping it wasn't someone trying to sell me life insurance or tell me that my home computer's security had been compromised.

"Oh, hello. Thanks for ringing back. It's Kevin Handleigh. We met quite recently at my school."

He was talking so quietly that I had to strain to make out what he was saying.

"Yes, I remember. As well as teaching, you're the chairman of the heritage society, as I recall?" I said, my mind racing to try to work out the reason for the call.

"That's right," he said, and there was a pause. "The thing is, I'm in a bit of a difficult position… a spot of bother you could say. Well, more than a spot, it could be a whole load of trouble, actually. I saw your article in the *Gazette* about the river and… well, we need to talk, but I can't talk right now. Any chance you could meet me later at the school, say five o'clock?"

I was guessing that this was related to the dodgy Douglas report, and our Mr Handleigh was concerned that things would start to unravel, implicating him. But this was the evening that Jenny and I had arranged to go out, so I wasn't at all keen on forgoing this… even in the interests of revealing another twist in the story.

"Sorry. I'm tied up this evening. How about I come round to the school tomorrow lunchtime?" I offered. Surely whatever it was would keep for a day.

There was another pause while he considered this.

"Well… I suppose that will be okay. I'll meet you outside the school main gate as soon after midday as I can. Maybe we can have a quiet chat over a coffee somewhere." The fear in his voice was palpable.

I agreed and he ended the call abruptly, leaving me worrying that I had been selfish. Was I making a big mistake in not meeting him sooner?

CHAPTER 15

I arrived at the office next morning tired, but feeling good. The evening with Jenny had been wonderful. We went to a riverfront restaurant and talked the night away, barely stopping to eat. And afterwards, in the car outside her house, we snogged like rampant teenagers enjoying being free from parental scrutiny for the very first time. When I finally got back to the flat I was buzzing with adrenaline… not to mention testosterone, and sleep seemed all but impossible.

As I walked into reception Tracy greeted me with a knowing smile.

"Someone had a good time last night! You look like you haven't slept. Dad wants to see you."

I smiled back, wondering if I really looked that rough, and tried to check out my appearance in the glass windows of the office next to Jack's. I ran my fingers through my hair and discovered what I always knew: fingers make a rubbish comb. Why was it that, whenever I was summoned to see Jack, my confidence level took a dive.

Jack's door was open, but I knocked anyway – a throwback to my school days, I think, when we all hoped that excessive politeness would help defuse any trouble brewing.

"Ah, Dan! You got my message… come in, take a seat." Jack was sitting with his feet up on his desk. He looked fairly relaxed, so I hoped that was a good sign.

"What's new?" he asked.

I recounted my attempts to track down Paul Connolly in some detail, and showed Jack the letter that Paul had sent to his wife announcing his emigration to the States. Jack listened attentively, and nodded occasionally. Like me, he thought that a typed letter was a strange way to communicate, and was suspicious that it might have been faked.

However, I could see that Jack had something of importance to say when he judged the time was right. And now it seemed, that time had come.

"You remember you told me about that history teacher at Castlebridge Grammar? The one you thought had something to do with doctoring the Douglas report?" said Jack, watching my reaction carefully.

This took me by surprise, and alarm bells immediately started to ring.

"Yes… I do remember. His name is Kevin Handleigh. He's also the chairman of the local heritage society. Coincidentally… or maybe not… he phoned me last night wanting to meet. I agreed to go round to the school at lunchtime today. Why are you asking?"

I was starting to get a really bad feeling in the pit of my stomach. Jack took his feet off the desk and sat upright, reaching for a piece of paper on his desk. Whatever he was about to impart was, from his altered expression, very serious.

"Ben put in a routine call to the police Corporate Comms Office this morning to see what was new. It seems like your Mr Handleigh was injured in a hit-and-run last night and is currently in Castlebridge Hospital being treated for some serious injuries. The police are appealing for witnesses and want us to run a piece today."

I was dumbstruck. Was this just a very unfortunate but unconnected event… or…?

He continued, "It happened at about five o'clock yesterday afternoon as Handleigh left the school. Eyewitnesses say that he was hit by a silver car, which it turns out was almost certainly a Skoda Octavia stolen from a car park in town earlier in the afternoon. Apparently, the police found the car abandoned late last night and are examining it forensically today."

In my mind I was replaying the phone call from Handleigh. Why had I so callously turned down his appeal for help? I could have probably seen him and still had time to go out with Jenny.

"Shit… I feel terrible! I should have gone to see him yesterday instead of putting it off. He phoned me and said that he was in some sort of trouble, but in my wildest dreams I never thought it would turn out this way."

"Well… no use in punishing yourself," he said. "Shit happens, as they say. We just need to work out why."

"I guess it's a consequence of my article, so I do feel very responsible."

Jack leaned forward and rested his elbows on the desk, fingers steepled together.

"I'm afraid, Dan, that's just something you're going to have to get used to. In our job, what we report often has unforeseen consequences, but we can't withhold the truth for fear it will offend someone, somewhere. And in today's world, with social media picking on and distorting the least offensive comment, it always will. On that you can be sure."

"I suppose so," I replied, not wholly convinced.

"Now, as far as Sam Hepworth is concerned, there were only three people who knew about the existence of historical references proving that Abbot's Meadow was prone to flooding: Sam himself, the report's author at Douglas and Partners, and whoever altered the report's findings. As far as we know, Douglas and co are still in the dark, so my guess is that your article in the paper has put our Mr Handleigh in the frame as a grass. And someone was either trying to punish him for talking, or maybe stop him talking altogether."

It seemed unthinkable, but I couldn't fault the logic.

"Do you think? Surely they wouldn't go as far as attempted murder over a bloody field. Would they…?"

Jack raised his eyebrows and shrugged. "Certainly beginning to look that way, though I can't for the life of me imagine why."

"Handleigh had read my article in the paper, and from the brief conversation we had, I think he had come to the same conclusion as you. He said he was in a load of trouble."

Jack lapsed into concentration for a few moments.

"Look, why don't you get on over to the hospital. I don't know just how seriously Handleigh's been hurt, but if you get a chance to speak with him, it could provide us with more ammunition against these guys. It's likely that the police will be there waiting to interview him, so you might be able to sus out whether they have any leads on the driver of the car. We'll run the story anyway, so if you have no luck getting to see him, see what you can find out from the locals where the incident happened."

"You know, if our suspicions about all of this turn out to be right, at some point we're going to have to bring the police up to speed," I said, worried that, as a small provincial newspaper, we were getting way out of our depth. "Shouldn't we just do that now?"

Jack frowned.

"Yes, you're right of course, but I'm not sure that now is the time. I mean, what have we got? There's some kind of caper going on over this damn field, but we have no idea what. The council may have been misled, but that would be a civil matter unless it can be proved to be misconduct. I doubt the police would be very interested unless some sort of financial gain can be proved. We think the Hepworths are running a cannabis farm, but we have zero actual proof. We think Handleigh's injuries were caused deliberately, but it may turn out that he was just in the wrong place at the wrong time, and was hit by a reckless joyrider. It's all supposition. We have absolutely nothing of any substance yet. I think we should just let things simmer a bit and see what happens. Don't forget that whatever the situation regarding Handleigh, Sam Hepworth has still got to deal with your article throwing a spanner in the works."

Jack was right of course, as usual.

"Okay, I take your point. I'll go and see what I can find out at the hospital."

I got up to leave and Jack held up a hand indicating that he wasn't done.

"Before you go, leave me that letter from this Connolly chap. I'll see what I can find out about his emigration."

I took out the letter and birthday card, and put them on his desk.

"How will you do that? I tried phoning the US Embassy, but they were clear that there is no way they will divulge any personal information due to data protection regulations."

"I have my sources," he said, smiling enigmatically. And I had no doubt he did.

*

The route to the hospital took me past Castlebridge Grammar School, and on the spur of the moment, I decided to take a chance and drop in to see whether I could have a word with the headteacher. I realised I knew absolutely nothing about Handleigh, and if he was married, it seemed quite likely that I would be bumping into his wife at the hospital. The fact was, I felt that by not agreeing to see him in his hour of need, I was partly to blame for his current state. Maybe his wife, if he had confided in her, would be less than pleased if I turned up. The least I could do was to try to find out just who Kevin Handleigh was, what made him tick, and who might be saying their prayers for his recovery.

I explained who I was and why I wished to see the headmaster to the lady at the school office. Her expression suggested that she wasn't in the least impressed by journalists in general, and maybe me in particular. She curtly informed me that the headmaster, Mr Gordon McBride, was indeed in his office and very busy, but she would see whether he could possibly spare me a few minutes. Thankfully, after a few minutes I was ushered through into his room, where he was seated at his desk quietly cursing his computer.

"Damn thing has frozen on me again! Sorry, please come in," he said, standing to shake hands.

He had one of those handshakes that lasted just a smidgen too long, which somehow managed to change the whole experience from friendly to just slightly creepy. He was a tall, thin man with short, neat hair, wearing gold wire-framed glasses halfway down his nose, over the top of which he peered imperiously. He wore a green tweed suit, which gave him a strangely old-fashioned look, as though he'd just stepped off the set of a 1950 Ealing Studios school comedy. I could imagine him as principal at a long-established public school, but he looked to be a peculiar appointment for a modern grammar school.

"You'll know that as a rule I don't normally see people without an appointment," he said in a thick Scottish accent, taking his seat once more. "However, I have made an exception on this occasion in view of the unfortunate events concerning Kevin. Please sit."

If this condescending opener was supposed to make me feel in some way honoured, he was pretty wide of the mark. "Thank you," I responded, biting my lip. My first reaction was that he was probably more at home lording it over obstreperous teenagers and obsequious staff. I could only imagine what some parents would make of his pomposity.

"I wondered whether you could tell me a little about Kevin Handleigh and your understanding of what happened last night?"

"Okay, but I can spare you ten minutes only. Let's start with what I know about the accident. From what I can gather, having spoken last night with the police, Kevin left the school at about five o'clock as usual and was hit by a car as he crossed the road in front of Gate 2. It seems there was an eyewitness who suggested that a car seemed to deliberately pull out towards him which he'd failed to spot, although I can't see that as being likely myself. Someone who watches too much TV, if you ask me. Why would anyone do that… to Kevin especially? I'm not sure whether he has too many friends, but I would be amazed if he has any enemies. It's much more likely that he just didn't see the car coming, and the driver was in a hurry… or intoxicated maybe. The policeman said Kevin has been very badly injured, but I don't have any more information just now. Fortunately, they don't think it's life-threatening."

"I see. Is Kevin married?" I asked.

"Kevin? No… not the marrying sort, I would have said. Much too wrapped up in his love of poking round ancient church records and monuments to have time to waste on the ladies. If he did have a lady friend, he certainly didn't ever bring her to the school."

"What about close family, brothers or sisters?" I said, hoping desperately that Handleigh wasn't such a lonely figure as McBride made out. If he was, it somehow made my callous treatment of him even more unforgivable.

McBride reflected for a moment, and said, "I believe he has one sister who lives in Jersey… or was it Guernsey? I really can't remember."

"So Kevin lives on his own?" I asked.

"Yes, and I don't know how he'll get on when he's released from hospital if there is no one to take care of him. I need him back here as soon as possible. It's all most inconvenient," he said, frowning.

"Indeed," I responded. "I imagine it's not great for him either."

McBride looked at me over his glasses, and I thought he was about to issue me with a reprimand for being facetious.

He seemed to check himself and stood up. "Quite so. Right… if you'll excuse me, I need to get on. My secretary will show you out." He proffered his bony hand once more, which I shook, reluctantly.

Once outside I walked along the pavement and found Gate 2.

Immediately opposite were several semi-detached houses, so I took pot luck and rang the bell of the first house. There was no answer, but as I turned to go, a voice called from the front garden of the adjacent house.

"They're not in. Won't be in till teatime. What was it you wanted?" said a middle-aged woman wearing a floral apron.

She had magically appeared, cloth in hand, and was making a half-hearted attempt to clean her front windows. I suspected that she had seen me walk up the path of her neighbour's house, and her curiosity got the better of her.

"Oh, hi there," I said, pulling a notebook from my pocket. "I'm with the *Gazette*. I'm trying to find anyone who might have seen the accident here last night."

If, as I suspected, this lady was a one-person Neighbourhood Watch, then seeing her name in the local newspaper would prove an irresistible prize.

"Well, look no further, dear," she replied, dropping any pretence at window cleaning, and moving closer to the low boundary fence separating the properties. "The name's Vera Patterson," she said, waiting to make sure I had written this down before proceeding. "Saw the whole thing, I did. Quite shook me up. I was just putting some recycling stuff in the bin – I am a big supporter of recycling, you know – and I heard a car revving up just down there by that streetlamp."

I turned to see where she was indicating, noting that the view was clear with no obstructions.

"Did you see what sort of car it was?" I asked, although I would have been surprised if she could identify it. Modern cars seemed to be losing their individuality nowadays as all designs seem to converge in the name of aerodynamics, safety and passenger trends.

"I'm not that good on car makes," she said, "but it was a silver-coloured car, like I told the police. The next thing I know the car accelerated, and when it got to just over there, there was an almighty bang, like it had hit something. I rushed up the drive in time to see it scream off down the road, and a man lying still on the ground."

The hedge along the front of the garden seemed to suggest that Vera couldn't have actually seen the moment of impact. She was not therefore an eyewitness in the truest sense, although I was sure that this subtlety of detail would escape her.

"That must have been a real shock," I sympathised. "I've been told that the man taught at the school, and was on his way home. So you were first on the scene?"

"I was, and I was shaking all over, I can tell you. Didn't know what to do. He was just lying there still, and there was lots of blood from his head, poor chap. I was joined by a motorist who came along just after it happened, and he phoned for the ambulance. It took about ten minutes to come. We didn't know what to do, and the man said we shouldn't try to move him, so I got a blanket from the house to put over him. Then the police arrived and closed the road."

I was making a few notes, but probably not writing half as much as Vera was anticipating.

"So, what was your impression of what happened?" I asked, trying not to put any words into her mouth.

Vera paused, clearly willing me to start writing again. "Looked like the driver meant to hit him to me, otherwise why did he suddenly pull out like that?"

"Could it just have been that the driver was in a hurry, and was too busy looking behind him to make sure that there was nothing coming before pulling out? He might have been concentrating on the traffic rather than pedestrians."

This possibility seemed to shake her confidence a little.

"Er… well, I suppose it is maybe possible… but the driver didn't hang around, which does make me think it was not an accident. Told the police officer as much."

I guess she did have a point there.

"And did the injured man say anything?" I asked.

"Not a word. He seemed to be unconscious. Had a nasty head wound. The ambulance team worked on him for maybe fifteen minutes before they moved him. Putting up drips and the like. And strapping him to some sort of board. Poor soul."

"And you say the police interviewed you?" I asked. She nodded. "Did they say anything about the car or the driver?"

"Not a word," she said. "They didn't seem to want to answer any of my questions."

I gave her a business card, and thanked her for her time.

"If you remember anything that you think could be important, feel free to give me a call. I can't promise that we can print many details of the accident while police enquiries are going on. We can't be seen to be prejudicing any subsequent criminal prosecution. I am sure you understand?"

Poor Vera looked at me, crestfallen. She didn't understand at all.

*

Castlebridge Hospital, like many town hospitals, grew with the town. It started life as more of a cottage hospital and some of those original Victorian buildings were still standing. But now these ornate brick buildings were surrounded by modern, featureless concrete blocks which were plain, but functional. The addition of an A&E department two years ago had been widely welcomed by the townsfolk, who previously had the horrific prospect of a thirty-minute ambulance ride should they have the misfortune to require urgent medical treatment. I parked my car in the hospital car park opposite the main entrance, noting that if I stayed too long there was a distinct likelihood that the parking charge could exceed the value of my car.

A pretty nurse on the reception desk was busy chatting to her colleague, and it seemed they had just got to a crucial moment in some unfolding scandal when I showed up. She gave her colleague a 'don't dare go anywhere until you've told me what happened next' look, and smiled at me sweetly.

"Hello," she said. "How can I help you today?"

"Hi. I'm Dan Curran. I was due to meet a chap called Kevin Handleigh in about two hours' time for coffee, but I gather he had an accident and was brought in here yesterday evening? I wondered how he was and whether it might be possible to speak with him?"

I wasn't sure whether Jack would approve of me not explaining fully who I was, and why I was interested, but under the circumstances, getting to speak with Kevin, if I was allowed to do so, seemed to be the most important consideration. The personal connection might just help. I didn't think a journalist fishing for a story would.

"Just one moment," she said, and tapped away on her terminal. "Ah yes, he was brought by ambulance into A&E at about six o'clock yesterday evening. He's been into surgery, and has been moved onto Ward 2 in the ICU. You can go along, but I imagine he is very poorly so you may not be allowed to see him. Do you know where the ICU is?"

"No… this is my first visit to this hospital since I came to Castlebridge," I replied.

In fact, I make it a rule in life not to visit doctors or hospitals unless absolutely necessary. One of my father's favourite observations on life is that hospitals are the best place to be if you want to be offered a whole smorgasbord of horrible diseases or illnesses to choose from. I guess the apple doesn't fall far from the tree after all. The nurse produced a photocopied plan of the hospital and indicated the route with her pen.

"The ICU is on the second floor of the Franklin Building, but when you get there the door will be locked, so you will have to ring the buzzer and wait."

I offered my thanks, although by this time she was deeply engrossed in her colleague's storytelling once more. Much as I would have liked to hang around, inquisitive to know whether hospital gossip was on a whole new level from your standard office gossip, I needed to get moving. I followed the map and her instructions, arriving at the door to the Intensive Care Unit, which was locked as she had said. I rang the buzzer and, after a short while, a nurse appeared.

"Hello, my name is Dan. I'm a reporter for the *Gazette*. I was due to meet up with Kevin Handleigh this morning for a coffee, but he's in a bad way after an accident, I gather. I wondered whether I could see him?"

The nurse spoke with a soft Irish accent, and I saw that her name tag said she was Staff Nurse Ciara O'Shea.

"Well, you will need to speak with the consultant who is dealing with Mr Handleigh, but I would doubt you will be allowed to see him. He is very poorly. He's been through a major trauma, so he has, and is heavily sedated. Still, would you come in and take a seat down here opposite the nurses' station, and we'll see what we can do."

As I followed her down the ward, I passed numerous dimly lit side rooms, accompanied by a soundtrack of sinister beeps and bongs which sent a shiver down my spine. The clinical ambiance and cloying smell of disinfectant made me feel distinctly queasy. We reached the chairs and she turned to look at me.

"I honestly have no idea when Dr Varma will do his next round, so you could be in for a long wait, I'm afraid. Sure, I said just the same thing to Mr Handleigh's brother not half an hour ago, but he got as far as this and then decided that he couldn't wait."

The alarm bells immediately started to ring. "You say Kevin's brother was here. Can you describe him?" I realised that this would seem an odd request, so added, "I didn't think that Kevin had a brother."

"Well, he was not at all like Mr Handleigh, and that's for sure. He was quite… well, thickset, if you know what I mean. I probably shouldn't say this, but he didn't have any hair to speak of. Oh, and he had quite a lot of tattoos… although, nowadays it seems, who doesn't?"

This sounded very much like Dean Lockwood, the Hepworth Landscaping thug that I had a run-in with on Abbot's Meadow. If it was, I doubted he was here to bring a bunch of grapes. I wondered whether I should tell Nurse O'Shea that this man was definitely not Handleigh's brother, but she was already making tracks down the corridor.

Sitting in one of the chairs was a uniformed police officer reading a well-thumbed copy of a car magazine, who introduced himself as PC Joe Harper. He asked me who I was, and I explained that Handleigh and I were meant to be having a coffee together later that morning. My conscience pricked me into adding that I worked for the *Gazette* and was following up the story of his injury. Thankfully, this didn't appear to faze him too much, but I guess he was used to bumping into the press at such times.

"I was the first officer on the scene," he said. "Poor guy was in quite a state. So how come you know him?"

"I don't really know him that well – we just met the once. I'm following up a story that has some historical aspects, from Anglo-Saxon times, in fact. Kevin is something of a local expert in such things. We were going to discuss it again this lunchtime."

It didn't seem prudent at this point to mention that Handleigh was scared of something, at least not until I knew whether or not he was just an innocent victim, caught up in an act of reckless driving. Plus, I was unprepared to be cross-examined on what we had discovered and what we suspected, and in any event, I would need Jack to give his blessing.

"Did anyone witness the accident?" I enquired, wondering whether he knew about Vera.

"Yes, I have a statement from someone who lives just opposite the school, but I'm afraid I can't share too many details with you while our enquiries are in progress," said Harper.

We were interrupted by the arrival of a doctor, clipboard in hand, accompanied by another nurse. The doctor, wearing the mandatory white coat with stethoscope 'necklace', turned to me and said, "Good morning. I am Dr Varma. I'm the consultant looking after Mr Handleigh. Are you next of kin?"

"No, I'm just a… well, a friend," I said, stuck for any

better description. If what I suspected was true, heaven knows Handleigh needed some friends just now.

The doctor looked up from his clipboard, having reached his conclusion quickly.

"In that case, I'm sorry but I can't let you see him. I'm going to let the police constable here see him just for five minutes, because it's important to find out how this happened, and whether any crime has been committed."

"I understand," I said, trying to hide my disappointment. "How badly injured is he?"

Dr Varma consulted his clipboard once more.

"He's got a fractured pelvis and broken right leg, several broken ribs, a nasty head injury, not to mention severe cuts and bruises. He's in a bad way, and we have sedated him… but he is conscious."

And with that the doctor turned to the policeman and indicated that he should follow him. PC Harper looked at me apologetically and said, "Never mind, mate. You'll be able to get information from our Corporate Comms Office later." He took a notebook out of his pocket, wrote down a number and tore out the page.

"Here," he said. "This is the incident number. It will make it much easier for whoever you speak with to access the info. I've put my mobile number there also. As I say, I am not allowed to give you information, but if you find out anything of interest, I'd be grateful if you could contact me."

He disappeared with the doctor and nurse into a side room. There was no point in my hanging around, and leaving the hospital seemed like an excellent idea. Nurse O'Shea came out of a side room carrying a bedpan, and nearly bumped into me as I made my way back down the corridor.

"Did ya have no luck?" she said, and I shook my head. "Aw… sorry. I thought that was going to be the case, so I did. Sure, you could always try tomorrow."

"Yes, I will probably do that," I replied. "Thanks."

I managed to get lost trying to retrace my steps, and ended up leaving by a side door some way from the main entrance. As I walked back along the service road to the car park, I saw a police patrol car parked up, and guessed that this belonged to PC Harper. Making my way between the cars I suddenly froze as I saw a familiar vehicle. Parked facing the main entrance was a white Ford Transit truck. As I approached from the rear right-hand side, I could see that there were two people inside. The driver had the window open and I could see a tattooed arm resting on the door. Making sure that I could not be seen in the wing mirror, I ducked down behind a car and rang PC Harper's phone.

After a couple of rings he picked up.

"Hello, PC 497, Harper speaking."

"Ah… PC Harper," I said, keeping my voice low. "This is Dan Curran from the *Gazette* again. There is something I think you should know. Nurse O'Shea who escorted me into the ICU said that Kevin Handleigh's brother tried to get to speak with him a little while ago, but refused to wait… very possibly because he saw you there. I know for a fact from talking to Kevin's headteacher at the school that Kevin doesn't have a brother. Furthermore, from the description that the nurse gave me, I think the man who purported to be his brother is sitting in a white Ford Transit truck in the car park about thirty yards from what I'm guessing is your patrol car. It looks as though he could be waiting for you to leave."

"I see," said Harper. "Well, I'm done here and just on my

way out. Thanks for the tip-off. I will go and have words with him."

About five minutes later, PC Harper appeared at the front door and made his way across the road to the car park, looking around at the cars either side of his car. His gaze fell upon the white truck and he started to walk towards it, but his movements were obviously being watched carefully. As he approached, the truck's diesel engine roared into life, and the truck moved forwards, mounted the curb, crossed a grass verge and bumped down onto the road, tyres screeching. Within no more than ten seconds it had disappeared completely, leaving PC Harper standing staring, with his hands on his hips.

I thought it best not to stick around and face awkward questions, but no sooner had I got into my car than my mobile rang. I saw that it was PC Harper.

"Mr Curran. It's PC Harper. The truck you described has just driven off in a hurry, and it looks as though I spooked the driver. Do you know who was in that truck?"

I didn't really want the police involved with the Hepworths… well, not just yet at least. That would run the risk that they closed down whatever it was they were up to, and covered their tracks. And of course, we had no proof of any wrongdoing as things currently stood. I couldn't even be sure it was Dean Lockwood that Nurse O'Shea saw. I decided to keep quiet.

"No I don't, but from Nurse O'Shea's description, it certainly could have been the same man who tried to get in to see Handleigh this morning."

I held my breath and waited, wondering whether he was going to buy this.

"Okay. I'm going to ring the ICU ward and advise them

not to let anyone in to see Mr Handleigh unless they can prove that they are family. Just while we conclude our investigation into his injury. After that… well, let's see," he said, and rang off.

As I drove back to the office, I couldn't help thinking about Dean Lockwood and what his plans might have been had he got to see Handleigh. Shivers ran down my spine as I realised that if he had been watching the hospital main entrance for PC Harper to leave, he probably also saw me arrive. In which case he would no doubt have concluded that I was becoming a bona fide, grade-A pain in the arse!

CHAPTER 16

I was quite late getting home that evening after staying to write up the story of Kevin Handleigh's accident – although I was firmly of the opinion that this was no accident. I was unable to obtain much more information from the police Corporate Communications Office, but it seemed highly likely from the careful wording of their limited statement that they too viewed the incident as a hit-and-run. The fact that the vehicle involved was stolen and then abandoned suggested that there was more than a hint of premeditation. In writing the piece I was mindful that investigations were ongoing and hence care was needed so as not to prejudice any legal case which may be brought. Reporting only the few indisputable facts I had resulted in just a few column inches of text. Unfortunately for Vera, who it seems wasn't actually an eyewitness to the event after all, this meant that her fifteen minutes of fame would have to remain on her bucket list.

I was looking despondently into the fridge, trying to work out how the meagre contents could possibly be turned into anything remotely filling, let alone appetising, when the phone rang. It was Jim Symonds.

"Hello, Daniel. I said I would ring you to let you know

how the Housing Committee meeting went today. Have I caught you at a bad time?"

"Not at all, Jim," I said, closing the fridge door, pleased for the distraction. "So how did it go?"

"Well, not like we thought, and that's for sure. The meeting was pretty much routine affairs as normal, but when it came to 'any other business', Sam Hepworth produced a copy of the *Gazette* and referred the committee to your article, so I didn't actually have to say anything. He passed round photocopies to the members. Took me by surprise, I can tell you. Hadn't seen that coming at all."

"That's interesting," I said, somehow slightly uncomfortable as I realised for the first time that people were actually taking note of what I had written.

"My guess is that he knew it might be coming, and decided on a pre-emptive strike to show himself in an honourable light," responded Jim. "Not that he knows the meaning of the word. Anyway, he expressed concern, and said that he would talk to Douglas and Partners to see why the issue over the river wasn't picked up in their report. He said that it was either an honest mistake by them in overlooking some important references, or maybe the references that you had used were inaccurate or had been disqualified as being unreliable."

"Clever… that last bit," I said. Suggesting that it may be me that got it wrong would stop other councillors from becoming too animated and baying for Douglas blood.

"I can't see that he would go as far as trashing what I had written. That would be way too risky. What was the reaction from the other members?"

"Well, there wasn't any reaction really. Total apathy, you might say. The chair thanked him for bringing it to everyone's attention so swiftly and opened the floor for questions. But no one seemed in the slightest bit interested or concerned. I was disappointed, but didn't see any mileage in being a lone voice raising my concerns, so I kept quiet and just observed. The chair asked that the committee be kept informed, and we moved on to other business. I just hope that he doesn't end up getting away with this, that's all."

"I think you're speaking for us all there, Jim," I replied. Although things had gone pretty much as expected, I still felt uneasy.

I thanked Jim for letting me know, and rang off. My first reaction was to bring Jack up to speed, even though he might not thank me for disturbing his evening. I dialled his number.

Jack answered almost straight away, and I was relieved that, far from being irritated, there was a note of concern in his voice.

"What's up, Dan? Have we got problems?" he said.

I brought him up to date on what had taken place at the council meeting, which he listened to without interruption. When I had finished, he stayed quiet and I began to wonder whether I was, in fact, still connected. I needed Jack once again to bring some clarity and direction.

"Okay," said Jack after a few moments. It looked like he wasn't going to disappoint. "So Hepworth is either going to stick to his guns, discredit what you have written, and see if it all goes away… or he's going to come clean, say that Douglas and Partners have admitted their oversight, and probably, after a week or two, table the original report which he will pass off as having been corrected."

"I guess they're the only options open to him," I conceded, wondering where this was leading.

Jack was now firing on all cylinders. "If he decides to rubbish your story about the field flooding… maybe saying that the references you used are not reliable… or worse still, that you made it all up, then he'll have the worry that we may not let him get away with it without a fight. He must be wondering just what we know about the report and worry we could simply pick up the phone to Douglas and Partners. The last thing he will want is to risk escalating the whole thing."

Part of me sympathised with Jim Symonds and wanted nothing more than to expose Hepworth, but Jack's instinct of playing the long game made a lot of sense.

Jack continued, "Now, if he decides to revert to the original version of the report, which I suspect he will, if only to try to silence us, then he runs the risk that the committee could then allow the Abbot's Meadow sale to go ahead… whatever 'risk' that involves, and we are still none the wiser about that. Assuming that Douglas and Partners never get to hear about all of this, that leaves Kevin Handleigh as the only fly in the ointment because he knows the truth. The Hepworths almost certainly think that Handleigh tipped you off about the report. My guess is that they have already tried to silence Handleigh and failed, and might perhaps be out to finish the job, just so that there are no loose ends, as it were."

Unfortunately, once again I couldn't fault Jack's forensic analysis. "So you think that Kevin might be in danger, even in hospital?"

This whole saga seemed to be getting more surreal by the minute, and I was having a job believing that it was all actually happening. In just a few short weeks, I had gone from leaving university as a fresh-faced and naive student, to discussing a possible attempted murder with my editor.

"You said yourself that one of his henchmen was at the hospital trying to visit. I can't imagine he was taking in flowers. They will try again, I feel sure, if only to satisfy themselves that Handleigh has got the message and will keep schtum. I reckon you should go straight to the hospital in the morning and camp there until you get to see him. If you can manage to get a statement, we might start to understand what the hell is going on here. And once they know Handleigh has spilled the beans, they will probably give up trying to get to him, and go into self-preservation mode. By that time the proverbial horse will have well and truly bolted and the shit will have hit the fan… if I'm allowed two metaphors."

"Okay, Jack. I'll go there first thing," I said. "And sorry to have disturbed your evening."

"No problem, Dan. You be careful now… By the way, I've got some information on Paul Connolly. It seems he didn't ever leave the UK, well, not by any legal route at least. Also, he doesn't have any sort of police record… not even for parking or speeding. His current whereabouts are unknown."

"I won't bother asking how you know all this. Maybe he just wanted to hide away from the Hepworths, and his wife. Start a new life somewhere else without being traced… do you think?"

In the case of the Hepworths, that would be completely understandable. Although I couldn't help thinking that he perhaps gave up too quickly on his wife, Laura. She seemed nice, and genuinely upset by her own foolishness. The romantic in me was hoping that I might have been able to do something about bringing them back together, but this was now looking unlikely.

"I've given up trying to make sense of people's idiosyncrasies,

Dan. When you've been reporting on them for as long as I have, very little surprises you. Oh… I nearly forgot. I asked a handwriting expert to look at the typed letter he sent to his wife announcing his intended emigration. He is as sure as he can be that the signature on the letter is that of Paul Connolly, but can't completely rule out a forgery as there is so little to work with. Anyway, I need to get back to my dinner. Just call anytime if you need me… and, as I said, take care."

I put down my mobile, my mind in overdrive, trying to process the last ten minutes of conversation. Suddenly I didn't feel very hungry.

*

The next morning, I set off early for the hospital once more. After my phone call with Jack, there was a distinct nervousness that I hadn't experienced before, and I slept badly. I was now acutely aware that, if our suspicions were true, I might be in some danger. In the restless small hours of the morning, these thoughts became more exaggerated with every passing minute as paranoia took hold.

I had with me a small rucksack containing my phone, a magazine, a plain grey baseball hat and a pair of almost zero-magnification reading glasses that I had bought during my student days because I thought they made me look more mature and studious. Maybe the vanity of youth might, after all, come in useful. I decided to wear jeans and a faded blue denim jacket that I had bought long ago because it was trendy, only to realise that I couldn't pull off trendy. The best I could manage was mildly dowdy. Still, with these few items I was hoping I could alter my appearance sufficiently to fool the thuggish

Dean Lockwood and his mates if the need arose. Strangely, my university education in journalism was also remarkably lacking in the arts of disguise and subterfuge. My feeble efforts felt ridiculous, and probably more likely to attract attention than to avoid it.

As I pulled into the car park, which was nearly empty, I scanned the parked vehicles to check that there were no white Ford trucks. Nevertheless, I decided to use the side entrance once more, and made my way to the ICU, cautiously observing any seating areas I passed for signs of someone loitering. Just how I was going to distinguish between someone waiting anxiously for news of a loved one and someone loitering suspiciously, was a step further than I had fully worked out.

I rang the bell outside the ICU and was pleased to see that the pleasant Irish nurse Ciara O'Shea was once more on duty.

She smiled warmly as she recognised me. "Well, hello again," she said. "Here to give it another go, are we?"

"Hopefully… If I'm allowed," I responded. She held open the door allowing me to enter. Out of the corner of my eye I could see that she was looking me up and down, no doubt quietly amused to see double denim worn so badly.

As we walked down the corridor the clinical smell again made me slightly nauseous. "Is Kevin any better today?"

"Yes, a little, although he's still a bit groggy from sedation. That policeman who was here yesterday evening apparently managed to get his statement. He also warned us to check anyone else trying to get to see Kevin… I don't know why, or quite how we are supposed to vet anyone. Anyway, I'm sure it's fine with you being here. Is he in some sort of trouble?"

"I think the police are just being especially cautious until they know more about how the accident occurred," I replied, not really wanting to get drawn into that particular discussion. "So, will I need to get the doctor's permission to speak with him? We have reported the accident in today's edition, but we had very few details so I'm not sure it was very enlightening for readers."

By now we had arrived at the seating area near the nurses' station, and I was relieved that all the chairs were vacant.

Nurse O'Shea smiled apologetically. "Yes, I'm afraid you will have to wait until the doctor has been round this morning. Could be a wee while, so I should make yourself comfortable. Unfortunately, you can't eat in here, but I can make you a tea or coffee if you would like one?"

"A coffee would be great, Ciara," I replied.

As the nurse had predicted, it proved to be a long wait, although it was not uneventful. After an hour or so, during which I had read pretty much everything of interest in the magazine, another nurse, more junior than Ciara, approached me looking concerned.

"Hello. I believe you're Dan?" she said.

"Yes, that's right," I replied, hoping this was going to be good news. "Can I see Kevin now?"

"Er… no, it's not that," she said. "There's a man at the entrance to the ward who wants to see Kevin, and Nurse O'Shea is not sure. She says that the police asked us to be careful with visitors, so she suggested that I ask you if it's okay? He says that he works with Kevin."

Alarm bells were ringing so loudly in my ears that I couldn't think straight.

"What does he look like?" I asked, before realising this must have sounded very strange to the young nurse. "I mean, I may know who it is from your description. And I think the doctor really only wanted immediate family to visit until Kevin is stronger."

By now I was obviously blustering, and the young girl looked even more confused. After all, I was not family, and I was there.

"Well… he isn't particularly tall, late forties, early fifties maybe… and he looks, well, you know… just a bit scruffy, if you take my meaning? I think Kevin is a schoolteacher, but this chap doesn't look anything like the teachers I had. I found him a bit scary actually. Anyway, I told him that Kevin already had one visitor waiting to see him, so it was unlikely he would be allowed to, but said I would check."

She looked at me for some reassurance that she had done the right thing.

"I see," I said, trying to remember what Lockwood's two buddies looked like when we had the confrontation on Abbot's Meadow. "As a matter of interest, did you mention my name to him?"

"No I didn't. I just said someone from the *Gazette*."

Shit! This was not what I wanted to hear, and the nurse picked up on my reaction.

"Did I do wrong?" she said, no doubt sensing that this wasn't going well and beginning to feel really uncomfortable.

"No, it's fine," I replied. "Could you just tell him that only family are allowed while Kevin is so poorly, although you have made an exception for the press to see him as it may help in tracking down the car driver. Would you mind? Sorry to put you on the spot, but I'm sure that's what the doctor would want."

Of course, what I really wanted her to do was to take a picture of him on her phone for me… but that would have really freaked her out. I sat and contemplated my predicament, wondering whether there would be someone waiting for me when I left. A familiar Irish voice interrupted my thoughts.

"Right, Dan," said a smiling Nurse O'Shea, "the doc's been round and is happy for you to see Kevin, but ten minutes only, mind. The poor fella needs his rest, so he does."

She led me to a side room, the door to which was wide open, revealing a hospital bed surrounded by electronic machines with wires and tubes attached. I approached the bed tentatively, trying to prepare myself mentally, not just for the sight of his horrible injuries, but also for the awkwardness of the conversation to come. Handleigh's body was covered from the waist down by a sheet draped over some sort of frame, and his head was swathed in bandages. There were also some facial injuries. He looked very different without his beard and wire-rimmed glasses. I was surprised to see that he was awake and watching my entrance, his face expressionless as if he didn't recognise me. He glanced towards the clock on the wall.

"You're late," he said. I thought there was a hint of a smile, but it was probably the pain of speaking.

"I'm sorry," I said, not quite knowing what to say. "We'll have to get that coffee another day. How are you feeling?"

"I've felt better," he replied. His voice was really quiet, and I had to get close to hear.

"Can you remember what happened?" I asked, taking out my notebook.

"Don't remember a thing. One minute I was on my way home, the next I'm in here like this. The police wanted a statement, but what could I say?" He started coughing, and winced with the pain from his ribs.

I thought I'd better get straight to the point before the nurse came back.

"Look... I know that you altered the report that Douglas and Partners produced about Abbot's Meadow, but what I don't understand is why?"

This seemed to deflate him, and he closed his eyes as if reliving the past. It looked as though he was struggling with some inner demons. After a few moments I started to worry that the shock of what I had said was having a serious medical impact. Breathing a heavy sigh, he opened his eyes and looked at me.

"So you know?"

I nodded and stayed quiet.

"I was heavily in debt... online gambling. Stupid idiot, I know, but when you're on your own it adds a bit of excitement to life... well, at first anyway. Then it got so I was borrowing a shedload on the credit card to pay off my losses. I was worried I'd lose my house... job even. They offered me money... easy money, really. I didn't think it would hurt anyone, and it seemed like the only way out..." His voice tailed off, and he closed his eyes again.

"I'm assuming that by 'they' you mean the Hepworths. Was it Chris or Sam that did the enticing?"

"It was Sam," he said quietly, trying to absorb the fact that his secret wasn't so secret after all. "How did you find out? I was going to tell you about it when we fixed up that lunchtime coffee, whenever that was?"

"It's a long story, and the nurse is going to chuck me out soon. The thing I need to know is what is it about Abbot's Meadow that requires them to go to such lengths to stop it being developed?"

"Dunno," he said. "That's the problem. Sam Hepworth just

said that my job was to make sure that the report concluded that the meadow was most likely an Anglo-Saxon burial site, and that proving it with GPR would be very expensive. They're up to no good, that I do know, and now I'm thinking they had something to do with my accident. That article you wrote about the river was good, by the way… but I knew as soon as I saw it that I was in trouble. Sam Hepworth was bound to think I'd talked to you. Do you think they might have deliberately tried to knock me down? Or, worse still…?"

"It does look suspiciously like it. What did you tell the police?" I asked, as that was going to have a big impact on Kevin's safety, I felt sure.

"Just said that I couldn't remember a thing, but it was possible I was a bit preoccupied and didn't look around properly before setting foot in the road."

"Good. Truthfully, I don't know whether there's any more to it than that, but that should help calm things down between you and the Hepworths. In the meantime, you just concentrate on getting better, and try not to worry. Rest assured, I'm on their case, and I'm going to find out what they're up to if it's the last thing I do."

"Let's hope it won't be," he said, trying hard to smile. "Famous last words and all that."

The relief in having unburdened his story on me was clear to see. Nurse O'Shea came into the room wheeling a drugs cabinet, which she left at the side of the bed. I guessed that was a signal that my time was up. Kevin began to cough again, evidently in a lot of pain.

"Thank you," he whispered. I was pretty sure it was my newspaper article that put him in here, so his thanks, though sincere, seemed wholly misplaced.

"Am I going to be in trouble with the police?" he asked.

"Hopefully not. If my suspicions are correct, they will have more important things to concern them. So just get better, and we'll go and have that coffee. You can tell me all about the heritage society. I might even join."

I left the room and waited outside until the nurse reappeared.

"Tell me, are the double doors where I came in the only way out? It's just that there might be a chap outside that I am not especially keen to see."

If she was at all alarmed by this request, she didn't show it, and more importantly, didn't ask me to explain.

"No. The doors at the other end down there go to the south staircase at the end of the Franklin Building. You can get out that way if you want."

I thanked her and made my way out of the ward, but instead of leaving the building I found the nearest toilets and put on my baseball cap and glasses. The weak lenses, which were really meant for reading, made everything look slightly fuzzy, but not so much that it prevented me from finding my way around with reasonable ease. I looked in the mirror at the bizarre image and wondered whether someone who had seen me only once would recognise me. Well, only one way to find out.

I went down to the ground floor and circled back via the main stairs towards the ICU. My curiosity had got the better of me and I was half hoping, half dreading that there would be someone stationed somewhere between the ICU and my car, waiting for me to appear. Exactly what would happen were this person and I to meet was unclear, but my instincts told me that it would be prudent not to put this to the test.

The corridor just before the ICU opened out into a small seating area with a coffee machine. A man in a dark jacket was sitting with his back to me reading a newspaper. Every few moments he would lower the paper and look at the ICU doors, clearly waiting for someone to appear. I bought a coffee and chose a seat which gave me a side view of him. I guessed he was maybe mid-fifties, so a bit older than the man the nurse had described. I wouldn't have described him as 'rough', although his weird choice of green shoes was definitely a crime against fashion… not that my current attire qualified me to be any sort of judge. Again, I racked my brains trying to put faces to the names of Dean Lockwood's two pals, Simon Kendall and Josh Townsend, but without success. Just then the ICU doors opened and a lady walked towards the man, who got up to meet her. They hugged tearfully, and it was clear that this man was definitely not my would-be tormentor.

I got up and made my way back towards the main exit. There were several seating areas along the route, and a number of people waiting in each. Most of them were looking at mobile phones, talking with others or reading, but there was one person that stood out sitting in the area near the reception desk. A thin-faced, middle-aged man was sitting separately, holding a newspaper, but clearly looking over the top of it at the traffic moving along the corridor towards the exit. I passed his line of sight, but there were no visual clues that he recognised me, and I walked straight past him to the doors. Once outside I stopped and tried to collect my thoughts. I hadn't really had a chance to take a good look at the guy, so it was impossible to say whether I had encountered him before. There was only one solution to this. I had to go back in… and maybe even try to get a photo.

I took out my phone and put it in camera mode, before

re-entering the building at the same time as several others, while ostensibly scrolling through messages. I managed to get a picture of his profile, but I needed to go further into the building and come back on myself to get a frontal shot. I knew this was risky as it gave him a second chance to spot me. I paused for ten minutes reading a noticeboard and then went back to the main entrance, again with my phone in front of me pretending to be deeply engaged once more. I got a much better picture this time, although I saw a brief flicker of doubt cross the man's face as he tried to work out who this nerdy-looking character in a baseball hat and glasses was. And hadn't he seen him a while ago leave the hospital? Thankfully, after a few moments, his attention reverted to the people behind me who were chatting noisily and animatedly. I left the building and breathed a sigh of relief.

Once back in my car I took off the cap and glasses, quietly pleased with myself for having successfully run the gauntlet. I found the photo of my mysterious stalker and zoomed in on the face. I couldn't be sure whether he was one of the men I had seen on Abbot's Meadow with Lockwood… either Kendall or Townsend. It definitely wasn't the balding Dean Lockwood. From memory the other two appeared to be younger. At times like this, social media is just wonderful, but I couldn't help reflecting on the sheer stupidity of people willing to display their private lives for all to see, particularly those engaged in nefarious activities which were best not shared. It didn't take me long to ascertain that this man wasn't either of the men who accompanied Lockwood. It was in fact the infamous Chris Hepworth, who I had yet to meet, although I had almost certainly heard talking from beneath the greenhouse staging during my clandestine adventure with Jenny.

I studied the images on my phone closely. Like his brother, Sam, he also appeared to be in his late forties or early fifties, but here any similarities ended. He had a lean, pale face and what, if it had been tidier, would nowadays be called designer stubble. His short brown hair was thinning leaving a widow's peak, but it was the eyes that stood out. While there were photographs showing him laughing or smiling, it was somehow only the mouth that changed. The eyes remained cold and piercing, which suggested a ruthlessness which people would no doubt ignore at their peril. Those haunting eyes sent a chill through me. I was glad that I seemed to have escaped a confrontation, at least for the moment.

As I drove back to the office, I thought about what Jack had discovered about Paul Connolly. I was convinced that finding Paul was the key to unlocking the Abbot's Meadow mystery. If he didn't go to the States, where exactly did he go?

CHAPTER 17

As it turned out, I didn't go straight back to the office. On the spur of the moment I decided to revisit Paul Connolly's friend, the plumber Kieron. I figured that he was my best bet at unravelling the mystery of Paul's whereabouts, although in truth, I had a very short list of options. I pulled onto the Bardon Pastures building site once more and made my way to the site office. The scary site foreman was sitting in his office poring over a large drawing, and seemingly not in the best of moods. I suspected my return would do nothing to brighten his day. He looked up with a wearisome expression.

"You again! You do know that this is a place of work and not a social club?" he said, reaching for his mobile phone. "I've got four brickies on the sick and two trainee chippies who don't know their arse from their elbow, and we're already a week behind schedule. And, as if my day wasn't bad enough, one of the mixers has broken down on its way here! So, what is it you want now?"

"Sorry. I just wanted another quick word with Kieron if I can?" I said, and then immediately kicked myself for sounding too apologetic. I couldn't imagine Jack being so mealy-mouthed.

He sighed somewhat theatrically and pointed to the visitors' book. "You know the drill. Sign the book. You've already read the health and safety sheet. Take a white hard hat and vest from the lower shelf, over there. He's currently on Plot 160… that's if he hasn't decided to bleedin' go off sick as well!"

Thankfully the roads were a little drier this time around, and I managed to locate Plot 160 with remarkably little collateral damage to my shoes. I found Kieron working in the kitchen of a small and featureless semi-detached house. This time I got a better reception, his eyes lighting up in expectation.

"Hi… have you found him?" he asked, putting down a pipe-bender on the sink draining board.

"Hello, Kieron," I replied, treading carefully over a floor strewn with pipes and fittings. "No, I haven't. But I have found out that he never did go to the States."

His expression changed instantly from expectation to incredulity, and then as the truth dawned on him, disappointment. "You're kidding me!" he said, the hurt in his eyes now obvious. "How did you find that out?"

How indeed? "We have our ways and means," I replied, quietly enjoying the role of seasoned, enigmatic journalist, but also hoping he didn't continue this line of questioning because I hadn't the faintest idea how. But I needn't have worried, because Kieron had by now reached his own reading of the situation.

"You mean to say he's still here… been here the whole fucking time but couldn't be arsed to get in touch with me?"

"Well, I wouldn't have put it that way exactly. The truth is that I don't know where he is or, for that matter, what his mental state is. And I don't know why he hasn't contacted you. Can you think back to the last time you saw him? Was he still living at the house with Laura?"

He considered this for a few moments.

"Er… no, he'd already left her, and he was staying in a cheap B&B off Bentley Street. He said it was just for a few nights until he got himself sorted."

"Can you remember the name of the B&B?" I asked, pleased to have at least one lead to follow up.

"Bentley Bed and Breakfast, I think. It's that white house next to the library. Bit crappy actually, but I guess he wanted to keep the cost down."

"Thanks, Kieron. Sorry to have troubled you again."

I turned to leave and then had a thought.

"As a matter of interest, I did go to see Paul's wife. She seemed very nice… and for what it's worth, is still devastated that she screwed up her marriage. And she knows and understands that you're not best pleased with her. I think it would mean a lot to her if you were to make contact."

He looked at me as if I was crazy.

"What! You've got to be fucking joking! That bitch ruined the life of my best pal… well, he used to be my best pal, I thought."

"Yes, I know. It's ruined her life as well. I think everyone deserves a second chance. She may not get Paul back, but I suspect it would mean a lot to her if you could forgive her. Just think about it, that's all I ask."

He stood and watched me as I left, too stunned to speak. The job was beginning to bring out the hopeless romantic in me, and I smiled as I wondered whether the *Gazette* had a resident agony aunt. I laughed out loud when I wondered what my dad would make of that. It might just finish him off.

*

Bentley Bed and Breakfast was exactly where Kieron had said it was, although not quite as he described it. The building may once have been white, but was now more of a scruffy grey colour, with peeling paintwork. It was a typical Victorian three-storey terraced house with stairs above a basement leading up to a wide, ornate front door, semi-glazed with geometric-patterned stained glass. The sign on the wall beside the door announced 'Vacancies', which didn't seem too surprising. I rang the bell and after a few moments, it was opened by a middle-aged woman with grey hair and purple-framed glasses, wearing a floral apron and a no-nonsense expression straight out of the landlady's handbook.

"Yes… can I help you?" she asked somewhat brusquely, arms folded beneath an impressive bosom.

"Hello. My name is Dan Curran. I'm from the *Castlebridge Gazette*. I wonder whether I might have a word with you about someone who I believe stayed here about a year ago? I'm trying to track him down and I'm hoping you might be able to help."

"That's a long time ago. I'm not sure I'll be of much use," she replied. Her hand moved to the door, preparing to terminate this intrusion.

"It is important, and shouldn't take long," I countered, offering her my card.

She studied the card and then looked back at me, trying to gauge whether I was to be trusted.

"Well, I suppose you'd better come in then," she said without any real enthusiasm.

She showed me into a sitting room which seemed clean, and nicer than I had expected, although I couldn't see it winning any design awards. We sat facing each other on slightly sagging armchairs either side of a fireplace with an old-fashioned screen in front. I could see that the room would once have been considered as tastefully decorated. Sadly, the passage of time had not been kind.

"I'm sorry, I don't know your name," I said, trying to establish a more friendly atmosphere.

"I'm Mrs Wincott," she said. "Dawn Wincott."

"Well, Dawn, the man who stayed here was called Paul Connolly, and as I said, it was roughly twelve months ago, probably in late summer from what I can gather. I'm afraid I don't have a picture of him... or an exact date."

I cursed myself for not asking his wife if I could have a reasonably up-to-date photograph and so had no idea what he looked like. I obviously hadn't even read Rule 101 of the 'how to track down a missing person' guide! First, identify your target and exactly when they went missing.

"I see. Well, you don't need no photograph cos I remember him well. He paid up front for two weeks and then left all of a sudden, like, after just a few days. Never heard no more from him. No goodbye, no explanation... nothing. Really strange. I mean, I get some odd people here at the best of times, but he's the first one I've had bugger off after paying in advance. They usually bugger off owing me money."

A worried expression flashed across her face, and I could see that she was wondering if she'd said too much, and whether she may end up having to fork out a refund to someone.

"I see," I replied, reaching for my notebook. "Did he leave a forwarding address... or say where he was intending to go when the two weeks were up?"

"Nope. And I remember that he didn't put an address in the register. I said that he needed to, and he said he didn't have no home at the moment. Wife fell out with him, I expect, and kicked him out. He looked sad, and I felt sorry for him."

"It wasn't quite like that... more the other way round actually. Did you contact anyone about his disappearance... like the police?" I asked. "They have a special Missing Persons Unit, I believe."

"No I didn't," she said quickly. "I didn't want no trouble... and he wasn't missing, he just left early. And in any case, what could I tell them other than his name? Didn't know where he used to live, didn't have no photograph, didn't have a contact number. It might not even have been his real name. Besides, at the time I didn't really think of him as missing. I thought of him as... well, just gone somewhere else. As I recall he mentioned moving away to a new job soon, and I just assumed he had done that sooner rather than later."

I could tell from her expression that, in retrospect, she now wondered whether she should have shown a bit more interest.

"That's a shame. I knew it was a bit of a long shot. I'm trying to track him down because he might be able to help me with an important story I'm working on," I said, trying not to sound as despondent as I felt.

"I see," she said, pausing in thought before inspiration suddenly struck. "Well, you could look through his things if you like?"

"What! You're not telling me you've still got his stuff here?" I said in disbelief.

"Yes... well, some at least. He left a few clothes and personal bits. Nothing much though. I just stuck it all in a black sack when I cleaned his room. Do you want to see it?"

"Yes please," I said, and my obviously pleased expression

visibly lifted her spirits. At least she had done the right thing in not getting rid of it.

She disappeared, and a minute or two later returned with a black bin liner, approximately half full, which she handed to me as though it were a prize. The contents were remarkably meagre… a clean, neatly folded pair of jeans, a polo shirt, a sweatshirt, underwear and socks, some assorted bits and pieces, a gents' wooden-backed hairbrush and a shaving bag. I don't know what I had expected to find, but it was certainly more than this. Like maybe some documents.

Sensing that the contents were a disappointment, she added, "He seemed to have more than that with him when he arrived, so he must have taken some of his stuff with him. There was another plastic carrier with a few bits of washing in… socks, underwear and suchlike. I waited a few weeks in case he got in touch, and then I put that in the bin."

What was surprising is that he left a shaving bag. A few clothes I could maybe understand, but a bag of toiletries did seem odd, unless he had decided on the unwashed, hirsute look. I took out the entire contents of the sack and laid them on the floor, still hoping for a clue to reveal itself. Dawn sat quietly. I got the impression that she ran the B&B on her own and was short of company… and very probably bookings too.

"Would you like a cup of tea?" she said with a smile.

"That would be lovely, Dawn," I said, and she disappeared into the back of the house.

I looked again at the items on the floor. From the label I could tell that the jeans were quite expensive. There were one or two small flecks of mud near the bottom hem which suggested that they had been worn, so I unfolded them and examined the pockets. They were all empty, save for one of the back pockets which contained a plastic card, much like a credit card, with the words 'BARRATT'S SELF STORE, CASTLEBRIDGE' printed on it. Maybe this would be the lead I needed. I put the card in my pocket and returned all of Paul's possessions to the sack.

Dawn appeared with a tray and mugs of tea, and we passed the next fifteen minutes chatting sociably. I learnt that her husband of thirty years had passed away a couple of years previously with lung cancer, leaving her to try to keep the business going. I sympathised and made small talk, wanting to leave, but trying to pick the right moment. It was obviously a real tonic to have someone to talk to, and I was not anxious to rob her of that brief respite from loneliness. Just then the telephone rang. The moment had come. I thanked her for sparing me her time and left her talking to a prospective guest. Maybe things were looking up for her. I hoped so.

*

Barratt's Self Store was a modern, bright yellow warehouse on an industrial estate on the outskirts of the town. The entrance to the car park had a barrier and gatehouse, but the gatekeeper appeared to be busy with his mobile phone, and the barrier was permanently raised. I drove in and parked close to the building entrance, which had a magnetic card reader alongside the door. I took out the card I had found in Paul Connolly's jeans and swiped it through the reader. There was a satisfying click as the door unlocked. I opened it and entered cautiously, expecting to be challenged at any minute.

As it happened, I needn't have worried. The building appeared to be completely devoid of staff, or indeed customers.

The inside was divided into dozens of white concrete breeze block cells of various sizes, the smallest being little more than a door's width, the largest maybe five metres wide. Alongside each bright yellow metal door was another card reader and a unit number. The problem was that I didn't know the number of Paul Connolly's unit, if indeed he had taken out a storage unit and not just picked up the card from somewhere.

I couldn't imagine Paul requiring a large storage space. It wasn't as if he needed to store the house furniture. I set off down the first corridor trying the swipe card on all of the narrow storage units. By the time I had got to the end of the third of the four corridors, which were arranged in a square, I was beginning to feel that this was a futile exercise, and that I was seeking something that perhaps didn't exist. Or maybe the card had expired. Just then a man appeared in the corridor in front of me, seemingly looking for his own unit.

"Hi," he said, smiling. "I'm not sure whether it's just me, but this place always gives me the creeps."

"Me too," I responded, with more honesty than he might have imagined.

I knew what he meant. Who knew what was behind all these innocent-looking doors? Family treasures, family closets… family skeletons? I smiled back and took out my phone as though I needed to make an urgent call. I didn't want him to see me trying different door locks. He walked on by, and with relief I turned the last corner which would take me back to the entrance, only to find myself face to face with a uniformed security guard.

"Hello, how are we doing?" he said brightly, clearly wanting to offer some help to break the boredom of the job.

"Good, thanks," I said. The last thing I wanted was to

engage in a conversation. Unfortunately, he seemed to be the opposite. He spotted the card in my hand.

"What number are you looking for?" he enquired, determined that I was going to be helped.

I froze inside, wondering how I was going to get out of this without raising suspicions.

"To tell the truth, I can't remember. I'm sure it's on this corridor and it's just a narrow unit." I held the card out for him to see. "Stupidly I forgot to look for the number on the agreement before I set out."

"That's no problem. There's only four narrow ones on this side. Let's just try them all."

And with that he took the card from me and proceeded to swipe the first of the door locks without success. He moved on and got the same result on the next two locks. I followed meekly, sweating profusely, and wondering if I was about to be rumbled. We came to the final narrow unit and he looked at me quizzically. The hint of doubt in his expression told me that he was starting to wonder whether I was a genuine customer. He swiped again, and to my surprise and great relief, there was a click as the door unlocked. The guard smiled and handed me back the card.

"There we go. Have a nice day," he said, and walked off happy to have been of service.

By now my heart was racing as I went in cautiously, not knowing what to expect. The room was in pitch blackness and, after a few minutes fumbling around, I cursed myself for not realising that the fluorescent strip light switch was on the outside, where it could be turned off by the security man.

The room was maybe three metres wide by five metres deep, and each side was furnished with tall grey industrial metal racking. Leaning against one of the racks was a smart carbon-fibre racing bicycle. Neatly arranged along the shelves were a number of cardboard boxes marked 'CDs', 'Books', Hi-Fi', 'Fishing' and 'Tools'. A bag of fishing rods was propped up against the wall at the far end, alongside a bag of golf clubs. The lower levels housed three large unlocked suitcases, which on closer inspection contained mainly clothes, coats and shoes. One shelf accommodated a Telecaster electric guitar and practice amplifier, and on another shelf were various expensive electrical tools in boxes. But it was a large cardboard box marked 'Various' that intrigued me most. I lifted it down onto the floor with some difficulty, and set about unpeeling the copious quantities of parcel tape with which it had been secured.

The contents of this box were, indeed, various. There was an assortment of personal effects, paperwork, box files, books, playing cards, batteries, various different chargers, earphones and a laptop computer. I anticipated that after presumably twelve months in there, the battery of the computer would be flat, and pressing the power button confirmed this. After rummaging around and some trial and error, I located a charger which appeared to have the right type of connector for the computer. There was a single power socket adjacent to the door, and after a few minutes, I had the computer charger hooked up and doing its thing.

I didn't know whether I should wait for a while before attempting to switch on, but after five minutes, the excitement got the better of me and I pressed the power button. The laptop sprang into life, and I was relieved to discover that there was no log-on password needed. Evidently Paul was very trusting… or foolhardy, depending on your point of view.

I started by looking at emails, but the last email on the hard drive was from a year ago. I noticed an email from Barratt's Self Store which had an agreement and invoice attached. The invoice showed that Paul had paid for the storage unit for two years, so he unquestionably didn't see this as a short-term measure. There were the usual junk emails from a myriad of companies trying to sell everything from half-price health foods to holidays in Tenerife, and some personal emails which all seemed quite innocuous.

I turned my attention to the Sent folder and noticed an email with several attachments and the title 'Request'. I clicked on it and as I read the words my heart skipped a beat.

Hi Ryan

I'm sending you some pictures… just so someone else has got them in case anything happens to me. I know that sounds a bit melodramatic but I have got mixed up with some bad stuff and some bad people. I have threatened to go to the police but not sure if that will make things even worse. Not that they can get much worse! I've left Laura… and it looks as though will now have to quit my job. Please don't show them to anyone for now. I will be in touch… and thanks.

Paul

I had no idea who this person Ryan was, and the email address was '*RyanTC371@gmail.co.uk*' which gave me no clues. From the message it was clear that Paul was a desperate man whose life was at rock bottom. The photo files had just a date reference and so gave nothing away, but I could feel my pulse racing as I opened each of them in turn.

The first picture was of a building I recognised instantly. It was the large brick building at the back of Hepworth Landscaping which I had observed during my early morning reconnaissance trip with Jenny, and which I'd heard voices refer to as 'the Block'.

The next few were apparently taken inside the entrance to the Block, and revealed that an industrial-quality mezzanine floor had been constructed, which was accessed by a set of galvanised steel steps. The ground floor was covered with rows of bright green plants, which I had no doubt were cannabis plants. Above each row was all the paraphernalia associated with a complete industrial heating, lighting, ventilation and hydroponics system. A mass of wires, pipes and ducts threaded their way through the building along girders, dropping down to ground level at intervals. There were close-up pictures of some of the plants in black polythene pots, the leaves having the characteristic symmetrical arrangement with serrated edges. Further pictures showed the upstairs gallery, which was also full of plants. Grey, spidery, flexible ventilation ducting rose up through the floor to one of the two large extraction fans at the top of the back wall.

The next photo showed a wooden board on which was mounted a very modern industrial electronic control system, with a mass of wiring leading off into trunking. This was obviously a no-expense-spared, professional installation, and must have needed a significant investment. It was difficult to see how many plants there were in total, but from the photos it was obviously hundreds. I'd read somewhere that the average street price of a full-grown cannabis plant was something like £1,000, so I estimated that this factory's current crop could be worth anything up to £1 million.

So here was evidence of crime on a major scale that Connolly had acquired, and for one reason only. This was the smoking gun he intended to show the police if the Hepworths didn't close the operation down. Knowing what I now knew about the brothers, Connolly was either very naive or very foolish to think that this was going to be an effective strategy. Probably both. The conversation I had overheard from inside the greenhouse suggested that, even if he had made the threat, Connolly was unsuccessful in getting the Hepworths to change their ways. Otherwise, why talk about installing more security cameras?

The final photo appeared to be taken from a distance using a zoom lens, and the quality was not as good as the others. It showed a male figure loading two blue plastic sacks into the back of a van. The significance of this photo was not immediately obvious and so I magnified the image to take a closer look. It came as a shock to see the name on the side of the van was Blaze Storage and Logistics, a name I had come across only a few days ago! This was the company situated next to Castle Cardstock, where I had covered the warehouse fire story.

Why would Paul Connolly be taking photos of a delivery van? Was this how the cannabis was distributed? The figure at the rear of the van was quite fuzzy and I wasn't sure that identification would be possible, even for someone who knew him well. I zoomed in on the blue plastic sacks and saw a white house-shaped logo with the initials CH inside. There was also some white writing underneath, but the picture was much too grainy to read what it said.

I took out my notebook and tore out a page, before writing a note for Connolly, should he by any chance return to the storage unit. Whether he had another electronic entry card I had no idea. The note explained that I had been trying to contact him and had removed the laptop for safe-keeping.

I placed one of my business cards with the note, picked up the laptop and charger, and left the storeroom. I was buzzing with excitement, feeling as though I might just be making progress.

CHAPTER 18

"There, what did I tell you?" said Jack triumphantly, as he clicked through the images of the Block cannabis factory on the laptop. "I knew that was what they were up to. I've seen a few of these operations over the years, but this one gets the prize for being the most professional. Must have cost a packet to set up, but then again, this stuff fetches big money… and not even among the underworld. Nowadays it's the posh middle and upper-class twenty-somethings that buy most of it. A little light relief with the Prosecco after a dinner party. And there are plenty of celebrities that boast on social media about their predilection for weed, normalising it for the young."

I agreed. "What amazes me is that they were able to find electricians, heating engineers and plumbers who were prepared to do the installation work when they must have known the purpose of the building. Or is that just me being naive?"

"I'm afraid it is, Dan," said Jack. "Sadly, there are plenty of tradesmen about who will do just about anything as long as they're paid in used notes and there's no trace on anyone's books. So the question is, what do we do now?"

I had been puzzling over this during the drive in to work, but drawn a blank.

"I tried emailing this Ryan character last night, but I've had no reply yet. And I'm pretty certain that there's no way we can discover his identity through Google, even though it's a Gmail account. I guess I could ask Connolly's wife if she's come across the name?"

But Jack's mind was elsewhere. He put his feet up on the desk, clasped his hands behind his silvery hair and looked at me, deep in thought. I had learnt by now that when Jack's brain was going at full tilt, his other systems went into dormant mode. I could now recognise that when he fixed you in that steely-eyed stare, it was not necessarily a sign that you were being judged or critically appraised, even though it still felt immensely uncomfortable. It was as though his eyes had shut down to leave more processing power for thinking. After a few moments he decided to share his thoughts with me.

"What I'm trying to figure is whether, with this new evidence, now is the right time to bring the police in? There is certainly enough here for the police to get a search warrant and nail Chris Hepworth on a Class B drugs charge, but my worry is that there is something bigger going on here which may not get uncovered. According to the cops, the Skoda that knocked down Kevin Handleigh was wiped clean of prints, which suggests that it was a professional job and someone wanted him either killed or injured. And we know that Chris Hepworth and his mates were trying to get to see Handleigh in hospital, so whatever's going on is major league."

"Certainly seems that way," I conceded. "And it's a big step from growing weed to attempted murder. So, what do we do?"

"The police have asked us to run the story of Handleigh's injury again, appealing for any motorists with dash-cams or cyclists with head-cams to come forward if they may have footage relating to the incident. Other than that, I'm not sure what we should do. Let's sleep on it. There is probably something we can do to try to flush out the truth, but I'm damned if I know what just at the moment. Come and see me in the morning and we'll devise a plan. In the meantime, see what you can find out about this company Blaze, and what this chap in the picture is up to. There has to be some reason why Connolly took the photo."

*

I went back to my desk and put the laptop in my desk drawer. Tomorrow I would back up those photographs onto a memory stick, just in case. Next, I phoned Laura Connolly to see if I could get any clues as to who Ryan might be.

"Hello, Laura. It's Dan Curran. I just wanted you to know that I'm trying to track down Paul and I've come across a reference to someone called Ryan. It's a long story, and complicated, so I won't go into details now. Would you have any idea who this Ryan might be?"

"Now you mention it I do seem to remember that he kept in touch with an old school friend called Ryan something-or-other, but I don't have any contact details. Paul grew up and went to school in Manchester, although I guess this guy could be anywhere after all these years. But how did you find out about him?"

"Well, as I say, it's complicated. But when I know something definite about Paul's whereabouts, you'll be the first to know, I promise."

After ringing off I set about trying to discover more about Blaze Storage and Logistics, and its association with CH…

whatever that was? Blaze's website seemed very professional, and the reviews from established industrial customers, if genuine, had nothing but praise for the service being offered. Thanks to the wonders of Google, it didn't take me long to discover that the blue sacks belonged to Castlebridge Hospice, and were used for doorstep charity collections.

Happy that I had some more leads to follow, I looked at my watch and decided it was time to go home.

*

Jenny and I were going out for dinner, and as I thought about her, I realised that I had been so wrapped up in work that we hadn't met for a few days. I decided to ring her on the way home. Her cheerful voice was just what I needed.

Had I not been so preoccupied by thoughts of my conversation with Jack, I might have noticed the black Audi Q8 with dark, tinted windows parked in the office car park behind the shops. The figure inside the car was observing the rear staircase leading up to our offices in the Albany Suite.

I got into my Mini and fitted my Bluetooth earpiece so that I could talk to Jenny on the way home. I longed for a more modern car with proper hands-free phone connectivity, but that seemed somewhat fanciful, given my current financial status. I clipped my phone into its dashboard holder, pulled up the contacts list and then headed out of the car park to join the traffic on Castlebridge High Street. Even a modest-sized town like Castlebridge can't escape rush-hour traffic, and progress was painfully slow. I jabbed Jenny's phone number. She picked up straight away.

"Hiya. I was beginning to think you had maybe emigrated," she said. Her voice suggested that she wasn't really chastising me, and just wanted to know that I was okay.

"Sorry, Jenny," I responded. "I've been a bit tied up with this story involving our friends, the Hepworths. It's nice to hear your voice. We're still okay for a meal tonight?"

"Of course. Looking forward to it. I left some of my lunch so I'd be good and hungry by this evening. How's it going... the Hepworth thing, I mean?"

I wasn't sure how much I wanted to share with Jenny, not because I was concerned about her keeping it quiet, but because a big part of me didn't want to drag her into anything that could turn nasty.

"Lots of developments, but still some massive question marks... hang on. We're at the Manor Street crossroads, and there's some idiot right up my exhaust pipe trying to force me out into the traffic."

When it was safe, I turned right into a space in the crossing traffic and was surprised to see that the car behind me had done the same, much to the annoyance of an approaching lorry driver. He was forced to brake sharply, smoke rising from the locked wheels, horn blaring as he vented his anger. I could see that the car was a big black SUV of some sort. We came to stationary traffic almost immediately, and looking into the rear-view mirror I began to imagine that it could be Chris Hepworth... maybe... possibly. Or was it just my overactive imagination again? The whole Abbot's Meadow saga was definitely making me paranoid. I needed to get a grip.

"Dan? Are you alright?"

Such was my concentration that, just for a few seconds, I'd forgotten we were on the phone. "Sorry, Jenny. Where were we?

Oh yes, the Hepworth story. I'll tell you all about it tonight. Probably should ring off and concentrate on my driving."

"Yes, do that," she replied instantly. "I want you in one piece for our meal. I'm starving. See you at seven. Bye."

The traffic seemed to be starting to move more freely. I made a left turn, heading towards my flat, and saw in the mirror that the car, which I could now determine was a big Audi, followed. We came to some more traffic lights and stopped long enough for me to get a better look at the driver. Although the reflection from the car's windscreen made it difficult to get a clear view, I was growing increasingly convinced that it was indeed Chris Hepworth. There was something disturbing about the eyes which were fixed on the back of my car.

I decided not to turn into the road where I lived and continued straight past, heading on towards the outskirts of the town. If it was Hepworth, I certainly didn't want him to know my address. I began to feel butterflies in the pit of my stomach, which grew steadily worse as we started to head out into the countryside and the traffic became lighter. I noticed that my speed was steadily increasing just to maintain what I considered to be a safe distance from the Audi, and I was starting to pay more attention to the view in the mirror than the road ahead. The traffic seemed to drop away and soon it seemed to be just me and my ominous black shadow.

The road came to a sharp, tree-lined bend, which took me by surprise, and the car struggled for grip on the loose gravel. Thankfully the front-wheel drive of my trusty Mini did me proud and pulled me round without any great drama, but I was now aware that this was starting to get really dangerous. And still, all I could see in my mirror was the large black bonnet and grille of the Audi, bearing down on me threateningly. If it was Hepworth at the wheel, he was seriously mad at me. If it wasn't, then the driver was just seriously mad. I glanced at the speedo and it showed 65mph, which for such a narrow, tortuous lane seemed suicidal... not to mention, illegal.

I passed a sign for a left-hand turn to West Lodgeford, which I remembered was where builder Bob Coldwell lived, and made a spur-of-the-moment decision to take it. The turning came up more quickly than I expected and again I stripped more rubber from my tyres as the car slewed round. To my relief, the Audi didn't follow me, but carried straight on. My heart rate began to slow, as did my speed. I decided to stay on the current road for another five minutes or so just to be sure, and to give my racing heart time to recover. I began to relax.

What I should have done was turn off again as soon as possible, which I realised too late. After little more than a minute, I felt a sharp bump on the back of the car and looked in the mirror to see the black Audi bonnet filling it once more. Shit! My heart was instantly racing again and I felt drenched in cold sweat. I wondered whether to just stop and confront the driver, but immediately dismissed the thought. I might be stupid, but out here in the middle of nowhere, I wasn't that stupid. This was becoming really scary, and I wondered who I could turn to for help. I found Bob Coldwell's mobile number in my contact list and punched the dial button, half expecting it to go straight onto voicemail. To my great relief, he picked up.

"Hi, it's Bob," he said in his usual jaunty manner.

"Hi, Bob, it's Dan Curran... of the *Gazette*," I said, probably sounding as though I was out of breath, which I was.

"Oh, hi, Dan. What can I do for you? You sound a bit bothered."

"Do you remember saying that if I ever needed the cavalry, to give you a call?" Please God, let this not have been just an idle comment or a show of bravado.

"Course I do. What's up, pal?" he said, his voice suggesting concern rather than regret.

Just then there was another bump as I realised that the Audi was plainly intent on forcing me off the road. I put my foot down harder.

"Dan. You okay? You've gone quiet."

"Sorry, Bob. I'm heading in your direction, being pursued at crazy speed by someone in a black Audi that is either trying to force me off the road or scare the shit out of me. He's nearly succeeded on both counts, and I don't know what to do. I'm pretty certain it's Chris Hepworth. It's a long story… but I have probably pissed off him and his brother big time. Sam Hepworth was responsible for the sale of Abbot's Meadow being withdrawn, and now I've ruined their plans."

Bob listened patiently without trying to interrupt.

"Okay, right…" There was a pause and I started to worry that I was sounding a bit pathetic. Maybe I should just man up and fight my own battles.

"Tell you what… me and the lads are working on a site about two miles past my house, going south away from town. It's just on the outskirts of the village of Brayfield. Before you go into the village there's a small building site on the right. Just half a dozen houses. Come into the site and stop in front of the blue Portakabin. You can't miss it. How far away are you?"

"I'll be passing your house in about a minute, I guess… so five minutes. Maybe less if this bastard keeps sitting on my tail and I don't wrap it round a tree or something."

"No worries. Just get here safely. We'll do the rest." The phone disconnected.

As I came towards Brayfield, still with the Audi tailing me, I began to worry about turning right onto the building site. Absurdly, I was trying to decide if I should use the indicators. Should I just turn in and risk a big rear-end collision if he couldn't stop in time, or give him warning of my intentions and risk… well, risk what? I didn't know if he would follow me, drive straight on, or realise that I was potentially moving into a more public space and try to prevent me turning. In the end I decided to brake as though I was going to stop, bringing both our speeds right down just before the turn, and then accelerate rapidly into the turn, hopefully taking the driver by surprise.

The building site was as Bob had described it, with just three large detached houses in various stages of construction on either side of a dead-end road. The Audi somehow managed to follow me, skidding at the entrance on the muddy tarmac. I pulled up in front of the Portakabin as Bob had instructed, and the Audi stopped behind me. I opened the door of the Mini quickly, not wanting to be caught in the car where my options were limited. If I had thought about it longer, I might have stayed put and locked the door, but adrenaline does strange things to the bit of the brain which is supposed to do the logic. I figured if I was going to get into a fight, it would be better standing up.

I looked around quickly, desperately hoping that I wasn't alone and that Bob would be as good as his word, but the site was eerily quiet. The Audi door opened and Chris Hepworth appeared looking positively homicidal. He was by no means a big man, but what he lacked in stature, it seemed he made up for in sheer meanness which appeared to exude from every pore. Jack's uncovering of his police record proved that he was no stranger to violence. I could imagine as a small boy his favourite pastime was pulling the legs off spiders, just to watch them suffer. It suddenly seemed that I was going to be the spider.

As he started to walk towards me, a yellow JCB digger, which had been sitting on the driveway of one of the houses, started up and moved out behind the Audi, blocking it in. The driver, a giant of a man with a big bushy beard, got down and stood beside the machine with his arms folded. Hepworth turned and eyed up the man. He was mentally calculating whether his original plan to cause me some serious pain would now need to be put on hold. Then the door of the Portakabin opened and Bob, accompanied by two equally burly builders, appeared, all wearing white hard hats and blue muddy overalls. The cavalry had arrived complete with uniforms, and boy was I pleased to see them.

Bob walked over and stood between me and Hepworth. "I think you're in the wrong place, Hepworth," he said. "This is my land and I don't remember inviting you onto it."

"Keep out of this, Coldwell," said Hepworth with a snarl. "This has got nothing to do with you."

"Oh but you're wrong there, matey. Dan here is a friend and I don't take kindly to people playing silly buggers with my friends. And your idiot brother has cost me a lot of money, screwing up the sale of Abbot's Meadow. So if you don't want a smack, I suggest that you get back into that Tonka toy and get off my land."

Hepworth looked from Bob to his workmen and the man behind him.

"Well, I guess I know when I'm outnumbered," he said

with just a hint of a smile that never got as far as the eyes. "But I still have a bone to pick with this arsehole here. He's become an itch that needs scratching."

Bob moved up closer to Hepworth and looked him straight in the eyes. He was a good six inches taller than Hepworth and built like the proverbial brick outhouse.

"If you know what's good for you, you will just go, crawl back under your rock… and stay there. I won't tell you again. Now are you going to move this thing, or shall I get Will over there to move it for you?"

The digger driver, Will, jumped up into his machine, started the engine and reversed back just a few yards so that the Audi could be moved. He left the engine running and dropped the bucket at the front down to ground level, a signal which didn't go unnoticed by Hepworth. He got back into the Audi, started the engine and lowered the window. He leaned out, looking directly at me.

"Seems like you had a lucky break, but never mind. How's that pretty girlfriend of yours? Keeping well, is she?" he said.

He watched my reaction closely, and I could tell that he knew he'd touched a nerve. In that moment I realised he wasn't going to bother with me anymore. He now had a more effective strategy. As I looked into those narrow, disturbing eyes, I realised that this was the first time in my life that I had ever met someone so completely devoid of decency and humanity. A man with no redeeming features whose moral compass, if he ever had one, had been demagnetised many years ago.

The window went back up, and the Audi reversed back to the lane in a flurry of gravel and disappeared.

Bob looked at me and I could see his lips moving, but I didn't hear the words. All I could hear were Hepworth's words about Jenny. The implication was clear. If he couldn't put a stop to my digging for information by threatening me, then he would turn his attentions to Jenny. This was after all what he and his thugs did so successfully with Councillor Sid Chisholm and his young girlfriend, Natalie.

"Dan? I was just asking if you're happy to drive back alone, or whether you wanted some company, just in case. Are you okay? Looks like that shook you up a bit."

"Sorry, Bob. What he just said has really got to me. Shit! That bastard will go after Jenny if I don't lay off." Suddenly, I realised how much she meant to me and knew that I couldn't put her at risk.

"You're still investigating the whole Abbot's Meadow issue then?" asked Bob. "Must be something really dark going on for him to get so pissed off."

"There is. And it goes far deeper than you can imagine… although we're still missing some pieces in the jigsaw. But I need to think seriously about whether I've bitten off more than I can chew here. Hepworth has found my Achilles heel. I can't risk Jenny being hurt. But, in answer to your question, yes, I'll be fine."

"Well, okay. Just shout if you need us. That goes for both you and Jenny," said Bob, still obviously concerned.

"I will do. I can't thank you and your guys enough for coming to my aid."

"No problem. We're only too happy to help, especially where the Hepworths are concerned." And with that, Major Bob led his troops away to resume their normal duties.

I got into the Mini and began the drive home wondering how I was going to face Jenny that evening.

CHAPTER 19

"So how are you, Dan?" asked Harry Swan.

We were sitting in his neat living room waiting for Jenny to appear, and I was having real problems looking him directly in the eye. I was acutely conscious that Jenny could now be a target for the Hepworths in their desire to stop me investigating their odious business activities. How could I, in all conscience, drag Jenny into my personal crusade to uncover their secrets, which, if I was honest, was as much about proving myself as a journalist as it was about righting wrongs. Harry was entrusting me with the most precious person in his life, the tangible link with his dearly loved but now departed wife. I decided that I was honour bound to say something, although exactly what I was going to say was eluding me at that moment.

"Um… okay I guess, Mr Swan, thank you. To tell the truth, I'm a bit preoccupied by a story I'm working on which has taken an unexpected, and… well, unpleasant turn. The thing is…"

"Hiya," said Jenny, cutting off my confession. She was standing in the doorway to the living room, smiling and looking as beautiful as ever in another of her floral dresses. She had restyled her lovely auburn hair, which was held back from her face by a black hairband.

"Hello," I replied, all other words failing me at that moment.

"So where are you two love birds off to tonight?" asked Harry, smiling broadly and obviously bursting with pride.

Jenny looked at her father blushing slightly, embarrassed, but seemingly not displeased by his summation of our relationship.

"I've booked a table at our favourite restaurant, the Riverside Bistro," I replied. "It's really nice there, and the food is great."

At that moment, food was the last thing I was thinking about. I was imagining the moment that Harry found out that I was bad news as far as his daughter was concerned. However, it now looked as though that moment would have to be postponed. There was no way I could say what I wanted to say with Jenny there. Well, not without creating a major scene.

During the drive to the restaurant, I was thankful that Jenny talked almost non-stop about what she had been doing during the week, sparing me the challenge of conversation more demanding than the occasional "Oh really?" and "That was nice". I tried hard to concentrate, but my mind was playing out the various scenarios for the discussion I knew was coming.

The restaurant was busy as usual, and as we made our way to the table I had booked overlooking the river, I couldn't help scanning the faces, on the lookout for any unwelcome interest in our arrival. I recognised that this bore all the hallmarks of paranoia, but keeping Jenny safe had suddenly become my top priority.

We sat facing each other alongside a plate glass window with fabulous views in both directions along the riverbank. The waiter came and took our order for food. To give the evening a sense of occasion, Jenny decided that she would like some wine. I ordered two glasses of red, determined that I would stop at a half glass to safeguard my driving licence. As soon as the waiter disappeared, Jenny placed a hand over mine to stop it fidgeting with the wine glass and fixed me with her big brown eyes.

"Okay, tell me," she said earnestly.

"Sorry? Tell you what?" I said, my voice sounding tense and unnatural, even to me.

"Don't give me that. There's obviously something on your mind. I can tell. You've been fidgeting since we sat down. Is it this Hepworths business and Abbot's Meadow? Or is it about us?"

I cursed myself for being so transparent. I would be the world's worst poker player. If I was going to be a successful investigative reporter, I needed to be more steely and enigmatic, like Jack. But in Jenny's gaze, I was putty.

"It's both actually," I replied.

And then I told her everything that had happened. And I mean everything, right down to Hepworth's threat on Bob's building site. I couldn't keep a secret from her if I tried, and the truth was that I didn't want to. I trusted her implicitly and wanted her to feel the same about me. So I decided to come clean and see where fate took us.

Jenny sat silently as I relayed the events of the last few days: the hit-and-run attack on Kevin Handleigh and my visits to the hospital, my attempts to locate the mysterious Hepworth 'third director', Paul Connolly, the discovery of Connolly's laptop with incriminating evidence of a cannabis factory on the land behind Chris Hepworth's house, and my run-in with him on Bob Coldwell's building site. Our wine arrived but remained untouched.

"Wow! You have been busy!" she said, her eyes wide, still trying to process what she had heard. "And you think this Paul Connolly is the key to understanding where Abbot's Meadow fits into the story?"

"It's a possibility. There has to be something more than the dispute as to whether the land was or wasn't an ancient burial ground. You don't try to murder somebody over something like that… don't you think?"

"Maybe once they've harvested their weed, they stash it in the meadow until it's sold?" said Jenny with a half-hearted laugh. She took a slurp of her wine and set the glass down, a look of determination on her face. "So, what's the plan?"

"The plan?" I replied incredulously and rather too loudly. The party at the next table looked across with a mixture of annoyance and curiosity. There is something of the schadenfreude about observing other people's arguments. I could sense them enjoying our discomfort, passing comments under their breath with the occasional furtive glance towards us and the odd smirk.

"Have you not been listening? If I persist with this investigation, they may try to get at you! The 'plan', as you put it, is that I see Jack first thing in the morning and recommend that we drop the whole investigation… either that or put someone else on it. Or maybe we just go to the police with what we have? These are not people we want to mess with, and I won't always be able to call on Bob to get me, or us, out of a fix."

"What! You have got to be kidding me!" said Jenny, her face suddenly deadly serious. "Am I in Groundhog Day or something? We seem to keep having the same conversation over and over again. I am involved, like it or not. You are going to see this through, Daniel Curran, so just get used to it! Okay?"

Her voice had risen, and her cheeks were beginning to flush.

We suddenly became aware that the waiter had arrived with our meals and was hovering alongside the table wondering if he should interrupt what looked like a heated argument. He pointedly cleared his throat to attract our attention.

"Excuse me. Are you ready for your meals now?" he said, plainly embarrassed by the situation.

"Yes, that's fine," I said, and added, "Don't worry, we love each other really."

It was meant to be light-hearted, a figure of speech said in jest to ease the tension of an awkward moment. I had said it without thinking, but now realised that it was true. I had indeed fallen in love with this spirited, auburn-haired firebrand.

The waiter placed our meals in front of us and retreated quickly, for fear of being caught in any crossfire. Jenny looked at me quizzically. "Well…?"

"Okay. Supposing, just supposing mind you, that we tip the police off about this Block building being a cannabis factory, and then run the story. Chris Hepworth will have his collar felt, but he's unlikely to be detained at His Majesty's pleasure while waiting for the case to come up. So he will still be at large, and I'm just guessing here, even more pissed off with me than he is now. And his brother, Sam, will presumably deny all knowledge and get off scot-free. I'm sure he will have covered his tracks financially to avoid implication if it all goes pear-shaped. He will doubtless lose a big slice of under-the-counter revenue from weed sales, so he will be pissed off with me as well. So we are none the wiser about Abbot's Meadow, and have two mean bastards out to use my testicles as ornaments. Not the best of results."

Jenny turned and looked out of the window, deep in thought. After a few moments she turned back and looked at me, her anger now replaced by excitement.

"Look. They don't know that you've rumbled their cannabis operation, do they?"

"No, I don't believe so," I replied. "I think they just want me to drop my investigation into the meadow business."

Jenny leaned forward, elbows on the table, her chin resting on her hands. "So… it's maybe best not to let on yet. So far, all the physical threats have been from Chris Hepworth or his gang of thugs. I wonder whether his brother knows what's been going on? As a councillor, he must want to distance himself from all that stuff… don't you think? The last thing Sam will want is to be implicated in anything illegal. He has his reputation as a humble public servant to think of, tirelessly working in the public interest."

"I guess so," I said. Suddenly Jenny reminded me of Jack, and his aptitude for forensic analysis.

"Maybe Chris is a loose cannon… totally out of control? Maybe Sam has no idea what's going on? Maybe, he doesn't even know about the hit-and-run? I'm no fan of Sam Hepworth, and I'm sure he's as dishonest as the day is long, but I'm willing to bet that even he would draw the line at such violence. His council days would come to a swift end if he were to be associated with any scandal, let alone major-league crime."

"You have a point there," I conceded.

"Maybe it's time to play one off against the other? Why don't you take the bull by the horns, and go and see Sam. You could suggest that his brother's aggression towards you and me is uncalled for over something so trivial as a piece of land…

maybe even mention involving the police. See what reaction that gets? My bet is that he will call off the dogs."

This all seemed to make sense to me, although getting to see Sam Hepworth might prove easier said than done.

"Okay," I said, reluctantly. "But I want to run it past Jack in the morning first. If he agrees then I'll give it a go. Do you know where Sam lives?"

"I'll text it to you in the morning. To hell with the normal protocol on privacy. Tomorrow is Friday so he should be at home. We rarely see him in the office on Fridays."

"Sounds like a plan," I said, suddenly feeling a bit more optimistic. "Shall we eat?"

"Yes, let's. I'm starving," Jenny replied.

We tucked into our food with relish, both sensing that all was good between us. The awkward moment had passed and we were now, once again, a team to be reckoned with. Yet again we talked effortlessly and enthusiastically about everything from politics to our favourite music, and the evening passed quickly. Jenny finished her wine more quickly than was perhaps wise, but it was good to see her enjoying herself so much, so I ordered a second glass for her. We decided to opt for the sticky toffee pudding dessert, and Jenny mischievously suggested that when the waiter brought it, we should be in the middle of another heated quarrel. In the event she proved to be a much better actor than I had given her credit for. When the waiter had placed our desserts down and retreated hastily once more, convinced that our relationship was doomed, we both laughed like a drain.

On the drive home we enjoyed each other's company without feeling the need to talk. The food had been excellent, and Jenny had probably drunk a little too much wine. When we got back to her house we kissed and cuddled in the car, not wanting the evening to finish, but aware that we both had work in the morning.

"I had a lovely evening," said Jenny, with the merest hint of slurred speech.

I watched her walk to her front door and began to wonder about her plan for me to confront Sam Hepworth. In the Bible, God protected Daniel in the lion's den. Sam Hepworth's house felt very much like a lion's den, so I hoped He was not preoccupied elsewhere when it came to looking after this particular Daniel.

*

The next morning, I got a text from Jenny with Sam Hepworth's address. I phoned Jack and he was okay with the plan to visit him because, despite sleeping on it, he'd got nothing better to suggest.

Sam Hepworth lived in a large, modern, Georgian-style house set back from the road in a leafy, prosperous suburb of Castlebridge called Brockwell. It had a sweeping drive lined on both sides with trees and shrubs. The large wrought iron gates were thankfully open, allowing me to drive right up to the house. I parked behind a flashy, almost new white Mercedes Cabriolet sports car. As I got out of the Mini, I could hear a dog barking somewhere, and looked around nervously before deciding that the noise was coming from inside the property. The front entrance was an ostentatious mock portico affair with columns either side, each guarded by a stone lion. On an older house it might have looked grand and imposing. On a relatively new build it just looked ridiculous.

I rang the bell and after a few moments was greeted by an elegant middle-aged woman, with neatly coiffed greying hair, wearing designer jeans and a white silk blouse tied at the waist. Her heavily but expertly applied make-up made it difficult to determine her age, but I was guessing that this was Mrs Hepworth.

"Hi, is Sam in?" I asked, trying to sound like I was a close acquaintance. I was also trying to exude confidence. Whether that worked on the outside I have no idea, but on the inside I was nervous as hell.

She paused, eyeing me up and down with a haughty expression. I could imagine that she revelled in her role as first lady to a district councillor, and was probably the doyenne of the bridge club. And when it came to visitors, there were certain standards to be upheld.

"Have you got an appointment with him? He didn't tell me he was expecting anyone." She was obviously not convinced that I was worthy of the great man's time.

"No I don't, but I'm sure he'll want to see me," I replied, presenting her with a business card. "If you could tell him it's about his brother."

She reluctantly took the card as though it was highly contaminated, and after looking at it and me for a few moments longer, disappeared back inside the house. The door was left partially open and as she moved away, I became aware of a large, jet-black Labrador sitting patiently in the hallway. Its dark orange-brown eyes glared at me, silently willing me to cross the threshold uninvited. The intimidation was definitely having the desired effect, and I didn't move a muscle for fear it may be seen as provocation. After a minute or so the woman reappeared.

"You'd better come in," she said, pushing the dog back none too gently with her foot.

The dog looked up at me knowingly, as if to say, 'You got lucky this time, matey... not my decision but I've been overruled', and it padded off down the hallway. The house appeared to be expensively decorated and furnished, and I wondered how much of this conspicuous wealth was funded by drugs... and whether the lady of the house had even an inkling of Sam's duplicity. I was shown into a study at the back of the house where Sam Hepworth sat in front of a large oak desk, tapping away on a laptop computer. He was dressed casually in jeans and a blue New York Giants sweatshirt, which was less than flattering to his pronounced beer belly. I noticed that he was wearing a pair of lurid green Crocs, for which I was unexpectedly grateful. This absurd and incongruous image alone did more for my confidence than any self-esteem coach pep talk ever could. It was all but impossible to take anyone looking like that seriously.

"Thank you, Polly. I'll take it from here," he said, encouraging his wife to leave us alone to talk.

She looked suspiciously from her husband to me, maybe sensing that there was something going on that she was not party to. Hepworth waited until Polly closed the door behind her.

"You've got some fucking balls, I'll give you that," he said. "Turning up here... I don't know what you've got to say, but it had better be good. I don't normally give the press the time of day, and in the case of your paper, I wouldn't even use it to wipe my arse."

Charming. And he wasn't finished.

"And what's all this about my brother? Just as well he isn't here, for your sake," he added, just to make sure I was under no illusions as to the intensity of his dislike.

I realised that I hadn't actually thought through what I was going to say, but the words came easily. I was starting to enjoy myself.

"Your brother? Ah… yes. This would presumably be the brother who tried to drive me off the road today, and could have killed me. The brother who is so big and tough that he likes to pick on vulnerable women and has now threatened to hurt my girlfriend. The brother who was so keen to get to see the unfortunate victim of a hit-and-run incident before anyone else, but mysteriously scarpered the moment he saw the police? Strange that. It almost makes you think he had something to do with it."

His eyes gave him away. Jenny was spot on in her assessment. There was that flicker of recognition, maybe even panic, signalling the realisation that his brother was out of control once again. I was sure that this was not the first time he'd been in this position.

"I don't know what you're talking about," he said dismissively, and I had no doubt that this bit was probably true. He didn't doubt that what I had said had actually happened, that much I could tell. I decided to press home the advantage.

"The thing is, I'm trying to decide whether it's time to get the police involved. Threats against me might go with the job to some extent, but threatening my girlfriend is just not on. I'm imagining the headline we could run. 'Councillor's brother threatens female council employee'. Sound good?"

I had to stop myself from adding, 'Councillor and brother caught running cannabis farm'. I couldn't let on that I knew about the goings-on in the Block. That bit of the story was for another day, hopefully after the brothers were arrested.

Hepworth glared at me, unable to think of an appropriate riposte, his face turning bright red in anger, or more likely frustration. I remembered the picture of him that the Traveller Rosa had shown me on her phone, the same bulging eyes as he struggled to keep himself in check. The fascinating throbbing vein on his temple was something the photo couldn't capture, however.

"You need to leave, now!" he said, not trusting himself to say anything further.

"I will. But just before I go, tell me what is it that makes Abbot's Meadow so important to you and your brother? Does Paul Conolly know? Is that why he left the business?"

It was as if he'd been poleaxed. At the mention of Paul Connolly's name his hands started flexing and he got up from his chair, visibly trembling with rage. I thought he was going to hit me but managed to restrain himself. After all, public servants were not supposed to go around hitting people. And I suspected that underneath all the bravado, he was just a coward, so used to getting his own way that he found any confrontation highly stressful.

"Get the fuck out!" he rasped, his vocal chords strained as panic was beginning to set in.

"Don't worry, I'm going. There's a stench of something rotten in here," I replied, pleased with myself for coming up with a line worthy of a film script, albeit a rather cheesy, low-budget 1960s one.

He marched to the door and held it open. The Labrador trotted up the hallway and stood looking up at his master, eagerly awaiting a signal to provide some exit encouragement. Fortunately, it didn't come, and I managed to beat a hasty retreat back to the front door. Polly heard me leaving and reappeared, oblivious to the goings-on in the study.

"Everything okay?" she asked innocently.

"That depends on whether you're talking about me or your husband," I replied enigmatically, and made my way to the car, leaving her watching with a bemused look.

*

Rather than go straight back to the office I swung out of the drive, drove a little way up the road, and pulled into a service road on the opposite side in front of a row of semi-detached houses. I did a three-point turn using a convenient driveway, and parked up. From here I had an uninterrupted view of the entrance to Hepworth's drive. My hunch was that, if Sam Hepworth was as shocked by my revelations as he appeared, there was a good chance that he would shortly be going to see his brother to find out what the hell he'd been up to.

However, after nearly an hour spent listening to the radio with no sign of anything happening, I decided that this was a complete waste of time. He had probably just phoned Chris. I was just about to start the car when a black Audi SUV appeared and turned into the Hepworth drive. It looked as though Sam had summoned Chris to come and explain himself in person… either that or Sam was a willing party to everything that had happened, and this was a family conference to decide what to do next. My curiosity was pushing me towards only one conclusion. I needed to find out which.

I left the car in the service road and walked down the road to the drive entrance. Fortunately, the slight bend in the drive, coupled with the dense trees and shrubs bordering either side, meant that maybe, by keeping to the side fence, I could get most of the way to the house without being seen. I moved into the shrubs and found a gap at the back adjacent to the fence that was just wide enough to squeeze through, taking me right the way up to the side of a detached double garage alongside the house. The Audi was parked behind the Mercedes and there was no sign of the driver. There was a wrought iron gate between the garage and the house which presumably led to the rear garden. Thankfully this was not locked and I went through, but as I closed the gate slowly, the rusted hinges squeaked, piercing the silence with a high-pitched noise that seemed deafening.

I froze, reluctant to proceed, but not wanting to risk opening the gate again to go back. I waited, listening intently for signs that someone had heard, my pulse racing. After a few minutes it seemed I was safe, and I made my way down the left-hand side of the house.

I was guessing that Chris and Sam would meet in the study, which I recollected was at the back of the house, to the left of the central hallway. As I came around the back of the house, I could just make out raised voices from the first room along. I inched along to the window frame, and flattened myself against the wall, confident that I couldn't be seen… unless someone were to come into the garden from the back door in the middle of the property, in which case I was toast. The sound carried quite well, thanks to a small top window in the study which conveniently had been opened.

It sounded as though Sam was going into meltdown over his brother, his voice strident.

"I mean, just what the fuck did you think you were doing!" There was the sound of something either being slammed down

– or maybe thrown. "Now that little prick is going to keep on digging around. He's got his sights on being an ace reporter… and he's threatening to go to the fucking police. And he knows about Paul. Jesus, what a fucking mess!"

"Well, that's it then, isn't it? That bastard needs sorting!"

"For fuck's sake, Chris! You just can't stop yourself, can you? Just use your fucking brain for once in your life. If you'd listened to me in the first place, it would have all blown over. But no, your answer to being in a hole is to keep on fucking digging. I can't go on covering up for you, Chris! This has got to stop. God knows what we're going to do now. He's not going to give up, and if he does go to the police we are in deep shit. Maybe we will have to…"

The conversation stopped abruptly as the dog starting barking loudly, and from the sound of it, quite near the window.

"What's up with him?"

"I dunno. What's up, boy? Have you heard something?" The voice sounded like Sam.

Suddenly I was in a state of panic. Maybe the dog had got a whiff of my scent. This was not looking good. If they let the dog out into the back garden, he'd think all his Christmases had come at once. I crept back along the side of the house and opened the gate just wide enough to get through, not bothering to shut it for fear of it squeaking again, and ran into the bushes alongside the drive. I could still hear the dog barking as I made my way back along the drive between the rear of the shrubs and the fence. I turned and looked through a gap in the branches to see the two brothers standing by the open wrought iron gate looking around. The dog was sniffing the ground, clearly agitated.

I reached the road and ran back to my car as fast as I could. I pulled back onto the road and floored the accelerator, the engine of my old Mini screaming in protest. A mixture of relief and elation washed over me, and I realised I was sweating profusely. It was a close-run thing, but I'd found out what I needed to know. Sam was the boss, trying desperately to restrain his reckless brother who was seemingly out of control. I had now poked the lion with a stick, and it was time to sit back and see what happened... preferably from a safe distance.

On the way back to the office I rang Jenny.

"Hi," she said. "How did it go? Did you manage to get to see him?"

"As planned... and you were bang on the money. Chris has been a law unto himself, and Sam is one very unhappy man. He's trying desperately to rein him in."

"Did he actually tell you that?" Jenny asked, her voice betraying incredulity.

"Not exactly. I'll tell you later," I said, realising that she was in the office, and hence talking might be difficult.

I suddenly wanted to put some space between myself, the brothers and the whole Abbot's Meadow thing, and just have some fun. Find a way of relieving the tension, I suppose.

"Tell you what. It's Saturday tomorrow. How about we go out somewhere for the day?"

"Okay," said Jenny. "That sounds like fun. And you can tell me what actually happened."

CHAPTER 20

The next morning I awoke at the crack of dawn after a restless night going over the events of the last couple of weeks in my mind, trying to fathom out the seemingly unfathomable. I couldn't shake the feeling that time was fast running out. Jack had suggested that if we couldn't make any progress on the Hepworth saga soon, we would have to go public with what we had and move on. One of my fellow reporters had gone on long-term sick leave following the discovery of a serious heart condition, and during the next few weeks, Jack needed me to step up and take on a more active role in the day-to-day stories that are the feedstock of a provincial newspaper.

With there being no prospect of getting any further sleep, I made a coffee and took a shower. For today at least, I resolved not to even think about Abbot's Meadow, or the Hepworths. Today was going to be a day for fun with my girl.

I picked Jenny up at seven o'clock, the plan being to drive across to the East Coast for the day. Sunshine was forecast, and an escape to the seaside would do us both the world of good, even if it was for only a few hours. Hopefully leaving early would enable us to put some miles in before the traffic built up, and the plan was to stop later for breakfast.

However, things did not quite go according to plan. We had been travelling for about twenty minutes when my mobile phone rang. Jenny answered it for me.

"Hello, Dan's phone." She listened intently. "Just one moment, please. He's driving, but I'll ask him."

"It's someone called John Manthorpe," she said. "Wants to speak with you? Says it's about something you might think is important."

"Ah yes, he runs the farm adjacent to Abbot's Meadow. I think I should speak with him."

My resolution not to think about Abbot's Meadow seemed to have gone out of the window. However, I knew that if I didn't speak with him, I would be thinking about it for the rest of the day. My day of fun would be ruined anyway. Things ended badly when I put off meeting up with Kevin Handleigh. I needed to find out why Manthorpe wanted to talk with me.

"Can you tell him I'll ring back in a few minutes after I've parked up somewhere?"

I wondered whether he had remembered something that could turn out to be a vital clue into the mystery surrounding the field. I saw a sign for a lay-by coming up and we pulled in. Jenny found the number, pressed the dial button and handed me the phone.

Manthorpe picked up after a couple of rings, and I immediately recognised his gruff West Country accent. "Last time I seen you, you says you was interested in those guys what were clearin' the ditches in the field next door."

"That's right. Did you remember something?"

"No… but I thought you'd want to know that they're in there again right now, same place give or take. Looks like they've brought the same kit… mini digger and suchlike. Arrived 'bout quarter hour ago."

"I see. Thank you for letting me know, Mr Manthorpe," I replied. "I'm actually some way away, but I'll see whether it's possible to come and take a look at what they're up to."

I explained what the call was about to Jenny and asked, "What do you think we should do?" I tried to stay cool, but I'm sure Jenny picked up on my sense of excitement.

She looked out of the window for a few moments and then turned towards me.

"The way I see it, the seaside isn't going anywhere. It will still be there another day. We need to go and see what these men are doing. I'm just as curious to find out as you are. I just hope we can get there before they leave."

I leant across and gave her a kiss. "Thanks. And as you say, there will be other days we can go. Plenty of them, I hope."

The implication in my comment didn't go unnoticed, and she replied smiling, "Yes. I hope so too."

I turned the car around and we headed back towards Castlebridge as fast as my old Mini could manage. On the way back I recounted my meeting with Sam Hepworth at his home, and my subsequent reconnaissance mission to find out just what the relationship between the brothers was. I decided not to mention that I was fairly close to becoming dog food, or that I overheard Sam Hepworth describe me as a 'little prick'. For men, there are some comments that just cut to the quick and prove, even when it comes to insults, size matters. Jenny sat quietly taking it all in.

"I'm just amazed! When you've got the bit between your teeth, you really go for it, don't you?" she said.

"I surprise myself sometimes," I admitted.

The traffic was just starting to build up as we reached the outskirts of town, and I was becoming increasingly frustrated with other drivers seemingly hell-bent on going nowhere very quickly. By now it was twenty minutes since I took John Manthorpe's call, and my imagination was in overdrive, wondering just what was taking place on Abbot's Meadow. Had my confrontation with Sam Hepworth provoked the brothers into some sort of action? With all the events of the last week or two, I realised that I had been so close to the minutiae of jigsaw piece clues that I hadn't really stood back to look at the overall picture. But now, the more I thought about it, the more a picture was beginning to take shape in my mind, and I found it difficult to escape the frightening conclusion that was starting to haunt me.

We crossed town and headed out towards Abbot's Meadow, taking care not to get caught by speed cameras. As we arrived at the entrance to the field, I saw that the large steel gate was open, and there were fresh vehicle tracks in the mud. A little way past the field entrance was a wide grass verge on the junction with a side road which provided a conveniently close parking spot. I turned the engine off and looked at Jenny.

"Well... we're here. You'd best stay in the car, and I'll go and take a look."

No sooner had the words left my mouth than I regretted them. Jenny's defiant look said it all.

"Okay, okay... let's both go and take a look, but just be careful."

Jenny opened her door and then paused. "Do you think you should let your editor know what's happening? From what you've told me he wants to be kept in the loop... and besides, it might be good to have some reinforcements."

"You're absolutely right, on both counts," I replied, and dialled Jack Marston's number. Unfortunately, it went to voicemail, so I left a quick message for him to call me and rang off.

We walked back to the field entrance and entered tentatively, keeping to the side close to the hedge. I pictured the layout on the map that Manthorpe had shown me. The area where he saw people working was to the left near the corner of the field. There was no sign of the Travellers, Mickey and Rosa. They must have packed up and moved on with their friends.

The hedgerow followed the curve in the road going past Abbot's Meadow towards Manthorpe's farm, and so it was not possible to see the corner in question without going further into the field. We edged our way along for maybe a hundred yards, keeping as close to the hedge as possible, and then pulled up sharp as a white Ford Transit truck came into view parked near the corner. Hitched to the back of the truck was a trailer, and behind both vehicles we could see there was a small digger at work, the arm rising and falling as earth was being scraped away. But from that distance it was impossible to make out exactly what was happening. I tried using the camera on my mobile phone and zooming in, but it didn't help. I needed to get closer to the action, and preferably with the view not blocked by the vehicles.

"It's no good. We can't see anything from here, and if we go any further they'll see us. They're digging only a matter of metres from the boundary hedge of Manthorpe's farm. How about you stay put here while I drive around to Manthorpe's and try to get up close? If you stay put, you'll be out of sight and perfectly safe, and getting two different views of what's happening should help. You'll know well in advance if they decide to pack up because they will have to reload the digger onto the trailer. So you'll have plenty of time to get back to where we parked at the first sign of danger. That'll be our rendezvous point. Keep in touch with me by text, and just make sure you keep out of sight."

"Sounds like a plan," said Jenny hesitantly, obviously not entirely convinced. "Please be careful though, and don't take any risks."

I promised to be careful, but stopped short of including the taking of risks. That was why I wanted Jenny not to come with me. If things turned ugly at least she would be safe, and who knows, maybe she could phone the police if it was necessary. One way or another, I had resolved to get to the bottom of this mystery, even if I had to clamber over Manthorpe's hedge and confront them. I retraced my steps back to the car and drove down the lane to the Manthorpe Farm entrance, where I stopped and phoned Manthorpe.

"Hi, Mr Manthorpe, it's Dan Curran. I'm at the entrance to your farm. Can I go across to the corner of your field to get a better look at what's going on next door?"

"Aye, lad. That's no problem. I'll come and join yer... if yer wants, like?"

"If you're willing to, that would be good, but just to warn you, it could turn nasty. I don't know what they're up to, but I'm pretty certain it won't be ditching."

"Best I do come then. Drive up the road till yer sees a large oak tree on the left-hand side. Stop there and wait for me."

Although I wasn't sure how effective he would be if it came to a violent confrontation, I nevertheless felt comforted by the prospect of some moral support. I followed his instructions and drove up the track, trying hard to avoid the numerous potholes and keep out of the ruts. There were fields on either side of the track, with wooden fences to keep in the livestock. A few moments later as I parked up by the tree, I saw Manthorpe coming down the track towards me on a muddy quad bike. Despite it being a warm late-summer morning, he was still dressed in the same ancient woolly jumper and wearing the same woollen hat. He stopped the bike in front of me and took a shotgun from a wooden box-like carrier on the rear of the machine. Maybe I had been too hasty in dismissing the support he could provide after all, although what he might do with the gun was a bit worrying.

Without a word he climbed over the fence and indicated I should follow. For a man of advancing years, I was amazed at how nimble he was. I did my best to climb the fence with equal aplomb, but failed miserably as my jeans snagged on a protruding splinter of wood. Fortunately, Manthorpe's focus remained on the far side of the field as I cursed and struggled to release myself. Just now I really didn't want to live up to the clueless city-boy stereotype.

As we walked across the field, I noticed that we weren't alone. There were maybe two dozen cows grazing, all of which turned to see what was so important as to interrupt the serious process of chewing grass. Now I have to admit that I am not good with cows. Spiders, rats, horses, snakes even… no problem. But cows are strange, enigmatic creatures, big, powerful and utterly unpredictable. And, in my own experience, able to smell fear at a hundred paces. However, at the sight of Manthorpe approaching, this lot just turned away in total disinterest and resumed their rumination. I tried desperately not to make eye contact with the animals as we walked through the middle of the herd and quietly approached the hedge which was adjacent to the corner of Abbot's

Meadow. Most of the hedgerow was a couple of metres high, but there was a short section that was a bit lower, which we might be able to see over. I was guessing that this was where Manthorpe originally challenged the men supposedly doing ditching, only to get a foul-mouthed tirade in return.

We edged our way along towards the lower section, and I could see and hear through the brambles that the digger was very close. A man was standing alongside the bucket of the digger directing operations. I recognised him as Josh Townsend, one of the Hepworth thugs who tried to evict the Travellers Mickey and Rosa from the meadow. As the arm of the digger swung round to empty the bucket, I could see that the digger driver was the repugnant Dean Lockwood, his heavily tattooed muscular arms protruding from a white vest.

Although there was a drainage ditch that ran alongside the hedgerow, the digger bucket was in fact creating a separate trench a few metres away. This trench was about three metres long by a metre and a half wide, and looked to be currently around a metre deep. The soil which had been removed had been expertly piled up alongside. Lockwood once more lowered the bucket into the trench and began retracting the arm to scrape out yet more soil when Townsend raised an arm signalling that excavation should stop.

As the noise from the digger engine died away, an eerie silence descended. Manthorpe and I both looked at each other and moved a little closer to get a better view, intrigued to discover what had been found. I panicked as I remembered my mobile phone, and hurriedly switched it to vibrate mode. The last thing we needed just now was my 'Smoke on the Water' ringtone as Jack returned my call. While I had the phone out, I quickly texted Jenny.

You OK?

Almost immediately an answer came back.

Yes... take care x

I looked at the bend of the hedge where she was hiding, relieved that she couldn't be seen.

Lockwood jumped down into the trench and started to remove more earth with a shovel, obviously working his way around some sort of object. After maybe ten minutes, he indicated that Townsend should join him, and together they wrestled what appeared to be a large roll of carpet out of the trench. They laid the carpet down alongside the trench and stood back to recover from their exertions.

At this point they were joined by a third person who got out of the truck, mobile phone in hand, and obviously deep in conversation. When he turned, I could see it was Simon Kendall, the third of the trio who I had previously encountered on the meadow. Then, Kendall rang off and the three of them stood alongside the object talking. We could hear the voices but, frustratingly, it was impossible to make out what they were saying.

Manthorpe and I exchanged glances, wondering what was going on. After a few minutes I began to wonder if he would decide that this was unproductive when he had a farm to run, animals to tend, sheep to shear... or whatever. These three didn't appear to be in any sort of hurry. Townsend lit up a cigarette. Someone cracked a joke and they all laughed. It was almost as though they were waiting for something... or someone!

I suddenly had a terrible sense that my plan was about to go horribly wrong, and that Jenny might not be safe where she was. I took my phone out and texted her again.

> Get out of the field now... and wait where we parked the car. I'll pick you up.

But it was too late. I looked across to the unfolding scene on the other side of Abbot's Meadow in total disbelief. A large black Audi SUV had appeared around the bend in the hedgerow, coming up fast across the field to where Jenny was. It was Chris Hepworth, and he had obviously seen her. Manthorpe picked up on my distress and looked at me for an explanation, but my mind was in a whirl, and conversation eluded me.

As we watched, the Audi pulled up abruptly and Chris Hepworth jumped out, leaving the door wide open. I could now see Jenny, who had broken cover and was running back towards the field entrance as fast as she could. But her flimsy sandals were intended for the beach, not for running across a bumpy grass field. Hepworth set off in chase and in no time had caught up with her, rugby-tackling her roughly to the ground.

Jenny was struggling and put up a good fight, but Hepworth was too strong for her, and in no mood to be nice. He hit her across the face and then manhandled her back to the car with her arms pinned behind her. I was more angry than I had ever experienced, and had I been able, I didn't doubt that I could at that moment have killed Hepworth with my bare hands. But I was not with Jenny, protecting her when she needed me. I was stuck behind an impenetrable hedge, frantic with concern for her, and with a mile drive between us. The girl I loved was being violently attacked and it was all my fault!

We watched helplessly as Hepworth lifted the tailgate of the Audi, brutally bundled Jenny into the boot, and slammed the tailgate down again. Manthorpe looked at me earnestly and said quietly so as not to be overheard, "Don't yer think we needs to get the police here, and quick, like? We're no match for this lot. These bastards mean business!"

He was right of course. I was completely out of my depth now and needed help big time. But if the police arrived, sirens blaring, it might warn Hepworth and his men, giving them just enough notice to escape. What they would do to Jenny didn't bear thinking about. She was at least safe as long as she was locked in the boot of the Audi and the Audi remained in the field.

No, what we needed was a quiet approach. And we did have one thing going for us. They didn't know that Manthorpe and I were watching their every move, and so might not be in an almighty hurry to leave. I thought of PC Griffiths, who was so helpful on the last occasion, and had given me his mobile number. I moved back from the hedge and dialled his number, desperately hoping he would be on duty.

After a couple of rings he picked up, and I immediately recognised the Welsh lilt in his voice.

"PC 267 Griffiths. Who am I speaking with?"

"Evan. It's Dan Curran from the *Gazette*… we've met a couple of times, once on Abbot's Meadow, if you recall?"

If he did recall, he didn't let on, so I continued breathlessly. "Well, it's a long story, but I'm at Abbot's Meadow again and those scumbags you sent packing last time are back here, and they mean business. They have just kidnapped my girlfriend and put her in a car boot. I'm really concerned for her safety. Also, I now have proof that these guys are involved in criminal activity involving Class B drugs at the very least, and probably much more."

"So exactly where are you?" he asked, obviously sceptical, and wondering why I was busy phoning rather than trying to rescue Jenny. "And, more to the point, why have they kidnapped your girlfriend?"

"I'm looking on from a field next door with the farmer, but the only way I can get there is by road, and it's about a mile away. My girlfriend was hiding in Abbot's Meadow, but they've rumbled her, and are probably going to use her as a hostage to get at me. The problem is I'm well outnumbered... there are four of them this time. I didn't want to dial 999 because it all sounds a bit far-fetched, but you know what they're like. Can you drum up some support and get here quickly... and quietly?"

It all sounded so garbled and unlikely. The line went silent for a few moments as PC Griffiths tried to decide whether I was under the influence of drink or drugs, possibly both, or maybe just delusional. Mercifully, he came to the conclusion that, far-fetched though it all sounded, I might actually be telling the truth.

"As it happens, I'm only a few miles away. We've just about finished up here dealing with an RTA. I'll report this in and get clearance to meet you there. Just don't go taking the law into your own hands. Understand?"

"Agreed, but please be quick!"

The line went dead. I looked across at Manthorpe and he gestured for me to join him again. The Audi was now parked alongside the truck, and Chris Hepworth was helping

Lockwood load the roll of carpet onto the back of the truck. Meanwhile, Townsend was in the digger, refilling the trench. It looked as though they were preparing to leave. I signalled to Manthorpe that I was going back to the car and ran across the field, daring any of the cows to stand in my way.

I had no idea how long it would take for the police to arrive and was worried sick that Hepworth would drive off with Jenny still locked in the boot. Reluctantly, I came to the conclusion that I once more needed some cavalry support, and phoned Bob Coldwell. Sadly, the call went straight to voicemail, but then again, it was well before eight o'clock on a Saturday morning. I didn't know whether he and his men would be working, although if they were, then an early start was not unusual in the building trade. I left a brief message and rang off.

On the drive back down the rough farm track to the road all I could think about was Jenny, and whether she was okay. Although I had never been especially religious, I found myself praying that she wasn't hurt and had sufficient air in such a confined space. It must be terrifying for her.

Back on the road I floored the accelerator and arrived back at the entrance to Abbot's Meadow within a couple of minutes. Common sense told me that I should wait at the gate for the police to arrive. If I blocked the gate with my car they couldn't get out. But I needed to try to help Jenny. She was all that mattered right now. I drove straight through the gate and onto the field, throwing caution to the wind. I was aware that I could now be seen, and hoped that the police wouldn't be too long in joining me. The uneven grass proved to be challenging for the little wheels on my Mini, and I was being thrown around wildly as the car bumped and pitched its way across the undulating ground. I made my way straight for the vehicles on the far side. The Audi was now parked behind the truck.

Chris Hepworth appeared alongside the Audi, and stood watching my approach, hands on hips, no doubt savouring the moment when he could at last get his hands on me. I considered driving straight into him, but knew in my heart that I couldn't bring myself to do this. Despite my bravado, I was not a murderer. I stopped short and got out.

"Let her out!" I shouted.

"Er… no, I don't think I will. So, let's see what you're going to do about it, shall we?"

He was smiling, but again the eyes told a different story. He started to walk towards me, banging one of his fists into the palm of the other hand, as if pumping up his aggression levels, and then stopped dead as he looked past me towards the field entrance. I turned around to see two police cars making their way across the grass at speed.

"Oh, you bastard!" he snarled, swivelling around to shout to the others, "It's the rozzers. Get the hell out of here!"

Hepworth jumped into the Audi, reversed back, and swung the car around to head off across the field, away from the oncoming police cars. Lockwood unhitched the trailer from the truck, and his mates piled in. Evidently, they were prepared to abandon the trailer and digger in their attempt to get away, but before they could move the truck there was a loud bang, followed a fraction of a second later by an even louder bang as the front offside tyre of the truck exploded. Behind the truck I could now see the barrel of Manthorpe's shotgun over the top of the hedge, with smoke drifting away in the breeze. The old boy's quick thinking had put paid to any chances of their escape. In that moment I could have kissed him, shaggy beard and all.

One of the police cars veered off in pursuit of the Audi, but unfortunately, the Skoda patrol car was no match for the powerful four-wheel-drive SUV in either speed or manoeuvrability on such terrain. The Audi snaked its way around the police car back towards the field entrance. It looked as though Chris Hepworth was going to get away! I couldn't believe my eyes. He was about to disappear with my precious Jenny.

However, incredibly, it looked as though my own private cavalry had once more come to the rescue. The gateway was now blocked by a blue van, in front of which stood three men. I could make out the white hard hats and blue overalls of Bob Coldwell and his chums. The Audi came to an abrupt halt in front of the entrance, and the men moved in quickly to extract Hepworth, none too gently, from the driver's seat.

Just then my phone vibrated, and I saw that it was Jack, returning my call.

"What's up, Dan? Have there been any developments?" he said.

"Um, yes... you could say that," I replied.

*

Ten minutes or so later we were all assembled over in the corner of the field beside the partly refilled trench and damaged truck. With a little assistance from Bob's boys, PC Griffiths and his three colleagues had handcuffed Hepworth and his three friends, and released Jenny from the boot of the Audi. She was very shaken, but remained head held high, gloriously defiant. She was definitely not going to be a victim. Her cheek was red where Hepworth had struck her, but otherwise seemed physically okay. We hugged each other, and I apologised to her for the hundredth time. Bob and his mates stood back watching proceedings, no doubt pleased that they had been able to play their part.

"Right," said PC Griffiths, notebook in hand. "So, who's going to tell me exactly what is going on here?"

To my surprise, Jenny spoke first. "Before we start, there's something I'd like to say to this gentleman here," she said, lacing the word 'gentleman' with heavy sarcasm.

She walked over to Chris Hepworth, placed a hand on each of his shoulders and moved close, almost as though she were about to kiss him. As she looked him straight in the eyes she brought her knee up sharply into his groin, causing him to let out a yowl of pain and bend over double. *That's my girl*, I thought proudly.

"Oh dear," Jenny said, walking back to stand beside me, her hand reaching out for mine. "It's completely slipped my mind now. That's women for you."

PC Griffiths tried to smother a smile as he said, "That's quite enough of that, young lady."

It was time for me to see whether my suspicions were correct. The drop-side of the truck was folded down, and I noticed that the muddy roll of carpet was now sitting on the flat bed. I turned to Bob and said, "Would you and your guys be so kind as to lift down that roll of carpet from the back of the truck?"

They quickly obliged, jumping up and manhandling the carpet down onto the ground.

"And if you could unroll it for us?"

The carpet was caked in mud and stuck together, but the three of them pushed and it began to unroll. Inside the carpet there were areas where a blue, green and cream criss-crossed pattern showed through the mud, but then a noticeable darkening suggested that there was something rotten inside.

An audible gasp came from several of the bystanders as the decaying remains of a human body were revealed. The grotesque image of a head, with some remnants of hair and decomposing flesh protruding above a grotesquely twisted body seared itself into my retinas. One side of the skull bore a large depression suggesting that it had received a forceable blow, either from striking – or being struck by – a blunt object. The corpse's lips and facial flesh had all but disappeared, and the rictus grin of teeth and hollowed-out eyes made it hard to comprehend that the thing before us was once a living, breathing person. Although I had anticipated this, the sight was still deeply shocking, and I felt physically sick. The remains of clothes were draped over a putrefied skeletal frame. One of the feet, still in its shoe, had separated from the leg, probably caused by the unrolling action. It was hideous… truly the very stuff of nightmares.

Jenny turned away unable to bear the sight any longer. I looked away also, desperately fighting the urge to throw up. After a few gulps of air to try to alleviate the feeling of nausea, I was able to continue.

"The sale of this land, Abbot's Meadow, was turned down on the basis that it is ostensibly the site of an Anglo-Saxon graveyard. The one bit of that argument which is evidently true was that this field is a graveyard, but not for the Anglo-Saxons. This sorry sight before you, I believe, is the mortal remains of one Paul Connolly, previously a director of Hepworth Landscaping. Furthermore, I suspect that Paul was killed by one or more of these men you have here because he threatened to blow the whistle on their illegal drugs operation. They managed to convince his estranged wife that he had emigrated to the States, so there was no one to worry at his disappearance. My guess is that they buried him here thinking that the field would remain in agricultural use and the body would never be found. Fortunately, that was a miscalculation. What they hadn't reckoned on was the council looking to sell the land, and Bob Coldwell and a housing association developing building plans! If you think back to when you last met them, Evan, the reason they were so uptight with the Travellers was that, quite by chance, they had previously dug a latrine close to this spot."

I looked across at Chris Hepworth, expecting to see an emotion of some sort… rage, defeat, fear even. However, his face remained totally impassive, or was that the trace of a smirk? Was he actually laughing at me? I found this unnerving, and cast a glance at PC Griffiths, hoping that he had fully bought in to my big reveal.

PC Griffiths had the look of a man suddenly out of his depth. He walked a little way away from the scene and spoke into his radio. He was going to need help. A lot of help.

CHAPTER 21

From that moment on things happened very quickly, and it all became a bit surreal, like watching a high-octane television police drama unfold before our eyes. Over the course of the next half hour more police vehicles arrived including a forensic team and an incident control centre van. Access to Abbot's Meadow was secured with blue and white tapes as a major crime scene was declared. Everywhere there were officers in hi-viz jackets and men in white overalls complete with masks, gloves and overshoes examining the corpse and conducting fingertip searches of the area. A police photographer was taking photographs of the body and the trench.

Chris Hepworth and his men were arrested on suspicion of murder, and taken away for questioning. Jenny and I were eventually taken to the police station for statements, a process which was to last for the rest of the day. The police wanted Jenny to go to hospital to be checked over, but she insisted that she was okay. In truth, the events of the last hour or so had taken their toll on both Jenny and me, and neither of us felt like talking as we sat holding hands in the back of the patrol car.

My main emotion was one of relief. Relief because Jenny seemed to be okay, and relief that the Abbot's Meadow question which had so preoccupied me since joining the *Gazette* now appeared to be answered.

At Castlebridge Police Station we were shown into a small, sparsely furnished interview room, where we were joined by a man in civilian dress who introduced himself as Detective Constable Nick Grant. He was probably in his late twenties and seemed relaxed and friendly, although a bit too laddish to my mind. He wore a neat, but inexpensive, grey suit and a light blue shirt which was let down by a crumpled collar and poorly tied dark blue tie. He had all the self-assurance of a man who knew he was good at his job, but I wondered whether his cockiness would cause him to struggle in later life when it came to promotion. No sooner had we sat down than the door opened and Jack was shown into the room, complete with Paul Connolly's laptop computer under his arm and the two copies of the Douglas report, one genuine, one falsified in a plastic wallet. Jack looked at Jenny's red cheek.

"What on earth happened? I got your message… too late, obviously."

"Hi, Jack. It's a long story, but I think we had better start at the beginning, for the benefit of Detective Grant here," I said.

And so with the interview recorder running, that's just what we did, starting with my visit to see Councillor Sid Chisholm. As I related all the events leading up to the discovery of Paul's body, the policeman's eyes widened slightly. If he was surprised by any of it, he certainly did his best not to let on. If it weren't for the fact that a very real dead body had indeed been uncovered, he would probably have dismissed my testimony as the delusional ramblings of a young and overactive imagination. Jack chipped in occasionally with small items of detail or context, all of which seemed to imbue my investigations with a sense of direction and logic which I certainly don't remember feeling at the time. We fired up the laptop and showed Grant the pictures of the Hepworths' drug factory and the desperate email to Connolly's friend, Ryan.

As the story unfolded I became increasingly concerned that we had no hard evidence to connect Sam Hepworth with growing cannabis illegally or the death of Paul Connolly. We only had the word of Kevin Handleigh that he was involved in falsifying the Douglas report. I thought of Jim Symonds and his fear that this might ultimately be the outcome. When the police got around to inspecting Sam's finances, whether they would discover that he received a lucrative income from the sale of cannabis depended on how clever he had been in covering his tracks.

I was certain that Sam knew about Paul Connolly's death, even if he had not, as I suspected, been personally involved. Having brushed with Chris Hepworth, I was also in no doubt that he had, either in cold blood or unintentionally, killed Paul Connolly and buried the body in Abbot's Meadow. Brother Sam had come to his aid and tried to prevent the field being sold and the body discovered. But if misleading the council was the most Sam could be charged with, then proper justice for Paul Connolly would be denied.

There was also no doubt in my mind that Chris Hepworth had tried, unsuccessfully, to take the life of Kevin Handleigh, most likely by engaging the services of a third party in a hit-and-run. I explained how Handleigh fitted into the picture and suggested that Chris Hepworth's mobile phone records might help track down the driver of the car.

Detective Grant informed us that Chris Hepworth and his three employees had all been remanded in police custody pending further investigations, and were currently being interrogated separately. In an off-the-record comment he added that treating the murder as a joint enterprise might help to uncover the principal offender. It all depended on whether any of them were prepared to spill the beans in the hope of a lighter sentence.

"Do you think they will be let out on bail?" asked Jenny, who was no doubt concerned about the prospect of bumping into Chris Hepworth. He would have painful memories of her last contact with him in the trouser department, not to mention his hurt pride.

Grant gave a half-hearted laugh.

"Knowing our custody officer, I should say there's about as much chance of that as a snowball in hell. For one thing, they've all got previous for violence, as you somehow seem to have already established." Grant looked at me enquiringly, and I looked at Jack. Jack looked at his shoes and chose to keep quiet.

He continued, "So, there is clearly a potential danger to the public. And don't forget we are dealing with a suspected murder here. There is also the strong possibility that they would do a runner given half a chance. No, we'll hold them on suspicion of murder, and put a file together for the CPS. The CPS will decide whether there is sufficient evidence for them to be charged with murder, and if so they will go to the magistrates' court, probably tomorrow morning… or the day after if we need to get an extension. The outcome will almost certainly be that bail is refused, and as this is an indictable offence, the magistrates will pass the case to the Crown Court, and the suspects will be remanded in custody pending trial. And, from what you have told me, it sounds as though we could later be making further charges for the production of cannabis, attempted kidnapping, assault, resisting arrest and the unlawful burial of a body, to name just a few."

A worrying thought suddenly flashed into my head. Suppose that the body was not in fact Paul Connolly, hard as that was to believe based on the evidence? That would throw a whole toolbox worth of spanners into the works.

"How will you determine the identity of the body?" I asked.

Grant read my worried expression and said, "Don't worry. That's usually the easy bit nowadays. With DNA profiling we can usually establish the victim's identity fairly quickly. Failing that, dental records are often a good fall-back, but I doubt that will be necessary. There will also be a Home Office post-mortem which, from the photographs I've seen of the body, should establish beyond doubt the cause of death. That can sometimes reveal extra identification details, dependent on the state of the body."

I told Grant about the bag of Paul's possessions at Dawn Wincott's B&B, which included a hairbrush from which hair samples could be obtained. The poor lady was going to have a fit when police arrived on her doorstep.

*

It was gone five o'clock in the afternoon before our statements were prepared and signed, and we were finally finished at the police station. It was the first time I had seen Jack look tired, and he was in a hurry to get back home. Jenny and I were both ravenous, having existed on nothing but coffee and a few biscuits since we woke up.

"Well, at times like this it's got to be fast food," said Jenny as we got into the Mini. "Plenty of calories, lots of grease to help it slide down."

We drove to McDonald's and were soon tucking into burgers and fries. It had been an eventful and incredibly stressful day. We'd both seen sights that would no doubt come back later to haunt us in our dreams. And my lovely Jenny had been struck and bundled into a car boot while I watched helplessly from a distance. Her cheek was still red and there was now the beginning of a black eye developing. Again, I felt an overwhelming sense of guilt that I wasn't able to protect her, and blamed myself for separating from her when we first got to Abbot's Meadow. I didn't dare think about what her father's reaction was going to be.

As we ate there wasn't much talking, but there was plenty of eye contact. Something had definitely changed between us. As she chewed, I felt that Jenny was almost looking into my soul with those big brown eyes, completely oblivious to her surroundings.

"Penny for them," I said, anxious to check that we were still good.

She smiled and put her hand on top of mine. "I was just thinking that, as we were originally intending to spend the day at the coast, my dad won't be expecting us to get back until later this evening. So we have a few hours to… amuse ourselves." There was a twinkle in her eye. Now I understood.

"Ah," I said, giving an acting masterclass of the penny dropping. "If I didn't know better, Miss Swan, I might be thinking that you are trying to seduce me."

She leaned forward, kissed me on the lips and stood up ready to go. "Best get your skates on then, sunshine. You really shouldn't keep a lady waiting."

*

I think we were both still smiling as we stood at the door of Jenny's house, preparing to confront her father. Given what had happened to her, and the horrors she had witnessed during the day, the both of us grinning like a pair of Cheshire cats was not going to be a good look.

Two hours ago, we had been energetically and passionately making love in the single bed at my flat, which proved to be the perfect antidote to a nightmarish day. It wasn't the first time for either of us, but for me it was unquestionably the first time it had been not just physical, but almost spiritual. Afterwards, as we lay blissfully in each other's arms, intoxicated by the afterglow of such an intense emotional and physical release, I knew that this was the person I was meant to be with. She completed me, gave my life purpose. From this point on I simply couldn't imagine a life without her.

But now, as we looked at each other, with Jenny trying to summon up the courage to put the door key in the lock, I was not at all confident that Harry Swan was going to see things in quite the same way. I put my hand under her chin and raised her head to examine her eye, which had a blue arc around the lower lid. There was no escaping the fact that his precious daughter had been injured on my watch. The evidence was there to see, as was the person responsible.

"Maybe he won't notice," she said without a shred of conviction.

"You think?" I said, dreading the inevitable questions that were coming my way.

We entered the living room to find Harry watching a football match on the TV. He looked up and greeted us, looked back at the screen, and then in a double-take, back at Jenny's face.

"What's happened? Your cheek is red... and your eye? Are you alright?" Harry looked at me inquisitively, his eyes making it clear an urgent explanation was required.

"It's okay, Dad," said Jenny. "We've had a bit of a challenging day. When you've finished with your football, we'll tell you all about it."

Harry reached for the remote control, turned off the TV and looked at Jenny with concern writ large across his face.

"I think you'd better tell me now, love."

So, for the second time that day, I started at the beginning and recounted everything that had happened... with the exception of the last couple of hours. Harry listened intently, looking alternately from me to Jenny, as though the two of us were playing tennis with some invisible ball. Occasionally Jenny interrupted, impressing on her father that she had been a willing accomplice to everything that had happened, despite my trying to keep her out of it. Harry's eyebrows rose in concern when we related our clandestine operation to find out what was in the greenhouses behind Chris Hepworth's house. And as I described the events on Abbot's Meadow that morning, his look of concern was replaced by outright shock, and maybe anger.

When we got to the point where we left the police station, Jenny looked across at me and smiled knowingly. I think Harry was too dumbstruck to notice, and just sat there staring at Jenny.

I found the silence unnerving.

"I'm really sorry, Mr Swan," I said, needing to break the silence. I felt overwhelmingly that I'd let him down in not protecting his daughter and keeping her out of harm's way. That's when I noticed that his eyes were glistening with tears welling up. Jenny noticed also, and went over to sit beside him, putting her arm around his shoulders lovingly.

"It's okay, Dad. I'm not hurt… and the bad guys are all in police cells."

Regrettably, that wasn't quite accurate. There was still one very bad guy likely to remain at large in the shape of Sam Hepworth, free at least for the moment to give us both a hard time. But this was definitely not the time to be negative.

Harry wiped his eyes. After a few moments to regain his composure, he looked at his daughter and spoke.

"You know, I've never told you this, but before we were married, your mum and I went and worked as volunteers at a kibbutz in Israel for a few months. It was what you did in those days. Nowadays kids go off on gap years, just touring the world and finding themselves. But back then, when you were young and radical, with strong socialist principles, that was the thing to do. And it was great. We had a wonderful time there, and it was one of the early shared experiences we both treasured. But there was a problem with a thief in the women's dormitory. Your mum was bothered a lot by it because most people there had very little money, and it was supposed to be a loving, sharing, caring community. She eventually caught the thief red-handed and made her put the money back, but not before there was a scuffle and punches were thrown. Your mum proudly sported a black eye for a week or two after that. She wasn't in the slightest bit bothered. Justice had prevailed. The culprit was exposed and made to apologise in front of everyone. In fact, your mum and the person involved became friends. When you came in and I saw your face, it took me right back…"

Harry was choked up and couldn't finish. It was such a touching thing to see and brought a lump to my throat. Eventually, after much hugging with Jenny, he looked across at me.

"Well, Dan, I'm not sure what to say to you. Do I hold you responsible for my daughter being hurt? Well, yes, I suppose I do. Could you have done anything to prevent it? I very much doubt it. Jenny is her mother's daughter. I see Debby in her every day, and never more than I do today. I'm just thankful she is with someone who appreciates that free spirit, that fearless determination to uphold what's right and good, which Jenny has in spades – like her mother had."

I couldn't argue with that.

*

Dusk was approaching as I said goodbye to Jenny and her dad and got into the Mini. I was overwhelmingly tired, but sat there for a few moments, troubled. When I was recounting the events of the day earlier to both DC Grant and Harry, on each occasion I got the strong feeling that I was missing something obvious. But what was it?

I thought again about watching Paul Connolly's body being uncovered. It was such a gruesome sight, holding my focus in a sort of morbid fascination, neither wanting to look... nor look away. I tried to replay the moment in my mind, but this time trying to recall as much of the whole picture as I could. What remained of the clothing did not appear to be especially remarkable or incongruous in any way. There were no objects visible on, or around, the body. But I was sure there was something I was just not seeing.

Some detail that was hiding in plain sight, if only I could figure out what it was.

And then it hit me! I knew what it was I had witnessed, but not properly noted. I started the car and set off for Sam Hepworth's house, hoping to get there while there was still some light. I didn't have a plan, and was not sure exactly how I was going to confront him, but seeing brother Chris in handcuffs had emboldened me. I was going to nail Sam Hepworth, or die trying. But with Jenny in my thoughts, I decided the first option was definitely preferable.

The light was fading fast as I got to the house, and rather than stop further down the road and sneak in as I did last time, I decided to be bold and pulled into the long drive. With his brother in police custody, I was suddenly not the least bit scared of Sam Hepworth. In fact, I was hoping I would be the first to tell him about Chris.

There was a large red van parked in front of the house with the rear doors open. A tall, thin-faced lugubrious-looking man wearing a flat cap was leaning against one of the doors. He watched me impassively as I pulled up behind the van. He was smoking in that weird way, where the cigarette is held in reverse with the tip pointing towards the palm of the hand. At each lungful of smoke, his eyes screwed up as though he was in great pain, only to be relieved by blowing out a plume of smoke, his body anxious to rid itself of this noxious substance. I decided that I would act as though I had every right to be there. I got out and approached him.

"What's going on? Is Sam having even more work done on the house? He's always spending a shitload of money. Dunno where he gets it all from."

"You can say that again!" agreed the man, his face lighting

up just a smidgen as he realised I might be a kindred spirit. "I mean, this stuff's still perfectly good. Why he wants it all taken out, and at this time on a Saturday night, is a mystery. Bloody daft if you ask me. More bleedin' money than sense. And his missus is in there doin' her nut. Still, the boss says that Sam is happy to pay us double time, so who am I to argue? Billy nobody, that's me."

I made as if to go to the front door and then turned back towards the van, noting that the writing on the side announced 'Carmichael Floorings – Established 1975' in large gold lettering.

"Just out of curiosity, what is it you're taking out?"

He stood back and pointed to the floor of the van where there were several rolls of carpet. My heart skipped a beat.

"Which one is it, not that really nice crimson one, I hope?" I asked, feigning an intimate knowledge of the house.

"Nah… it's this one what we put in only last year."

He unrolled a little of the carpet to reveal a tartan design in blue, green and cream. A design that I had seen twice before. Once when I had been in Sam Hepworth's study confronting him about his brother's behaviour towards me, and once a few hours ago wrapped around a human corpse.

Obviously, the news of the discovery of Paul Connolly's body had reached Sam, and he realised he could be implicated. Removing any traces of the carpet so urgently was an act of desperation… a race against time before the police arrived to talk with Sam, which they most surely would.

Trying to suppress my excitement, I observed, "Oh, that one."

"Yeah. Three bleedin' rooms of it, and we've got to replace it all with this beige stuff tonight, can you believe? Why it couldn't wait, Christ only knows. Says he's got some important visitors on Monday and wants the place looking its best. I guess when you've got that much money you can do anything you want."

"Is it very expensive then? Always looked a bit naff to me, him being from Yorkshire, not Scotland."

"Bloody well is! We had to get it specially made by a company in Scotland. A hundred and fifty quid a square metre, made to order. I mean who pays 150 quid a metre and then bins it after a year? Sam didn't know it cost that much, mind you. His missus was in charge and made us promise not to tell him… I bet she's told him now though. You should hear the barney goin' off in there! Cussin' and blindin'. Not very ladylike if you ask me. Come out 'ere for a bit of peace and quiet, I did. Give me earholes a rest."

I nodded sympathetically. "As a matter of interest, when you fitted the carpet originally, was there any left over?"

The man lifted up his cap and scratched his mousey hair.

"Now I think of it, there was quite a large piece. He got us to put it in his garage. Said it might come in useful if they had an accident, or that dog of theirs crapped all over it."

Just then another man came out of the front door and stood with his hands on his hips, visibly annoyed by his colleague. He was older and more brawny than his mate, and had sweat on his brow.

"There you are! Why are you out here? Quit gassing and get your arse in here! I need some help lifting this last one."

The man looked at me curiously, and then back to his mate, perhaps in search of an explanation. After a few seconds, it was obvious this wasn't going to happen, and he disappeared back into the house, grumbling as he went.

Flat-cap man looked even more miserable as he dropped his cigarette, ground it under his boot and made his way inside the house, muttering to himself. "Well, once more into the… wotsit."

I had seen enough. It was time for me to leave while the going was good. The longer I stayed, the more chance I had of being confronted by Sam Hepworth's dog. I pulled out my phone and took a couple of photos of the carpet. When I got home I would email these to DC Grant.

As I drove back home, I smiled to myself. So, Sam Hepworth had supplied the carpet used in the burial of Paul Connolly, not realising that it wasn't an off-the-shelf item, and that it could be directly traced back to him. I would love to have seen his face when his wife told him the carpet was specially made and totally unique.

Sam would have known that Abbot's Meadow was owned by the council and probably thought that it would be a safe place to dispose of the body. And there would be nobody to see or object to the presence of his men and their equipment. No doubt he was trying to save his brother from being tried for murder, either out of brotherly love, or more likely the thought that their nice-little-earner drugs operation might come to a sudden end.

Maybe the carpet was not definitive proof that Sam either took part in, or was an accessory to, a murder, but as circumstantial evidence goes, it looked pretty strong to me. Maybe Kevin Handleigh might be persuaded to testify against Sam, although I was guessing that he would prefer to keep a low profile. Once Sam's finances had been crawled over by an expert, I felt sure the police could put together a case that would see him put behind bars for some time.

CHAPTER 22

I arrived at the office on Monday morning full of enthusiasm for the job, for life, for love. Everything seemed to be working out just fine and I felt on top of the world. I couldn't wait to get cracking with Jack on deciding what to run in the paper… and when. Timing was everything in such situations, and we needed to plan the phased release of the story over a number of days to get good traction among the readership. This was going to be one of the biggest stories the *Gazette* had run for some years.

However, my bubble of joy was about to be unceremoniously burst. Jack called me into his office.

"I've just been speaking with the police," he said, indicating that I should take a seat. "It seems that the DNA from the hairbrush and the body did not match. Although they have only got the results of the rapid test so far, and still need to wait for the full forensic test, the results seem to be pretty conclusive. The police also obtained some other physical characteristics from the body for corroboration. They don't believe that the body you uncovered was that of Paul Connolly after all!"

Jack watched me carefully, his fingers steepled together, his face expressionless. He was no doubt interested to know how I would react. A test of my resilience.

I felt as though I had been punched in the gut. It appeared that all of my ace detective work which had led me so surely to the one inescapable conclusion, the only possible interpretation which fitted all of the facts, the logical explanation which made perfect sense, was in fact complete fiction! I suddenly felt rather foolish. Like a boy caught unsuccessfully trying to do a man's job. After a few seconds I summoned up enough composure to be able to at least respond like an adult.

"Seriously? I can scarcely believe it. So who the hell was it that they dug up?"

"Good question. However, the fact that this Hepworth gang set out to deliberately dig up a body bearing all the indications of having been murdered will ensure they are kept under lock and key while further investigations establish the identity of the person."

"So, if Paul Connolly is still alive, and he didn't go to the States, maybe he just decided to disappear and start a new life?" I ventured, even now struggling to come to terms with the news. I remembered the look on Chris Hepworth's face during my graveside exposé and realised that he was actually amused by my miscalculation.

"Looks like you've got more work to do," said Jack with a knowing glint in his eye. I had the distinct feeling that he was quietly enjoying seeing the enthusiasm of youth brought down to earth with a bump. This was how journalism was meant to be… lots of graft and sweat, punctuated with setbacks and red herrings.

When I got back to my desk, I jotted down the different pieces of information I had discovered and mentally tried rearranging them into a narrative that pointed towards a different conclusion. However, I still had two pieces of information which didn't fit anywhere:

1. Paul Connolly had taken a photograph of a man with a Blaze Storage and Logistics van… loading bags marked Castlebridge Hospice.
2. Before his disappearance, Paul Connolly had reached out to someone called Ryan who was an old school friend.

At the moment, I couldn't do much about the second point, so I decided that it was time I paid Blaze Storage and Logistics a visit.

*

I pulled into the industrial estate and as I drove past Castle Cardstock, I noticed that the fire had resulted in quite severe damage to about half of the warehouse section. The Blaze premises were identical in arrangement – a small two-storey office block at one end butting up against a large warehouse. Fortunately, there were several empty visitor car parking spaces.

I pushed the intercom button and announced my arrival. I had made an appointment to meet the managing director, a Mr Dimitris Castellanos, who, according to the secretary, would be delighted to see me. The door lock clicked and I entered into a small, tidy reception area with a desk and visitor book. A very pleasant young lady with long dark hair, Mediterranean looks and a stunning smile came down the stairs to greet me. She looked as though she could have Greek blood, and I wondered whether she was related to the MD. After I had signed in, she escorted me upstairs to Castellanos's office which was at the end of the corridor.

Castellanos was standing looking through a window behind his desk down onto the warehouse floor and loading bays. He beamed as he held out a hand to greet me.

"Mr Curran. Very nice to meet you, and welcome to Blaze. You've met my daughter Rhea, I see. Please take a seat."

Castellanos was probably in his late fifties but had the bearing of a much younger man. He was lean and handsome in a craggy sort of way, with a deep, even tan. His full head of thick grey hair was matched by a bushy grey moustache. There was still the trace of a Greek accent, but I was guessing he had been in the UK for many years.

"Thank you for seeing me at short notice. I just wanted to ask you a few questions in connection with a story I'm working on," I said, encouraged by the friendliness of his reception.

"That's no problem at all," he replied. "Would you like a coffee?"

"No, I'm fine thanks," I said, not knowing whether I would run out of questions very quickly, in which case a hot coffee would be an embarrassment. The news that I was completely wrong about the Abbot's Meadow body had knocked my confidence for six.

"So how can I help you?"

"Can you tell me what your relationship with Castlebridge Hospice is," I enquired, carefully watching his expression.

"Yes, of course. My business supports the hospice in its fundraising activities. We carry out a doorstep collection service about once every two months, usuualy at weeeknds, delivering plastic sacks and collecting voluntary donations for the charity. Things like clothes, shoes, books and toys. It's something I and my staff feel strongly about, and we all give our time freely to help ensure that this terrific place remains available for those in need. My wife spent some time in there a few years ago, and the staff were simply wonderful."

A veil of sadness passed across his face for a brief moment, and I guessed that the hospice was where his wife passed away. The smile returned almost as fast as it disappeared and he looked at me enquiringly.

"Can I ask why you want to know this?"

I pulled out a paper print of the photograph taken by Paul Connolly showing a man loading bags into a Blaze van, and placed it before him.

"I just wondered whether you recognise this person? We came across this photograph while following up a story which involves a missing person."

He looked at the photograph for no more than a few seconds, and I could see displeasure written across his face. His demeanour changed suddenly, from friendliness to uneasiness.

"I'm afraid I do know who it is. It is a man called Steven Trindle who used to work for me up until about a year ago. I regret I had to sack him. It turned out he was using one of our vans to collect sacks which were… well, shall we say not connected with the hospice. I don't really want to go into detail, I'm afraid. Just take it from me that Blaze is an honourable company, and we expect all our staff to behave with integrity. Regrettably, this individual did not live up to that standard. Can I ask how you came across this picture?"

"It was taken by the person I'm trying to track down. How did you discover what was going on?"

"This isn't the first time I have seen this picture. I got a copy anonymously through the post last year. On the photo was written the date it was taken, which I knew was not an agreed collection date. I approached Steven to clarify what was taking place and he was unable to offer a satisfactory explanation."

"Did you suspect that it had something to do with drugs?"

The bluntness of my question threw him, and his eyes gave

him away. He took a few moments to compose himself, his face now etched with anxiety.

"If I'm honest, yes I did… although I had no proof, you understand? I put two and two together. One of my other drivers had previously complained that there was a strange smell in one of the vans, which he thought was reminiscent of cannabis. I checked the records and it was the same van that Steven had been driving. I asked him outright if he had been distributing cannabis, and he denied it… but he was a really poor liar. I didn't ask any more questions. I just told him he was fired with immediate effect. I should have gone to the police, I know, but I didn't want the good name of Blaze to be tarnished. And equally, I didn't want the reputation of the hospice to be damaged in any way. I just wanted him gone… quickly."

"I quite understand," I replied. "But I'm afraid I am not the only person to have this photograph. The police have it also, and unfortunately you may well be getting a visit from them. It's just that I have had a head start, so to speak. I'm sorry."

Castellanos looked crestfallen, and I couldn't think of any words which would ease his worries.

"Am I going to get into trouble?" he asked.

"Just tell the police exactly what you've told me, and I'm sure it will be okay. Do you know where Steven Trindle lives?"

"Well, I can give you his address when he was working for us, but whether he is still there I have no idea. A few days after he had gone my secretary tried ringing him to discuss some personal possessions he had left behind, but there was no answer. Whether she tried again later I don't know."

He got up from his desk and disappeared down the corridor. I took the opportunity to have a quick look down into the warehouse and was impressed by how efficient and professional it all appeared. At the back half of the building were huge storage racks served by a high-lift forklift truck which trundled up and down the aisles. The front half of the building was devoted to loading bays and there were several vans in the process of being either loaded or unloaded. It looked to be an excellent operation, and I could understand why Castellanos would feel so protective.

A few moments later he returned with a slip of paper on which was written an address and mobile telephone number.

"As far as I know he lived alone and didn't have any close family. As I said, he may not be there anymore."

As he handed me the slip he asked, "Is this all going to come out in the newspaper?"

"I wouldn't worry too much," I replied, not at all sure just what would ever find its way into print. "This is just a tiny part of a much bigger picture, which frankly should be of far greater interest."

I thanked him for his time and co-operation, and made my way back downstairs to the car. I felt saddened by the corrosive effect that a few bad apples could have on those doing their best to be good law-abiding citizens.

I went back to the office and phoned the number that Castellanos had given me for Steven Trindle, only to find that it was no longer in use. I contemplated driving to the address that Castellanos wrote down, but it seemed likely that this would be a wasted journey. I then checked my emails, but still nothing from the mysterious Ryan, Paul Connolly's old school friend. There was no 'failed' error message, so it seemed that the account was probably still active. My email to him had given away very little, so I thought I would raise the stakes and see if that provoked a response.

Hi Ryan

I believe you may know the whereabouts of Paul Connolly. Please tell him that I now know the secret of Abbot's Meadow, what goes on in the Block and why he photographed Steven Trindle. We need to talk urgently. Ask him to phone me on the number below.

Dan

Maybe, just maybe…

*

The sudden noise of my phone ringing made me jump. It was a number I didn't recognise.

"Hello. Dan speaking."

The line remained quiet for a few seconds. I was beginning to think it was maybe some foreign call centre telling me that my computer security had been compromised… or something else equally improbable.

"You sent me an email a few minutes ago. I'm Ryan."

My heart skipped a beat as I realised who it was. It seemed that raising the stakes had paid off.

"Ryan! Am I pleased to hear from you… even though we don't know one another. But you know Paul Connolly, and I feel as though I know him. I've been trying to track him down for some time. I need to talk with him."

There was another long pause, and I had a horrible feeling that we had been cut off… or worse still, he was about to deliberately put the phone down on me. Eventually he broke the silence.

"Paul's in America."

"You and I both know that isn't true."

Jack seemed pretty sure that Paul didn't leave the UK, so I thought I'd chance my arm. There was another silence.

"Are you responsible for the email I got this morning from the police?"

Shit! The police were now on the case and had no doubt scared him.

"Well, in a roundabout way, yes I am, but it's a long story, and let me stress that Paul is in no danger. All I ask is that you give him a message from me. Can you do that?"

"Perhaps," he replied, clearly not yet convinced. "What do you want me to say?"

"Please can you write down what I'm about to tell you?"

"Go ahead."

"Tell Paul that Chris Hepworth and his three employees have all been arrested on suspicion of murder, and other charges including Class B drugs production are about to follow. Sam Hepworth's arrest as accomplice is imminent, if it hasn't already taken place. Tell him that with the help of a key card left in his jeans at the Bentley B&B, I managed to get access to his storage unit. His laptop has been handed over to the police, along with those images he took. Ask him to phone me. Did you get all that?"

"Yes I did. I'll pass the message on, but I'm making no promises. If Paul doesn't want to talk to you… so be it."

Ryan rang off abruptly without waiting for me to reply. I was so close.

CHAPTER 23

The call, when it came, was from Ryan again, not Paul. Apparently, Paul had agreed to meet me at the M6 Knutsford Services Southbound coffee shop at 2pm that afternoon. It looked as though he might still be living somewhere near Manchester where he grew up. Ryan explained that he needed me to email a self-portrait photograph, and said that Paul would make contact with me. It was starting to feel like the script for a second-rate spy movie. After having disappeared for over a year, he was obviously being very guarded about breaking cover.

The first thing I needed to do was phone Laura Connolly to honour my promise that she would be the first to know when I had news of her husband.

*

The motorway traffic was worse than usual, but I arrived with time to spare and made my way to the coffee shop. I had to cross over to the southbound side, which presumably was the direction from which Paul would arrive. I ordered a coffee and sat facing the entrance so that I could observe people coming in. What I hadn't twigged was that I also had been observed as I came in. A voice alongside me made me jump.

"You'll be Dan then… from the *Gazette*? You spoke with Ryan."

I'm not sure what I was expecting, except to say that it wasn't this. He was a tall, handsome forty-something athletic-looking man who could have just stepped out of a shoot for a men's aftershave advert. He had a deep suntan and dark brown hair, which was greying at the temples making him look distinguished, and sported fashionable designer stubble. The bulge of biceps easily discernible beneath his white shirt suggested that he worked out regularly, or at least was no stranger to physical activity.

"Paul, am I glad to meet you!" I said, offering a hand. "You have been a real challenge to track down."

He ignored my outstretched hand and sat down opposite me with an expression bordering on hostile. He obviously hadn't wanted to be found, and now held me responsible for whatever troubles his reappearance would bring.

"Can I get you a drink?" I asked, still recovering my composure slightly from the abruptness of our meeting.

"No thanks. I just need to know why you're here?"

And so I told him. I started by explaining that I had discovered that the Hepworths were running a drugs business and, with help from his best mate, Kieron, I had found the photos of the Block factory on his laptop. I went on to describe how Abbot's Meadow fitted into the picture, and how I and the police had managed to catch Chris Hepworth and his chums digging up a body. Even as I said the words, I couldn't help but be amazed at how blasé I had become about events which not long ago would have seemed the stuff of fiction.

"I was convinced that the body was in fact you… because in the email to Ryan, you discussed going to the police if they didn't stop. Having met Chris this seemed like a course of action that was always destined to end badly. There was also the note saying that you were going to the States which was all very strange, and smacked of an attempt by Chris Hepworth to deter anyone who might come looking for you, like your wife… or the police, maybe."

"Well, as you can see, I'm still very much alive," he said with a faint smile.

"You don't look to me like a man that needs to hide away from the likes of Chris Hepworth, but the important thing for you to know is that Chris and his friends are currently being detained by the police while they investigate exactly what charges they need to bring. And Sam Hepworth should by now have been arrested as an accomplice. As far as I can see, that means that you don't have to hide away any longer… surely?"

"I'm not sure it's that simple," he said. And then he told me his story.

"I found out about the drugs operation quite by chance when the door to the Block was accidentally left open while contractors were installing some additional heating lamps. I confronted Chris Hepworth and said that I didn't want any part of it. Chris told me to just get on with the landscaping work and forget what I had seen. But I couldn't just forget it. How could I?"

"Well, looking on the positive side, I'm not sure how the police could prove that you were an accomplice, were they to discover what was going on," I ventured.

"Maybe so, I don't know. I was a director of the business, remember. Anyhow, the operation continued to get bigger and draw in more people. A distribution network was set up which involved shipping the dried plants to various middlemen who cured and processed the plants, before delivering the cannabis in packs to dealers across the county. This was by now a major-scale operation, and I felt I was caught up in it!"

It was like releasing the floodgates. I had provided an outlet for all of the pent-up anger and frustration, and it all came pouring out.

"Then, about a year ago, as part of this expansion, they recruited another guy into the team called Steven Trindle. Steven's day job was delivering parcels for Blaze Storage and Logistics. Blaze had an agreement with a local hospice which meant that their drivers used the company vans to collect doorstep charity bag donations, typically every month or two. It was supposed to be an act of kindness on behalf of Blaze. Hepworth just saw it as the perfect cover to move the charity bags containing dried cannabis plants around without suspicion. I later discovered that Trindle kept a few bags of clothes ready to put at the front of the van cargo space whenever he was ferrying so that if he was stopped by the police, the drugs wouldn't be found.

"I was worried someone would get careless and that the police would eventually crack the drugs operation. A lot of money was being made, although as far as I know, it all went to the two Hepworth brothers. But everyone in the company was obviously benefitting to some degree, me included. The above-average pay for all of Hepworths' employees was the price of silence. I think most of the other guys knew exactly what was going on. The really good lads soon left, and we were left with the likes of Dean Lockwood. I felt I was implicated whether I liked it or not."

"I guess you could just have gone to the police like you threatened?" I offered. "The company might have collapsed, but you would hopefully be in the clear."

"I know, but I liked the work. It was well paid, and it kept me and Laura enjoying a reasonable standard of living. And finding a new job would have been very difficult for me. I'm not that good with reading and writing and that kind of stuff."

"I know. Laura told me."

At the mention of Laura, I saw a flicker of sadness in his eyes.

"Well, I regret now that I didn't do that, especially as things with Laura all went wrong. I decided I would collect incriminating evidence and then confront Chris and get him to stop. Now I think about it, I was so bloody naive it was laughable. He was never going to take any notice of me. I would probably have ended up under that field, as you at first suspected. The guy is a total headcase!"

"Yes, I know what you mean," I said, still picturing his smirk as we stood in front of the exhumed corpse.

"One day when everyone else was out on a landscaping job, I came back to get a rotavator. Seeing the key to the Block on a hook by the back door of the office, I seized my chance and let myself into the building, where I took lots of photos on my phone. A few days later I saw Steven Trindle arrive in a Blaze van and caught Chris Hepworth and him deep in conversation, both obviously nervous in case there were prying eyes. A number of charity bags were loaded into the van and it drove off. I jumped in my car and followed it at a safe distance. Trindle stopped at what I suspected was his own house and removed two of the bags. I managed to get a long-range picture of him as he turned to take them into the house. I thought at the time that he might be skimming some off the top as it were, but I couldn't be sure. If he was, then he certainly had balls, I'll give him that. Chris is a guy you wouldn't want to cheat on."

He looked away for a few moments, lost in his thoughts as the memories flooded back. "I felt sorry for Blaze and the charity… so I sent a dated photo through the post to Blaze anonymously, hoping that they would investigate and take action. Even if Blaze went to the police, I knew that Trindle would never grass on Hepworth, or his life wouldn't have been worth living. He would keep silent and take the rap."

"Well, it certainly worked," I said, anxious to let Paul know that his actions did do some good. "I went to Blaze and spoke to the boss. Trindle got fired on the spot, although unfortunately he didn't pursue it with the cops."

"It was about this time that I discovered that Laura had been two-timing me. Completely took the rug from under my feet. I felt completely fucked, although… looking back, I guess I should have seen it coming. I was definitely not a nice person to be around just then. I drank way too much and was always in a foul mood. Anyway, pride – foolish pride, I suppose – drove me to move out of the house, even though I had nowhere to go. I put all of my personal stuff into storage and took a room at a B&B while I got myself together… but then you know that, don't you?"

The sadness in his eyes was plain to see as he recalled what I supposed were the darkest days of his life.

"So what happened next?" I enquired, anxious to keep him talking.

"A day or two later, Chris Hepworth called a team meeting at his house, and I decided that it was crunch time. Shit or bust! I realised that I couldn't stay on with the business but felt it was my duty to offer the Hepworths an ultimatum… either wind down the weed operation or I would take the evidence I had collected to the police. I know it sounds foolish – that's because it was. I don't know what I was thinking really. I guess after Laura, my head was turned. I was just kind of giving up…"

"Brave rather than foolish I would have said. So then what happened?"

"Well, things took an unexpected turn. Steven Trindle rocked up to announce that he had been sacked from Blaze. He was very cagey about explaining why. It turned out that Chris Hepworth already had his suspicions about Trindle after discovering that bags were going missing. Chris confronted him in his normal, cold, calculating style. You just knew that underneath he was seething and ready to launch. Trindle blustered that Chris was mistaken, but it was obvious to everyone that he was guilty as sin."

He paused and looked down at his feet, reliving the experience.

"There was a scuffle and Chris threw a fearsome punch which knocked Trindle clean off his feet. As he fell backwards he hit his head hard against the corner of a metal filing cabinet and died a minute or so later. His head had a huge gash with blood everywhere. At this point I just panicked and went into self-preservation mode. I wasn't scared of the Hepworths or their bully boys, that bastard Dean Lockwood included, but there was no way I was going to be accused of complicity in manslaughter, or even murder. I just turned and left the scene without a word and headed north to seek refuge with my long-time school pal, Ryan. From there I sent a note to Laura saying that I had gone to the States, hoping that this subterfuge would help my disappearing act."

So the mysterious body in Abbot's Meadow was that of Steven Trindle and not Paul. In my mind I saw again that gruesome cadaver, unceremoniously ejected from a roll of carpet.

"And you've been here ever since?"

"That's right," said Paul, no doubt relieved at having been able at last to share his story. "I thought that they would maybe rip out all of the stuff from the Block and then own up to an accidental death. It never occurred to me that they would get rid of the body, but as time went on, it was clear that this is what must have happened. I watched the news and searched the internet daily for a long time, expecting the truth to come out. I suppose the weed income was simply too important to them."

"So how have you managed to survive for the past year, seeing as how you don't in theory live in this country?" I asked, incredulous that anyone could manage to disappear from any authorities for a year.

"I've got Ryan to thank for that. He's put me up in one of his spare rooms, and in return I help him out on site with his building business. As it's a one-man band, he pays himself more, and then pays me a bit out of his own pocket as it were. Means he pays a shedload more tax, but in theory he's not breaking the law, tax-wise. Well that's what he reckons, anyway. Although I'm sure there must be some employment laws he's breaking somewhere along the line. And of course, I'm probably not likely to be too popular with the Inland Revenue. It was only going to be for a few weeks, but it's sort of drifted on. Suppose I needed someone like you to come and knock some sense into me…"

"I'm glad to have been of service," I replied.

"The thing is, now I've dug this hole, I don't quite know how to get out of it."

"Well, if you want my advice, I think you should go to the police that are investigating the case and come clean before they catch up with you. Tell them exactly what you've told me. They already know that you took the pictures… because they have your laptop. In my mind that shows that you weren't involved in any of the drugs stuff. Also, I don't know whether Ryan has told you, but they've sent him an email regarding your whereabouts… so it really does look like you're now on borrowed time."

He looked at me for a few seconds trying to weigh up the options, and I could see from the look of resignation that he hadn't found many other options… none at all, to be precise.

"Okay. I'll go back to Ryan's place, collect the few things I have and then get the train down."

I wrote down DC Grant's contact details on a serviette and handed it over.

"Now, there is one other thing I have to do before I go," I said, hoping that the goodwill I seemed to have built up wasn't about to evaporate. I picked up my phone and sent a single word text. Paul looked at me suspiciously, and there was something approaching panic in his eyes.

"What are you doing?" he said sharply. Maybe he thought I'd been 'wired' like they do in the movies. Was it a sting operation where the police would appear and handcuff him?

"I'm sorry that I didn't quite follow your instructions regarding coming alone," I confessed.

A voice from behind startled him.

"Hello, Paul."

He turned to see Laura standing behind his chair, tears in her eyes. Almost immediately I could also see tears welling up in his eyes. I knew then I had done the right thing.

CHAPTER 24

My mother was waiting with the door open as we got out of the Mini and made our way up the drive. She looked as if she were about to burst, such was her excitement.

"Come in, come in… it's so nice to see you both," she gushed. "And how are you, Jenny?"

"I'm fine thank you, Mrs Curran. Lovely to see you also," Jenny replied, smiling as they hugged.

It was a week since that unforgettable day on Abbot's Meadow, and any signs remaining of Jenny's black eye were easily covered by make-up. She looked lovely in her pale blue summer dress which showed off her suntan. I still found it hard to believe that she had actually chosen to hook up with me, an insecure, slightly nerdy young man, still with the last vestiges of awkward teenager inside. She was so out of my league it brought a lump to my throat.

My mother had put on one of her best frocks and done something with her hair. Unusually she had applied make-up which took me a little by surprise. Maybe she had put the mascara and lipstick on early in the morning while it was still dark? I was deeply touched that she wanted to make an extra special effort for me and my girl, and I gave her a warm hug.

We were ushered through into the kitchen where my sister, Emily, was busy helping with food preparations. After more hugs and kisses, my mother took great delight in showing Jenny the feast that was being prepared. Emily seized her chance and pulled me excitedly to one side.

"Well?" she whispered, looking at me enquiringly.

"Well what?" I replied, although I had a feeling I knew where this was going.

"Don't give me that 'well what' crap, bro. You know perfectly well what I'm talking about. Are you two...? Have you...? Will you...?" She embellished each staccato question with a facial expression and a swivelling of eyes that somehow managed to perfectly convey the meaning.

"If you mean, are we an item, yes we are. As for the rest, mind your own business!"

"Ah... you have then," she said knowingly, with a look of satisfaction. "That's good. She is lovely. And definitely a keeper."

From anyone else, making Jenny sound like a possession, a chattel to be either kept or discarded, could have seemed somewhat offensive, but Em and I were so close that I was just pleased that she was pleased. And she was right. I definitely intended to do my damnedest to keep her. We smiled at each other conspiratorially, and rejoined Jenny and my mother, who was taking Jenny through the finer points of making a charlotte russe.

Just then my father entered the kitchen from the back door and padded across to greet us in his socks. His gardening shoes no doubt had been left outside, in accordance with my mother's strict house rules. We shook hands, both feeling slightly awkward. My dad and I didn't really do tactile, but we seemed to have turned a corner in our relationship. Our eyes each told their own story. My fear of returning like the prodigal son had now been replaced with a certain confidence and feeling of pride. My job seemed to be working out, and while I may have left home still very much a boy inside, thanks to Jenny and the recent events, I felt that I was coming back as a man. I sensed that my father's blatant antipathy to my chosen career had been replaced with an uncharacteristic humility. We looked at each other, both trying to find the right thing to say. Once again, Jenny came to our rescue and gave him a kiss on the cheek.

"It's lovely to see you again, Mr Curran," she said, smiling warmly and sliding an arm around his waist as she gave him a quick hug.

My mother was impatient to get on to the business of the day and herded us all into the lounge. We sat down and exchanged brief pleasantries while my mother produced mugs of tea, the national lubricant for important events. Finally, it was time for me to take centre stage. I produced several copies of the *Castlebridge Gazette* and distributed them around.

"As you can see, the story made the front page, and also pages two and three. It even got some coverage in a couple of the nationals."

I had also had an interview for the local TV news, but I decided that my mum's blood pressure was best protected by keeping quiet. Plus, this would have been proof absolute that she was destined to be meeting that nice Trevor McDonald even sooner!

The room went quiet as my family read the words written by '*Our investigative journalist, Dan Curran*'. We put together the story the day after the incident on Abbot's Meadow but had to take great care to report only indisputable facts about what had happened, because of the danger of prejudicing the criminal investigation and forthcoming trial. Jack had the paper's retained legal adviser cast an eye over the story just to be sure we were safe.

Some details needed to be left for another day, and while this was in many ways disappointing, the story did nevertheless make compulsive reading. Castlebridge was a backwater, a sleepy town where, on a quiet day, the theft of a car could make the front page. News of council irregularities, kidnapping, a murder or manslaughter, a clandestine burial and a cannabis farm in the town caused sales to rocket, and Jack was ecstatic. Maybe, just maybe, he might start to replace some of his lost life savings and contemplate retirement someday. And we would also get more bites of the cherry when further charges were made, and then again later when the trial was finally under way. No doubt the direct involvement of a councillor in deception and crime was going to create a whole new wave of interest in the workings of local government, something I was looking forward to exploring further.

Over the next few hours, including an extended lunch, I went through the entire story in some detail, aided by Jenny who chipped in occasionally. She took great delight in adding details and nuances which I'd either glossed over or made light of. As I described the reuniting of Laura and Paul Connolly my mother was in tears, and even my father had to look down at his feet, lest his face gave away any unmanly emotions. But for the most part the family sat silently taking it all in, with looks which alternated between admiration, astonishment, incredulity and, occasionally, horror.

Although, that wasn't quite true. My father's main

expression was one of pride. A pride that even beat winning the Best Bloom Award at the annual meeting of the Luton Dahlia Society… or Luton Town beating Watford at home in the FA Cup. We smiled at each other. Job done. His son was going to do just fine.

This book is printed on paper from sustainable sources managed under the Forest Stewardship Council (FSC) scheme.

It has been printed in the UK to reduce transportation miles and their impact upon the environment.

For every new title that Troubador publishes, we plant a tree to offset CO_2, partnering with the More Trees scheme.

For more about how Troubador offsets its environmental impact, see www.troubador.co.uk/sustainability-and-community